"YOU DEVOUR ME. . . ."

"If you were in my shoes, what do you think you would do, Katie?" Julius asked.

"In your place," she said, her voice very small, "I would turn me away. I have no place here, Julius."

"I disagree." He brought his thumb gently down to trace the outline of her ear. His breathing was beginning to quicken, and so, he noted with satisfaction, was hers.

"You've set a fire in me, little Katie, and I don't know how I'll quench it."

"It's not possible to quench volcanoes," she said, with a small smile on her lips. "Didn't you know that? They just burn hotter and hotter until they explode."

Harper
Monogram

Brimstone

SONIA SIMONE

HarperPaperbacks
A Division of HarperCollins*Publishers*

This is a work of fiction. The characters, incidents, and dialogues are products of the author's imagination and are not to be construed as real. Any resemblance to actual events or persons, living or dead, is entirely coincidental.

HarperPaperbacks   *A Division of* HarperCollins*Publishers*
10 East 53rd Street, New York, N.Y. 10022

Cover illustration by Bob Berran

First printing: October 1995

Printed in the United States of America

HarperPaperbacks, HarperMonogram, and colophon are trademarks of HarperCollins*Publishers*

❖ 10 9 8 7 6 5 4 3 2 1

For Robert, who brings me cocoa when I'm on deadline. I love you, sweetie.

1

Katie Starr studied the Brimstone Earl with senses sharpened in the wildest hells of London. The earl was coldly handsome, arrogant, and about to lose thirty thousand pounds. Katie thought the experience would do him a world of good.

She was sitting at a small table in Lady Odcombe's card room, directly facing a wall with too many paintings. Airless landscapes and pinch-faced portraits of long-dead relations, the kind of paintings no normal person would want even *one* of, much less the two dozen crowded together on the wall.

Everything was that way in this country. The parks were too big, the streets too narrow. The *ton* was too brilliant, too debauched, too bored. The poor were appallingly poor. The streets were surpassingly filthy.

And the ninth earl of Brynston, sitting across the card table from her, was far, far too rich. But Katie was doing everything she could to remedy that fact.

He can afford it. Her cards formed a comfortable fan in her hands, and she tilted her face up to bat her eyelashes at the earl. Brynston was no fool—before she joined the table, he had turned a thousand pounds into thirty thousand in less than four hours. But he wasn't any match for Katie, either. She smiled vapidly at him, and fanned herself with the studied foolishness of the most paper-skulled chit in London.

A hulking figure materialized behind the earl's shoulder, holding a silver tray in massive white-gloved hands. A long scar in the shape of a two-pronged fork curved down the side of his face, distorting his left cheek and partly obscuring his left eye. He was impeccably dressed in emerald sateen livery, his wig powdered and trimmed, every detail correct. It all looked as incongruous on him as a party dress would have looked on a circus bear.

"Your lordship?" the man murmured to the earl.

Brynston glanced up at him, scarcely noticing. "No, no, nothing," he said with a careless wave.

Katie was careful not to show her disappointment. Sooner or later, the earl was going to get thirsty. And when he did, she'd be ready for him. She glanced at the big man, willing him to bide his time a little longer.

But it seemed Katie wouldn't have to wait to pluck her pigeon, after all. Brynston gestured absently to the scarred man. "No, now that I think of it, fetch me a rum punch."

Katie didn't try to contain her excitement, but let it bubble away in a particularly foolish giggle. "I should very much like a glass of champagne," she told the scarred man, who nodded and silently retreated.

Katie glanced around the room, taking in the heavy glitter of the chandeliers, the discreet whisking of the servants amid the throng of guests, and table after table of titled sapskulls throwing their money away at cards. Throwing their money away, perhaps, to players very much like Katie herself.

She turned her attention back to her own opponent, slowly flicking her fan, presenting the very picture of a frivolous, wealthy American heiress. It wasn't difficult. She caught the earl's glance with a renewed batting of her eyelashes. "I declare, all these elegant lords and ladies make a simple American girl feel positively *provincial.*"

The smoldering look Brynston gave her almost made her drop her cards. He was the perfect representative of high *ton*, everything a gentleman was supposed to be, even if he was a little too serious to be entirely fashionable. And he had a history to offset even that small flaw. The earl of Brynston, before coming into the title, had been one of the most hell-born rakes ever to raise the eyebrows of the West End.

His coat was cut to the very inch of fashion, but there was nothing of the dandy in his face. His eyes were an intense, pale blue, the color of a match flame, and seemed to burn right through Katie to the years of false names and temporary addresses. The planes of his face were severe, not at all what she'd thought of as the typical soft English man of leisure. His hands were large and strong. Only his mouth, generous and full, held any suggestion of warmth. "Don't be foolish, my dear. I assure you, you are the picture of fashion."

Katie recovered her composure in an instant. "I must say, Lord Brynston, that dark countenance of yours positively gives a girl the shivers." She giggled again for good measure. "You put Lord Byron himself to shame. Are all English gentlemen so forbidding?"

His look seemed to whip away all possibility of falsehood. Katie was beginning to appreciate how the Brimstone Earl had earned his nickname.

"I daresay not," he finally drawled, lowering heavy lids over those hard blue eyes. "You'd doubtless find most of the peerage more to your taste. A flock of partridges, begging to be plucked."

Katie's throat went dry as paper, and she wondered if he hadn't guessed her game. But no, it wasn't possible— she'd been losing all evening, nearly coming to the bottom of the five thousand pounds she'd brought expressly for that purpose.

She tilted her gaze up to meet his in an approximation

of fawning adoration, lowering her lashes a fraction and sliding the faintest suggestion of huskiness into her voice. "Not at all, my lord. I'm quite sure I've never met a more fascinating gentleman in all of England."

His reactions were subtle, exquisitely controlled, but Katie had taught herself to read even the smallest change in a man's face. His pupils dilated a fraction, and there was an almost imperceptible softening in the hard lines of his mouth.

She had him.

"And how long *have* you been in England, Miss Feathering?" he asked, his voice as cold as iced champagne as he reined in his own reaction to her.

"Ten weeks," she said, brightening a little as she fluttered her fan. "I must say, the experience has been most . . . educational. We've nothing like this in Philadelphia, I assure you." Her gesture took in the distinctive mix of luxury and decadence so characteristic of Lady Odcombe's notorious card room.

"A droll diversion for a pretty young heiress," Brynston drawled, leaning back in his chair with apparent ease. His dark hair curled across his forehead in a seemingly careless tumble, and his faint smile was that of a man without a thought for this world or the next. But Katie had done enough play-acting to recognize a pose when she saw one. Brynston's nonchalance was a sham; there was nothing free and easy about the Brimstone Earl.

She shot him a daring glance and giggled again. Katie loathed women who giggled, but it seemed to have a soothing, almost stupefying effect on the male brain. "When in Rome, my lord, one simply *must* do as the Romans do! Especially when it's so awfully amusing."

He fixed her again with those burning eyes. Suddenly Katie was angry—angry at men like him, whose yearly incomes could easily feed a thousand of the hungry children who stole to survive in London's streets. Men who would look right through a common cheat like Katie Starr as if she were made of glass.

Katie fanned herself, unnerved, and forced herself to remember who she was and why she was here. If she found the earl distasteful, she had only to wait a few more hours, when so much of his lovely money would be hers. Until then, she could play the rich, pretty fool a while longer.

The scarred man appeared again, his silver tray now laden with glasses and several new decks of cards. "Refresh your cards, sir?"

"I suppose so," Brynston said absently. He took his rum punch and tilted it back with the lack of concern of a man very much accustomed to drink. Katie could have purred with pleasure. Rum punch was a strong-flavored drink, one that could conceal any number of additional ingredients.

The servant replaced the deck with one freshly wrapped in paper and made his way around the table, stopping at Katie's side. "Miss," he offered neutrally, revealing nothing as he handed her a glass of champagne. She had to admit, for all his frightening looks, Manners was the best man in London for this sort of business. There wasn't a blackleg alive with more discretion—or a more generous heart.

"Oh thanks *awfully*," she said, gazing at his right shoulder to keep any spark of recognition from lighting her eye.

Manners tilted the glass just enough to let a few drops scatter across Katie's gown. "Oh!" she cried with a little jump, feeling the familiar flutter in her palm as her friend expertly palmed her a thin stack of cards.

"I do beg yer pardon, Miss," the man said, his scarred face a thoroughly convincing picture of abject apology.

She slipped the cards into the hidden pocket of her flounced gown as she dabbed at herself with a handkerchief. "Idiot! You've ruined my dress!"

"Fetch the lady a clean serviette, you lackwit," the earl said, exasperated.

"Of course, your lordship," the scarred man mumbled, disappearing from the room.

Perfect. Katie could feel the edges of the cards in her pocket, the small weight pleasant and reassuring. The playing cards were identical to the originals she held in her hand, but for the fact that they lacked the usual complement of numbered cards. Her pocket held nothing but knaves, queens, kings, and aces, including four of a suit. She was closing in on her prey, could all but feel him in her jaws, and the thought brought her extreme pleasure.

The earl had downed his drink. It would take some minutes for the drug to take effect, and Katie spent the time throwing away a few hundred pounds, giggling and asking the earl to explain the rules of the game to her again. By the time he had done so, she detected a faint but definite blurring of his faculties.

"You feeling quite the thing, Brynston?" a beak-nosed baron named Darconville asked at the earl's elbow.

Katie could have killed the interfering fool. She couldn't afford to lose her pigeon now—she had five thousand pounds invested in tonight's game. It was critical that she win it back again, and more. Much more.

The earl shook Darconville off with a frosty glower. "I'm as fit as I've ever been, you noddycock. Do I look addled to you?"

Brynston glanced discreetly at the night's winnings— thirty thousand pounds, in cash.

That was convenient. Katie didn't always find it comfortable to collect IOUs, especially for large sums. She was even now holding the vowels of a rash buck named Willowby, and she had no idea how long it would take the young hothead to raise the cash.

It was time to tighten the snare. "Do you know, I think I have finally gotten the knack of this game!" she said brightly, with what she hoped was the final bat of her eyelashes for the evening. "I can see my difficulty now—I've been far too cautious."

An insolent smile whipped across Brynston's face, and for a moment she hated him. It had been so easy to convince him she was one of *them*—one of the useless, vapid females of the *ton*, cursed with too much money and not enough sense.

"My dear, you astonish me," he said dryly.

"Do I, my lord?" Katie fanned herself languidly, with a glancing brush of her free hand to check the cards in her pocket. "I'm sure if I were to risk a really *dashing* quantity of money, it would focus my concentration most marvelously."

The earl exchanged glances with Darconville, as if to smirk over what a plump little American goose he'd snared. He turned to Katie with a smug smile. "A fascinating theory, my dear, but I daresay you'd do best to call it a night and return tomorrow. Perhaps your luck will have turned by then."

He was being indulgent, paternal, and she could have punched him for it.

"No, no," she insisted instead, lowering her voice and concentrating every ounce of her will on convincing him. It was a knack she'd picked up over the years, a more important skill even than the instant recalculation of odds, or the smooth, well-practiced palming of cards and coins and false dice. "Indulge me in this, my lord. It's only money, after all, nothing more than a silly pile of coins and notes. Just metal and paper, Lord Brynston, metal and paper."

He might not have succumbed without the drug. He was well ahead, and not a man to be bamboozled easily, even by a woman of Katie's special talents. But the intoxicants Manners had mixed into his drink were making the earl both pliant and brash, giving him the sense that he was invincible. Katie had never known Manners's cocktail to be anything but highly effective.

"You promise not to be vexed with me afterwards? In the unlikely event that you lose, I mean." He flashed her a smile, a smile Katie hadn't seen before. It nearly undid her. The room suddenly seemed lit more brightly than by the glittering chandelier, and Brynston himself was transformed from an rich, arrogant, unfeeling Englishman into a man with a soul, a man of strength and compassion.

She collected her wits in an instant. Damn it, what the hell was she doing? Thinking like a pigeon, at the very time when she needed to remember that she was a wary, careful cat. She looked deeply into the earl's eyes, steeling herself against their flame-blue depths. "I positively promise, my lord," she said softly.

Brynston had had the devil of a time concentrating on anything but the girl all night, and the effect was becoming more pronounced. She was not at all to his taste, physically or mentally. He tended to prefer intelligent, dark women, and had enjoyed any number of mistresses fitting that description during his years on the Continent.

The heiress in front of him was a frothy, spun-sugar confection with great green saucers for eyes and hair that was almost too blond. Brynston had a superstitious aversion to blondes. And she was tiny, reminding him of a Dresden shepherdess—very delicate, very lovely, and utterly useless.

Katherine Feathering was also vulgarly rich. Which was why Brynston was willing to take the pretty child's money, which she lost with perfect carelessness. She played atrociously, without consideration for the odds or the risks. But then, Brynston supposed one could scarcely expect sophistication from an American.

His ears had begun to buzz annoyingly, and the room seemed almost to dim, though the china shepherdess glowed like a lantern. There was something deuced odd about the creature's eyes—they scarcely seemed to suit the rest of her person. They were wild, wary, as if they'd seen too much.

He shook his head to clear his thoughts. It wasn't like him to allow a single rum punch to affect him this way, but the room had grown warm, and he was no longer accustomed to deep play. It had been a long time since his rakehell days had seen him at a gaming table, looking over tens of thousands of pounds in winnings. The sensation was more intoxicating than he cared to admit.

He brought his attention to the subject at hand—the strangely appetizing little heiress who seemed addicted to the pleasure of throwing her money about.

Never let it be said that the earl of Brynston was one to disoblige a lady. "Very well, my dear. By all means, then—another hand."

She gathered the cards he'd dealt with a gleam in those wide green eyes, an eagerness that for an instant seemed almost lascivious.

Brynston scowled at his own idiocy. What the devil was the matter with him tonight? His wits seemed to have all but deserted him. He'd come here for a reason—a damned good reason—and the days when he'd played cards for mere pleasure were long behind him.

"Wait—" she said, before Brynston could pick up his hand. "I'm having one of my feelings, and that means I'm about to run into a delightful bit of luck. Shall we place our bets now?"

He checked his urge to snap at the girl. Really, the stupid child made taking her money almost unsportingly easy. "Are you very sure you wouldn't rather cast an eye over your hand first?"

"I tell you, that's been my problem all evening," she said with a delectable pout. "Overcaution, I'm sure of it. I shall just have to trust in fate." She eyed his winnings the way a child might eye the counter of a pastry shop. "Thirty thousand pounds says I take this hand."

Brynston coughed to cover his astonishment. The girl was completely mad.

Darconville leaned his prominent nose over the table to drawl, "Mind, gel, ain't you diggin' yourself rather deep?"

"I'll tell you what," Brynston offered, rather magnanimously, he thought. "Let's have a look at our hands and we'll decide after, shall we?"

She frowned, her rosy lower lip thrust out enticingly.

"Oh very well, if you must be *conventional*." Her eye caught his, and that sparkling look she'd been giving him all night seemed to betray an almost carnal curiosity. He very much doubted the bubble-headed creature even understood her own feelings—or how gravely they were clouding her judgment.

"Won't your papa get himself a trifle out of sorts if you should lose?" Brynston asked, gathering his hand and glancing down at it. It was liberally peppered with knaves and queens, and a decent sextet to seal the silly chit's fate. He felt almost guilty.

Miss Feathering laughed. "Oh, Daddy never gets grumpy with me! He'll frown and tweak my nose and say something about how fast children grow up. I shouldn't worry a bit about Daddy."

Brynston's hand was excellent, and he had yet to win all he needed. His scapegrace little brother had gotten himself sunk past the ears in debt, and the china shepherdess was offering an enticingly convenient way to get Valentine out again.

"Thirty thousand, then," Brynston agreed, with only the faintest twinge at taking Miss Feathering's money. Winning this hand would give him enough to pay Val's debts, and leave him an attractive surplus as a souvenir. And the girl really did have it coming to her. Perhaps it would teach her to look after her affairs with greater care, though Brynston doubted it.

The green eyes flashed. "How perfectly thrilling of you, my lord." The girl's voice was a sultry purr that seemed to aggravate Brynston's muddled faculties.

"I suppose you'll think me a terrible fool, to go against one of your . . . *feelings*." Brynston kept his voice as icy as he could manage, and all the while those wild green eyes threatened to shred his composure into tiny, useless bits. But he had no intention of allowing the girl to know how she affected him. As long as she was the only one making sheep's eyes, he retained control of the table—and of her.

"Thirty thousand, then," she said, flickering her delicately painted fan.

He discarded his seven and eight and drew a pair. A ten and another queen, rounding out his hand admirably.

The girl frowned down at her cards, chewed nervously at a fingernail, and threw down the maximum of five, taking five more from the stock. The hand she'd drawn hadn't been a strong one, then. He felt another twinge— poor little idiot. Surely her papa would have something to say at her losing thirty thousand on a single weak hand. "Are you very sure you want to do this?" Brynston heard himself asking, cursing himself for a fool.

She gave him an impatient little glower. "Of course I am! I'll walk away from this table with your entire winnings, see if I don't."

The cheek of the wench! Very well then, if the child insisted on being infuriating, Brynston would teach her the lesson she sorely needed.

The room seemed to grow steadily darker, and Brynston snarled, "Dash it, can't someone do something about the blasted lights? A fellow can scarcely see what he's winning."

They began the bidding, the girl frowning over her cards as if trying to remember just what constituted a meld. Her lips moved as she silently counted out her hand. Finally she said, "Point of five."

Brynston looked down. "How high?"

"Queen," she said, smiling foolishly.

Blast. "It's good," he said, scowling. So the child had picked up a few decent cards after all, what did it matter? Even if she'd been lucky enough to draw a capot, she wouldn't know how to play it to win.

But she scored another declaration off him, a quint. Suddenly he found himself behind twenty points. He was about to make a sharp remark about her newfound luck when a thunderous crash came from behind him, the sound of a full tray of glasses hitting the marble floor.

Bits of wet glass pelted his feet, and he started up from

his chair. The scarred manservant was cringing behind Brynston's chair, picking shards off the floor. "I do beg yer pardon, yer lordship, ever so sorry. Go on with your pleasure, sir, if you would. I'll have this up in a jot."

"Not like that, man, you're cutting yourself to pieces," Brynston said roughly. It was true, even through the white gloves the fellow had opened a nasty cut in his hand.

The servant looked up at him, the broad, scarred face abject. "I'm ever so sorry to have disturbed your lordship. It won't take me but a trice to clean it up, sir, I promise you."

Brynston shut his eyes against the strangely pounding headache that was building in his temples. The rum punch had left a stale, almost metallic taste in his mouth, and no one had done a damned thing about the lights. "After you've finished here, see if someone can do something about this infernal darkness, man. Lady Odcombe means to put us all to bed at this rate."

"As you wish, your lordship," the man said, his voice a quiet grovel.

Poor wretch. Brynston turned back to his game. "I say, then, where were we?"

"About to begin the play, as I recall," the girl said brightly. She led the first trick, hearts.

Brynston followed suit, feeling oddly tired. He would make this his last hand. Even the excitement of risking— and winning —such an obscene sum of money was beginning to pall, and he half wondered if it wouldn't be more honorable to simply let the chit keep her money. He had no taste for taking candy from gullible infants, even if they *did* seem bent on throwing it at him.

"The trick is mine. Twenty-one points. My lead." She led again with another heart, a ten this time.

Brynston looked stupidly down at his hand. What was the matter with him? Had he followed with the knave? There was a perfectly good eight in his hand, and he'd been saving the knave for— He couldn't quite remember now. His head ached horribly.

"My lord? Lord Brynston?" The girl's voice drifted to him from far away.

"Yes, yes, what is it?" he muttered, gathering his wits. Blast it, he was letting his intellectuals get into a perfect scramble. He needed only a few more moments of concentration, and then he'd be able to go home. To hell with the girl's money, he could make up the rest of Val's debt from the family coffers. He would let the girl off with a warning to watch herself more closely next time.

"My lord, will you follow suit?"

Brynston stared at the trick on the table, and then at his hand. The faces on the cards seemed to stare evilly at him. Hearts? He had one left. "Yes, yes, there." He laid down his eight and looked up at her, almost as if to reassure himself that had been the right thing to do.

For a moment the girl's blond curls tangled to a riot of strawberry ringlets, and the green eyes melted into pale blue. Brynston felt his heart contract painfully. "Josephine?" he whispered.

The girl smiled dazzlingly, scooping up the pair of cards on the table. "I take that one as well, is that right?"

Her voice, with its strange, flat American accent, kicked Brynston savagely back to the present. He was horrified by his lapse, and pulled himself straight as a blade in his chair. Josephine was gone, she would never come back. And the silly little female in front of him was *nothing* like Jo. Nothing.

"Oh, I absolutely *knew* my luck was about to change," the girl prattled, her face bright with pleasure.

The eight lay there like an insult. Idiot! Brynston *had* to gather his wits.

But she took the next trick, and the next, as his mind refused to behave itself. One moment he had held a surefire hand, and the next she was gathering the cards and shuffling them as prettily as you please.

Brynston blinked, carried again for an instant into another time, facing another pretty young blonde. So long ago.

Then Darconville was at his elbow, shouting some nonsense about Brynston's being ill. Brynston shook off the baron's grip. There was no question of admitting the shameful weakness that had overcome him. "Never felt more the thing, Darconville, and I'll thank you to keep your blasted hands off me."

He drew himself up, staring at the china shepherdess, whose eyes shone like leaves wet with rain. She'd won. The silly American fribble had beaten him to the tune of thirty thousand pounds.

And through the murderous pounding in his head, Brynston wondered just how the hell she'd managed it.

2

Katie waited for the exhilaration that should have come from so thoroughly besting Brynston, but it never appeared. She didn't feel it in the curricle on the brief ride home, though Alex Manners was as pleased as his cautious nature allowed. Nor did she feel it as she shrugged out of her unflattering, expensive gown and went to bed.

And she didn't feel it the next morning, as she dressed for another day of mingling with London's high *ton*.

Katie studied herself in the gilt mirror. She was wearing another of her new gowns, all of which she despised. This morning's was a pale green muslin lavishly sprinkled with pastel ribbon flounces. The maid stood in the center of the room, ironing the pelisse of slightly darker and heavier merino.

"I'll freeze solid if I go out in this," Katie muttered, casting a disgruntled glance at the iron-gray sky outside her window.

"Aye, miss," murmured the young maid, Hannah. "But it's a pretty thing. You'll be the handsomest heiress in all London."

The thought made Katie want to throw something across the room. She tugged on a pair of pale yellow morning-gloves instead.

It wasn't fair to take out her frustrations on Hannah. The maid was gentle and utterly loyal, a strict Methodist, but that Katie could forgive. She was a pretty girl, with dark hair and a round, rosy face that seemed incongruous with her picket-thin frame. Years ago she had been a prostitute, but her religious conversion had forced her out of the profession. Katie's entire household was a kind of charitable house for such discards from the criminal classes.

Hannah had finished the pelisse and moved to stand behind Katie's back. The girl's mouth was full of hairpins as she motioned for Katie to turn her head slightly to the left.

Katie suppressed a small sigh as Hannah settled the pale blond wig over Katie's natural curls, combing the thing into an artful tumble of ringlets. If she thought about it objectively, the wig was quite lovely, making her look even younger and more delicate. More *gullible*, she corrected herself, remembering the smug look on the earl's face the night before.

Brynston's eyes still seemed to carve into her, the high-handed voice still mocked her in that patronizing drawl. She had completely gulled the Brimstone Earl, and she was quite sure he'd never suspected what had hit him. But her victory was bringing her no pleasure.

Katie all but tripped over a trio of brawny footmen rolling dice in the hallway, and she read them a stern lecture about the perils of neglecting their duties before she shooed them off to the servants' hall.

Breakfast had been served in the front parlor. Her father and Alex Manners were already sipping coffee by the time she made her way downstairs.

Katie had her mother's eyes, but she'd inherited her

height—or lack of it—from her father, who was only an inch or two taller than she was, a plump little quail of a man in a chestnut-colored coat.

"Morning, Dad," she said, greeting her father with a kiss. "Scuttlesby has managed to turn you out very presentably this morning." Scuttlesby was her father's valet, and he was almost entirely blind.

"I had to scratch four choices before he happened on this one," Phineas said, grumbling. "Don't know why we hired him. It's a damned idiotic notion, having a blind valet."

"We hired him because he couldn't do his other work," Katie reminded him firmly. "Who ever heard of a blind resurrection man? It takes sharp eyes to find the right gravestone, and in the middle of the night at that." Scuttlesby's former profession involved the illicit sale of fresh corpses to medical students. He had been quite good at it, before his eyes began to cloud and fail.

She turned to Alex Manners, who was impeccably turned out in a butler's black superfine, the effect marred only by the bandage on his hand. "That get-up does suit you," she said with a grin.

Alex's face flushed with embarrassment. "A bit of gristle wrapped as steak."

She patted his good hand comfortingly. "Don't be silly, you're terribly handsome. Anyway, we're two of a kind, a pair of ostensibly sensible people masquerading as teacakes."

"You sound very ungrateful, Katherine," her father said severely. "It's not many girls who have lovely things like you do, or who get to live exciting lives."

"Sorry," she said, feeling guilty as she poured a cup of coffee from the silver service. It wasn't like her to chafe at a cover this way. Usually this part was an entertaining masquerade, a game that challenged every ounce of nerve and wit she had. But this time the game was beginning to pall, and the night before had left a bad taste in her mouth.

Her father's face gentled. "That was a fine piece of

work last night, girl. Manners tells me you handled yourself like a champion."

She frowned as she gathered her skirts and sat back on the divan. "We won't be able to stay in London much longer. Between Val Willowby's fifteen thousand last week and Lord Brynston's thirty, I'm afraid Katherine Feathering's reputation as a goosecap is in severe jeopardy."

"Well, for forty-five thousand pounds, I say it's worthwhile wearing a bit of a hole in our welcome, eh?" Her father gave a contented sigh as he eased himself into the brocade of the upholstered chair. "Forty-five thousand pounds. I've raised myself a champion, that's what I've done. My little Katie, better than any damned racehorse."

She smiled faintly, but she was still troubled. "We need fifty-five more to pay off the Turks," she pointed out, taking a pastry from the silver tray. "We'd have done better to move more slowly. After last night, we won't be able to find a gudgeon in the seediest hell in London."

"You saw your mark and you pounced on him, girl, just like you'd been taught. That's called taking initiative. That's called being a *winner*. I'm proud of you, child, and that's the end of it. Anyway, thirty thousand will hold those bastards off for months, maybe longer."

"*Thirty* thousand? Dad, you aren't thinking—" She broke off, frustrated.

Her father waved his hands impatiently, as if to whisk aside her concerns. He'd always made that gesture, ever since she could remember. Phineas Starr was not a man to concern himself with the possibility of failure. Unfortunately, failure seemed to raise its stubborn, troublesome head every time her reckless father walked into the room.

"It's an investment, child, don't you see? You're telling me we'll need to start over, to invent a new cover—very well, then, a new cover we shall have. More splendid and extravagant than anything we've contrived before!" Phineas had that gleam in his eye that usually prefigured the loss of a large sum of money.

Katie shot Alex a helpless look. At this rate, they'd be running from the Turks forever. She could all but feel them closing in on her, as if they were hounds and she and her father were a pair of scrawny, tired foxes.

She tried again. "But fifteen thousand pounds? Surely there's no need—"

"You've got to think big, child," her father insisted, leaning forward in his chair, his plump face suddenly serious. "We can turn fifteen into two hundred, if we keep our wits about us, which would keep us in fine feather for a good long time."

It wouldn't, she knew. Even if they could win such a large sum of money, it would be gone within a year, dribbled away on gaming debts and outlandish extravagances.

"Dad, we have to concentrate on the Turks. Remember what you always taught me—don't get greedy. That's for the flats."

Her father's face twisted into one of his rare scowls. "Don't lecture your old man, Katherine."

Don't lecture me. It's what he used to say to her mother. Her mother. Katie felt a hollow pain in her chest, as if her heart had been kicked black and blue.

Alex cleared his throat heavily. "If you're nearly finished with your breakfast, Katie, I'll tell the driver to prepare the coach."

She blinked rapidly, startled from her thoughts, and nodded with a faint smile. Alex had come to her rescue, as he always did. When Katie was younger, his frequent small kindnesses had often brought the sharp sting of tears to her eyes.

But Katie was a tough little street rat, and she'd outgrown tears a long time ago. "Yes, I'm ready. Thanks, Alex."

"Where are you two off to today?" Phineas asked, reaching with some effort toward the tray of pastries.

Katie pushed the tray a few inches toward her father. "I believe Miss Katherine Feathering would find the Frost Fair *awfully* amusing."

Phineas frowned, studying the pink icing on a marzipan cake. "The Frost Fair? Seems a little vulgar. Doesn't do to show yourself as anything but class, Katherine."

She downed the last of her coffee—she never had been able to abide tea—and stood, brushing the crumbs from her pelisse. She grimaced as she caught a glimpse of herself in the large mirror above the mantel. The artful tumble of ice-blond ringlets might make her look delightfully feminine, but it also made her look pale and silly, and Katie hated it.

She pasted on a pleasant expression. "There will be a great number of vulgar people there, but all the *ton*'s mad with curiosity over it. Anyway, I'm supposed to be an enthusiastic naive, remember? Miss Feathering will find it all terribly *exciting*."

Her father gave a good-natured snort. "Yes, I suppose she will. Well, mind your reticule, Katie. The place'll be full of sharps and pickpockets." He laughed expansively at his own joke.

She arranged her trifle of a hat over the blond curls, tilting the lemon-yellow ostrich plume rakishly forward. Everything about her appearance suggested a high-spirited female who spent money as if it were water. "Sharps and pickpockets?" she said, arching an eyebrow and smiling at her father. "Fiddle faddle! I'm sure I never saw any such thing in all my life."

Both Alex Manners and the maid Hannah accompanied Katie to the fair. Katie had decided she didn't care if it *was* fashionable to nearly freeze to death, and she'd brought a snowy white fur-trimmed mantle. She pulled it around her shoulders now, breathing in the sharp tang of frost and wood smoke in the air. The Thames had completely frozen over, and a jumble of untidy booths and tents had promptly sprung up on the ice, each vying with the next to be more gaudy, more exciting.

For the first time that day, she felt good. The fair—part fairy wonderland, part squabbling East End market—seemed to mirror her own troubled heart. She was neither fish nor fowl, but some strange hybrid that belonged in neither world. And like the rowdy little fair, she wouldn't last much longer in London. She and her father would board a boat to Italy within a week or two, and then perhaps on to Paris after the peace was signed. On to a new name, a new identity.

A new collection of lies.

A chill wind blew over the back of her neck and she shivered, pulling the mantle up to protect her nape. "Come on, Alex," she said, plucking at his elbow. "Let's see the sights, shall we? We've no end of diversions to amuse ourselves with, and I'm simply dying for a ginger nut."

They had been at the fair no more than five minutes before Katie insisted they each buy a pair of ice skates, rather than slipping pell-mell on their boots. Ice skating had not been part of Alex's education, and Katie was at some pains to spare his dignity while she taught him to make his way without falling.

"Here," she said, demonstrating. "Do you see how I've used my toe to stop? Now you try."

Alex's expression was at its most painfully dignified as he struggled to keep his huge body upright. "I believe I'd rather walk on my boot-soles, if you don't mind."

Katie fought to keep from smiling. "If you're sure you won't slip and fall."

"I've been walking on leather soles from an extremely early age," Alex said, his face flushing darkly beneath the pale scar. "I've come to believe it suits me very well."

Hannah laughed girlishly, taking a turn on her skates. "It ain't so hard. Look, see? Right smart, and quick as you please. It don't take long to get the knack, Mr. Manners, if you'll just give it a try."

He gave Hannah his stoniest glower. "All this sliding

around may be very well for young girls, but upper staff must have a care for their dignity, Hannah."

Hannah blushed pink as a peony as she looked down at her quaking skates. "Of course, Mr. Manners, just as you say. I weren't meanin' no disrespect."

Katie frowned at her old friend. At times he really could be a little *too* prickly. "Alex," she said, trying to smooth the waters. "Could you possibly see if you can find me a ginger nut? I declare, I'm positively faint with hunger."

"Oh, I'll fetch one for you, miss!" Hannah chirped.

"You stay with me, Hannah," Katie said firmly. "I'd skate rings around Alex, and as we can see, that puts him in a wretched temper."

Alex lifted an eyebrow and gave another little bow. "Of course, Katie."

Katie and Hannah skated on, past the rows of toyshops and butchers and bookstalls, until Katie slid to a stop in front of the skittle alley.

"Penny a ball, tuppence for three!" the barker bawled. "Tips the pins and wins a prize!"

"That looks like fun," Katie mused aloud. "Do you know how to play, Hannah?"

Hannah shook her head violently. "Not skittles, miss. It's gambling, and a terrible sin!"

Katie raised one skeptical eyebrow at her maid. "You do remember what I do for a living, Hannah?"

Hannah blushed. "Aye, and may Heaven preserve you. But skittles is frightful common, miss, no kind of game for a proper young lady."

Katie wrinkled her nose. "You sound as grouchy as Alex. I think it looks perfectly interesting." She closed one eye and peered at the ninepins arranged in a neat diamond. "All I have to do is knock those things over with this wooden ball, is that right?"

"If anyone was to see you, miss," Hannah said pleadingly. "And you lookin' so ladylike in that pretty dress. It ain't the thing, miss, Lord preserve me it ain't."

Katie had already pressed her tuppence into the barker's hand. Steadying herself on her skates, she flung the ball down the alley in imitation of the brawny young men on either side of her, but it rolled uselessly down a ridge to the left of the pins. "Damn!" she muttered beneath her breath.

"Oh, miss, your language," Hannah murmured pleadingly.

"Sorry, Hannah. I get two more chances, though."

The barker was watching her with frank amusement. "You needs a bit more of a flick in yer wrist, milady," he said, demonstrating. The ball sailed in a perfectly straight line, bouncing once before knocking down every pin. "Easy once you gets the knack. I'll gives you another ball, free an' gratis."

The barker set the pins up again, and Katie hurled her second ball. This one did manage to hit a few of the pins, knocking four of them down.

The barker's face split into a grin. "You've got natural talent, milady, natural talent."

Katie shot Hannah a triumphant look. "You see? I have natural talent. Now all I need to do is knock the others down."

She wedged the toe of her skate firmly into the ice, took careful aim, and flung the ball down the alley. The wooden ball wobbled and spun off at an angle, shooting over three alleys into another player's gutter. "Oy!" came an angry voice, until the player realized who his opponent was and muttered, "Beg yer pardon, milady."

Katie frowned. "Drat, that one seems to have gone a bit awry."

She felt rather than saw the imposing figure that swooped up behind her, accompanied by the sound of skate blades over ice. A dry, masculine voice came from over her left shoulder. "You bowl with admirable force, my dear, but your aim wants improving." The voice belonged to the Brimstone Earl.

Katie's knees wobbled beneath her, and suddenly she

felt far too warm beneath the fur-trimmed mantle. She gripped the side of the booth for support and mentally commanded her skated feet not to slide out from under her.

"Lord Brynston," she said in greeting, forcing a coolness she did not feel.

"Will you allow me?" he asked, holding out his hand for the last wooden ball.

Wordlessly she handed it to him, hardly trusting herself with even the slightest pleasantry.

Brynston took careful aim. "Thirty thousand pounds says I can take out the remaining pins."

Katie felt the blood drain from her face.

"Lord preserve us!" Hannah murmured.

"My lord jests, of course," Katie managed.

The earl flashed another of those smiles that discomposed her utterly. "Of course," he said, then threw the ball smoothly down the alley. It knocked over the remaining pins with ease. "A pity you're not as reckless this morning as you were last night, Miss Feathering."

Hannah was harrumphing vigorously, torn between respect for an earl and loyalty to her mistress, however sinful that mistress might be.

Katie struggled with the urge to bolt. A champion, her father had called her, and he'd been right. She wedged her toe firmly into the ice. She was far too tough to allow this . . . this *Englishman* to intimidate her.

She tilted her face up toward his. Her feet wobbled a little on her skates, but her eyes met his with perfect steadiness. "I suppose we were both caught up in the events of last night, my lord. Thinking back on it, I can see I behaved like a perfect ninny. I do hope your losses haven't inconvenienced you."

He gently pushed off on his skates, gliding until he was very close to her. "Inconvenienced me? Don't be foolish, my dear. English earls are all crammed to the gills with cash—or doesn't one know that, in the wilds of America?"

Katie could feel a kind of heat coming off him, despite the winter day's chill, and she freed herself to glide backwards a few inches, moving away from him. "We hear all sorts of stories in my country," she said, trying for the greatest possible flippancy. "I suppose you'll think us all frightfully naive."

He tilted his head to one side, and his eyes drilled into her. "Naive? How interesting. Do you know, Miss Feathering, I've just learned this morning of the most fascinating coincidence. We have a mutual acquaintance."

"Do we?" she asked, letting herself slide back to put a few more inches between them. There had to be some way to put an end to this uncomfortable conversation, but her mind had become as tangled as a knitting basket full of kittens.

"Rather more than an acquaintance, on my side, actually." An almost imperceptible movement brought him closer. "Lord Willowby—Valentine Willowby."

Willowby. The reckless buck she'd taken for fifteen thousand pounds last week. She felt her palms grow faintly damp. The earl couldn't help but realize that Katie was not the simpering fool she'd pretended to be, if he knew Val Willowby.

"He's my brother," the earl drawled. He showed no overt sign of suspicion or anger, but his pale eyes narrowed faintly.

She worked to think of an appropriate remark, but her mind refused to cooperate.

"Milord?" the barker broke in. "Milord?"

Brynston turned irritably to the man. "Yes, what is it?"

"You won a prize, milord. Anyfing you wants. Might I suggest sumfing pretty for milady?" The barker grinned engagingly.

"For *milady*," Brynston repeated, the ghost of a smile on his lips. "Yes, I quite agree." He stared up at the rack of prizes, past the rows of cheap, brightly painted toy drums and wooden puppets. His eye lit on a rack of gaudy ear bobs. "I'd like those, please, the green."

The barker handed him a pair of ear bobs made from two parrot-green glass beads, swirled through with stripes of scarlet and blue. They were something a gypsy girl might wear, cheap and flashy and very much out of keeping with the frosted confectionery gowns Katie wore as Katherine Feathering.

Brynston handed them to her with a flourish. "Emeralds for my lady," he said dryly. "From her most humble and obedient servant."

She was at a loss for anything remotely intelligent to say. But Brynston's eyes held an almost playful spark, and she decided there was no harm in playing along. "Emeralds! My lord is too kind." She held the ear bobs up, and the cheap beads glittered in the weak winter sun. "And of the very first water." She looked up at him and ventured a smile.

He returned it with a faint mocking smile of his own that made her pulses race like a first place trotter at Newmarket.

"Now then, about this matter of my scapegrace little brother—"

From behind her came a shuffle, a muffled grunt, and then a thump as someone hit the ice. Katie turned to see Alex Manners sitting squarely on his rear end, packages sprinkled around him as he scowled in disgust.

Katie sucked in her breath. *Not now, Alex. Any time but now.*

Alex's eyes met Katie's for no more than half a second before he turned away, bending his face low as he gathered up his packages. Katie flicked her glance dismissively over her friend, then turned away. "Your brother, my lord?"

"Miss Feathering?" Hannah said, puzzled. "Here's Mr. Manners, miss!" Hannah bent down to help the man up. "Now then, sir, you're right as rain, praise be to God. Look there, you managed to save them ginger nuts!"

"Hannah, get up from there immediately!" Katie said, too quickly. *Damn it, damn it all to hell.*

Hannah looked up at her, her round face pink with surprise. "But miss—"

Manners was looking past Katie's shoulder, and she could not keep herself from following his gaze. It led her directly to the furious countenance of the Brimstone Earl. The stark planes of Brynston's face had become as rigid as granite, and all the harshness had returned to the piercing eyes.

When he finally spoke, his voice was little more than a low whisper. "I have been wracking my brain all morning over the vexatious riddles you've posed, my dear. A ninny-hammer scarcely out of the schoolroom one instant, a shrewd gamestress the next. But now it appears I have the answer I've been looking for."

Katie's ankles wobbled as if they would give way beneath her, but she managed to regain control in an instant. "I beg your pardon, my lord, I really must be going. I have an appointment with my dressmaker at two o'clock. Good day."

Brynston continued as if he hadn't heard her. "I can only perceive one possible conclusion. Appearances would suggest, Miss Feathering, that you are scarcely better than a dishonorable, lying little cheat."

3

Brynston could scarcely speak for his rage. He'd allowed an unprincipled slip of an American girl to deceive him by fluttering her eyelashes and pretending to be a paper-skulled fool. And he had believed it, every bit of it. He could have murdered her.

But he was far more disgusted with himself. For God's sake, he was no green boy, ready to make an ass of himself over a pretty girl. The duplicitous Miss Feathering had more than her fair share of charms, it was true, but the ninth earl of Brynston had long prided himself on his ability to resist the attempts of mere females to muddle his thinking.

Brynston watched as the girl scrambled to help her servant to his feet, the scarred wretch she'd called "Manners." A damned civilized name for a blackguard and a thief. The fellow had been at the tables last night—he still wore the bandages of that nasty cut. An accomplice of some sort, then.

No doubt this was all some amusing game to her, a

diversion for the bored little heiress who could have anything she pleased. And Brynston, ass that he was, had fallen for her scheme.

"I haven't the first idea what you might mean by that odious remark." Katie sniffed, having recovered her dignity, though her face was still dangerously pale. "I can only infer that, despite your title and your fancy English manners, you are no gentleman. Good day, Lord Brynston." She tucked her arm quickly beneath Manners's and made to glide away, the scandalized abigail coming up behind them.

But Manners was slow and clumsy on his boot-soles, and they were no match for Brynston. He closed the gap between them in a few strokes of his skates, and murmured in Katie's ear, "I shouldn't be so quick to take leave if I were you, my dear."

Manners turned on the earl, the scarred face twisting into a savage snarl. "You wouldn't be threatening the young lady, now would you, sir? I'm afraid I can't allow that."

Brynston assessed the situation. He was a tall man by anyone's standards, standing above six feet, but despite his skates this hulking creature towered over him. Lord Brynston was no mean hand in the boxing ring, and he suspected he could take the blackguard, but he would not be able to dispatch the massive brute quickly.

And it would not do for the earl of Brynston to be seen brawling like a commoner in the public streets. Surely there were more effective ways to put an end to this pair's disgraceful thievery.

"I would hardly call it a threat," Brynston said, meeting the man's steady gaze with his own. "Perhaps you might consider it a warning. I don't know how cheats are viewed in your country, but in mine, the practice is quite beyond the pale. I daresay you shan't find another victim to rook by night's end. And the young lady's chances of snaring a titled husband would seem to be somewhat imperiled."

Katie fixed Brynston with those clear green eyes, and for an instant he caught a glimpse of something startling, as if he'd caught the eye of some wild creature before it slipped back into the forest.

The girl herself brought him quickly to his senses. "I wouldn't give two cents for the richest lord in England," she said, haughty despite that abominable American accent. "Especially if you are a typical example of the species. Good day, sir."

She pushed off roughly on her skates, the scarred fellow Manners struggling along behind her on the slick ice. The round-faced abigail skated beside her mistress, chittering like an outraged squirrel.

Brynston watched them for a few seconds. The girl's snowy mantle waved behind her like a battle standard, and the yellow plume on her hat caught the breeze jauntily. She looked the very picture of a delightfully carefree young lady of fashion.

And she was a damned sharper. A cheat who had all but stolen forty-five thousand pounds from his family. No, Brynston corrected himself: twice that. That was what the Willowbys rightfully would have won if the baggage hadn't resorted to false play.

The earl scowled and pushed off on his skates, moving through the busy crowd toward his carriage. There was little to be gained in following them, but he was not about to give up. Somehow, he'd think of a way to bring that unscrupulous little hoyden to heel, and get his family's money back in the bargain. He considered it a matter of honor.

And in matters of honor, the Brimstone Earl always had his way.

Brynston was in a vile temper by the time he came home, anger settling around him like a blue-black cloud. It had been years since he'd given his rages free rein, but the stories about him had persisted. The downstairs parlor maid had blanched with fear, as if she might faint dead away at his glower as he prowled the house.

Finally he'd shut himself up in his library, unwilling to submit himself to any further displays of terror. Only his valet, Edward Graves, had dared interrupt him. The man had set himself to dusting the already immaculate book-shelves, ignoring the fact that household dusting was quite beyond the purview of a gentleman's valet.

"You are quite certain, your lordship?" Graves was blinking rapidly, the only sign that he was uncomfortable at Brynston's pronouncement.

"I'd recognize the fellow anywhere. His face is hideously scarred, there couldn't be another like him in all of England. His hand was still bandaged from the cut he'd given himself. He served our drinks last night, and I ended up feeling duecedly queer all evening. Have you ever known me to get foxed on a single rum punch, Graves?"

"Not since your lordship's days in the schoolroom," Graves conceded. "And early days, at that."

"There was a commotion over her gown—he'd spilled something. That must have been the moment when he palmed her the cards. And that hugger-mugger with the tray of glasses—I'd lay odds it was some kind of diversion. Old tricks, but I didn't recognize them dressed in such pretty feathers."

Graves lifted a skeptical eyebrow. "The young lady *is* an heiress of some considerable fortune, sir. It seems doubtful that such a person would condescend to cheating at cards."

"She's one of those spoilt American girls—savages, every one of 'em," Brynston said. "And there's something about her—the look of a bird in a gilded cage. I shouldn't be surprised if she were quite miserable."

"So your lordship feels pity for the unscrupulous creature?" Graves ventured. He applied the duster to Pliny's *Historia Naturalis* as if trying to scrub the gilt off the binding.

Brynston scowled. "Not an ounce of it. She cheated at cards. The single most dishonorable thing a gentleman can do. And that's the trouble of it."

Graves looked up from his dusting. "Sir?"

Brynston brought his fist down on a small table with a clatter. "She's not a bloody gentleman, is she? If she were, I could call her out and be done with it. She's a female, an infernal female who's got ninety thousand pounds that by rights belongs to me. And I want it back."

"The young lady might be somewhat averse to returning such a sum," Graves pointed out helpfully.

Brynston shot his valet a withering look. "Thank you, Graves, I had considered that fact. The baggage seems completely unconcerned at being unmasked as a nasty little fraud. But damn it all, she won't profit by this chicanery. Anyway, there's Val to consider."

"Indeed, sir," Graves murmured, "I daresay young Valentine would make himself quite insufferable if he were to discover your lordship had forfeited thirty thousand at deep play. In light of your lordship's recent discussion with the boy, that is."

Brynston's withering look turned to scorching poison. "Damn it, Graves, that's not what I meant."

The valet blinked owlishly and nodded. "Of course not, sir."

Brynston's scowl would have made a lesser man quake, but he knew from long experience that Graves was perfectly unflappable. It was among the man's chief qualifications as the earl's valet. Brynston couldn't abide by a man who cringed every time a fellow displayed a touch of bad temper.

"Right then," Brynston said, satisfied. "We're agreed. Extreme measures are called for."

Graves's eyebrow raised a fraction of an inch. "As your lordship thinks best."

Brynston noted Graves's failure to concede agreement, and chose to ignore it. His valet had always tended toward an almost cowardly overcaution. "The girl seems to give no thought to her reputation, no thought to civilized custom, and certainly no thought to honor."

"It would seem not, sir."

"She's a damned bit of cheeky American fluff, a spoilt child severely in want of discipline."

Graves said nothing, but nodded faintly.

Brynston twisted his calfskin gloves absently in his hands, half wishing they were the American baggage's pretty neck. "If rich Yankee papas aren't in the habit of keeping their progeny in line, I know one man who damned well will."

"Am I to assume that your lordship is formulating a plan to recover the funds?" Graves asked.

Brynston tossed the gloves aside, impatient to begin. "This isn't about money. Bugger the bloody money."

"Indeed, sir," Graves said, doubtless mortified to his toes by the earl's vulgar remark.

But Brynston was in no humor to coddle Graves's tender sensibilities. "God help me, Graves, but money aside, I intend to teach Katherine Feathering a lesson she will never forget."

Katie had to sit on her hands on the drive home to keep herself from biting her nails down to the quick. This fiasco with Brynston would completely overturn their plans. Now they would have to leave for the Continent immediately—tomorrow at first light would not be too soon. Val Willowby certainly wouldn't be paying his debt, now that his brother had found Katie out.

London was a dangerous city for those who made their living outside the law. She'd once seen a boy hanged at Newgate for having stolen a watch chain. She shuddered to think what the barbarous English might do to a sham heiress who'd cheated a peer out of thirty thousand pounds.

Suddenly the carriage seemed oppressively dark and close, a rolling cage rattling its way to the gallows. If only she'd taken another assistant that night! Competent sharpers were a dime a dozen in London, and she should have known it was reckless to use Manners. It *was* difficult to forget him, once one had seen his face. But lately she'd been playing for high stakes—obscenely high—and she'd been nervous. Having Manners close at hand had soothed her, allowed her to keep a cool head.

It had been a stupid move. Katie was tough. Tough enough to have taken Brynston for his expensive ride by herself, and laughed all the way home. Now she'd brought all the fury of the English peerage down on their heads, in the form of one dangerous-looking Brimstone Earl. Because she'd been weak.

Cardsharps couldn't afford to be weak.

Heartsick, Katie looked out the window of the careening carriage. Another midnight disappearance, another cutting of every tie. But Katie would walk away from the name, the house, the clothes—all of it, and without a backward glance. She'd done it many times before. She'd just never realized how much she hated it.

Katie nearly wrenched the handle off the carriage door when they pulled to a stop in front of their Berkeley Square lodgings. Alex appeared in an instant, towering over her. He was the only person in the world Katie could tolerate looming over her like some mother bear. "Your eyes, child," he said in a low whisper, laying a comforting hand on her shoulder. "You've got to learn to keep the trapped look out of your eyes. You mustn't be afraid, we'll get out of this like we have a hundred times before."

Katie nodded, pasting on a bright expression. "Sorry," she whispered. "I'm all right now."

"There's my girl," Alex said with a smile. "Now, let's go in there and explain things to your father."

When they had told Phineas Starr the news, he was not pleased that they were once again on the run, but he was not terribly surprised either. "Bound to happen once in awhile," he said, not unpleasantly. "No good letting the grass grow under our feet, is it, girl? That's not what Starrs are made for!"

No, Katie thought. *Starrs are made to cheat and steal.*

But she said nothing, only kept the smile stuck firmly to her lips. When Katie was a child and the family had had to decamp quickly, her father had always said they were going away on an "adventure." Katie's mother would shoot him a look that could have felled a pack of wild beasts. The older Katie got, the more she understood her late mother. This was not an adventure. This was simply running away.

Packing did not take long. It rarely did when one was leaving everything behind. Katie tucked a handful of personal effects into her bag: a small bottle of scent, her clean underthings, and the few items that had followed her gypsy existence since late childhood—a heavy silver-backed hairbrush, a small hand mirror, a pair of modest tortoise and topaz combs that were of little use on her now close-cropped hair.

And a silver locket enameled with violets that Katie wore on a long ribbon, hidden beneath her gowns or tucked into her reticule. The locket swung open to reveal a miniature portrait of her mother, painted during one of her family's more stable periods. She thought there was some chance her father had actually paid the painter's bill. The trifling ornament was far too shabby to be worn by an heiress like Katherine Feathering. But the grubbing little thief Katie Starr found it oddly comforting.

And she had one last trinket to add—the green glass ear bobs Brynston had won for her at the Frost Fair. She had intended to leave them on her dressing table, but something in her resisted the idea. She tucked them into her jewelry box with the rest of her paste and trumpery. They would remind her of the time she'd let herself get a bit too close to the fire—close enough to singe her toes. It would be a valuable lesson.

By late that evening they were finished. Alex had booked passage on a ship leaving at dawn the next morning. Katie's few possessions were packed, and Phineas was positively gleeful at the prospect of another "adventure."

Katie kept her apprehension carefully hidden until after dinner, but excused herself early to go to bed. Her richly appointed room, with its tasteful, unimaginative watercolors and frilly bed hangings, depressed her even more. She turned out the lamp almost immediately, although it was some time before she could fall asleep.

Katie had just begun a fitful dream when she was startled awake again by a small noise near the ewer stand. The night was dark and moonless, and she could make out nothing but a few black shadows. Her heart slammed to a gallop, and her throat felt dry and tight. She sprang to a sitting position, her hands gripping the bedclothes. "Who's there?" she cried sharply.

A calfskin-gloved hand clamped over her mouth, and she began to struggle furiously. For a moment she was as wild with fear as a trapped animal, unable to think or breathe as she thrashed. Her hands were pinned to her sides by a man of considerable strength. She finally gained the presence of mind to bite at the hand over her mouth, but the leather gloves kept the assailant from feeling her teeth. Working quickly, the man thrust a cloth gag into her mouth, tying it in a hard, bulky knot behind her head.

Katie felt a tide of panic so strong she nearly fainted. She fought it, willing herself to think clearly. Who could want to abduct her—the Turks? Whoever was responsible for this attack, she'd have to keep her wits about her if she were going to come out of it in one piece.

"My apologies for the inconvenience, Miss Feathering," came a soft, dry voice in Katie's ear when the brute had finished tying the gag, his hands moving to secure her arms behind her back with a rough length of rope.

Katie was horrified to recognize the voice of the Brimstone Earl.

4

Brynston quickly forced Katie's hands behind her back and tied them with a cloth. She fought him hard, thrashing in earnest now, trying to knock over the heavy silver pitcher on the ewer stand. Anything to alert the household and get her out of this.

"I'm afraid I can't let you do that, my dear," he said quietly, gathering her tightly in his arms. She worked to smash her heel on his instep, but he simply lifted her a few inches off the ground. His strength was absolute, and he had the advantage of two free hands.

His voice continued its relentless soft assault of her ear. "I realize it's a bit harsh, but you've left me with no other choice." A blindfold came down over her eyes, and Katie's stomach lurched with fear. "The truth of it is," he continued, sounding oddly rational, "you've practically forced me to kidnap you. You've brought this on yourself, girl, and I hope it teaches you a lesson."

If Katie hadn't been bound up like a trussed chicken, and gagged to boot, she honestly thought she would have laughed. The man was lecturing her as if he were some kind of schoolmaster. Was he completely mad? Earls didn't go around just kidnapping women, even women who happened to have fleeced them for a bit of cash. Weren't they supposed to go by some kind of code of honor?

Honor doesn't apply to women like you, Katie. The thought came before she could chase it away, and she knew it was true. She had been born into a den of thieves, and their lives had twisted and warped her until she was fully one of them. She could lay no claim to the tenderness due a lady.

It took him a long time to get her out the window, during which it was something of a miracle she wasn't physically ill. Only long years of extricating herself from tricky situations kept her from panicking now. She had a bad moment when, after he had fitted her into some rope cradle contraption, she had felt herself free-fall for an instant. But the cradle held her and she was lowered to safety without further incident. Brynston heaved her into a carriage, muttered a few words to the driver, and they lurched on into the night.

When Brynston's large hands finally removed the blindfold from her eyes, Katie winced at the blaze of light. Two men stood over her: the earl and an impeccably dressed, gaunt young man with a long, serious face.

"Graves, turn the lamps down, won't you?" Brynston said quickly.

"Of course, sir," the long-faced young man said, making haste to dim the harsh lights.

The small room was permeated with a stale, rancid smell. From beneath Katie's feet she could hear the sounds of men laughing too loudly. Brynston had brought her to an inn of some kind, and a none-too-reputable one, from the grimy look of it.

Katie would have scowled if she hadn't been constricted by that awful gag, so she contented herself with glaring murderously at Brynston. If he thought he could make up for this barbaric treatment with a tiny kindness like dimming the lights, he had better think again.

"English beast!" she finally spat out when he'd removed the gag. "In America, no man would be so despicable and cowardly and—ow!"

As Brynston worked to untie her ankles, he gave her a sharp pinch on her bare instep. "Sorry, my dear, just wanted to be sure the blood was circulating properly."

Katie's pulse was pounding so violently that she thought it must surely be visible in her throat. But the earl had not really harmed her, and it seemed from his relatively gentle treatment that he had no intention of doing so. It was just possible that he could be bullied into letting her go. "Circulating, my eye! You pinched me on purpose! I'll have you thrown into prison for this, see if I don't! My father will have every Runner in London out looking for me, and when they discover what you've done—"

"Rather a lot of fuss over a little pinch, wouldn't you say, Graves?" Brynston's eyebrow tilted in the most despicably arrogant way.

Graves's gaunt face kept its neutral expression. "Perhaps a trifle more fuss than is customary, your lordship."

Katie wriggled her wrists against the ties. "It isn't the pinch, you . . . you scoundrel! It's kidnapping me this way, without the slightest regard for—"

Brynston's blue eyes narrowed, and the harshness returned to the cold, severe planes of his face. Katie swallowed hard, suddenly doubting that she'd be able to bully the man. He had murder in his eyes, and she decided it might be wiser to hold her tongue for the moment.

"Regard?" he said, his voice bone-dry. "A pretty word from a shameless card cheat."

"I don't have the first idea what you're talking about," she said quietly. "Take me home at once."

Graves lifted his sandy eyebrows in silent surprise.

"Not the first idea? Really?" Brynston's voice was pure ice. "Allow me to fill you in, then. Last week you won fifteen thousand pounds off my brother. Now I'll be the first to admit that Val's a rash little idiot, but he's no fool at the tables. I'd assumed the silly pup was foxed, or let his pride overcome his intellectuals, or some such damned thing. There was a time when I was susceptible to such stupidities myself."

"No longer?" she said tartly, regretting it the next instant. The last thing she ought to be doing was taunting this insane Englishman.

He studied her for a long, thoughtful moment. "You ought to sack your maid, you know. Or set her to peeling potatoes. She hasn't a clue as to what to do for your looks."

Katie shouldn't have felt stung by the criticism, but she did. She was suddenly acutely aware of her plain, voluminous linen nightgown and the unfeminine short-ness of her cropped hair. Yesterday she had been silly, perhaps, but glamorous, a songbird in flashy feathers. But tonight Brynston had discovered small, plain Katie Starr. Not surprisingly, he'd found her lacking.

Katie squashed her hurt feelings. "Don't find me to your liking, my lord? What a pity. You might as well let me go, then. It would damage your reputation to no end to be known to have abducted such a loathsome antidote."

Brynston raised an eyebrow, visibly amused. He walked over to a small table and poured himself a sherry, studying her as if she were a painting he was considering buying. "You misunderstand me, Miss Feathering. I meant only that your maid is gilding the lily to your detri-ment. You are too small to wear ruffles and bows, they make you look like a snuffbox."

"Are all English earls such flatterers?" she snapped.

"And the contrast between the boyish hair and that delightfully feminine body," he continued, passing his eyes insolently over her. "You should exploit it, Miss Feathering, not hide beneath that silly blonde wig. The combination is most . . . piquant."

She looked quickly down at the floor to keep him from seeing the surprise in her eyes. She should not be here, he should not be saying such things. And she should most definitely not be finding herself strangely flattered. She looked up at him again and managed a cold smile. "If I had but known my lord preferred short hair on ladies, I should never have cut it off."

He took a sip of his sherry, pretending not to hear her. "In a classical dress, with a few carefully chosen adornments, you would turn every titled head in London, married or no. That's what you want, isn't it? To convince some sapskull to overlook your lack of manners, your lack of pedigree, even that appalling accent, and make you into a duchess? Or a marchioness at the very least. I daresay you'll manage it, the bait's tempting enough."

Katie pulled hard at the ropes tying her down. "You'll forgive me if I don't giggle and blush, my lord. Something about being tied to a chair always interferes with my pleasure at a compliment."

Brynston shrugged and tilted back the last of his sherry. "It's not a compliment. I never pay compliments to spoilt girls, it only encourages them. It is simply the truth."

"I'll thank you to keep the truth—your opinion of the truth—to yourself," she said.

He set his empty glass back on the table. "Irritable little thing, aren't you?"

"Only when I've been abducted by a skulking English brute with a chunk of burnt sulfur where his heart ought to be," Katie said, tilting her chin up to meet his gaze. She profoundly wished her hands were free, and not tied behind her.

Brynston laughed and stepped toward her, taking her chin lightly in his hand. His eyes tore away her defenses as they had over the card table, and suddenly she needed all her will to keep up her pretense. She was Katherine Feathering, a foolish child who took nothing seriously, least of all the dishonorable victory she'd snatched from Brynston the night before. However disconcerting she might find the Brimstone Earl, she could not afford to forget that.

His eyes narrowed as he released her. "Am I truly such a monster?"

"How am I supposed to reply?" she answered, mustering every snippet of courage she possessed. "You break into my rooms in the middle of the night—"

"Actually, it wasn't much past ten," he drawled. "You get to bed awfully early for such a felonious little creature. I wonder why that should be. Planning on being up at the crack of dawn tomorrow, are you?"

"I am not felonious," she said irritably. "I should say you're the felon, here, not me. Or isn't abduction a crime in this horrible country? Perhaps rich English earls are beyond the law."

"Forty-five thousand pounds poorer, actually, thanks to you," he said, pouring himself another sherry. "Though I daresay honor does not strictly require Val to make good his debt, considering. Did you run the same scheme with him? Down to your beastly accomplice dropping a plateful of drinks virtually in his ear? No doubt the clamor gave you some kind of cover—what was it? Marked cards? An ace or two up those pretty sleeves? Just to satisfy my curiosity, mind."

"You're mad," she said, tucking her chin stubbornly. "You are quite insane and I think I shall do best by praying for God's mercy to deliver me from you."

He ignored her. "The thirty thousand pounds is nothing to me, of course. It was nothing more than the matter of an evening's work. An *honest* evening's work," he said significantly.

Katie did her best not to look at him, murmuring pointedly, " . . . who art in heaven, hallowed be Thy name, Thy kingdom come . . ."

He downed the sherry in a swift, decisive movement. "But I find I can't let this squalid little business go. It's a matter of honor, you see. Something I realize you know nothing about, but I'll do what I can to explain the concept to you. When a person—even a female person—has revealed herself to be nothing but a low, common, filthy cheat, a fellow has to do what he can to unmask the fraud for what she is."

Katie cast him a furious look. " . . . and forgive me my trespasses, as I forgive those who trespass against me," she murmured, "and deliver me—"

Brynston blithely continued. "Because if he doesn't, the wretched creature shall never know when she has gone too damned far."

Katie wrenched again at her arms, wanting to be out of this, wanting the blasted Brimstone Earl to make his point and let her go. Surely he was only trying to teach her a lesson, as if she were a silly little girl caught pinching penny candy from a sweetshop. "You're right, I went a little too far, my lord. I'm very sorry for all the trouble I've caused your family. If you'll just drive me home now, we can all—"

"Silence!" he whispered, and the whisper was more frightening than the most thunderous shouting would have been. "You went more than a little too far, Miss Feathering, and I have no intention of letting you off with a tweak on the nose and the admonition to be a good girl."

Katie, who'd hoped he was about to do just that, felt her temper begin to fray. "You can't just keep me here. What do you intend to do with me? Just what is it that you want?"

Graves looked expectantly at Brynston, his gaunt face hanging politely on the earl's answer.

Brynston scowled. "If I wish to keep you here until you are a hundred and seven, that's what I'll bloody well do."

"Shall I make arrangements for an extended visit, then, your lordship?" Graves asked, with an almost excruciating politeness.

"You're an excellent fellow, Graves," Brynston muttered. "And one of these days I vow I'll strangle you."

"Very good, sir," Graves said blandly.

"If I want you to make arrangements, I'll inform you. Now, as to our larcenous heiress—"

Katie thumped her chair with her heels in protest. "I am *not* larcenous."

"Criminally high-spirited, then," Brynston said with a nasty smile. "Before I can even consider letting you go, I must have my money back."

"Your money?" His money. Of course he would want his blasted money. And Katie absolutely could not afford to give it to him.

"My money," Brynston repeated. "You remember. A nice, round sum you won from me last night. I'd like it back now. As a matter of fact, I want sixty thousand—that's what I would have walked away with if you hadn't cheated. We will consider my brother's debt to be null and void."

Katie smiled weakly. "I see. I'd love to, my lord, all in the interest of good will, but I . . . I don't have your money any more."

Brynston twisted his leather gloves in his hands in a motion that made Katie wince. "What d'you mean, you don't have it? You've had your pretty paws on it for less than twenty-four hours! You can't possibly have spent it yet."

"Not spent it, my lord, no, of course not," Katie babbled, forcing herself to think quickly. The earl didn't seem about to murder her in the near future, and her father absolutely needed that money. "I lost it. On a horse race."

Graves busied himself at straightening the decanter and glasses.

Brynston's eyes blazed for a moment before he regained his composure. "You're lying. A cheat doesn't lose that kind of money in gaming. Anyway, thirty thousand on a single race? It's preposterous."

Katie forced her hands to stop their fidgeting behind her back, as she took measure of the situation. Brynston knew she was not quite the bubble-headed thing she'd appeared last night. What he didn't know was that she was no more an heiress than she was the Queen of Spain. "I met a funny little man at the track who told me the horse would win, and I wagered the whole sum on it. I quite like wagering large sums of money—it makes life interesting."

"It's rather more interesting when you don't know how it'll all turn out," Brynston said dryly. "Someday I hope you will try the experience for yourself. In the meantime, I need not regain the precise notes I lost to you, as I hadn't the time to form much attachment to them. But in one form or another, you will return the thirty thousand pounds you won through shameless and unlawful trickery, and you will augment it with the thirty thousand you wagered against mine. Before you do, there can be no question of your release."

Katie nearly wrenched her shoulder out of the socket trying to twist free of the bonds he'd tied. It seemed the more she struggled, the more tightly the ropes held her. When she was free of this horrible Englishman, she vowed to herself she'd make him sorry he ever set eyes on her. "I can't give you the money, my lord. I haven't got it."

His voice was dry and nonchalant, but he paced the room as restlessly as a cat. "Of course you do, my dear. Surely your doting father will cough up the cash, when you've explained matters to him."

"Daddy won't give it to me. He's already got his nose out of joint over the horse race."

She looked into his eyes and willed him to believe her. Her old gift might be somewhat impaired here, with her hands tied behind her and the earl on the verge of coming to a boil, but she had to try. "I cannot return your money, my lord, and you cannot continue to keep me here." *Believe me. Let me go.* "I don't know what you were intending, but—"

He interrupted her, his eyes shining dangerously. He stopped suddenly in front of her, his body an overwhelming wall of muscle and sinew. "Do you know, Miss Feathering, what pretty young ladies usually do when they can't pay their gambling debts?"

Katie shivered. Had the room gone suddenly cold? But the fireplace blazed bright and hot. "I don't suppose I do."

Brynston leaned over her as he stroked the side of her face. "They negotiate."

Graves coughed, polishing the glasses as if his life depended on it.

Katie felt her mouth go dry. "Negotiate, my lord?"

Brynston's eyes burned harshly. He was suddenly close enough that she could feel the gentle warmth of his breath on her own lips. "What d'you think you might have that would be worth sixty thousand pounds to a young man of healthy . . . appetites?"

For one awful moment, Katie was not sure she could still breathe. "I'm sure I can't imagine, my lord."

The tip of his finger traced a line from her temple down to her collarbone, and across it to the base of her throat, where her pulse was racing. "Not an inkling, my dear? Not the first tiny glimmering? I'd thought you were a creature of more imagination."

This was a threat. It had to be. But Katie was not feeling like a young woman who'd just been threatened. The butterflies in her stomach were threatening to lift her clear off the ground, and her heart was pounding in a way that was not at all as unpleasant as it ought to be. She knew this muddle was his fault somehow. "Have you poisoned me?" she blurted.

Brynston threw back his head and laughed. "Not yet, but it's a fine idea. Graves, did you take note of that? The girl wants to know if she's been poisoned. Somewhere in this vile neighborhood we ought to be able to find a competent poisoner, I daresay."

"Undoubtedly, my lord," Graves said.

"Would you like a slow poisoning, my pretty, or a quick one?" Brynston asked.

The doorknob turned, and a wicked-looking, pinch-nosed face peered into the room. "Everything as it should be, your lordship?" the pinched face asked. "You wouldn't care for another bottle of the sherry?"

"Good God, no, the last was execrable," Brynston muttered, but in a louder voice he said, "Lyme, come in here for a moment, won't you?"

The pinched nose made its way into the room, followed by a face and body of extraordinary unpleasantness. The man was dressed entirely in black, with long, skinny limbs like a spider's. "Yes, your lordship?"

Behind him was a boy, no more than ten, wearing an oversized black chapeau bras. The hat's points were worn side-to-side, making him look like an even scrawnier version of Napoleon. His thin face was a mass of freckles beneath the ludicrous hat.

Brynston stooped to take a lump of coal from the coal scuttle, and before Lyme could move to stop him, he began drawing a straight line at waist level along the entire circumference of the room.

The freckled boy worked to keep a grin from splitting his face, but Lyme's black eyes glittered angrily.

Lyme said only, "Yer lordship'll pay to have the room repapered?"

"Don't be impertinent, man," Graves said crisply. "His lordship will make all appropriate compensation when he sees you've done your job."

Brynston looked up from his artistic pursuits, a faint smile on his lips. "Fear not, Lyme. You will profit exceedingly from your exercises here. Now then, and you mark this as well, Finch. This young lady is to be at perfect liberty and comfort, with the exception that she may not cross this line. Do I make myself clear?"

The freckled boy eyed Katie suspiciously, and Lyme looked down at her as if he'd like to gobble her for dessert. "Clear as glass, yer lordship," said Lyme.

"You and your evil band are not to lay a hand on her while she's here. Her well-being, so long as she confines herself to this room, is worth your life to you."

The nasty gleam in Lyme's eye dimmed a bit, but he said, "Don't you worry, yer lordship. The young lady's as safe with me as with her blessed mother, gawd help me if she in't."

"You'll need more than God's help if she comes to any ill," Brynston said, his voice lowering to that icy dryness Katie was coming to know all too well.

"Mr. Lyme," Katie said, putting on her haughtiest manner, "you should know that this supposed gentleman is a perfect lunatic, keeping me here quite against my will. I expect the Bow Street Runners will be here any instant, they won't hesitate to break the door down. If you've got any sense at all, you won't believe a word of this man's promises."

Lyme looked as if he might strike her to the ground. "Here, now, I in't gonna listen to any cheek from a stuck-up soss brangle, see?" His eyes glittered menacingly.

The freckled boy frowned at the spidery villain, but said nothing.

Brynston gave Lyme a look to make the devil himself quake in his boots. "You'll take whatever cheek the young lady chooses to dispense. If I hear you've so much as laid a single sooty finger on her, I'll thrash you to within a half-inch of your life."

The boy's face relaxed slightly, though he still wrung his huge hat in his hands. Lyme transformed into the picture of servility. "I'll treat her like I would me own daughter, yer lordship, gawd strike me down if I don't."

"I hope you'll do a little better than that," Brynston said. "Now then, Graves, we'll be on our way."

"You can't mean you're leaving me here!" Katie cried, the fear in her voice not entirely false. She glanced out the window, onto a warren of twisting streets, filthy with dung and offal. A high-pitched giggle came, muted, through the wall.

Suddenly it became clear to her. She'd assumed this was some dirty, remote little inn, but it was something worse than that. A flash house, where thieves met to congregate and recruit young boys into their profession. From the sounds on the other side of that wall, this one doubled as a brothel.

She had to get out of here. Katie was more familiar

with the grimy brutality of the underworld than Brynston could have guessed, and she knew just how treacherous such places could be. Lyme was untrustworthy and dangerous, and could not be counted on to refrain from hurting her.

The giggle came through the wall again. Katie could not, under any circumstances, spend the night in a place like this. She'd rather have been stuffed in some filthy dungeon.

Brynston smiled faintly. "Don't you care for your accommodations? They're the very finest I could procure, I assure you. No one from the *ton* will ever catch a scandalized glimpse of you here. And so long as you don't get any foolish ideas about escaping, you'll be perfectly safe. Of course, take one dainty step outside that black line and you'll be murdered in a trice—or worse. That trinket 'round your neck would be more than cause enough," Brynston said, reaching down to examine her locket.

"Don't!" she cried, moving to pull away from him. But she was bound securely, and she could do little more than scoot her chair noisily a few inches to one side.

The movement was enough to brush her breast roughly against his hand, and the room seemed to swim for a moment. The look on Brynston's own face was unreadable, as if he were a marble statue. "My apologies, my dear."

She nodded, not trusting herself to speak.

Brynston lifted the locket gently from around her head. "I shouldn't bother clouting her over the head for this, Lyme. It wouldn't bring you two shillings. I wonder, Miss Feathering, whatever could possess you to wear such a shabby ornament. I shouldn't have thought it would be at all to your taste."

Katie turned her face away from him, not quite trusting her expression. "It has sentimental value. Something you obviously could never understand, since you appear not to have a heart in your wicked breast."

Brynston laughed again, the laugh of the devil himself.

"Quite correct, Miss Feathering. A present from an admirer? What is he—a stable boy? The gardener, perhaps?"

"You're unspeakable," she said.

Brynston pried the locket open. "Who's this, then? Not your lover. A rather beautiful woman, though with an expression that could sour good milk."

"Take your hands off that," she said, her throat tight.

He looked up at her, surprised. "Is she your mother? You have her eyes—I didn't see it at first."

"Just give it back, please," Katie said, working to keep her defenses from giving way. Stupid, to let a little thing like his offhand remark get to her, but her throat was beginning to constrict in a way that threatened tears. Damn this unfeeling bastard of an English lord, damn his questions, and damn the whole stupid mess that had brought her here.

"I'm sorry," he said quietly, his manner suddenly very different. The sardonic bitterness was gone, and his pale eyes had gentled. He replaced the locket around her neck, his fingers lightly brushing her neckline.

The unexpected moment of kindness caught her by surprise, and a single traitorous tear burned at the corner of her eye. Damn it! She was furious with herself, disgusted for letting him rattle her and disgusted for displaying her own weakness. "Just go away and leave me here to be murdered, if you please," she said, when she'd regained some measure of control. "I'm quite certain I'll prefer the company of these thieves and brutes to your own."

The boy looked entirely put out, but Lyme only licked his lips—in anticipation of profits or wickedness, Katie couldn't tell.

"Yes, I daresay you shall," Brynston said, the old aristocratic arrogance returning in full force. "Very well, then. Graves, untie the chit, will you? I shouldn't want her to be uncomfortable."

Katie's elbows and shoulders all but creaked in protest as Graves worked the ties. "Take me home, Lord Brynston.

You can't keep me here, you know you can't. This is madness."

"Not at all, my dear," he said pleasantly. "You will remain in this room until I have received sixty thousand pounds. I'll be writing a note—unsigned, naturally enough—to your father tonight, explaining the situation."

"He'll never pay you!" Katie said quickly. "He'd rather die than give in to the demands of a kidnapping blackguard."

"You would do well to pray he has more sense," the earl said dryly.

"I shall grow old and die here, and to the devil with you," she said, wincing as the ropes slid from her hands.

"As you please," he said. "I have more than ample means to keep you here forever, if that's what you prefer."

"English beast," she spat.

"A fitting match for a dishonorable American savage, then," he replied. "Good day, my dear. Do try and keep from annoying Lyme."

"Shall I remain with the young lady," Graves asked, "Or will your lordship require my presence?"

"No, come with me, Graves," Brynston said brusquely. "Surely a horrid English beast has need of his valet to spoonfeed him his pudding and wipe his nose."

"I can't fathom how you stay with such a hateful person, Graves," Katie said. "You seem like a decent enough fellow. Too decent to participate in this murderous business."

"Oh, I shouldn't think he'll murder you, miss," said Graves mildly. "At least, not if you conduct yourself as you ought."

"Thanks for your assurances," she said acidly.

"Remember what I said," Brynston said, his hand on the doorknob. "This is quite a ferocious neighborhood, Miss Feathering. If you take a single step outside the line

I've drawn for you, you will come to a sudden and deeply unfortunate end. Good day."

"No, wait!" she cried, furious. "Oh . . . *damn* you!" But the Brimstone Earl was gone.

5

That night, in the first small hours of the morning, it began to snow. By dawn, the snow had silenced London's streets and lanes, a clean white cloak to hide the city's sins.

Alexander Manners woke early, as he always did. He never slept very deeply—the old pains prevented that. But last night he had slept more fitfully than usual. Today the Starrs would pack up and move again. It was a hard time for Katie, having to work harder and more cleverly than ever. And Phineas Starr didn't seem to realize the toll this business was taking on his daughter. Katie was a good sharper, better than any Alex had ever seen, but she had a surprisingly tender heart. And Alex was worried about her.

The other servants would be awake soon, and Alex dressed quickly. He washed his face, wincing at the cold water on his scars. Even now, so many years later, they ached. Even now they reminded him of the bond between him and Katie. She was like a daughter to him. A thought flashed through his mind, unbidden—Alex felt

more protectively paternal of her than the girl's own
father did.

If things had only been different—

Alex smothered the thought ruthlessly. There was no
sense in bringing all that up again. He was nothing but an
old family friend, and it would be best for everyone if he
remembered his place. God knew Katie didn't need him
meddling in her family's business.

Hannah's feet in the hallway pittered to Katie's door,
and from his room Alex could just hear the maid's tentative knock. She knocked once, then again, then a third
time.

"The girl's picked a fine day to lie abed," Alex muttered to himself, squinting at the mirror to tie his cravat.
Strange, though. Not like Katie at all. Usually the girl had
nightmares the whole night before they'd decamp, and
wake up before even Alex himself did. The child turned
her back on the old memories in the daytime, but they
came back to haunt her at night. Alex fretted for a
moment, as he always did when he considered this problem. He'd have given his life for Katie, if need be, but
that didn't seem to be what she needed at all.

Alex froze, unable for a long instant to move at all,
when he heard Hannah's scream of dismay.

The maid's voice was a frightened, plaintive wail.
"She's gone! She was here last night, I swear it! Lord
defend and preserve us all! That lovely girl's done and
gone!"

Brynston enjoyed a tolerable breakfast, consisting of an
unimaginative but decently prepared steak-and-kidney
pie. The freckled boy, Finch, had ventured in with a tray
of kippers. But if there was one thing Brynston positively
could not abide, it was a plateful of kippers before a man
had drunk his morning tea.

"Remind me, Graves," he said offhandedly, "to make
sure that Miss Feathering is provided with something

other than kippers for breakfast. I don't believe Americans care for kippers."

Brynston had for the time being taken a room in the flash house, and this one comfortable enough, though the green and gilt wallpaper was beginning to grate on his nerves. From time to time in the night, he'd heard feminine giggling in the hallway, accompanied by the drunken babblings of young men. Odd that the infuriating Feathering creature should lead him once again to a place like this, a den of thieves and whores and swindlers. Before he'd come into his title, the underworld had been far more attractive to Brynston than the conscribed world of honor and respectability he now occupied.

Graves was studiously engaged in the business of pressing Brynston's best buckskins. The valet made no response to Brynston's suggestion, and his long, gaunt face was troubled. When Graves was troubled, Brynston himself would invariably pay the price for it.

Finally Brynston could stand no more of his valet's discreetly silent concern. "What is it, damn you? You look like a cat who's swallowed a poisoned mouse."

Graves inclined his head with the faintest of bows. "I beg your pardon, your lordship."

Brynston fixed him with a cold stare, thrusting his breakfast dishes roughly to one side and scattering crumbs all over the morning paper. "Don't be an ass, man, if you've got something to say then say it."

Graves looked up at him with those impassive gray eyes. "I was not under the impression that your lordship desired advice in the matter."

The matter. Graves meant the girl, of course. "I don't, especially, but I'll be damned if I let you go about making reproachful eyes at me."

Graves blinked. "My apologies, sir. I hadn't realized my eyes were giving offense. I shall correct my demeanor at once."

Brynston let out an exasperated cry and stood up from

the table. "You disapprove of my methods with the girl, I take it?"

"Is your lordship seeking my counsel?"

"I'm asking you a bloody direct question, confound you. Yes or no? Do you or do you not approve of the way I've dealt with the Feathering chit?"

"A direct question, your lordship?" Graves asked, as if to reassure himself.

"Point blank. Yes or no."

"No, sir. I regret to say I do not." Graves returned to his ironing, his face a perfect mask of studious concentration.

Brynston briefly entertained the notion of hurling the tea service through the small glass window, but thought better of it. "You can't very well leave it at that, Graves. What d'you mean *no*?"

"May I speak freely, sir?"

It took Brynston an almost superhuman effort to keep from bellowing. "For God's sake, I wish to high heaven you would."

Graves set the iron neatly to one side. "Young master Valentine is clearly freed of his obligation to the young lady. Your lordship has lost a shocking sum, but as that sum was won at the tables only a few hours previously, it would seem that your lordship had lost very little. To that end, your lordship's behavior seems somewhat . . . beyond the strictly necessary."

Brynston poured himself a third cup of tea, his annoyance subsiding into something else. Guilt? Nonsense, he had nothing to feel guilty about. "It's not a matter of money, it's a matter of principle."

"I see, sir." Graves resumed his ironing. "Abducting an heiress, then, is a principled response to a questionable evening's play at cards?"

Brynston took a swallow of his tea. It was decent stuff, but it had been sitting far too long, and it tasted acridly astringent in his mouth. "There's damned little more dishonorable than cheating at cards, Graves, you know it as well as I do. If the brat had been a man, she would have had to call me out at my merest suggestion of such a thing. Of course, she's not."

"Sir?"

"A man," Brynston said, thinking of the green fire in Miss Feathering's eyes. "For all she styles her hair like one. I must say, I fancy her natural color over that blond wig she wears."

"The young lady is indeed quite charming," Graves said blandly.

Charming. Graves had a way with understatement. Charming was the word for Katherine Feathering as she had been in Lady Odcombe's card room—the flounced and ribboned china shepherdess. Last night, in her voluminous white nightgown and her natural short curls the color of tawny vintage port, she was a startling beauty.

"Charming, if you like vipers," Brynston said finally, brushing aside his musings as he downed his tea.

"If I might, sir, she seems more a high-spirited girl than a genuinely treacherous one," Graves ventured with unusual directness.

Brynston scowled. "She hasn't got an ounce of shame. It's not as if she needed that money, Graves. She's rumored to have something like fifty thousand a year—a damned sight more than I do. She just cheats for the fun of it. I can't abide that, and I daresay no Englishman with an ounce of self-respect could abide it either."

"She may be unfamiliar with English custom," Graves said.

What the devil was the man on about? This wasn't at all like the usually reticent Graves, who often took twenty minutes of discreet waffling to get around to saying he thought one's cravat might need retying. This morning he insisted on openly defending that Feathering creature. The girl had driven everyone around her mad.

"Then it's time someone showed her how damned serious this business is," Brynston said crisply, in a tone to suggest that his opinion was not subject to revision.

"She doesn't give a fig for her honor or her reputation. At this rate, she'd be ruined in the *ton* before springtime. I'm doing her a favor—she'll end by thanking me for it, Graves, see if she doesn't."

"But surely it would be a great tragedy if something untoward were to happen to the girl," Graves insisted. The man had become positively blunt.

The thought of the girl coming to harm twisted Brynston's stomach into a surprising, painful knot. "You heard Lyme, the girl's perfectly safe."

Graves coughed discreetly. "Is it entirely wise, sir, to trust Mr. Lyme?"

"The man's a brute, of course, but he won't harm the girl unless it's in his interest. And he knows very well that it is most emphatically not in his interest."

Brynston could feel the disapproval that seemed to radiate from his valet in great waves, though Graves's face remained perfectly impassive.

"Damn it, don't you see?" Brynston continued. "He's enough of a bastard to keep the rest of these flash-house blackguards at bay, which is the important thing. God knows I don't want every bully and bawd in Pinchpye Close coming 'round. With Katherine Feathering's moral fiber, no doubt she'd be plying her charms in Covent Garden by the end of the week."

Graves's expression grew even longer and more pained, but still he said nothing, returning to his study of Brynston's buckskins.

"Damn it, man, cease your infernal glowering," Brynston snapped. "I said nothing would happen to the brat and I meant it. Lyme will look after her better than she deserves."

"As your lordship thinks best," Graves said mildly.

Brynston watched his valet bend over the ironing table as if he were inspecting diamonds. "Look here, I give you my word, upon my honor. That little American monster will come to no harm under my care. Is that good enough for you, you miserable blackmailer?"

Graves allowed himself a smile so faint it was almost invisible. "I'm sure that will be very satisfactory, sir."

A muffled knock came at the door, and Graves turned from his pressing to open it. It was the boy again.

"Hallo, there," Brynston said, doing his best not to seem intimidating. Somehow he invariably seemed to frighten children. Except his own rowdy pack of siblings—those he could hardly keep from taking over his house like a gang of monkeys. "What can I do for you, Finch?"

The boy tilted his chin up with the suggestion of bravado. "Mister Lyme done sent me with a message."

Brynston smiled amiably. "Oh yes? What would that be, then?"

"It's the lady. She says—" The boy cleared his throat, as if preparing to repeat a memorized speech. "She says she won't have nuffin' to do with nuffin' given her by a great unfeeling English bastard—beggin' yer pardon, yer lordship, it's what she said—and she won't touch a bite of food nor a drop of wine neither 'til she gets her freedom, seein' as she ain't done nuffin' wrong."

"What the hell—" Brynston broke off when he caught Graves's warning look. He did his best to reassemble his features into an expression of paternal kindness. "What I mean to say is, are you telling me the young lady declines to eat?"

"If I may make so bold, sir, there was the question of the suitability of kippers to the American palate," Graves said earnestly.

"Don't be a damned fool, Graves," Brynston snapped. "This has nothing to do with kippers. The girl's obviously trying to tell me she's not happy with our . . . arrangement."

"That's it exactly, yer lordship," Finch offered. "Says she'd rather die than give in to a brute such as yerself. Them's her words just as she spoke 'em."

Brynston would have been delighted to take a cane to the spoiled chit—or even better, to let her bloody well starve—but Graves's brow was furrowed into an expression of grievous concern. "If your lordship might recall his promise . . . " Graves said.

The man was becoming positively impertinent.

"Of course I remember my promise, damn your eyes!" Brynston snarled. "I made it no more than sixty seconds ago."

"Perhaps your lordship will be able to convince the young lady—" Graves suggested, his pale eyebrows lifted expectantly.

Finch stood in the doorway, his face defiantly courageous. Brynston wondered if the boy had taken the same inexplicable liking to Miss Feathering that Graves had. "Very well. I'll go see if I can reason with the creature."

Graves and Finch both looked markedly happier. "Very good, sir," Graves said.

Brynston stalked down the hall, swallowing his urge to curse a streak that would make a sailor blush. He'd known that duplicitous bit of American fluff for less than forty-eight hours, and she'd already turned his life completely topsy-turvy, bringing him back to this world of shadows and vice he'd have sworn he'd left behind forever.

Brynston stopped to collect himself as his hand rested on the doorknob. In an instant, his composure had returned to its usual icy, stern correctness.

It was a pity he'd ever laid eyes on the brat. But he promised himself now, by the time the Brimstone Earl was done with Katherine Feathering, she would rue the day every bit as much as he did.

6

Brynston opened the door, ready to verbally tear the girl into small, remorseful bits. But she stood there with her back to him, her short curls revealing her bare nape. She'd wrapped a gray wool blanket tightly around her voluminous nightgown as if to shield herself, and the cool morning light made her skin shine like an angel's. For an instant he could not move, struck by her terrible fragility, by the sweetness of those few inches of bare flesh at the back of her neck.

She wheeled to face him and chased all such madness from his mind. Miss Feathering's eyes blazed with a peculiarly intense green flame, and there was nothing fragile about the determined set of her mouth.

"Finch tells me you won't eat your breakfast," Brynston said, drawling the words in his most intentionally annoying aristocratic fashion.

Finch slipped in from under his elbow, and was now looking up at the girl entreatingly. "It ain't the kippers, is it, milady? I ain't one for kippers meself. More fit for a cat than a pretty young lady. Bloody unappetizin', that's what they is." He blushed quickly. "Pardon me language, milady."

"No, Tom," she said gently. "It isn't the kippers. It's *him*." She looked balefully at Brynston. "You don't frighten me, you know. For all your wretched threats, you can't force me to eat. And if I don't eat, I shall die, and you will be entirely responsible."

Brynston leaned nonchalantly against the door frame. So the girl had a touch of the tragic romantic about her. Fascinating. "I hadn't seen it in you before," he mused.

Her eyes narrowed. "Hadn't seen what?"

"The impulse to martyrdom. You have a neck very like Marie Antoinette's—absolutely made for the block."

The girl's hand fluttered nervously to her neck.

"I must say, my dear," Brynston continued, enjoying himself, "that such displays work to far more suitable effect in genuinely virtuous young ladies. But I will allow, you give the role a certain piquancy."

"I would rather burn at the stake than pique your interests, my lord," she said evenly.

Finch moved between the two of them and began fussing at the breakfast tray.

Brynston laughed. "There now, you see, that's precisely what I mean. If you were some ladylike milksop, such a speech would suggest there'd be no sport in chasing you at all. But in an ill-mannered hellion like yourself, the protests only spur a man's curiosity."

She turned away from him again, unaware of the effect her delectably unprotected nape was having on his self-control. "I promise you, my lord, if you chase me I will drop down as dead as an opossum, and you won't find me to your liking at all."

He found himself crossing the floor, wanting very much to be next to her, to catch the subtle fragrance of her perfume, an intoxicating mix of spice and roses. He'd caught a hint of it when he'd struggled with her to take her from her rooms. Now he needed to breathe it again, there on her pale, bare neck. "I haven't the first idea what an opossum might be, my dear, and I beg you to refrain from enlightening me."

Finch's thin shoulders were tight as he clattered the plates and teacups on Miss Feathering's tray.

She pulled the blanket tighter around her arms. "It's a disagreeable little animal in America, with beady eyes and a tail like a rat." She shot him a furious glare. "And it bites."

Brynston reached out to brush the rough wool blanket away from the tender flesh above her nightgown's high neckline. "I can see that begging spoilt American brats does a man not a whit of good. Therefore, you may consider my next statement a direct order. You will eat your meals like a well-behaved little girl, or I'll turn you over my knee and give you the spanking you so richly deserve."

Her breath quickened almost imperceptibly, and he imagined her pulse would be like a small bird's, rapid and fluttering. But her voice was surprisingly clear and strong. "Your threats don't frighten me, my lord. You may torture me if you like, but I will not eat until I have been returned to my father."

"Oh, I don't intend to torture you, Miss Feathering," he said, feeling a hungry smile curve over his lips. "Not precisely. But you will do as you are told, or I promise you'll regret it very much."

Finch brought the teapot down on the breakfast tray so hard that Brynston was surprised the plates didn't crack in half.

Katherine swallowed, but held Brynston's gaze. "I won't."

He reached up to trace the high line of her cheekbone. "You will."

Her cheeks stained bright rose, then she pulled sharply away, as if she'd suddenly come to her senses and realized that they were far, far too close. "I'll die before I submit my will to that of an unfeeling Englishman!"

Finch cleared his throat discreetly.

"Yes, boy, what is it?" Brynston asked sharply. He had

been on the verge of possessing her will, he was sure of it. She was only a girl, after all, a green twig to be bent to whatever shape he might desire. But it was a delicate business, and one sensitive to inappropriate interruptions.

"A thousand pardons, milord, but I wondered if her ladyship might fancy a bit of broth. Seein' as how she don't take to them kippers."

Brynston frowned. The boy had heard for himself that Miss Feathering had refused to eat anything, so why make this impertinently ill-timed offer? "Ask her yourself, then," he said, still facing the girl.

The boy cleared his throat and made a bow Graves would have been proud of. "If I might make so bold, yer ladyship, seein' as how a delicate flower of ladyhood like yerself needs her nourishment, I'd be honored to serve yer ladyship the house's finest light repast. If you can find a clearer broth in all o' London, milady, me name ain't Thomas Percival Quincy Ezekiah Finch. An' I can talk Cook into a nice persimmon pudding as well."

"She's not a lady, you know," Brynston put in, annoyed. "She's an American, there aren't any titles over there. They seem to find the notion of peerage undemocratic."

Katherine frowned at him and turned her attention to the boy. "You're very kind, Tom. I know you're worried about me. But as long as *he*"—she motioned to Brynston with a stubborn movement of her chin—"is holding me hostage, I can't touch a bite, much as I'd like to. It's a matter of principle."

Brynston snorted. "I had no idea you were so principled, my dear. A pity your nobler side damned well deserted you two nights ago."

Miss Feathering's eyes chilled to green ice. "You may curse in my presence 'til you turn blue in the face—it's no more than I'd expect from a hypocritical English blackguard. But I'll thank you to set a proper example in front of the boy."

Finch stood in the middle of the carpet with his hands jammed into his pockets, his bravado deserting him entirely. He looked as embarrassed and painfully smitten as any ten-year-old boy who ever breathed.

It was well past time to set the child straight about his beloved captive. "Do you know what she's done, Finch?" Brynston asked.

"I'm sure as how it ain't my business, sir," he said, his thin, dirty face the picture of reproachful indignation.

"For heaven's sake, boy, you're as bad as Graves. This spoilt American creature has stolen from me. Quite a lot of money, actually. And all she has to do to get out of here is give it back."

"I'm sure it ain't my business," the boy repeated, tucking his chin stubbornly.

"You wouldn't let some girl steal from you, now would you, Tom?" Brynston asked reasonably. "Of course you wouldn't. You'd get your money back and there'd be no hard feelings. Isn't that right?"

The boy looked up at him, his eyes shining fiercely in the grubby face. "Tom Finch might not be no gentleman, but I'll put a chivey in the heart of any man what says I don't know how to treat a lady."

Brynston was taken aback by this, but he noticed that Miss Feathering had acquired a distinctly triumphant gleam in her eye. "Matters of honor are often complicated by pretty ladies," Brynston finally said, hoping the boy would leave it at that and refrain from attempting to defend Katherine Feathering's precarious honor. Children really were deucedly peculiar creatures.

"That's as may be, milord," the boy said flatly, folding his thin arms over his chest. But he added nothing further, satisfied to have made his point.

Brynston cast a glance at the cold breakfast tray. "My old nurse would have forced you to eat that, no matter how unappetizing a plate of cold kippers might be. And I daresay it would do you a world of good," he added with a scowl. "But as even I am more lenient than my former nurse, I will permit the boy to bring you a fresh breakfast.

And I expect you to eat every crumb of it. Have I made myself quite clear?"

Miss Feathering shot him a venomous glower. "I will never submit to you!"

Brynston smiled wryly. "Of course you will, my dear. Good day." And with that he turned the doorknob and walked out of the room.

Finch whistled through his teeth. "The toff's a rum 'un, ain't he milady?"

"He's a despicable fiend," Katie said flatly, "and I'm glad he's gone. But he's right about one thing, you know."

"That yer ladyship ought to be eatin' her breakfast?" Tom asked hopefully.

She sat on the bed. "That I'm not anyone's ladyship. Why don't you call me Katherine? I'll agree it's a rather stuffy name, but it is the one I'm used to. Or you could call me Katie, that's what all my friends call me."

Tom looked at her, his blue eyes shining. "Oh miss, I couldn't do that. Not what it ain't the most elegant name in London town, hang me if it ain't."

Katie smiled wryly. "How about Miss Feathering, then? You know, it makes me feel like one of *his* kind when people call me *my lady* or *her ladyship*." She gestured toward the door with a thrust of her chin.

Tom nodded gravely. "I understand, me— that is, Miss Feathering. You don't want nothin' to do with the likes of him, and no mistake. But ain't there no way your people could see you out of this pickle, miss? It tears me heart in half to see you this way."

"Don't you worry about me for a second," she said, smiling. "These fancy gentlemen think they're awfully clever, but they're no match for me."

Tom grinned. "No, miss. You've got sumfin' up that pretty sleeve, don't tell me you ain't."

Katie pulled the blanket up around her shoulders. "I wouldn't want you to get into any kind of trouble because of me, Tom. I can see that brute Lyme is very dangerous."

"That old sod!" Tom said contemptuously. "He's so sotted half the time he don't know who he is. Dreamin' about the blunt his lordship'll be tossin' his way. Meanwhile, it's Tom Finch what does all the work. You won't be seein' no more o' Lyme, me— Miss Feathering. He's done his part, and that's to take his lordship's purse."

"You won't see a penny from this, then?" Katie asked. "It seems you're taking a terrible risk."

Tom pulled a gold watch from his pocket, admiring its polished gleam in the pale winter light. "I wouldn't say as how I won't see a penny, miss. Tom Finch is a lad what knows how to take care of himself."

Katie blinked, startled. "Surely that doesn't belong to Lyme?"

Tom grinned anew. "No, miss. Belongs to me now. But it was the earl what I done nipped it from, not Lyme. Old Lyme don't have nothin' half so flash."

"You picked the earl's pocket?" Katie asked, astonished. "But I was watching you the whole while—"

"Not precisely, miss. You was watchin' him, and he was watchin' you, and whenever there's a bit of a dust-up, Tom Finch knows he can profit by it."

Katie was still skeptical. "You must be awfully good. You're sure you took it just now?"

"As I live and breathe, Miss Feathering." Tom was grinning with all the cocksure self-confidence of a bantam rooster.

"I take it you don't feel any sense of . . . loyalty . . . to the earl, then?" Katie asked, trying to be as delicate as possible. The boy's sense of honor was, in his way, as prickly as Brynston's, and it would never do to affront him.

Tom suddenly looked painfully earnest. "I could never feel loyal toward a man what treated a lady so ill, miss. He's a right villain, and no mistake."

Katie nodded thoughtfully. "I see."

Tom brightened. "I has an idea, me—Miss Feathering. How about if I sneaks you a bit of somethin' nice—Cook makes some lovely pies—on the quiet, like? Old grumble-guts won't be none the wiser."

"I couldn't do that, Tom," Katie said. "It wouldn't be principled." Nor would it fit Tom's enamored image of her. And with any luck at all, Katie wouldn't be around long enough for her hunger strike to cause her more than a few twinges. "But I'm glad to know I've got a friend here. It makes it all much less frightening."

The boy's cockiness vanished as his freckled ears reddened. "If there's anything I can do—anything at all, miss—I hope as you'll let me know. Tom Finch's your man in a pinch, miss, knacker me if I ain't."

As Tom took the breakfast tray, removing from the room the truly disagreeable odor of cold kippers, Katie smiled weakly to herself. She was in a harsh and dangerous milieu, but it was one she knew well. Her hunger strike had begun to throw Brynston off his stride, for all he tried to hide it. And she had an unswerving ally. Nothing in the world could stop her now, not even the Brimstone Earl.

7

Alex Manners had been afraid that it would take all morning to quiet the hysterical Hannah, but the girl regained her composure moments after Alex had dashed into Katie's room.

The little maid had been chalk white when she'd stammered that Miss Katie was missing from her bed, and she was still deathly pale these two hours later, her usual bright demeanor dulled. They'd searched every inch of the house, picking through the attic and cellar and pantry as if they were looking for a thimble and not a full-grown young woman.

They had missed their morning ship, of course. But if they could not find Katie, none of that mattered. Not Phineas's debt to the Turks, not the complication with Lord Brynston, nothing. By late morning, the footmen had usually finished their early duties and started fighting or throwing dice, the servants' hall resembling a particularly rowdy tavern. But today the house was silent as a church.

Alex sat now in the parlor with Phineas Starr and

Hannah, the three staring morosely at the carpet and wracking their brains.

The pinch-faced cook appeared at the parlor door. "I'm sorry to disturb, sir," she murmured to Phineas. "I know it ain't my place to bring messages, but seein' as how Mr. Manners was in here with you—" To finish she held out a white envelope. "This come a moment ago, sir."

Alex sprang to his feet. "Did you get a good look at the man who sent it? What did he look like? Was he confident or did he seem ready to slink off?"

The cook shook her head. She'd been a prime fence in earlier days, but a stint in the prison hulks had left her too terrified to steal so much as a linen handkerchief. When Katie had found her, begging quietly in the streets, she'd been a few days at most from starvation. "He was a boy, Mr. Manners, the kind what runs errands."

Hannah leapt to her feet, her dark eyes wide. "Oh Mr. Manners! Do you think it might have somethin' to do with Miss Katie?"

The cook retreated after she'd given the note to Manners, who in turn handed it to Phineas.

Phineas puffed out his cheeks as he examined the envelope, holding it at arm's length to read the address. "Hmmph, nothing unusual there, old boy. Seems a letter like any other."

"Perhaps you should open it," Alex said gently. *It might have news of your missing daughter, you heartless bastard.* But Alex kept his face carefully neutral.

Phineas hummed to himself as he slit the envelope and removed a single sheet of expensive paper.

"Well?" Hannah asked, almost beside herself.

Phineas held the page out again, squinted, and began to read. "'Dear Mr. Phineas Feathering'—ah, etcetera, etcetera, etcetera, here we are—'It may have escaped your attention that your beloved daughter owes a debt of honor that has yet to be paid. Until such time as you may make such reparations'—ah, etcetera, etcetera—'namely in the sum of sixty thousand pounds, to be given to the keeper of the Dun Cow Inn on Pinchpye Close near the Billings Gate, to be held in keeping for Mr. Blunt—ah, I say, that's good, isn't it? D'you get it? Blunt. It's their word for money over here, don't you recall, Manners?"

Alex worked to control his impatience. Like it or not, he probably needed Phineas's help if he wanted to get Katie back. "Does it say where she is? Does it say if she's all right?"

"Well of course she's all right, you ass. She's a champion, that girl. Always could take care of herself. A damned sight better than her old man ever could, and that's a fact. Now then—" Phineas peered at the letter again. "You see? Says here in black and white, 'The girl will be perfectly safe if our demands are met.' Now that's clear enough, ain't it?"

"There's just one problem, Phineas. We don't have the money."

Phineas waved Alex's concerns away. "It's that earl that's got her, that Brynston, and he won't hurt her. He doesn't have the guts. I'll tell him some damned thing about refusing to deal with someone so dishonorable, he'll get bored, and let her go."

"Oh, but Mister Starr, what if some harm should come to her?" Hannah asked, wringing her small hands. "She was worried about that 'un, said she never should have fleeced him. Which, of course, she shouldn't have, seein' as how it's a sin and against God's will."

"Stop your gab, Hannah," Phineas said irritably. "It's a hazard of the occupation, that once in awhile a gudgeon will take offense. Katie can take care of herself."

Alex found himself wondering what it would feel like to wrap his hands around Phineas's fat throat and squeeze the life out of the little dung-sack. He squelched the thought. For now, Phineas was Alex's line to Brynston, and he couldn't afford to let that line be severed.

"We've got to throw him a bone," Alex argued, when he could trust his voice not to reveal his anger. "Tell him we can't get the funds yet, but that they're on the way. In the meantime we can work on discovering where he's taken her. Send a few of our footmen over to charm Brynston's parlor maids. Dick Barker's a fine, handsome fellow, he could charm milk into butter."

Phineas huffed as he pushed his stout body out of his chair. "Even if Brynston's got more gumption than we thought, he won't hurt her if he thinks he can get money back. And Katie's too smart to let him hold her for long. Ten to one she finds her own way back here by nightfall."

"I'm not interested in gambling with Katie's safety," Alex said through gritted teeth. "You send him a note telling him we're working on getting the funds. I'll send Barker over right away. Once he's charmed his way into the kitchen, maybe he'll hear something."

"Maybe," Phineas said, distracted. "Worth a try, I suppose. I'm off to the club."

"Aren't you worried about her at all?" Alex asked, ready himself to tear the city apart looking for her.

"Course I am. She *is* my daughter, man, I'd be unnatural not to. But I might hear something. These gentlemen's clubs, you know, are breeding grounds for gossip."

"Oh, Mr. Manners," Hannah wailed, twisting her apron in her hands. "I don't know what I'll do if that girl's been harmed. If it weren't for her, half of us would be dead by now, or on the hulks which is near as bad."

Alex felt a protective pang. "Don't you worry, Hannah. We'll find her. You say a few prayers to that God of yours, and see if he'll give us a hand. You'll see, everything will work out very well."

But Alex's heart was ice cold for fear that everything might not work out well at all.

Katie stared at the glass of wine on her tray for a long moment before hurling it across the room. It flew through the air, sending a satisfying arc of wine splashing across the wallpaper to mix with the ugly black coal streak Brynston had scribbled on the wall.

She was going mad in here. Stark, raving mad.

Outside the window it had begun to snow again, falling in a claustrophobic blanket that seemed to smother her in its whiteness. How could she possibly make her way back to her father and Alex in nothing but a thin nightgown, a blanket, and a pair of flimsy slippers?

She pulled the blanket more tightly around her shoulders, repressing a shiver. The snow was the least of her problems. This neighborhood was overrun with footpads, rapists, and murderers. Somewhere in the flash house, Lyme was lurking, waiting for her to do something foolish. She was trapped here.

Trapped.

The thought tightened Katie's throat until she could scarcely breathe through the panic. She had to get out of here, before her senses deserted her completely. She would not remain here to waste away in this cage.

The dinner tray seemed almost to call out to her, enticing her with the smells of good, simple food. But the thought of Brynston's smirk chased her hunger away. She wouldn't give him the satisfaction even of knowing she'd taken a single nibble before escaping this prison.

The door to her room was locked, of course, but it took her no more than half a minute to pick the lock with a hairpin. She shook her head with faint disgust. Lyme must not be much of a crook, if he couldn't manage to put better locks than that on the doors.

The hallway was long and ill lit, wall sconces throwing weird shadows on the gaudy wallpaper. Another giggle came from behind one of the doors, and then a muffled thump. Katie squelched her panic decisively, pulling her blanket protectively around her.

The stairs were long and narrow, and they seemed to lead to a fearful din of shrieking and fighting. There were two doors at the bottom of the steps, and she put her ear to the door to her right. She drew back a little as some ruffian hurled an ugly curse, seemingly right at her. That must be the main room, then.

At the door on her left, she heard nothing. That might be the kitchens, or another passageway. Whatever it was, it sounded deserted. Katie took a deep breath to calm herself, and twisted the doorknob.

The door led to a large kitchen that was surprisingly clean. There was not so much as a lone scullery maid to interfere with her progress. At the far end of the kitchen, a wooden door with a small window led out onto the street.

Katie could have laughed aloud. She crossed the kitchen floor quickly and peered out the tiny window. All she had to do now was negotiate the snarled tangle of streets and find her way back to her fashionable Berkeley Square rooms.

So long as she didn't get murdered—or worse—along the way.

Katie pulled the blanket over her head like a hood, and bent her back to resemble that of a withered crone's. She could take care of herself. She always had before.

The next instant she was out in the street, blinking in the light. Snow seeped instantly into her useless, flimsy slippers. She pulled the blanket so it covered her completely, bent her hunched back a few more pitiable inches, and began the long walk home.

Before she had taken three steps, a woman rounded the corner, both elbows laden with baskets. The woman's face was so strikingly pointed and rat-like that Katie almost expected her to have a long, scaly tail dragging behind her.

"Here now, what's this? What are ye doin' here, ye old cow?" the woman asked, suspicious.

Katie acted purely on instinct. "Alms for the poor, milady?" she croaked. The address was gross flattery— the rat-faced woman was dressed neatly enough, but the most innocent child would never take her for a lady.

"Get off!" the woman cried, nose twitching. "I won't have no dirty beggars hangin' round me clean kitchen! Get off, then!" The woman shooed her as if Katie were a crippled dog.

Katie pulled her blanket closer around her face and cringed away from the woman, limping off toward the alley. She held her breath, but the woman did not follow her.

She limped along, hoping she looked too pitiful even to rob. The inch of white nightgown was incongruous below her makeshift disguise, and the blanket wasn't nearly as filthy and torn as it should have been.

Katie glanced around. The grimy alley was deserted. She quickly knelt and scooped up a handful of muddy slush from the ground, smearing it liberally over the blanket. If she smelled and looked disgusting enough, she just might escape notice. The hem of her nightgown was already becoming a tattered rag in the filth of the streets.

She had just begun to arrange the blanket over her head again when a black, spidery figure appeared at the mouth of the alley. Lyme.

"Hey!" he cried.

Katie cringed again, sinking into an abject hunch, and began limping away from him.

"Hey! Hang on!" Lyme cried. "I'm lookin' for a girl, she done run away. It's a farthing if you can tell me where she went."

Katie did not trust her voice, so she shrugged beneath the filthy blanket and made for the other direction as if her life depended on it. Which it probably did.

"Didn't you hear me, you old bitch?" Lyme cried, his voice ugly. "I'll teach you to ignore Quentin Lyme."

He caught up with her in an instant, grabbing her roughly by the elbow. Katie thrust a stinking, blanket-covered arm up toward his face, hoping to disgust him into releasing her.

"Pah! You stink to hell, you mangy cow!" Lyme cried, shaking her roughly.

The blanket threatened to slip from her head, and Katie clutched desperately at it. "Eh?" she croaked. "Alms for a poor, deaf old woman?"

Lyme thrust her away in disgust, sending her sprawling into a pile of old rags.

Katie clawed at the blanket, trying to keep herself covered, but it was too late. Lyme goggled as he caught a glimpse of her clean, short curls. "Why you lying little slut!"

Katie scrabbled away from Lyme, narrowly escaping his grasping claws. She threw the dirty blanket over him and ran straight toward and past him, hoping to throw him off for an instant.

It worked, but only for the briefest of moments. Lyme disengaged himself from the blanket, looked around, and gave a shout like the bark of a hound when he spotted her behind him.

Katie ran for all she was worth. The muddy slush on the ground was slippery beneath her feet, but she managed to keep her footing as she raced down the alley. When she reached the street, she turned blindly to the right, not knowing where she was going and not caring.

She smashed into a grubby little boy, all but knocking him over, and she could hear Lyme's curses behind her as he tripped over the child. She winced at the child's yelp, knowing that Lyme had cuffed the poor thing.

Her lungs burned. The street nearly curled around onto itself before meeting another crooked corner. She turned left this time, coming on a footpad relieving a frightened-looking young gentleman of his purse. She scooted past the pair, Lyme hot on her heels.

"Bitch!" Lyme cried, shockingly close behind her. He was gaining ground, and everything would be lost. Katie ran faster, not knowing where she found the strength, feeling the ground threatening at every step to slide from beneath her feet.

At the corner she turned right, and she collided with a massive, unyielding wall of flesh. All but blind with the instinct to escape, she tried to wriggle past the man.

"Oh, I shouldn't think that was a good idea, my dear," came a horribly familiar voice.

Katie blinked twice before she gasped and tried again to dart past the figure. Brynston.

He took her easily by the elbow. "This really wasn't very clever of you, Miss Feathering. I believe I did tell you that this quarter was most dangerous for proper young ladies. You're quite lucky to have found me." His voice was controlled, but his eyes were deadly.

"Let me go!" she cried, trying desperately to twist free of him.

"And let him catch you?" Brynston gestured to Lyme, who was panting twenty feet away, scowling murderously at her.

"Better him than *you*," Katie spat. She had lost. He'd caught her, and would return her to that stifling prison. Suddenly she felt the defeat, heavy on her shoulders. Damn him, damn this crazy, arrogant Englishman.

Brynston took her face roughly in his hand, forcing her to meet his gaze. "Oh, I don't think so," he said softly. "I wonder if you have the first idea what that monster would have done to you."

Katie winced from his touch as if his fingers were branding irons, but she straightened her back. He could keep her like a bird in a cage, but she would never let him think he'd defeated her spirit. "I don't care," she said coldly. "It would have been worth it, for the chance of getting away from you."

"You little idiot," he whispered harshly. "You haven't the first idea what you're saying. Look here, I don't give a damn if you get that pretty little throat cut, or worse, but unfortunately I've given my word you'll come to no harm. D'you understand me? Do you?" He gave her a furious shake, his face a tight mask.

"Go to hell!" she snarled, steeling herself against his rage. He was dangerous, she could see, truly dangerous, but right now nothing mattered more than defying him. It was insanity and she knew it, but she couldn't help herself.

He visibly tightened his rein on his self-control, until

the only remaining sign of his anger was the deadly fire in his eyes. "You will never escape me. I will give you your freedom when your debt of honor is paid, and not before. Accustom yourself to that fact." He hauled her roughly through the streets, brushing Lyme aside with a furious snarl.

She wouldn't have been able to find the flash house again if her life depended on it, but as it happened they were no more than a minute away. In the tangle of streets, she had been moving in a rough circle, getting no further away no matter how fast she'd run. Brynston was right. She would never escape him. And her father did not have the money to pay her ransom. She was snared.

A choked sob escaped her throat before she could stop it, but she ruthlessly clamped down on her emotions. She would not let another sign of weakness escape her lips.

"Tears," Brynston said in disgust. "I would have thought such a cheap trick beyond even your duplicitous wiles. It appears I have overestimated you."

They trudged the rest of the way back in silence.

8

When Brynston slammed the door shut behind her, Katie almost felt ready to give in to the tears that were jabbing her throat like knives. It was snowing harder now, muffling the raucous sounds of the awakening street. The ugly black line that Brynston had scrawled across the wallpaper seemed to mock her feeble attempts to escape. She was utterly alone.

After some minutes a knock came at the door, soft as the timid scratchings of a rabbit.

"Leave me alone!" she cried. The last thing she wanted to face now was Lord Brynston's recriminations. She was sure the only reason he'd left her was that he didn't trust himself not to do her bodily harm.

"Please, Miss Feathering, it's Tom Finch." The boy's voice quivered with worry.

Katie smiled wanly despite herself. "Come in, Tom."

His pointed little chin thrust itself into the room. His expression was cocky and defiant, but his eyes betrayed the depth of his concern. "His Lordship's makin' an awful row below stairs. When he heard that Missus

Baggitt let you walk right past her, I thought he might go off like a bleedin' rocket."

"Mrs. Baggitt—is she the one with the face like a rat?"

Tom's ears shone bright red. "That's the one. Horrible bad tempered, she is, but now she knows what it's like from the other side. His Lordship was fit to murder her, hang me if he wasn't."

"She seems like a perfectly dreadful person," Katie said, remembering the woman's curses.

"Did he treat you rough, then?" Tom asked timidly.

Katie shook her head. "Not really. It's just . . . " She was quiet a moment, not trusting herself to go on. It was impossible to explain, to Tom or anyone, why being locked in this place affected her as it did.

"He thinks he can give me orders," she began again. "I'm sure he's used to it, lord of the manor ordering the peasants around. But he can't order me. Does that make sense?"

Tom's eyes were shining. "I know just what you means, Miss. Tom Finch don't let no gentry cove put on airs, neither, an' I don't care who his bloomin' dad was. In Pinchpye Close, all what matters is how quick a bloke is, with his fists or with his wits. The toffs don't know nothin' about the ways of the street."

"You're quite right," Katie said, though privately she thought that Lord Brynston seemed more than quick enough to match wits *or* fists with any of the denizens of this place.

"I tell you, Miss, I don't feel right about what he's doin'. You don't deserve to be in no rich man's clutches."

Katie smiled at him. He really was a gallant little creature, with his reverent ways and his dignified demeanor. "You're quite the gentleman, Tom Finch. I mean that in the truest way. You're nothing like *him*." She gestured with her chin toward the door—toward Lord Brynston and all the privilege and arrogance he represented.

Tom couldn't suppress his grin. "I'd do anything to get you out of this pickle, I swears I would."

Katie frowned and bit her lower lip. She wouldn't have jeopardized Tom for all the world.

She glanced out the window at the mounting snow-banks. Her situation was growing ever more desperate. She *must* get out of here. "Anything? Truly?"

"Hang me if I lie, miss," he said solemnly.

"Would you—" She broke off. It was appalling and unfair, and she wouldn't do it. She wouldn't use a child to solve her problems. There had been too many times when she'd been called on to rescue her father from his scrapes.

Tom thrust his chin out proudly. "You can count on me, miss. You want me to take on that bastard Lyme for you? I'd cut his throat, I swear it. It'd be doin' the world a favor. He's an evil one, and no mistakin'."

"No, no, nothing like that!" Katie was horrified. "I could never ask you to do anything wicked!"

Tom shrugged. "You wouldn't be the first, miss, nor the last neither. I've done what I ain't proud of. You'd make me happy to let me help—then I'd have done at least one thing in me life that was good."

She frowned again. She shouldn't let him talk her into this.

She thought suddenly of Alex, of how frantic he would be. His shoulders would hunch with worry, and he would shuffle aimlessly around the house, wringing his big hands. Alex went to pieces when she had so much as a case of the sniffles; he'd be out of his mind over her kidnapping.

"If— What I mean to say is, perhaps—"

"Yes, miss?" Tom looked at her eagerly.

"Are you free to come and go here? Can you slip away without anyone noticing?"

Tom jammed his hands in his pockets and assumed a pose of sullen defiance. "I goes where I please. I'm the best nipper they has. If I wants to go right up to bleedin' Carlton House, ain't no one to tell me no."

"Do you think you could take my family a message?"

"Neck and crop, miss. Won't take me above an hour. You sure there ain't nothing else I can do?"

"That's more than enough," Katie said firmly. "I wouldn't ask this much, if I could think of any other way to get help."

"It's an honor and a privilege, miss," Tom said proudly.

Katie lifted her mother's locket over her head and handed it to him, drilling him on what he must say. Satisfied that he would repeat her words absolutely faithfully, she sent him off into the snowy day.

She sank back onto her narrow bed after he'd left, staring at the sodden wine and coal stain on the wallpaper. Alex wouldn't let her rot in this madhouse much longer. In a matter of hours, she'd be free.

Alex Manners had never been so miserable. The snow piling up beneath the parlor windows seemed to mock the despair that was settling over him. If they didn't come up with sixty thousand pounds, God only knew what Lord Brynston would do.

Not harm her. Surely not harm her. But Alex had seen a dangerous gleam in the man's eye at the Frost Fair. The best that Katie could do would be to sit quietly until Alex and Phineas could figure something out, but sitting quietly was not something Katie did well.

"Sit tight, little one," Alex murmured, almost like a prayer. "We'll come for you, girl, don't you be frightened." But it was Alex himself who was frightened.

The cook made a baleful entrance at the parlor door. "There's two men come to see you, sir. Asked for you specially."

Alex all but jumped to his feet. "Is it about Katie?"

"I can't rightly say sir," said the cook, frown lines appearing between her eyebrows. "They're foreign gentlemen."

"Show them in," he said, straightening his waistcoat and flexing the tired muscles in his shoulders.

She showed two men into the parlor, one tall and fat,

with an air of fastidious grace, the other small and sly. Both were impeccably dressed in the English style, though their impassive faces were as brown as walnuts.

Alex drew himself to his full height, fixing the men with his most unswerving glower. "What the hell are you two doing here? We don't have time for your games today. Tell Ali he'll get his damned money when we have it, and not before."

The fat man, Khalil, flashed a brief, cold smile as he removed his gloves. "There has been talk around the city, that the charming young lady has achieved an impressive victory. Ali wishes only to ensure that he shares in your joy."

Alex snarled. Ali wished only to get the money Phineas owed him. "You've been misinformed. She was found out, and had to give the money back."

The men exchanged glances, and Khalil spoke again. "We have heard no such word. If you please, we will discuss this matter with the young lady."

The parlor was silent for a long moment before Alex could answer. "She isn't here."

The man's eyes narrowed to suspicious slits as he all but hissed, "She seeks perhaps to escape her father's debt?"

Alex could have torn their miserable black hearts from their bodies. "She's been abducted. I don't suppose the two of you would have anything to do with that, now would you?"

For a moment, the men looked entirely taken aback. A few muttered words in Turkish passed between them before they recovered their composure. Khalil turned again to Alex. "We are not fools, Mr. Manners. The girl is, how do you say, our goose that lays eggs that are gold. Ali has no wish to harm her. He wants only what is honorable."

Alex squeezed his eyes shut, pressing his palms to his temples. "You can see we're busy here. We'll be in touch when we have your money, not before. You can tell Ali he'll just have to wait a little longer."

The fat man smiled again, revealing strangely pointed teeth. "Ali has demonstrated great patience. He believes that perhaps it is the moment to demonstrate something other than patience. We would not wish Mr. Starr to underestimate the depth of Ali's commitment."

Khalil was tall, but Alex loomed over him. Ali's henchmen were carefully trained to be cool and impassive, but Alex could see the tiny beads of sweat begin to appear on the fat man's forehead as Alex stared down at him. "Tell Ali that if he took the lot of us right now and held a pistol to our heads, we'd have nothing to give him. We have nothing without the girl. If he wants his damned money so badly, get him to find her for us. I'll tell you who's got her—the earl of Brynston, Julius Willowby."

The small, sly one, whose name was Mehmet, squinted pugnaciously up at Alex as if relishing the thought of sparring with the much larger man. But Khalil nodded his head and took a half-step back. "Ali will grant you another fortnight. No more. After that point, we must consider extreme measures."

"Get the hell out of this house," Alex said, suddenly feeling as though the weight of the world sat squarely on his shoulders. The Turks were dangerous, and meant business, but there was nothing he could do about them now. He'd been right when he'd said that without Katie, they had nothing. Less than nothing.

Alex felt the guilt tighten around his throat in a strangler's grip. Once before he'd failed to protect Katie, and she'd paid the price. Every time she had a nightmare, every time fear haunted her eyes, Alex felt the old shame settle on him. And it was happening again, despite all his efforts. He'd worked hard, so hard to shield her, and now everything was ashes.

The men melted away like wraiths. Ali was an ugly man with an ugly mind, exactly the sort of person you didn't want to owe a hundred thousand pounds to. But when Alex had tried to get Phineas to see this, the little man had only puffed his chest and cleared his throat and said something inane about the need in life to take risks.

The cook showed up again at the parlor door, her mouth looking like she'd been sucking on lemons. "There's another one, Mr. Manners. Another messenger to see you. Says he can't speak with anyone else." Disapproval stood out as clearly on her face as the deep lines between her forehead.

"Show him in," Alex said wearily.

A child stood at the door, a rail-thin boy with eyes too old for his small face. Every inch of visible skin was dusted with freckles. He swept off his hat—an outrageous black chapeau bras, far too big for him—in a surprisingly grand gesture. "Beg yer pardon, sir, is you Mr. Alexander Manners?"

"Yes," Alex said gruffly. "What is it, boy? We're busy here."

The boy slipped in the door, closing it softly behind him. He dangled a white and violet enameled locket from his thin fingers. "Me name's Tom Finch, sir, and I has a message from Miss Katherine Feathering."

9

Lord Brynston felt the curricle pull slightly to the left, and he made a minor correction to the reins. Daisy was letting Bruno do all the work again, while she tossed her pretty head and accepted the admiration of the fashionable throng in Hyde Park.

"What's wrong, Jules?" Portia asked. Her voice was gentle, as it always was.

"He's wearing his Thundering Jehovah look today, isn't he?" Titania mused, adjusting her bonnet so that it showed her delicate features to best advantage.

Brynston scowled. "You're a pillar of support as always, Ti."

Titania ignored him, nodding coldly to a lovesick baron who had offered for her only last week. "I can't help it, brother darling. What's wrong, did one of the maidservants tip over the coal scuttle? Or perhaps your breakfast porridge was scorched this morning."

"Or perhaps I've just had to deal with another one of your bloodthirsty suitors," Julius drawled. "Look, there's Waxcomb. I heard he called another one out last week.

You're a menace to society, Ti. You'll reduce the upper ten thousand by a hundred or two at least."

"If men are so pigheaded as to demand satisfaction for every imagined slight, that is hardly my fault," Titania sniffed.

"Hush, Ti," Portia said. "Jules is truly upset about something, can't you see that?"

Julius sometimes wished his middle sister were a little less perceptive. She was an unfailing barometer of other people's feelings, though she paid scant enough attention to her own. "Never mind, Portia. A minor brangle with a scoundrel, that's all. It's weighed on my mind these past days, but I'll forget all about it soon enough."

"A scoundrel?" Titania asked, lifting one eyebrow. "Male or female?"

Portia was instantly on the alert, like a mouse twitching her sensitive whiskers. "Female?"

"My dear, didn't Val tell you? Julius lost thirty thousand last week to a very pretty, very scatterbrained chit from the colonies," Titania said with a wicked grin.

"The matter is not open to discussion," Julius said. "Tibby, I must insist that you refrain from leaning out the carriage that way. You will do yourself some form of permanent damage."

Julius's youngest brother sat upright, clapping his hands together to dust them off. Julius had given the boy's governess the afternoon off, wanting to have his family to himself for a few hours.

"May I drive, then, Julius?" he asked politely. "It will alleviate my boredom, and as we know, I am prone to troublesome escapades when I am bored."

Julius shuddered faintly. "No, you most certainly may not drive."

"We are going very slowly," Tibby pointed out with extreme reasonableness. "It is therefore most unlikely that I would crash into any objects, or tip over the carriage."

"I appreciate your arguments, Tibby. The answer is still no."

Tibby made a small noise of impatience, then sat back in his seat.

"I would let you play with my watch," Julius offered, a little sorry for the boy. Julius himself had hardly been able to sit still when he was Tibby's age. "Only I haven't a clue as to where I could have left it."

"I have already taken your watch apart and put it back together," Tibby said, with an air of extreme boredom. "It is no longer interesting to me."

Julius, who did not know Tibby had done this, smiled to himself. He felt a fierce, protective warmth toward all his family, but there was something special about Tibby. Their mother had died a few weeks after the boy's birth, and their father had followed her that winter, leaving Brynston the earl. Leaving him to take care of this half wild, harebrained family by himself.

Sometimes that responsibility struck him anew with all the force of a bolt of lightning. "If you are very good," he said, "you may drive the carriage for a few minutes when we return home. The roads will be quiet, and the horses will be easier to manage."

"I'm afraid he talked the coachman into letting him drive most of the way between Oxford and London," Portia said.

"He did what?" Brynston's alarm transmitted itself to the horses, who tossed their heads aggravatedly.

"The fellow was quite drunk," Tibby put in. "He reeked dreadfully of gin, Julius. I did not think it was safe to let him drive."

"I think the little monster may have set a new speed record," Titania said, not without admiration.

Julius worked hard to erase every trace of softness from his voice. "I expressly forbid you ever to do something so foolish again, Tibby. You might have all been killed."

Titania laughed. "Really, Julius, there's no sense threatening the little beast with mortality. He scoffs at death."

Julius glanced back at his brother, whose face was lit with a sly smile, as if he truly *did* scoff at death.

Titania shut her eyes and leaned delicately back in her seat. "I hope I wasn't so vile at that age."

"You were far worse," Julius said, a slow smile creeping across his face. "I still remember the night you somehow got into mother's jewelry box, and came downstairs to a ball wearing a hundred thousand pounds in rubies and not a thing else."

Titania sat bolt upright. "You're making that up!"

Julius's face split in a grin. "I'm not. I watched from the upstairs balcony. You don't remember father shouting? I'll never forget it."

"You're wretched, and if you ever repeat that filthy lie to anyone else, I'll—"

"You'd even managed to get rid of your nappy, though God knows how you managed it. Just your little pink bum for all the world to see, and a fortune in rubies hanging off your skinny neck." Julius felt twelve years old again, delighting in taunting his much younger sister.

"My neck was never skinny!" Titania hissed, looking thoroughly put out. "I was an adorably plump child, everyone says so."

"You certainly had a plump little bottom," Julius said wickedly. "And a fat belly like a puppy's."

"I'm never speaking to you again as long as I live," Titania said, her eyes sparkling with venom.

"Don't tease her, Julius," Portia said, though she looked ready to burst into laughter at any second. "You know Titania blushes easily."

It was true—Titania's cheeks blazed red. "He's just trying to change the subject," she said crossly. "He doesn't want to tell us about this American female who gulled him out of all that money."

Brynston's mood came crashing down like a felled oak. "That is not a matter open to discussion."

"You were jolly well willing to discuss it with Val when she fleeced him first," Titania said, relentless.

"Val told you that?"

"Of course he did. Said you'd gone out to win the great pile of money he owed, and ended up digging your-self even deeper to the same girl. Lucky creature, I'd say. Two reckless Willowby brothers in the space of a week."

"She must be terribly good at cards," Portia said gravely.

Titania laughed. "Oh yes, terribly. Good enough that she's made our eldest a little suspicious, I'd say. Am I right, Julius? Do we suspect the giggling colonist is a cheat?"

"Leave it, Ti," he said, his voice a warning growl. He turned out of the gate and onto the road home. "I'm not going to discuss this with you."

"Come on, Julius, tell us your plans for her. Boiling her in oil, are you? Giving her a squeeze in the Iron Maiden?"

"Didn't anyone ever tell you how unattractive yam-mering is in a woman?" Julius felt uneasy as the wall between his two lives began to fragment. On one side was the flash house and his insane decision to abduct Katherine Feathering. His mind filled with a sudden and most uncomfortable image of the seductive curve of the back of her neck.

And on the other side were family and title and sober duty. The real world, with no room for beautiful card cheats.

"Perhaps he's tossed her down the oubliette and left her there to rot. You'd better run and check on her, Julius, or she'll waste away and you'll never get your money back."

"Damn it, Titania, will you just shut up?" he shouted.

No one in the curricle said a word. Portia looked at him, blinking her eyes in surprise.

Julius stared angrily at the road in front of him. He'd lost his temper. He *never* lost his temper, not since—

His mind skidded away from the memory.

"She upsets you that much, does she?" Titania asked, never one to back down in the name of tact.

"I think he'd rather not talk about it," Portia said, biting her lower lip.

Blast. He didn't mind—much—shouting at Titania from time to time. As often as not it was the only way to get her to hear. But Julius truly disliked disturbing Portia.

"Don't fret, Portia, I'm sorry I lost my temper," he said.

"Why are you apologizing to her? I'm the one who got screeched at," Titania sniffed.

"Because you deserved it," Julius said brusquely. "The girl is none of your business, Ti, and I don't want to hear another word out of your mouth."

"But—" Titania began.

"Not another word," he said, putting a full measure of ice behind the words.

Even Titania knew when she was beaten. She smoothed the ruffles of her skirt. "Will you be home for Easter?"

"I don't know, yes, I suppose so," he said, slowing the carriage to turn into a narrow lane.

He was distracted, plagued by thoughts of the girl. Graves had been right, his reaction to Miss Feathering's duplicity was beyond all reason. Every minute he spent on her was a minute away from his duties.

And, if he were honest with himself, he recoiled at keeping her like a bird in a cage. She refused to eat, which infuriated him, but it worried him too. Half of his heart wanted to strangle her for refusing to give way to his wishes. The other half wanted to protect her and be sure she came to no harm, to lock the lovely Dresden shepherdess in an exquisite china cabinet.

He had to let her go. The flash house had been the only place he could think of where she positively would not be discovered by some *ton* busybody, but his scheme worked only so long as she was too frightened to try to escape. His chest constricted as he thought of what might have happened this morning. Her throat could have been cut, or she might have been mauled by one of the snarling young men who roamed the street like rabid dogs. The mere thought of it threatened to drive him half out of his mind.

A crowd of street children had begun to run after their carriage, and Julius glanced over his shoulder to see why. Tibby, feet wedged under the seat and leaning out of the carriage like a cantilever, was handing pennies to the children, making a game of reaching out to meet their grasping hands with his own.

Portia and Titania noisily wrestled Tibby back into the carriage as Julius turned a corner and pulled up to the gray brick facade of his terrace house.

Despite the clamor of his sisters scolding Tibby as they stood down from the curricle, Brynston could not shake the matter of Miss Feathering from his mind. He could hardly release her before showing her the error of her ways. To cheat at cards was to become little better than a common thief, and she would eventually be spurned by decent society. If he could devise a way to get that fact through her annoyingly stubborn head, eventually she would fade into some sensible marriage and life would go on as it should always have done.

Tonight, he thought, as they climbed the stone steps to the house. A scolding Titania was leading Tibby by the ear. Julius had his unruly feelings well in hand now. Tonight he would teach Miss Katherine Feathering the consequences of her reckless behavior.

And the consequences of tangling with the Brimstone Earl.

10

Katie paced her prison, waiting. What was taking Alex so long? True, it would take time for Tom to travel the city on foot, but the sun had set two hours ago. She stared at the ugly black coal line scrawled on the wall. As the night wore on, the brothel would pick up life, and the sounds of drinking and laughing would begin to come through the walls. She had to get out of here. Soon.

A fast knock came at the door, and before Katie could compose herself, Brynston walked in, a strange, shadowed expression on his face.

"Come with me," he said.

"Go to the devil," she said coolly, arranging her blanket neatly around her shoulders.

He took her arm and half hauled her toward the door, so that she had to hop to keep from stubbing her toes. "I said, come with me," he replied.

"You are the most uncivilized, ill mannered, arrogant, unfeeling—" Katie began, furious.

"Yes, yes, you're repeating yourself, my dear," he said, his voice a perfect cultured drawl. He turned her around by the shoulders, so she faced away from him, and lowered a blindfold around her eyes.

"No!" she cried, pushing the thing away from her face.

"If you don't like the blindfold, I could always knock you unconscious instead," he said softly in her ear.

She forced her hands down to her sides. "So I have no choice."

"You always have a choice. However, the least disagreeable will always be to follow my wishes," he said, his voice infuriatingly reasonable.

"You are a horrible person," she said.

"I believe you covered that already, under uncivilized, arrogant, and unfeeling."

"Where are you taking me now? Off to be murdered, I suppose."

"If I'd wanted you murdered, I would have left you out there in the street this morning," he said, his voice all ice. "That was a stupid and unnecessary thing to do."

"It was necessary that I get away from you," she said.

"Enough. You are really becoming quite tiresome. Come along."

He took her by the arm, less roughly than before, and led her out of the room and down a long corridor. The floor was cold beneath her thin slippers, but she did not protest. His hand was large and warm, and seemed almost to burn through the fabric of her nightgown as he held her high on the arm. She ignored his touch, walked as far away from him as she could to keep the knuckles of his hand from brushing her body.

The sound of prostitutes entertaining their clients filtered through the walls, and Katie willed herself not to hear it. She chanted a litany to herself. *It's different now. This isn't like before. I can take care of myself.*

And yet she wanted desperately to bolt. The sounds of high-pitched laughter and the clinking of glasses constricted her throat, and she forced herself to take deep gulps of air.

Finally he opened a door and pushed her in ahead of him, shutting the door behind them. His fingers were at the back of her head, untying the blindfold, and she blinked at the bright blaze of candlelight.

The room was large and shabbily sumptuous, the walls hung with faded red silk. What seemed like hundreds of paintings, ranging in subject from demure nymphs to blatantly obscene satyrs, surrounded her on all sides. In the middle of the room was a mahogany table, its legs chipped and scarred.

And, God help her, on the table was food. The linen tablecloth was spread with a dazzling array of meats and cheeses, carafes of wine and delicate silver bowls of chocolates and ripe fruit.

"I specifically asked them to omit the kippers," Brynston said softly. "In deference to your delicate American palate."

Katie swallowed hard. A large joint of beef lay on a massive silver platter, cut to reveal the juicy pinkness within. The steam coming from the platter carried the unmistakable odor of roast meat to her nose.

"I told you," she said, her hands balled into fists at her sides, "I won't eat until you release me."

"Did you? I must have forgotten." Brynston locked the door behind her and slid the tiny brass key into his watch pocket. "Very well, then, you may simply stand there and watch me."

There were no chairs, no place she could have sat quietly as she tried to think of something other than stewed chicken and artichoke pie. She backed slowly into a corner, and a wall sconce poked her in the back. She turned her head to see that it was formed of two copulating figures worked in gilded plaster.

"This was a rotten trick, Brynston," Katie said, turning her eyes quickly away from the sconce.

"Hmm, it was, wasn't it?" he said, sounding pleased with himself. "Let me see now, poached salmon with leeks and morels. That looks rather decent. I can't decide if I'd rather have that or the lobster. I'm rather partial to lobster. What do you think?"

He turned the full force of his gaze on her, and it was like being struck by lightning.

"I think I want to go back to my room," Katie said evenly.

"Come now, I thought you wanted to go home," he said, his voice all silk and gravel. "You must make up your mind, you know."

"I want to go home, but if you will not let me do that, I want to leave this room."

"Certainly," he said smoothly. "Directly after dinner. If you won't eat, you must at least come over here and help me choose."

"I'd rather not."

"I will happily drag you to the table, Miss Feathering." His voice had lost none of its honeyed sweetness.

And she was hungry. She was desperately hungry.

She stepped reluctantly to the table, keeping her hands folded in front of her like a child saying her prayers. "Perhaps you ought to try the cod," she said sweetly.

Brynston raised one black eyebrow. "Do you think so?"

"It's supposed to be very easy to choke on those tiny bones," she said, no less sweetly.

He laughed.

Katie was weak from lack of food, and the candlelight all around her seemed to flicker eerily. The strains of a gypsy violin, accompanied by much drunken singing, seeped through the silk-paneled walls. She took a deep breath to clear her head. Her ears rang faintly but insistently. She needed to sit down, but there was no place but the floor. In another moment, she was afraid she'd be lying on it in a dead faint.

"The lobster, I think, to start," Brynston said, ignoring her distress. He speared a white creamy chunk with a silver fork, dipped it in butter, and brought it to his lips.

She had never wanted anything as much as she wanted to taste that lobster. She could imagine it on her tongue, imagine the rich, faintly salty flesh and the creamy sweetness of the butter.

It would not be such a terrible thing. What would it harm, if she gave in to him? Alex would be here to rescue her any moment now. To be sure, she would lose face in front of Brynston, but what did that matter? In a day, two at most, she'd be on a ship bound for Portugal, and the earl of Brynston would be nothing but an unpleasant memory.

He looked down at her, the flame blue of his eyes flickering over her. He was pure darkness except for the fierce light in those eyes. Around her the candles glittered, and the food on the table was calling up to her with a riot of seductive scent.

"Come now, Miss Feathering," he said, his voice soft as a kiss. "A bite. Surely a bite won't hurt you."

She gripped the side of the table hard enough to hurt. "No, thank you," she said, and wondered what in hell kept her from giving in to him.

"You can't keep this up, you'll faint with hunger," he said.

As if in response, the ringing in her ears rose to a dangerous clang, and she could feel her knees begin to buckle.

"No, thank you," she said through gritted teeth, and locked her knees even as a prickle of white dots began to fill her field of vision. She was going to faint. Damn.

He caught her neatly, and scooped her up in his arms as if she'd been no heavier than a child. "You ought to let a fellow know if you're about to succumb to the vapors, Miss Feathering. Next time I might not be quick enough to catch you."

"I just need some fresh air," she said, fighting the urge to sink into the sanctuary of his arms. Now that she was off her feet, her mind should have begun to clear, but she was becoming muddled in a new, more dangerous way.

"You need to eat," he said, all but nuzzling the words in her ear. "Here, just take a bite."

With his fingertips, he brought a morsel of the lobster
to her lips. Her senses were at a razor's edge, and she
could smell the faint creaminess of butter. The lobster
was moist with it, and the moistness brushed her mouth.

Damn him. Damn him to hell.

Though every ounce of pride screamed in protest, she
opened her mouth and received him, greedily taking
what he had to offer.

Her resistance tumbled like the walls of Jericho. He
fed her a few more morsels of lobster, as tenderly as if
she were a wounded bird, then rare, juicy bites of roast
beef and a spicy fricassee of salmon, thick with cream.
He fed her asparagus tips and the sultry rich earthiness of
morels. He fed her the buttery crusts from a hot rabbit
pie, and a few tender little cakes, fragrant with nutmeg
and rose water.

And he fed her strawberries. They tasted of the
promise of spring, of a man so powerful that spring gave
up its fruits out of turn for his pleasure. Their fragrance
was like the most sensual perfume, their sweetness was
enough to make her drunk. She *was* drunk, drunk on the
sensation of hunger sated, and on the sensation of being
surrounded by his arms.

He lifted a strawberry to his own lips, and the scent
seemed to waft between them. And then his mouth was
on hers, and their breaths mingled, perfumed with the
sweetness of winter strawberries.

Part of her had known this was coming, had waited for
it as her body had waited for the food it needed to sustain
itself. But she had expected the Brimstone Earl to be hard,
demanding.

Instead he explored her gently, his mouth as sweet
and lush as the ripe fruit. He ran his tongue across her
lips and opened her, then tasted her more fully, as she
tasted him.

She could feel herself melting like sugar in hot tea.
The blood sang in her ears as she curled her arm around
his neck and rose to meet him, wanting to blend the

sweetness of his mouth with her own until they were one breath, one perfumed ripeness rising and falling together.

He growled softly as she moved against him, not a growl of anger, but one of animal contentment.

She was conscious of her body as she had never been before, conscious of its contours in the thin fabric of her nightgown as she curled against him. The buttons of his waistcoat bit into her, and she pressed herself harder against him.

He made a sudden movement, and silver dishes hit the floor with a ferocious clatter as he swept them from the table. He lowered her onto the table as if she were some rare, prized dish, kissing her all the while in hungry nibbles.

Her heart pounded with a wildness of need, and with fear. No man had ever opened her mouth before to fill her with the sweetness of crushed strawberries, and no man had bent over her as Brynston did now, heavy and hard and gentle all at once. He left her mouth for a moment, to look into her eyes and stroke her cheek with his hand. "So sweet," he murmured, bending down to kiss her again. "So fresh and sweet."

The notes of the gypsy tune were marred by the sound of a harshly feminine giggle coming through the wall, and a rumbling masculine echo. The woman shrieked, and giggled again, and there was a loud thump against the adjoining wall.

Not just a woman's laugh. A whore's. Because that was what this place was, a house where whores entertained their clients.

Katie stiffened as the memories stabbed at her, more painful than before because she was open now, and vulnerable.

Panic smothered her and she struggled, forgetting where she was or who bent over her, remembering only the need to escape.

She was in the old place again, in the dark halls where she had once played children's games, before the thing had happened that had taken childhood from her forever.

The blood, all around her the blood, and the cloying sound of a whore's laugh.

Brynston bit off a curse as she punched at him with her fists. She wrenched a hand free of the circle of his arms, and grabbed for a weapon. The drunken songs downstairs rang in her ears like funeral bells.

She'd expected to find a knife there, but her hands closed around a heavy silver candlestick instead. Half blind with panic and rage, she swung it up at him. He stepped back neatly, or it would have broken his nose. As it was, she dealt him a glancing blow off his right cheek.

She swung at him again, pushing forward with her entire weight. The gypsy music sobbed in her: *Escape! Escape!* If she crushed the fragile bones of his face he would not be able to hurt her.

"Mother of— What the hell is wrong with you?" He leaped back well away from her and touched gingerly at the tender place on his cheek.

She scooted off the table and grabbed at the blanket lying forgotten on the floor, holding it in front of her. "I'm not for sale," she snarled. "Find yourself another damned whore."

"What are you talking about?" As she watched him, his features assumed a carefully controlled expression. "I beg your pardon. You need have no fear of me. I will not touch you again. I have acted in a deplorable fashion, and can find no excuse for my behavior."

Katie blinked, and the red haze of panic began to clear. She had been caught in another time, another place, with a stinking drunk who did not make genteel apologies for anything. But here in front of her was another man, handsome and honorable. A man who had not tried to hurt her.

She looked down at the candlestick in one hand, and the blanket clenched in the other. Then she looked at his face, where an ugly red mark was already blackening into a bruise. "I'm—you shouldn't have done that."

He looked at her levelly, though the faintest shadow of pain seemed to flicker across his eyes. It was not the mark on his cheek that hurt him, she knew. His wound went deeper than that. "You're right. I shouldn't have."

The woman's giggle floated through the wall again, and the man's coarse laugh followed.

"I can't . . . I can't be in a place like this," Katie said, working hard to regain her composure. She had lost control utterly, forgotten where she was and who she was with. To lose control in a jungle was to invite the wild animals to tear her to pieces. She must never, never make such a mistake again.

In the adjoining room, the woman's voice lowered to a kind of playful reproach. Katie knew all about women like her. She knew what their flimsy costumes of *déshabille* would look like, how they would lie abed until two then get up to breakfast on a cup of gin and a plate of sweets. She knew what was on their dressing tables, the silvered mirrors and jars of perfumed unguents.

And she knew how they treated their children. A slap one minute, smothering kisses the next. The whores' daughters, she knew, would be dressed like little Puritans, as plainly and wholesomely as possible—for awhile. Never long enough.

"I— I lost track of myself," she said finally, after what seemed like an achingly long moment.

"So did I," Brynston said, his gaze steady.

"I would like to go back to my room now."

"I think that would be a good idea."

The air in the room all but crackled with what was still unsaid. But it was impossible to tell him the truth. He was an English earl, and she a wily American street rat. There were a thousand differences between them, ten thousand reasons they could never understand each other. The sudden desire she felt to trust him, to tell him the truth, was weakness. Nothing more.

She gathered her blanket around her with great dignity and allowed him to lead her from the room, without a blindfold this time. She walked past the rows of doors without turning her head, but as she passed each door, she counted it. Fourteen, fifteen, sixteen. Sixteen closed doors, sixteen girls who had not run fast enough away from danger. There would be no one to weep for them now except for Katie.

As her door closed behind her and she sank down onto the bed, she realized she was too tired even to weep for herself.

An hour later, the earl of Brynston was home again, working on getting drunk.

What had he been thinking? What in blazes could he have been thinking?

A discreet knock came at the door. Julius ignored it. He was in no mood for company. He was too full of self-loathing for having manhandled Katherine Feathering into a full-fledged panic.

What had happened to his self-control? For nine years now he had been the model of aristocratic restraint. He knew too well what happened when men lost control of themselves. He had been a man to do so, once, and his family's name had nearly suffered for it. Another woman, so long ago, who had cheated at cards. A young man who had allowed himself to be ruled by base passions.

Julius poured himself another drink, though more brandy would just worsen his inclination to wallow in the mire of past sins. There was nothing he could do now about the mess that Jo Cargill had once made of his life, but he could certainly keep himself from getting into another tangle over a woman.

A confusing woman, with a genuine streak of savagery. And green eyes that reminded him of the wild, rocky dells near Willowby.

The brandy slid down his throat as easily as the others had. Julius wanted to forget Katherine Feathering, to forget the taste of hothouse strawberries on her lips and the spark of real fear in her eyes as she'd swung viciously at him with the candlestick.

He had terrorized her. Somewhere this evening he had lost control, had let himself be swept away in the tide of lust that had seemed to carry them both, and he had frightened the daylights out of her.

And he had dishonored her. That, above all others, was the thought he tried to chase away with brandy. She was an innocent, in the ways of the body at least, and he had plucked innocence from her waiting mouth like a ripe peach. And devoured it.

He had to let her go. It struck him now with new force. But would letting her go be enough? He did not know what else to give her.

The knock came again at the door, and he cursed. "Whoever it is, I'm not at home!"

He could hear a throat clearing in the hallway, and he knew it was his valet. No one could clear his throat with greater expression of feeling than Graves.

"I do beg your pardon for disturbing you, your lordship—"

"It'll wait til the morning! For God's sake, go to bed and leave me in peace!" Julius snarled. Perhaps the brandy was beginning to take effect after all. He did not normally permit himself to bellow at the servants like some burlesque version of Henry VIII.

"If you would open the door, sir, it is indeed very important news."

Julius cursed again and stood, swaying only marginally, to open the door. When he had slid the lock, he found Graves outside looking as worried as a mother cat who'd misplaced her kittens.

"Thank you, sir," Graves said.

"What the hell do you want?" Julius slurred the words. He was most definitely drunk.

"It's the—" Graves cleared his throat again, indicating delicacy this time. "It's the young lady, sir."

Julius wasn't sure if he wanted to laugh or put his fist through the wall. The young lady. "Isn't it always?" he asked, his voice heavy with irony. "Come in and pour yourself a drink."

Graves slipped into the study and shut the door softly behind him. "No thank you, sir. I only wanted to relay the news."

Julius hardly heard him. "Nothing but trouble. You tried to tell me that, Graves, but I wouldn't listen." He poured himself another brandy and sank heavily into a chair. "What is it about me, d'you think, that invites treacherous women to cross my path? I never went looking for 'em, Graves, you know that."

"Er, yes, your lordship," Graves said, looking concerned. "About the lady—"

"Course, Lady Milvia's not treacherous," Julius mused, bringing the brandy to his lips. Its fire had built up a blaze that warmed him like the brightest hearth. "She's correct and predictable and all that a lady ought to be. But the poor creature's got no spark in her at all."

He wondered where the rest of his brandy had gone. He couldn't possibly have drunk the glass already. He reached out for the bottle, but it was almost too far away to bother. "Pour me another, Graves. There's a good fellow."

Graves wrung his hands, and his long face was abject. "It's about the young lady, your lordship."

The young lady. Julius thought again of how Katherine had eaten greedily from his fingers. How she had met his tongue with her own, pressing up against him. She had not been frightened then. He would have sworn she'd burned as hotly as he had.

"We'll let her go in the morning," he said abruptly. "If the little idiot keeps trying to run off, she'll land us all in the scandal sheets." Julius frowned. "Damn it, Graves, you aren't going to be tiresome about that brandy, are you? I'm in no mood for morality plays."

Graves looked pained as he crossed to the cut crystal decanter on the sideboard. "I've been trying to tell you, your lordship—"

"You haven't been trying very hard," Julius said, stretching his legs out in front of him and shutting his eyes. "Just pour the damned drink and spit it out, man."

Graves cleared his throat again. "The young lady, your lordship. She's gone."

11

The breeze came up off the Thames in a stiff, cold bluster, and Katie pulled her cloak tighter around herself. The wind carried tobacco and rum, and the harsh stench of hides. Men teemed around her, wheeling hand trucks or rolling casks, and one frustrated-looking sailor was trying to teach a caged green parrot to curse.

Phineas was still in the city, tying up loose ends, and Alex had gone off with some unsavory-looking person to inquire as to which of the massive, bobbing ships they would be boarding. Katie paced the dock nervously. At the moment, her immediate concern was to get out of this wretched country as quickly as possible. Just where she'd be going was a question she didn't want to think about quite yet.

The wind tore the hood from her head as a bowlegged little man, positively encrusted with brass buttons, was making his way toward her.

Accompanying him was a disgruntled-looking Alex Manners. "Beg your pardon, miss, but the captain seems to feel there's a problem."

Alex looked as if he would have cheerfully slit the

captain from guts to gullet, but the bowlegged little person merely peered into Katie's eyes and blinked quickly. "Good day to you, miss," he said, with an air of careful dignity. "I understand you wish to proceed to the, ah, Continent."

"Yes, that's right," Katie said coolly. "Surely there's no difficulty in that."

"The only matter for concern, that is to say . . . " The little man cleared his throat with weighty harrumph. "It is to be understood, miss, that you are a citizen of the former American colonies?"

"Yes, I'm an American. What of it?" she said, a little curtly.

The captain coughed discreetly into his handkerchief. Clearly he had something distasteful to tell her, and just as clearly he didn't want to risk her displeasure by saying it. Or perhaps it was the looming Alex Manners whose ill will he feared. He rocked back on his bandy legs. "Ah, well, you must understand, according to the precise disposition of American citizens whilst traveling in the British Isles as opposed to their status within the larger—"

Katie had realized long ago that there was positively no sense in allowing such a person to blather. "You're saying there'll be some delay? How long?"

The man's face fell a little, but he pasted on another bright smile. "Ah, yes. Precisely. The exact nature of the particular departure, in order to perfectly comply with all statutes national and local, in as much—"

"How long?" she repeated, interrupting him. Her tone was as frosty and unyielding as she could make it, and she held her spine flat and straight as a broadsword.

The captain blinked again, as if to signal his apology. "Two weeks, miss. I apologize most profusely for the delay, but there really can be no question as to the—"

"Manners?" Katie snapped, turning away from the little bandy-legged person. "Why haven't Prince Schwartzenberg's aides informed us of this possibility?"

Alex, bless him, was as cool as lemon ice. "I'm sure

it's not their fault, miss. It's the war, you know, very difficult to find clever young men to fill these posts. It's a matter of the correct documents to satisfy the requirements of this . . . " Alex looked disdainfully down at the bowlegged captain, as if regarding a rather grubby piglet. "This . . . person. Of course, the Prince will be *most* disappointed."

Katie gave what she hoped was a convincing little shiver. "Surely the Prince can't fault this man for wanting to obey regulations? Even Schwartzie could hardly be so unfair."

She glanced over at the captain. *Do this*, she willed. *For once in your life, bend your precious rules.*

Alex smiled evilly. "You know how it does put him in a temper to be kept waiting, miss. He might well simply confiscate the ship, just to be done with the whole wretched mess. The Prince is, after all, most anxious for you to be abroad." Alex gave Katie a significant look, one not lost on the bandy-legged captain.

"Ah—confiscate?" The captain's reedy voice quavered a bit. "Surely there's no need to be hasty. These are difficult times," he intoned, shaking his head gravely. "Very difficult times, and measures must be taken."

"Difficult measures," Katie suggested, fixing the captain with a penetrating look. She turned the full force of her silent will on him. *Let us onto this ship without delay.*

The captain blinked rapidly. "Precisely, my dear. Difficult measures. In such a case, given that the, ah, Prince's need is so very great, perhaps we could see our way clear to a certain flexibility."

"Absolutely not," Katie said firmly. "Schwartzie is so very particular about details, I couldn't possibly ask you to disobey regulations. I simply don't know what I'm going to tell him. Manners? Dispatch a note to the Prince notifying him of the difficulty. And *do* be sure to mention the zeal of this Captain—I am sorry, Captain, your name again?"

Despite the morning's chill, the captain was beginning

to sweat, rivulets slipping down his plump neck and beneath the folds of his collar. "I really think—" he squeaked, then cleared his throat and began again. "I must insist—I wouldn't dream of it, my dear. It would be unpatriotic of me to insist on a foolish adherence to the letter of regulation, when the young lady is so obviously on a mission of . . . "

Katie fixed him with another icy look, daring him to complete the sentence. The poor man didn't know what she was to the Prince. Spy? Mistress?

" . . . of the utmost importance," he finished, looking briefly pleased with himself.

"As you wish, captain," she said brusquely. "I'll arrange to have my trunks carried to your vessel. Good day."

The captain's face was the picture of gratitude, and he broke out in a fresh sweat, his collar beginning to look rather limp. "Very good, miss. Yes, very good indeed. I look forward to your presence on our journey."

Katie stared at him as coldly as if he'd been an insect invading her parlor. "Quite," she said.

Katie had no difficulty finding a cab to take her to the ship. It was surpassingly sturdy for a simple hack, but perhaps the damp and bustle of the docks called for a more substantial vehicle than the flimsy hansoms that scuttled about the streets of the city.

Alex and the footman had loaded her trunk into the cab, then gone in the opposite direction with the captain to thrash out the last of the paperwork.

Katie stepped into the dark cab, glad to be getting out of England. The place smacked of ill omens and cruel reversals. Fifteen thousand pounds, plucked deftly from Val Willowby, that she would never see.

Her mind skittered away from the true ill omen of her voyage here—those days with Brynston. Not only had she been found out, she had been given a small taste of an English earl's idea of revenge. Kidnapping had not been enough for him. Her mind went over and over that strange meal with him, the table laden with delicacies, the dark hunger in his eyes. Hunger for Katie's humiliation, hunger for her ruin.

She gripped her reticule so tightly her knuckles hurt. Some small, idiotic part of her wanted to believe he'd truly desired her. But she would not let herself go down that foolish road. A kiss to a man like the Brimstone Earl was a weapon. He'd wanted only to destroy her, hurling her own shameful desires in her face. Perhaps he'd even wanted to boast his conquest as if she were a new race-horse he'd bought.

Because Brynston hated her. She had to remember that, it was the only thing that linked her to sanity. She did not know why his eyes smoked with such volcanic fervor when he looked at her. But they did, and Katie could only hope that by leaving this wretched country, she could truly escape him, and in time forget the strange effect he'd had on her.

The cab rocked violently, and Katie shouted out in protest, "Hey! Mind what you're doing up there!" She had no intention of getting her neck broken in some carriage accident. Wherever she was when she finally gave up the ghost, she vowed it wasn't going to be on English soil.

The cab jolted forward, unheeding, the great wheels squeaking and clattering on the wooden dock. Katie felt a twinge of unease. "Hey!" she shouted again, bracing herself to stand and rap on the ceiling. "Are you some kind of madman? Slow this carriage down immediately!"

The cab swerved sharply to the left, as the horses whinnied in protest and the driver cursed them, forcing them onward. Katie began to feel distinctly nervous. Surely there was no reason to ride like Satan himself merely to reach the other side of the dock. And her tap should have stopped the cab—instead, if anything, it had seemed to urge the driver to go even faster.

Probably the driver was drunk, or worse, and hadn't noticed her tapping. She thumped at the ceiling again, louder this time. The driver made no response. Katie pushed at the window to open it and shout up to the lunatic. But the window was shut tight, as if it had never been opened.

"This is ridiculous," Katie muttered, breathing deeply to control the twinges of fear in her stomach. Public coaches were notoriously dangerous, and Katie had no desire to end up with her neck broken in some English ditch. Perhaps the driver had been thrown, the horses thundering along without him.

Katie sat for a moment, gripping the seat with her hands to keep herself from being thrown bodily around the dark cab, and decided there was no sense in waiting like a duck in a pond. She slid toward the door, meaning to wrench it open and at least see if she could assess the situation more clearly.

She frowned as she twisted the door latch. It refused to budge. She gave it a sharp shove, pushing all her weight against it. The effort sent her off balance, nearly throwing her to the floor. But the door handle did not move a fraction of an inch.

Panic began to snake its fingers around Katie's throat, pressing against her windpipe until she felt she could hardly breathe. Suddenly the cab seemed too dark and close to endure, the walls coming in around her. She was trapped as surely as a rabbit in a snare.

She threw herself at the carriage door, wrenching furiously at the handle, slamming her body against it in hopes of crashing through it entirely. It didn't matter that they were careening down the road at obscene speed. All that mattered was escape, freedom from the suffocating darkness.

The door was sturdy, strangely so for a common hack, and refused to yield. The carriage hit a dip in the road, then veered sharply up again, throwing Katie backwards. Katie swore under her breath and pulled herself back to her seat, not daring to release her grip even to rub her bruised and aching muscles.

The next minutes dragged on like hours. Katie tried several more times to force the door, but the cab was built like a fortress, and seemed made of iron and stone rather than mere wood. She strained her ears, listening for any sound from the driver, and once she thought she heard the crack of the whip, but the noise of the wheels was too ferocious for her to be sure of much of anything. She shouted herself hoarse crying to the driver for help, but if he heard her, he showed no sign. Finally she gave up, wedging herself tightly into a corner, clutching at the seat with white, strained fingers. All she could do now was wait.

Katie did not know how long she rode that way, but eventually the carriage began to slow. The metallic taste of fear filled her mouth as she wondered who would be waiting there for her. Horses might shy, or even run away with a carriage, but they did not lock the windows and fortify the doors. Someone had wanted her badly enough to kidnap her, and Katie could think of only two possibilities. Either Brynston had found her, which seemed unlikely, or the Turks had decided they would wait no longer for her father to repay his debt.

She swallowed roughly as the carriage further slowed its pace. It would take every scrap of her wits to come out of the Turks' clutches in one piece. She would have to compose herself. Painfully she straightened her legs, wincing at the pain shooting from her hips to her heels, and she smoothed her skirts. She wiped her palms and forehead with a handkerchief she dug from her reticule, and ate a peppermint to chase the taste of fear from her mouth.

The horses clopped to a stop, making a wide circle. Katie could hear men's voices from outside—English voices. Katie bit her lip, forcing herself to concentrate.

The door swung open, and she blinked at the blaze of sunlight. She could not make out the features of the dark shape outlined against the yellow wash of light, but her heart gave a strange, aching twist at the breadth of shoulders that all but filled the carriage door frame.

"D'you know, Miss Feathering, I believe you are beginning to make me angry." The voice was cold and hard as an iron spike.

"It's not possible—" Katie broke off, her voice choking. She didn't know whether to laugh in relief or burst into tears, and for a wild moment she thought she might succumb to her lightheadedness and faint.

Her plans and her scheming had come to nothing. She was once again a prisoner of the Brimstone Earl.

12

When the earl of Brynston stepped into the dark hansom and finally clapped eyes on a frightened but defiant Katherine Feathering, he didn't know whether to box her ears or collapse in relief. He had combed the streets until three that morning looking for her, hauling ruffians by the collar and slamming them against brick walls, demanding to know if they had seen the girl.

"Miss Feathering," he said coldly. "Delightful to see you again. You don't mind if we share the cab, do you?" He stepped up into the hansom and closed the door behind him.

"How dare you!" she said. Even in the darkness her eyes blazed with indignant fire. "You frightened the wits out of me. Remove yourself at once, and instruct that lunatic driver to return me to the docks."

Julius tapped at the roof with his cane, and the cab rumbled on. The driver had instructions to take them to an ill-traveled inn a mile or two out of town, from where Brynston would send a message back to the girl's father to pick her up.

But first, he was going to blister her hoydenish ears. He

had been wild with worry before a giggling tribe of street urchins had finally told him yes, they'd seen a pretty, short-haired girl in a fine wool cloak and dirty slippers. No, she did not look frightened. She was with a great hulk of a man, taller even than Julius, and some of the children had thought he was the devil. The man had a scar twisting down his face, in the shape of a two-pronged fork.

"I frightened you, did I?" Julius asked, trying to rein in his fury. "Do you have the faintest idea what was going through my mind after you left last night? I had thought I was quite clear on the subject of the dangers of Pinchpye Close."

Her eyes were murderous. "Is this supposed to be an apology for kidnapping me? Because I must tell you, my lord, it lacks something in the way of grace."

Julius felt a guilty twinge. He had been nearly undone by self-recrimination last night, as his imagination invented ever more horrid fates that Miss Feathering might be enduring behind the closed, dirty doors.

"My behavior was unforgivable," he said curtly. "However, we are not talking about *my* behavior. We are discussing how even the most innocent heiress could be so grossly stupid as to waltz through a London slum as if it were Almack's?"

He caught a flash of something in her eyes—that wounded forest creature he had seen before.

"I could not stay in that . . . place any longer," she said in a small voice.

"Don't you realize what could have happened? Forgive the indelicacy, Miss Feathering, but you could quite easily have been forced into a brothel, where they would have wasted no time in selling you to the highest bidder."

She stiffened at that, her small hands whitening as she clutched her reticule. "I would not be so foolish as to travel alone. My father sent a man for me."

Julius leaned back in his seat. His temper had been getting the best of him all morning. He had mobilized an army of Pinchpye Close brats to fan out and comb the city for Miss Feathering. Reason and cool common sense would dictate that he let her go where she pleased, and to the devil with all his unanswered questions. The money meant nothing to him, and the sting of wounded pride weighed little against the shocking potential for scandal that seemed to float around Miss Feathering like a cloud of expensive scent.

But he had allowed his temper to erupt, and he did not seem to be able to call it back again. "Ah yes," he said. "Your man—Manners, wasn't it? A few of the street urchins took him for Old Nick himself."

Miss Feathering nodded faintly. "He frightens some people. I am accustomed to him, and know that he is gentle and kind."

"The intriguing thing is," Julius said, leaning forward to capture her gaze with his own. "Some of the other urchins recognized him. They call him The Knacker. Shall I tell you why?"

Miss Feathering frowned and pulled away from Julius's penetrating gaze. "Children can be very cruel about physical disfigurements."

"I don't think so, Miss Feathering. Your man, a man I know very well for a sharper's apprentice, is known in the worst quarters of London as a fellow who'll cut throats as readily as he plants the books."

Miss Feathering's expression was haughty as she turned her chin toward the closed window. "You are being ridiculous, Lord Brynston. They must have mistaken him for someone else."

"Your Mr. Manners is a difficult man to mistake," Julius said.

"Mr. Manners is as gentle as a lamb."

"Mr. Manners is a cold-blooded assassin, as well as a common thief," Julius countered. "What I want to know is why you keep such a person in your employ."

Miss Feathering shifted an inch toward the window, tilting her chin in a martyred attitude. "You are clearly a ravening lunatic, Lord Brynston. I suppose you shall murder me, that's what ravening lunatics do, isn't it?"

"You make it sound very tempting," he growled softly, "but no, I'm not going to murder you. However, you will tell me why you are going about London fleecing wealthy gentlemen for large sums of money. You will also tell me why you employ such a dangerous criminal as your Mr. Manners. I suppose while you are at it, you may tell me where you were going when I apprehended you."

She shot him a poisoned look. "I do not make explanations to lunatics."

Before he could answer, the cab gave a sudden lurch. Men's voices came from outside, sharp and angry, speaking an unfamiliar language.

Across from him, Miss Feathering went white as a handkerchief.

"What is it?" Julius asked, suddenly wary. "Are you frightened by something?"

The voices from outside came louder, and two pistol shots were fired in rapid succession. The horses went wild, and for a gut-wrenching moment, Julius was certain the cab would overturn. It rocked violently from side to side, then settled down to a lurching stop.

"Whatever you do, don't tell them I'm here!" Miss Feathering said, working to see if she could pry up her seat.

"Tell whom? Do you know those men outside?"

She slid her heavy trunk out from under her seat, so that she might wedge herself in its place.

Julius felt in his coat for his own pistol. He was glad he'd brought it now, as he tested its weight in his hand. "I'm going out to see what in blazes is going on."

Miss Feathering shot him a terrified look. "No, you mustn't!" she hissed. "They'll surely kill you if you confront them."

Julius narrowed his eyes. "We will discuss this later." He cocked the pistol, then slowly eased open the hansom door.

Two swarthy men on horseback, one elegant and fat, one rangy and thin, held pistols trained on Julius's valet. Graves in turn had the fat one in his sites, his pale hands steady. The hansom's driver slumped in an untidy heap on his seat, looking quite dead.

Neither Graves nor the highwaymen noticed Julius, who, shielded by the bulky body of the cab, was moving with a cat's grace and silence to position himself where he could get a clear shot.

"You need not share the fate of your unfortunate driver," the fat one said, his voice a silky purr. "We do not relish the shedding of life. Simply release to us the American female, and you may continue unmolested."

Julius's blood chilled. He remembered the stricken look on Miss Feathering's face when she'd heard the men's voices.

"We have no such person on board this coach," Graves said evenly. "You have killed this man in vain. I suggest you not compound your crimes by pursuing the matter."

The fat one smiled with a torturer's bland grace. "It is most inadvisable to toy with us, my friend. Do not think you do the girl a kindness by your stubbornness. I personally would not harm her for the world, but my friend Mehmet is easily angered."

The skinny one, Mehmet, gave a crazed, malicious smile that made Julius think of a stoat.

Julius fingered a heavy sovereign coin in his pocket. He remembered an idiotic tavern game he used to play, when he was a bored young buck with nothing better to occupy his time: the flicking of coins into mugs of ale, on which all manner of complicated wager had been made. Julius had been surpassingly good at it. The stakes were higher now, and it had been ten years, but it was the best chance he had.

He cast a glance at Graves. The man was as still as if he were carved out of granite. Unexpected depths, that chap.

Julius closed one eye to aim, and flicked the coin expertly in the direction of Mehmet's horse's left flank. The coin hit the animal with an audible slap, and the animal screamed and reared on its hind legs as if it had been trained to do so.

The fat one's horse caught the other's fright, and skittered back and around in a circle like a child's mechanical toy. The fat one fired his pistol, and it ricocheted off the cab with a nasty ring, quite near Brynston's left shoulder.

The nags pulling the cab would have none of this, and tried to jump back from the blood and thunder. The hansom lurched hard to the right.

Graves did not hesitate. He took aim as best he could and fired, managing to send Mehmet's pistol flying into the air. Mehmet's horse wheeled and jumped, screaming in fright.

As Graves fired, Julius set his sites on the fat one. Not at the man's firing hand, but at his black heart. He didn't know who this bastard was, but he had already killed a man, and Miss Feathering was terrified of him. Julius held his breath and squeezed the trigger.

And, unfortunately, missed. The man clutched at his arm rather than his chest, his jaw slack with shock. His hand began to well with blood. The pistol slid forgotten to the ground, where the horse took it as yet another demon and jumped well clear, shaking its head and skipping sideways.

All this took no longer than an instant, though the events unreeled in Julius's mind with an unnatural slow calm.

The hansom's horses tore off down the road, willing to endure no more of this bedlam. Graves steadied himself in his seat and began to reload with ruthless efficiency. Julius pulled himself up onto the seat with the dead driver and stepped over the unfortunate man to join his valet.

The highwaymen worked to regain control of their horses, casting a nervous eye at Graves as he rammed another ball into his pistol. Julius took the hansom's reins and worked to ease the terrified horses to a stop. He had no wish to escape those assassins, quite the contrary.

But it was the assassins who made their escape, galloping in the opposite direction as if fleeing hellfire. As the hansom slowed to a stop, Graves turned, cocked his pistol and fired, but the ball landed far short of its mark.

Julius's heart felt as if it would leap from his chest, but he managed to compose himself. "Waste of a shot, there, old man."

Graves blinked and nodded his head in agreement. "Quite right, sir. I was taken by the spirit of the moment."

"Perfectly natural," Julius said, securing the reins so that he could reload his own pistol.

Graves stepped over him to inspect the driver. "I am afraid the poor fellow is quite dead," he said, wiping his hands on a clean corner of the man's coat.

"You don't mind taking the reins, do you, Graves?" Julius said, replacing his pistol in his pocket. His heart was still hammering in his chest, and his ears still rang from the shot he'd fired. He stepped down lightly from the driver's seat. Control, control.

"If I may ask, sir, where are you going?" Graves asked, reloading.

Julius took a deep breath through his nose and smoothed his lapels. "I believe it is time for a stern conversation with Miss Feathering."

13

Katie had extricated herself from the hansom and was headed as quickly and quietly as she could manage for the woods when Brynston's hand gripped her arm. "Suppose you tell me, Miss Feathering, just what the devil all that was about."

She wheeled and tried to yank her arm free. "Please, my lord, this has nothing to do with you."

"It has everything to do with me," he said. His breath fogged in the winter air, and his voice was as hushed and cold as the snowdrifts banking the road.

Katie swallowed hard. She looked up at him, and wished she hadn't. The bruise where she had struck him last night was vivid purple, and an ugly blot of the driver's blood stained his white shirt. His eyes were, if anything, colder than his voice.

"It is a private matter, one I am not free to discuss with you," she said, willing him to let the matter go.

"I am a surpassingly patient man, Miss Feathering, when I've a mind to be. I will happily stand here in the snow all day, and into tomorrow, if you prefer."

Katie stared at the ground as she wracked her brains. "I'm—I'm being blackmailed."

Brynston released his grip, visibly astonished. "You're being what?"

Katie took heart. This might work, after all. "Those men are angry because I . . . missed a payment. They follow me everywhere, I can't find a moment's peace. I had hoped to escape them by fleeing the country, when you apprehended me on the dock." She looked into Brynston's eyes, daring him to disbelieve her.

The Brimstone Earl was a man who dared a great deal. "And the matter between you and myself was of no consequence in that flight?"

"You were a complication, my lord, that is all. I needed money to pay the blackmailers and you were at hand. I regret it." Katie enjoyed letting the high and mighty Brimstone think he was nothing but a moment's inconvenience. It would serve him right. *Believe me*, she willed. *For once, you infuriating English bastard, believe me.*

Brimstone held her gaze for a long moment, searching her face for the lie. She matched his gaze with her own fierce one.

"Forgive me, my dear, but I must ask. What is it you are being blackmailed for?"

She looked away. Damn the man, Bonaparte himself couldn't match him for arrogance. "It is a personal matter, my lord."

He took her chin in his hand and brought her gaze to his. His touch was not harsh, not cruel, but it was inescapable. "You will tell me."

She was afraid of him. Afraid of the hot blue flame of his eyes and afraid of his doggedness. He would never let her alone, never.

"M—my mother," she stammered. "She took a lover. Before she had me. My father is not my father." Where in blazes had *that* come from? But it would work, it would work admirably. There was disgrace in it, but nothing compared to the truth. "She wrote some indiscreet letters, which landed in the hands of those rogues."

Brynston abruptly released his hold on her chin, biting back a curse. "Forgive me," he said. "But I needed to know."

She looked down at the snowy ground, refusing to meet his eyes as she mentally invented a list of details, checking them against one another for soundness.

"And you are your father's only heir," Brynston said after a brief pause. "May I take it your papa is not the kind of man to turn an indulgent eye upon such a matter?"

Katie firmly suppressed the desire to laugh aloud. If there was a man alive to turn an indulgent eye, it was her poor, silly father. "He is a ruthless man, and hard," she said, speaking the lie as if it were gospel. "If he knew, I should be thrown in the street without a penny, without any means to support myself."

Brynston made a sound of disgust. "Surely the man's not such an ass as to throw his fortune away on some distant third cousin, when his own daughter could inherit?"

"He would die before he permitted his fortune to fall into the hands of a bastard," Katie said evenly. "My cousin . . . Jamie is a drunkard and a fool, but he is a Feathering, and he is legitimate." Her cousin? Jamie? Her mind galloped like an Arabian racehorse.

Brynston swiped one hand along the back of his head as he looked up at the gray sky. "Good God, I have been the worst species of idiot. What can your father have to say about this—" He gestured around him, to the lonely road and the bloodstained hansom, and in a larger sense to the dangerous dance between the two of them. "I have compromised you unforgivably. Your father knows I've abducted you—not once now, but twice. I had assumed your family at least would have the sense—not to mention the natural feeling—to welcome you home. With their cooperation, you could retain your reputation. Without it . . . " He trailed off, his mouth a hard, tight line.

Alarms were ringing in Katie's mind. "I—I feel certain I can explain things, my lord."

Brynston shook his head impatiently. "If your father would throw his fortune away on a distant relation, he would throw you away as well. Surely he will not be more forgiving of the daughter than of the mother."

"I have committed no sin, Lord Brynston!" Katie said, feeling her cheeks go hot.

"Not in my eyes, or in your own, but in the eyes of society you are nothing less than ruined. Think, girl. You've spent above three days and nights in my company, with no more chaperon than a freckled pickpocket. With your father's care, the matter could have been hidden, your reputation preserved, but now—"

Brynston wiped the back of his hand across his mouth, swallowing another curse. "Da— Dash me and my bloody stubbornness." He turned a sudden, surprised look on her. "But what did your father say when you returned home?"

Katie's heart sank. "My father?" Damn.

"Yes, your father," Brynston said brusquely. "He must know where you've been all this time. What did he say when you returned?"

"He's been away. In India," she said smoothly. India? That was a bit farfetched. She should have said something plausible, like Cornwall. "He's only just come back last night. Alex has sworn not to tell him."

"So you would have been safe, if I hadn't taken you again today," Brynston said, sounding like a man reading the warrant for his own execution.

Katie cursed herself silently. Why did she have to say last night? It could have been tomorrow night just as easily.

"Confound me for a clumsy blockhead," Brynston said. "Why in blazes didn't you say something sooner?"

"I thought I'd been quite explicit on the matter," Katie said frostily, folding her arms in front of her. "I did demand several times that you release me."

"Well of course you did, you silly goose, who wouldn't have? But you should have confided in me as to your father's unforgiving nature, if not as to—ah, your own predicament."

She gave him a frozen look. "Surely the matter is none of your business, my lord."

"Gad, but you're the most mule-headed chit alive." He was exasperated, but there was no harshness in his voice, only concern. "You said it yourself, there can be nothing for you now. No marriage, no fortune. Surely that was worth a moment's embarrassment. If you'd told me that first night in the flash house, I would have taken you home that instant. How will you live?"

Katie struggled to smother her guilt. It had been easier to deal with the Brimstone Earl when he was being an unfeeling brute. Katie had no defenses at all against this man with gentle, worried eyes. "Pray do not concern yourself, my lord. I'm not so delicate as all that."

He took in the set of her jaw and the straightness of her back. "There was never anything of the fribble about you, was there? It was nothing but a performance, to fleece me out of my money."

She suddenly longed to explain everything to him. The cheating, the lies. Even the reason she'd lashed out at him in the flash house.

She stifled the idea as soon as it appeared. It was an idiotic notion, and a dangerous one. If he discovered the truth, he'd see her hang before he would ever forgive her. "I was desperate, my lord," she said, mastering herself. "I will not ask for your forgiveness, or even for your understanding, but that is the truth."

"You should have told me," he repeated. "If I had known, if you had given me some clue—" He broke off, the moment's softness in his eyes disappearing. He looked every inch the Brimstone Earl again, unyielding as a chunk of obsidian. "I have done you an unforgivable harm. You say you will not ask for my forgiveness or my understanding, and I will not ask for yours. But do not doubt that I will repay you."

Katie felt a wave of panic all but steal her voice away. "I do not need your repayment, and I do not want it. Return me to my family, that is all the payment I ask."

"You are gallant in your way, but you must learn to set aside your willfulness," Brynston said, taking her hand abruptly and leading her back to the grim hansom, where Graves waited patiently in the driver's seat. He had clearly decided what he was going to do, and Katie's wishes on the subject be damned. "You will prepare yourself. We are to be married as quickly as possible. We shall tell the world it was a love match, and we could not bear to wait. Everyone will assume you are breeding, naturally, but their tongues should quiet when they see you have waited the correct period of time to give me an heir."

Katie stopped in her tracks, momentarily stunned into silence. "Married?" she said, when she had regained her voice. "Do you think I'm completely mad? Why on earth would I consent to marry you?"

Brynston's pale eyes narrowed dangerously. "You speak too quickly, Miss Feathering. Once you have considered the situation, I do not think you will reject my generous offer so rashly."

Katie pulled her hand free of his, and stared down at the ground. Her throat scratched with the tears she would never shed. Marry him? It was impossible, insane. Worse than insane. "There is no explanation on earth that could convince me, my lord. Please do not speak of this again."

"You are quite ruined," he said, as calmly as if he'd said *I do not care for sugar in my tea*. "It is entirely my fault, but what is done cannot be undone. You have no choice."

The words made her angry, and the anger was enough to chase the hard knot of tears from her throat. She gave him a savage look. "How dare you make assumptions for me? If I have to choose between marrying you and living the rest of my life without some overbearing English husband, I think my choice is very clear."

Brynston's jaw twitched faintly, a certain sign that his temper was building. "Surely marrying an earl can be no worse a fate than stealing money to pay blackmailers, Miss Feathering."

"Isn't it?" She was speaking too harshly, too quickly, but she couldn't help it. He had thrown her off balance with his casual pronouncement. *We are to be married as quickly as possible.* He had no idea who she was, what marrying her would truly mean. And the thought of telling him the truth filled her with sick panic. He would despise her, as he had every right to do.

"Look here," he said brusquely, "I'm not so bad a catch as all that, you know. Your father will doubtless be very pleased."

Katie found herself laughing, and had to stop herself before she gave way to full-fledged hysteria. "My father? My father is the least of my concerns at the moment, I assure you, Lord Brynston. I do not wish to marry you, I *will* not marry you, and I do not wish to speak of this any further."

"Why the devil not, if I may ask?"

Katie allowed herself a glance at him, taking in the flame-blue, forbidding eyes, the breadth of his shoulders beneath his coat, the powerful legs in their snug inexpressibles. Despite the bruised cheek and the bloody shirt, he was quite perfect. And he had just asked her to marry him.

She gathered together the small scraps of pride she had left. "Let me see now." She ticked on her fingers. "You've kidnapped me twice, threatened me more times than I can number, held me against my will in a dangerous and scandalous environment, risked my neck in that hellish ride up here—shall I continue?"

Brynston narrowed his eyes, his mouth twisting into a snarl. "I know we have had our differences, but—"

Katie laughed again, she couldn't help it. But there was no warmth, no humor in it. It was the laugh of a desperate creature, a treed fox with the hounds baying and snapping at its tail. "I think I'd call them something more than that. You're mad to suggest it, as mad as I've always suspected. I'm not marrying you, ever, so you may as well disabuse yourself of the notion." She pulled her shawl more tightly around her shoulders and made to move past him.

Brynston caught her arm as she tried to pass. "I gave my word of honor you would come to no harm because of me. You may not give a damn for the concept yourself, but you will not hinder me from my duty. I will not be known as a man who has ruined a young woman's reputation and left her in the lurch. This is the most sensible solution, and you will do as you are told."

Katie worked to twist her arm free of his grip, but he held her tight. "What colossal arrogance you English have!"

"It cannot match the egregious stupidity of certain hell-born young American ladies," Brynston said through gritted teeth. "I've made up my mind. You will accustom yourself to the matter immediately. We can take the cab as far as the nearest inn, where we should be able to procure a carriage for Scotland."

"I will not!" she said hotly. "I presume even in this barbaric country, a man may not force a woman to marry against her will." Katie was clutching at straws, and one floated into her grasp. "My father won't give you a penny if we elope, you know. He'll be out of his mind with rage. If you steal me this way, I'll come to you quite penniless."

Brynston gave her an evil smile. "I see you are growing accustomed the idea. Fear not, Miss Feathering—I suppose I may call you Katherine, now that we are affianced. I have more than enough money for both of us. If your father chooses to be disagreeable, that is his affair. But I believe he will come around, once he understands the situation."

Katie could hardly breathe, the cold air suddenly seeming thick and noxious. "I will never agree to marry you," she said, shaking her head.

"You will, or it won't matter," Brynston said negligently, taking her arm again and hauling her, none too gently, toward the darkness of the hansom cab. "I've made up my mind, Katherine, for your own good. You'll see the wisdom of it eventually. And once I make up my mind, I always have my way."

Early that evening, Phineas Starr was reclining in the sitting room of his London apartments, about to launch into a platter of cakes. Manners was dashing around the house, assembling maps and charts to try to deduce where Katie had been taken.

It was all very clear to Phineas—Brynston had snatched her again. It couldn't have been the Turks, they would have made more noise over it. So it must be the earl. He'd treated the girl gently enough the first time he'd snagged her, and Phineas wasn't over concerned this time. Brynston would tip his hand soon enough, and Manners would run and fetch her again. It was inconvenient, but not much more than that.

For some reason, the earl hadn't made a peep about Katie fleecing him at Lady Odcombe's. Phineas was ready to flee to Italy if Brynston did, but in the meantime, there was no sense in getting their feathers ruffled. That was the trouble with Manners—the man never knew how to sit and wait. Always itching to run off and *do* something.

The cook knocked at the door, and held out an envelope. "This just come, sir. The boy's downstairs, he says they want a reply immediately, if it's convenient."

Phineas gave a satisfied smile. He took the envelope off the tray, and turned it to check the seal. Sure enough, the earl of Brynston. "I'll have a reply directly," he muttered.

He scanned the note, and his eyes widened. Surely it couldn't be? He read it again, and laughed out loud. It was. His daughter had landed a fish Jonah himself would have been proud of. It was almost too perfect.

"Manners!" Phineas bellowed, pushing himself with

some difficulty to his feet and rummaging in the writing desk for an inkwell and a scrap of paper. Clever girl, he'd always known she'd come to something great.

His Katie, his own little champion. Better than any damned racehorse, any day of the week.

14

Katie sat straight-backed on the coach squabs, trying to concentrate on the brisk air coming in through the open window, fighting panic with every shred of courage she could muster. They'd been traveling for days, and every night had been worse than the last. Brynston all but kept her under lock and key, knowing very well that if she were given the slightest chance to escape, she would.

The noose was tightening with every clip of the horses' hooves toward Scotland, until Katie was ready to kick, scream, anything to escape. Perhaps she could convince him she was mad. Perhaps she truly was.

Brynston had not ridden in the carriage with her, had done nothing that might seem improper, with the notable exception of abducting her by force. He paid guards to stand outside her door, and more guards to lurk beneath her windows. She was his prisoner, and he had no intention of letting her go.

The carriage took a turn from the rutted road, and Katie peered out at the darkening sky. They would be stopping for the night, then. Another inn. More thick-fingered young hog farmers paid a guinea apiece to make sure she didn't slip out the window to her freedom.

And every night there was Lord Brynston, pouring her wine, smiling his cool, elegant smile, ignoring her curses and her pleas. They never ate in the common rooms any more; she made too much trouble, and Brynston wanted to keep a low profile in case the Turks returned.

Lord Brynston opened the carriage door to escort her to her room, his arm firmly on hers. He had insisted that she wear a bonnet with a heavy veil ever since the Turks had come looking for her, and Katie shuddered as the black thing fell over her face. Trapped, and no way to free herself from the web.

Brynston moved quickly up the stairs, his powerful frame guiding her, and she had no choice but to follow. She had resisted him the first night, and had been forcibly dragged upstairs for her trouble, her ankles and shins bruised from where she'd struck the railings as she kicked.

"Are you feeling well, my dear?" he asked solicitously, opening the door in front of her.

"I feel horrible. I wouldn't be at all surprised if I hadn't caught some dangerous fever. Maybe a fatal one. I think it would be best to wait here until it passes." Katie did what she could to sound convincing, but he would not believe her. She had concocted a thousand stories over the past days, and he hadn't believed a one of them.

"You look very well to me," he said mildly. "But I'll have the landlord bring you a nice bowl of gruel. There is nothing more restorative, I find."

Katie shuddered. "That won't be necessary, thank you."

The Brimstone Earl gave her a faint smile. "As you please, my dear."

Thank goodness he'd let up. The night before, spurred by her invented complaints of chilblains, he'd decided that the snowy weather required her to be wrapped in blankets, and she had lain all but immobilized under a heap of them, panting from the heat as he built up the fire. Her attempts to free herself were met with a stern warning that he would sit on her if she did not cease her wriggling.

The fact was, Katie had all but given up. Manners would not be able to find her while they were inexorably on the move; there were too many inns, too many possible paths. The last place Alex would expect Brynston to take her was to Gretna Green, that notorious refuge of eloping couples. Probably even now he was combing London's underworld, wringing his big hands and wondering where she could be.

I'm safe, Alex, she thought, as if she could communicate with him merely by wishing so strongly that she could. And she was, she supposed, safe enough, as far as her body went. Her gaze wandered to Brynston, who was even now checking the latches on the doors and windows.

So far as her heart was concerned—that was another matter entirely.

Julius dared a glance over at Katie, and was surprised to see that much of the fight had already gone out of her. He'd been afraid she would try another hunger strike, but all mention of the time in the flash house seemed to send her into a peculiar melancholy. She doubtless thought back with disgust of his shocking behavior toward her, of the way he had swept the dishes from the table and lowered himself onto her—

Julius's vision clouded. For a moment all he could think of was the way she had clung to him, her mouth fierce beneath his, her wildness calling out to his own, sparking like a tinder in a stack of dry wood.

He shook his head to clear his mind, and looked at her again, his vision clearer now. He had dishonored her in the flash house, behaved disgracefully, but he would make it up to her.

He tried to look at her objectively. She was nothing

but a small, spoiled American girl, rather the worse for wear for having been traveling at this breakneck pace. Fear of his humors had made her demure and silent. He should have been pleased by his handiwork. He *was* pleased by it. Perhaps she would not make such a bad wife to him after all.

He frowned. "Are you very sure you feel well, Katherine?"

She shut her eyes and pressed her fingers to her temples. "If I say I am not, you'll no doubt try to poison me with cod liver oil, or something far more noxious. I have the headache, that's all. And I do wish to dear God you would stop calling me Katherine."

"But what should I call you? Miss Feathering seems oddly formal for one's fiancée, and you do not strike me as possessing an overly formal character."

"Just call me Katie. Everyone calls me Katie."

"Katie." He should not have liked it—it was a name for a parlor maid, or an apple seller. But it suited her, suited the green wildness in her eyes that was just now beginning to be tamed. "Very well, then, Katie it shall be."

Katie sat back in her chair, her head bent down to hide her face. In her dusty traveling dress, she looked small and worn and far too thin.

"Does that not please you?"

She looked up at him then, and every scrap of fierceness suddenly resurfaced in her eyes. Julius felt almost relieved to see it. "Nothing you do pleases me, and it never will. I will not marry you, not if you hold a pistol to my head. I will never submit my will to yours, never do as you command, and you would be wisest to release me at once. If you send a note to my father, he will send a man for me."

"I don't think it's as easy as that, Katie," Julius said.

She went on, emboldened. "Your reputation need not suffer, my lord, I will disappear so completely that you will forget I was ever in England."

He smiled wryly, and passed his hand across the back

of his neck, wondering how to break the uncomfortable news to her. "I've had news from your father, you see."

Katie bolted to her feet. "News? How? Does he know where I am? It's not possible!"

Julius felt the now familiar pangs of guilt nibble around the edges of his heart. "I sent him a letter."

"A letter!" Katie closed her eyes, and for a moment Julius thought she would faint. "I see," she said, composing herself. "And did you tell him of your intentions?"

"Of course," Julius said, faintly offended. "I know you are unhappy at the prospect of this marriage, Katie, but I am not a brute. I would not leave your father to worry himself insensible over your safety."

She arched one eyebrow. "Am I supposed to thank you for that, my lord?"

"Heaven forfend you should exert yourself in social niceties, my dear," he said dryly. "But I think you have underestimated the man."

"What do you mean?" She was wary now, bracing herself as if for flight.

"He is as proud as any papa would be, to hear that his hell-born commoner daughter is to marry a man of both fortune and title. Indeed, he was positively gleeful. Count yourself lucky you weren't auctioned off to some ancient marquess with bad breath and false teeth."

"At least I could count on an elderly marquess to take himself off that much sooner," she said, her voice chill with fury.

"Ah, there's my old disagreeable girl. I wondered where all that ill temper had gone."

"Don't you see? You're ruining your life as completely as you are ruining mine. I will always be wretched to you, always taunt you and fight you and spit in your eye. Let me go, my lord. Find a wife you can love."

Julius felt his heart contract. "Pray do not speak like an idiot, Katie. It is not an earl's portion to love. And do not think you will make my life so unhappy as all that. If you are troublesome, I shall spend only such time with you as is necessary for the begetting of my heirs."

Katie paled. "You're a monster."

"I'm the earl of Brynston," he repeated. "Only children believe in monsters. If you have no further need of me, my dear, I shall take my leave. Good evening." With a small bow, Julius removed himself from the disturbing presence of his unwilling betrothed.

15

Katie Starr sat in her small room at the inn, staring into the mirror and wishing she were dead. Brynston had arranged for a maid, had even managed to find a dress, an old-fashioned midnight blue gown, heavy with beads and very beautiful. To Katie it was nothing better than a joke in very bad taste.

Brynston had not quite dared marry her in Gretna Green. There had been too many witnesses, even a few gallant swells who might have tried to defend her. Katie had fought to keep her calm since that last terrible conversation, in which the noose she had knotted for herself had slipped so conveniently around her neck. Her father had approved the marriage.

Well, of course, he would have. To Phineas Starr, it was just another way to fiddle Brynston out of his cash. But Phineas was not the one getting married. Katie thought of what the earl would expect. Surely he would not force himself on her? Not the first night, at any rate. But Katie knew she was fooling herself. Brynston would take whatever he pleased, as he had done his entire life, and no protest Katie could make would stop him.

Which is why she had stopped protesting. She thought there was just some small chance that she could escape him, if he thought she had accepted her situation. Most girls in her position would have been thrilled. Perhaps he would think she had given way to normal sentiment at last, that she was pleased at this marriage. He was rich, richer even than she pretended to be. And he was young and titled, and he was handsome.

Her breath caught at that. Because the earl of Brynston was something more than handsome. He was the embodiment of everything cruel and dark and dangerous, wrapped up in a breathtaking package, from the powerful sweep of his shoulders to the eyes that burned like blue flames.

She choked at the thought of him, and turned away from her own image in disgust. She was as beautiful as the maid's skill could make her, her short, modern curls contrasting piquantly with the old-fashioned gown. Her corset had been laced tightly, as if she were bound with ropes.

She ran to the door and tried it again. It was locked and bolted, as she knew very well. She had tried it several times since her maid had left her. Brynston had no intention of relaxing his guard until she was safely wed to him—perhaps until she was safely bedded. The thought made her weak at the knees.

She sat on the edge of the bed and tried to calm herself, to think. She had to get out of this. The wedding would not be a legal one, of course. In the first place, she would never consent, and in any event she was giving a false name. Which meant she would go to Brynston's bed not as his treacherous wife, but as his unwilling whore.

"Oh, Dad, what have you done?" she whispered, burying her face in her hands.

The bolt scraped outside the door, and Katie sat rigidly upright, her hands gripping the coverlet.

"Plain Kate and bonny Kate, and sometimes Kate the curs'd," Brynston said softly, filling the door frame in that unnerving way he had.

"Do not make the mistake of thinking I can be tamed," Katie said dangerously.

"It's hard to imaging taming you," he admitted. "Your eyes are as wild as the jungles of Borneo. Having a case of wedding-day collywobbles?"

"I cannot bear the sight of you," she said quietly. "You are shackling yourself to a woman who despises you, who will only disrupt your life and make it a misery. There is no reason for this, Brynston!"

"You may call me Julius when we are wed," he said sweetly. "The gown suits you very well. I knew it would. I hope it is not too old fashioned to please you, but I have never thought weddings an occasion that required strict adherence to fashion."

"Listen to me!" Katie was shouting now. "You wouldn't want this any more than I do if you knew—" Katie broke off, her courage flagging for a moment. She took a deep breath and found it again. "If you knew who I truly am."

"I know you are a dishonorable American hoyden with a greedy father," he said. "I cannot see that there is anything you can say to further dissuade me." Then, more gently, "Katie, the matter is settled. I know you are frightened, but you needn't be."

"I'm a fraud!" she stammered, the truth burning like vitriol in her mouth. "It was all a lie, from the beginning. I'm no heiress, I'm nothing better than a common criminal, and neither is my father."

Brynston's eyes turned hard. "You are becoming annoying. It is time to go downstairs and meet your destiny, Katherine. In a half hour's time, you will be the countess of Brynston."

"Didn't you hear what I said? I lied, Brynston. All of it, my family's fortune, my background, everything. You are marrying a lie."

"Gentlemen?" He tapped his cane on the floor, and two burly farm boys appeared at the door. He must have kept them in wait in case she was reluctant. "Now, my dear, I think your gown would show itself to advantage if you were to walk downstairs, rather than being dragged."

She shook her head fiercely. "No more lies, Lord Brynston. I will not marry you, I will not go through with this farce. If you want to destroy both our lives, you'll have to bind and gag me to do it, because I swear to you I will never go to you willingly."

He was perfectly still, his face a mask of composure, but she knew him well enough now to see the rage burning in his eyes. She forced herself to look at him, to try somehow to cross the gulf that separated them. *Believe me*, she willed. *For both our sakes.*

"As you wish," he said finally, his voice wintry.

She breathed a sigh of relief.

"Gentlemen, you heard the lady. Bind and gag her."

The young men's faces were stark with astonishment. "My lord?" the taller of the two said.

"This is not what you want, Brynston," she said, stiffening as the farm boys touched her. "Damn you, can't you see I'm trying to do you a favor? Take your hands off me, you ape!" she snapped at the boy who was trying ineffectually to bring her arms behind her back.

"You act like you've never done this before, gentlemen," Brynston said, his voice low and sharp. He crossed the room and grasped her wrists tightly, bringing them together in front of her body. "Here's how it's done, boys. More merciful to do it quickly, like killing a goose. Here, bring me that."

One of the young men handed him a silk wrapper that had been laid carelessly across a chair. Brynston took one end of it in his teeth, and pulled down hard with his free hand, tearing off a long strip. He wrapped the silk tightly around Katie's hands, tying it in a distressingly competent-looking knot.

She recognized the look on his face. It was the same look he'd worn in the flash house, the way his head tucked like a vicious stallion's, ready to trample anything that stood in his way.

"You're insane," she whispered. "Good God, what kind of man are you to do this? Haven't you heard a word I've said?"

"I gave my word," he said, tearing off another strip of silk. "You were to come to no harm under my care. It has become clear that the only repair that can be done to your name is through marriage, and so, wild Katie—" He paused a moment to thrust the length of silk into her mouth, gagging her. "We shall marry."

She tried to curse him, but it came out as nothing but a strangled cry. She kicked savagely at his shins, but he sidestepped her neatly, hooking his leg behind hers to send her flying onto the bed on her back.

She kicked at him again, wild with panic, but not so wild that she did not think to aim straight between his legs.

He caught her kicking feet neatly in his hands, and had them tied in an instant. "Let's to church, gentlemen. Do have a care for the lady, she's a delicate creature."

Katie could not shout words, but she could scream, and she did. She screamed until her throat was raw as the farm boys carried her down the wooden stairs, and screamed as they brought her into the chapel. The village folk exchanged looks, but Brynston looked and acted like the devil himself, and no one opposed him.

A swell of music accompanied her cries as she was carried down the aisle. By thrusting her feet, she managed to land a solid thumping kick at the thigh of the taller of the farm boys, but he merely grunted. The chapel aisle was narrow, and Brynston walked ahead of her, acknowledging nothing amiss. Everything about him was flawless, while Katie could feel the wildness of her hair and the dishevelment of her heavy dress.

No one filled the pews to witness this travesty. Only

the parson, as somber and resplendent as robes could make him, stood at the head of the aisle, utterly dumb-founded.

The couple stood before him, Brynston looking composed and rather bored, Katie propped up by the two farm boys.

"My lord, I cannot—" the parson began in a mild voice.

"We have discussed this. Begin!" Brynston snapped. The sound was like a pistol shot in the all but empty chapel.

The parson looked pleadingly at him, then at Katie with what seemed to be an unspoken apology. "Dear friends, we are gathered here today . . . "

Katie remembered little of the ceremony, except that at one point her vision had blurred, and she'd sagged against one of the farm boys, mercifully unconscious. She woke in a few moments, the parson still droning, Brynston staring straight ahead and looking every inch the civilized, faultless young gentleman.

"Wilt thou love her," intoned the parson, "comfort her, honor and keep her in sickness and in health? And forsaking all other, keep thee only unto her, so long as ye both shall live?"

Katie twisted her head to catch his eye, to make one last, silent plea.

He ignored it. "I will."

"And wilt thou, Katherine Feathering, have this man to thy wedded husband, to live together after God's ordinance, in the holy estate of matrimony? Wilt thou obey him, serve him, love, honor and keep him in sickness and in health, and forsaking all other, keep thee only unto him, so long as ye both shall live?"

Brynston motioned to the young man at his elbow, and the gag was lowered an inch to free Katie to speak.

"Go to the devil, you damned English bastard!" she

cried. "I hate you! I will make every day of your life a hell, if it kills—"

Brynston frowned and motioned for the young man to replace the gag, which he did. "She will," Brynston said quietly, over her inarticulate cries.

The parson's watery eyes goggled, and he licked his lips nervously. "Ah, yes, I see. Are you quite sure—?"

"Continue," Brynston said, as if Katie were a radiantly demure and blushing bride.

The parson looked at her for a long moment, then at Brynston. He sighed quietly.

The two boys were at some pains to wrestle the ring onto Katie's finger, and her muffled shouts echoed through the church so loudly that the parson cut short the usual prayers. He merely clasped her right hand firmly and joined it to Brynston's, shooting her one last guilty glance as he said, "Those whom, ah, God hath joined together, let no man put asunder."

The boys held her so tightly that she was able to lift her bound feet and land a satisfying kick at the parson's midsection, chasing the breath from him in a pained huff.

"Under the circumstances," Brynston drawled, flicking an imaginary spot of lint from his coat, "I believe I shall decline to kiss the bride."

Brynston did not ride in the carriage with his new bride, instead riding on ahead. He'd procured a passable mare from the inn at the edge of town, and commanded the beast on, pushing her, pushing himself.

This was, he had to confess, not the wedding day he would have imagined for himself. He was not such a fool as to have had romantic notions of a blushing girl in a white gown and veil, but he would have liked to see his family there, his sisters sniffling, as they always did at weddings.

And the bride who had knocked the wind out of the

parson, and cursed Brynston blue the instant her gag was removed?

Brynston urged the mare on, feeling the ground pound beneath him. He swept any trace of remorse from his mind. He had not allowed Katie to force him into dishonor, that was the important thing. He had kept his word and he had preserved her name and his own.

But she is the countess now, Brynston. You have permitted another flighty, dishonorable woman into your life.

Brynston forced the doubts from his mind, forced himself to mind the horse and the road. Katie would mend her ways. He would see to that.

And if she does not?

He had done what honor required, and it could not be undone. He would force Katie Feathering to bend herself to his will, to become a suitable countess, if he had to kill them both trying.

Katie had not said a word since the travesty of a wedding that morning. She had said nothing as he'd unbound her, nothing as he'd escorted her, gently enough, into the carriage-prison she had come to hate. She stared dully out the small windows now, watching the bleak landscape unfold like an endless bolt of dun cloth. It had stopped snowing, and the world was gray and brown, the remains of the snow lying in untidy heaps like forgotten laundry.

Katie Starr, who slipped free of traps as readily as the slyest fox, was being shipped in this rolling prison to her new cage. A great manor, with footmen and a carriage house and a dining table to seat fifty. The urchin had become a countess. The thought made her physically sick.

Brynston had ridden on ahead, pushing his horse like the madman he was. Perhaps he would break his damnable arrogant neck, and spare her the remainder of this farce.

But even as she thought it, she leaned out the window, craning to catch a glimpse of him. She did not want him to come to any harm. She simply wanted to slip free, to sail off to Italy or France and leave all the wretchedness of England behind her. To slip the noose and walk off with her hands in her pockets, whistling her defiance.

For the first time in days she spared a thought for her father without wanting to thump him. The Turks would be pressing him in earnest by now. Would he have the wits to put them off a while longer? Would Alex?

The thought of Alex, her old friend, her gentle protector, made her heart constrict. He would not have approved of this dangerous game, he would have seen it for what it was—a gamble with her body, with her maidenhead. Even with her grubby urchin's heart.

Katie leaned against the wall, staring at the browns and grays outside the window, and shut her eyes. If her waking life was to be spent as a prisoner, she would find a few moments freedom in dreams.

Katie sucked in her breath as she stepped from her prison out into the clear, cold winter's light. She did not know what she had expected, exactly. Brynston was wealthy even for an earl, she knew that. Of course he would own a large, well-appointed house.

But Willowby Hall was something more than a house. The facade was of smooth, gray-green stone, echoing the winter grays of the sky and earth. Twin curving staircases led up to an ornately carved stone entryway and massive double doors of dark-polished wood. Flanking the door on either side were broad wings, glazed with what seemed to be thousands of small windows.

Graves stepped quickly down from the carriage and conferred with a mass of servants. Two liveried footmen, a sour-looking man in a dark coat, a tiny, roly-poly maid in apron and white mob cap. And behind them all was the most elegant woman Katie had ever seen.

"Julius, darling," the elegant woman said, walking swiftly down the steps to greet Brynston. She wore a flawlessly cut sea-green gown that made her slim, tall frame look even slimmer. "Welcome home, my love."

16

Katie felt the words rather than heard them, like a sharp blow to the stomach. *My love*. Brynston had never mentioned a flawlessly elegant woman who called him *my love*.

Brynston extricated himself from the woman's grasp and held her hands at arm's length. "Milvia, it's wonderful to see you, as always. There is someone you will have to meet."

Milvia smiled and looked over his shoulder at Katie. Suddenly Katie wished very much that she could have brushed her hair and washed her face. Brynston, though he had been riding most of the day, managed to look every inch an earl.

"Julius, darling, you mustn't make me guess," Milvia said, her voice low and cool.

"Katie, this is Lady Milvia Trowsedale. Milvia, allow me to introduce you to Katherine Feathering, now Katherine Willowby." His voice was soft, with a gentleness Katie had rarely heard. "Katie is my wife."

Milvia's mouth pulled to an ashen line. "Julius, pray do not play foolish tricks on me, it is unbecoming."

Brynston handed his hat and coat to a footman. "I'm sorry, I should have written to tell you, but it seemed a dashed awkward thing to put in a letter. Katie and I were married this morning."

Katie felt as gray as Milvia now looked. There was another woman who had loved him, who had clearly intended to marry him. And Katie had stolen that away, though she did not want it at all.

"This is not possible, Julius," Milvia said, her voice like an ice pond.

"It is possible, and it has happened." Brynston spoke quietly, and took Milvia's hands in his own to comfort her. "I'm sorry, Mil, you know I would never have wanted to hurt you."

"You cannot do this," Milvia said, yanking her hands free and addressing herself to Katie. "I don't know who you are—" she paused to flick a dismissive glance over Katie's disheveled traveling costume, "—but this man is not some village farm boy to marry wherever the whim takes him. Julius Willowby is the earl of Brynston, and he must have a care whom he takes as his countess."

Milvia was white with fury, Katie could see that, but she could not keep from responding with anger of her own. "This is hardly my doing, Lady Milvia. Place the blame where it belongs—on Lord Brynston himself."

"Good God, Julius, an American," Milvia said with a shudder. She pressed her hands to her temples and shut her eyes. "You cannot, you simply cannot."

"Perhaps you misunderstood me, Lady Milvia," Brynston said. His voice was quiet, but it echoed in the stone entry yard like the crack of a falling oak. "This young lady is the countess of Brynston, and she is my wife. She will be treated with the courtesy due her station, or you are welcome to remove yourself from Willowby Hall until such time as you regain your customary good manners. Have I explained myself clearly?"

Milvia's nostrils flared, and her cheeks flushed with two hot red spots of anger, but after a long moment she broke her gaze and nodded. "Forgive me, Julius. I cannot imagine what can have overtaken me." She walked to the carriage and extended both hands to Katie, helping her down. "I have behaved monstrously, and I apologize. The shock—I suppose I was overwrought."

"I understand," Katie said softly.

"It will not be mentioned again," Brynston said flatly. "Come, Katie. I will show you where you are to live. I do not think you will be too disappointed."

He held out his arm, waiting for her to come and claim it. Half wondering why she did it, Katie stepped up to him and rested her arm warily on his.

The two walked up the stone steps together, and as they did, Katie could feel Milvia staring daggers into her back.

Katie quickly grew uncomfortable at the touch of his arm beneath hers. He was covered in mud and sweat from his ride, but somehow that did not make him less attractive. An unnerving animal vigor pulsed beneath his usual proud grace.

But the opportunity to annoy Lady Milvia steeled Katie's resolve. The thin, elegant woman was such a picture-perfect counterpoint to Brynston, elegant gray to his unyielding black, both of them disgustingly *correct*. It was clear that Milvia had grown up with servants and horses and governesses well versed in the social niceties. She was, in short, perfect. And Katie found to her own chagrin that she rather hated her for it.

Willowby Hall was palatial, far grander than anything Katie had seen in London. They walked through room after room of ancient portraits and sedate landscapes, of a quality several notches above the paintings in Lady Odcombe's card room. A rosy-cheeked, laughing young woman smiled from what looked to be a Titian, and unless Katie was very much mistaken, the quiet, glowing portrait in the corner was a Rembrandt.

There was a very good, if flattering, likeness of the Regent himself in the main drawing room.

"This is the Royal Room," Brynston explained. "It irks Prinny to no end that I include the pretenders."

Katie nodded, only half comprehending, but feeling oppressed by the weight of all those serious faces looking down on her from their heavy gilt frames. "I can't live here."

"You haven't seen it yet," Brynston said reasonably.

"I don't belong here," Katie whispered, her voice harsh. "It should be *her* here next to you, not me."

"That is irrelevant. You will learn to belong here." His expression allowed no room for protest.

Katie felt a tiny stab that he had not denied her words. It was true. She didn't belong here. "This isn't the dark ages. You could force that parson to do your will, but you will never force me."

He touched her back lightly, guiding her into the library. "I should tell you, this house was built during the War of the Roses. It's something of a fortress, I'm afraid. You might have escaped me in the past, countess, but you will not be able to slip away from Willowby. I will post additional footmen at your door, and beneath your window, in case you become restless."

"You won't win this, Brynston," Katie warned.

"We shall see, little countess," he said pleasantly. "We shall see."

By the time he had left his wife to her bedchamber, Julius was exhausted. She was still bitterly angry with him, the result, no doubt, of failing to get her way. His bride had a most unattractive obsinate streak, one that Brynston would have to break her of. Not, he suspected, that it would be easy. She seemed to delight in displeasing him, to go out of her way to defy him.

He rang for Graves, and his valet appeared so quickly Brynston wondered if the man had been lying in wait for him. "Her ladyship is well, I trust?" Graves asked, visibly anxious.

"Her ladyship is an ill-mannered, ungrateful brat who desperately needs a good spanking," Brynston said, loosening his cravat. "And it's all your damned fault, Graves. If you hadn't extracted that stupid promise from me . . ."

"Your lordship would still have followed his conscience," Graves said mildly.

"There are days when I could horsewhip you, Graves," Brynston said irritably.

"Quite right, your lordship," Graves said neutrally, buttoning Brynston's cuffs with all the careful attention of a diamond cutter. "And will Lady Milvia be staying to dinner?"

Brynston shut his eyes at the thought. "I suppose we must invite her, if she cares to stay. She was shocking with Katie in the entry yard—I can't understand it. Milvia was always so dependable."

"Disappointment in love may render a person temporarily . . . disagreeable, my lord," Graves said. His voice was admirably neutral, since Brynston knew for a fact that Graves loathed Lady Milvia. He considered her bloodless and cold, an odd criticism from a man like Graves. Brynston had only managed to secure his valet's honest opinion by virtue of the direst threats.

Graves finished tying his master's fresh cravat, stepping back to admire his handiwork. "No matter how well turned out one manages to be while traveling," he said with immense satisfaction, "there is really nothing like one's own proper home."

"You are the soul of domestic bliss, Graves," Brynston said, pausing to listen to the sound of breaking glass that was coming from the vicinity of his wife's bedroom. "As such, I hope you will pray for mine."

The rumble of the elegantly fitted carriage on the winter-rutted roads was causing Phineas Starr's digestion no end of trouble. Just how, he wondered, was a man supposed to digest his lunch when the roads were fit to shake a man's teeth out of his skull?

Luckily, English inns were close together and well appointed. They had been able to stop every time Phineas felt peaked, to refresh themselves with a mug of ale or the tiniest sip of rum punch.

"Do you think you would like to stop soon for a snack, Manners?" Phineas asked his traveling companion, who hunched in the corner. Next to him, the little maid Hannah was asleep in her seat, her head bobbing with the motion of the carriage.

"I just want to get there. We've been on this miserable road for four days now, and God knows what's happened to Katie."

"What's happened to her is that she's married a god-damned twenty-four-carat English earl," Phineas said, chuckling at the thought. "I love that little girl, she's sharper than a fistful of tacks."

"I don't like it," Manners said, as he'd been saying for four days now. "Why would the earl marry Katie? It can't be love, the man's not capable of it. He knows she cheated him at cards, and Brynston's a man of honor. He won't forgive that easily."

Phineas shrugged. "You know Katie, she's got the gift. That girl could talk a cat out of its whiskers. She gave him a line, and he swallowed it like a good little fish."

Manners shook his head. "I don't know what happened between them when he kidnapped her, but it was bad enough that she wouldn't talk to me about it. The man is dangerous, Phineas, and I can't help wondering what he's got up his sleeve."

Phineas squirmed uncomfortably on the squabs. This was *supposed* to be a first-rate carriage, but the seats were harder than they'd felt at first, and his backside was beginning to go numb. "They were falling in love, man! Or rather *he* was. Our Katie's too sensible for that kind of game. Do you think these seats are getting harder?"

"I think you've got rocks in your head," Manners

muttered, but he sank back into his corner, scowling out the window and drumming his huge fingers on the edge of his seat.

Phineas wriggled to try and find a comfortable position. He was beginning to wonder how much longer he'd be able to employ Alex Manners. True, the man was the best there was at every criminal practice in the book. He was even a first-rate pickpocket, a rare quality in a big man.

But there was always the past, looming there between them like some nasty Punch and Judy show. That wretched business in Boston, with Katie's mother. Phineas felt a twinge. He missed Molly himself, of course he did. It would be unnatural if he didn't. But there was no going back to fix the past.

Katie was fond enough of Manners, what child wouldn't be? The fellow had been a faithful servant and accomplice to the Starrs since before she'd been born. He was almost like a father to her.

Phineas frowned. No, that wasn't right. An uncle, Manners was like Katie's uncle. Phineas tapped on the carriage ceiling with the carved ivory head of his cane.

The sleeping maid Hannah fluttered her eyes open at the sound, and blinked, confused.

"What now?" asked Manners gruffly.

"I require some refreshment at the next inn," Phineas said with a delicate sniff. "My stomach has begun to feel distinctly queasy."

17

Katie looked at the pretty Limoges pitcher with some regret. It was delicately made, creamy white with a gilt handle. Katie had fenced just such expensive trifles, and knew what this one must have cost.

The thought pricked at her. All the more reason she could not stay here. A street rat could not be a countess, it was impossible.

She took aim at the window and sent the pitcher crashing down to the stone-flagged courtyard below.

The doorknob twisted violently, and when the intruder found it locked, he began to pound on the door. "What in blazes do you think you're doing in there?" came Brynston's voice.

Katie bit her lip to keep her courage, and tossed a heavy, expensive-looking vase out after the pitcher. So far she had not touched the books or the pictures, but the day was not over yet. There was a great deal Katie would do to keep from becoming the countess of Brynston.

Brynston threw his weight at the door, and Katie eyed it nervously. It looked solid enough, but Brynston was a large man and, from the sound of it, a determined one. She had already wedged a chair beneath the knob, and now Katie scooted the writing desk in front of it for good measure.

Now then, the carpets. They would just fit out the window if they were rolled, and though the fall would not really damage them, with any luck it would irritate Brynston enormously.

She had the largest of them halfway out the window when Brynston finally crashed his way through the door. The blasted carpet had become stuck on something, and Brynston found Katie giving it a vigorous shove in hopes of dislodging it.

Katie had to admit, he looked ruffled. A small army of footmen stood behind him, and it appeared it had taken all of them to break the door open. Brynston's coatsleeve was torn, and there was a small cut beneath his left eye, right above the fading bruise she had given him in the flash house. It only served to make him look uncharacteristically rakish.

"I repeat," he said, breathing hard. "What in blazes are you doing?"

Katie lifted her chin and looked him dead in the eye. "I'm throwing all this trash into the courtyard," she said.

Brynston let out a long, slow breath, and raked his palm over the back of his head. "I suppose it would have been too much trouble to simply *open* the windows?" he asked, gesturing to the jagged panes where Katie had dashed out the glass with a chair.

"Much too much trouble," she said evenly, picking up a Louis XIV chamber pot and hurling it toward his head.

Brynston ducked neatly, and the chamber pot crashed behind his head. "At least it was empty. You have an excellent arm, Katie," he said, smoothing his lapels as he stood straight. "But as I've told you before, your aim wants improving."

She stood in the far corner of the room, looking like she wished she had not already pitched her weapon at him. Or at least like she wished she hadn't missed. The curtains billowed behind her.

"I have not given you permission to enter my bedroom," she said, crossing her arms like some imperious foreign princess.

Brynston gave her a practiced smile. "Forgive me, madame. I pray you will accustom yourself."

"I will never accustom myself," she said, her eyes glowing fiercely. "You do not own me, Lord Brynston. I am not a mare or an heirloom rug or a . . . " She waved her hands, groping for the word. "A china figurine."

"No," he mused, studying her. She was wearing one of Portia's dresses—they were of a size, and Portia had asked the maid to bring in a selection. The butter-yellow muslin set off the warm sherry color of Katie's hair and the creamy sweetness of her skin. She looked more feminine, more delicate, than she had since the night she'd cheated him of thirty thousand pounds in Lady Odcombe's card room. "Not a china figurine. Though once I thought you resembled one exceedingly."

"It would be best for both of us if you let such illusions die, Lord Brynston," she said coldly. "Release me from this marriage, release yourself from the ignominy of being married to a dishonorable harpy. It would not be difficult."

"It would not be difficult for you, perhaps," he corrected. "You have not given your word, you do not feel yourself bound by honor."

"How can this be honorable? You *abducted* me!"

Brynston waved his hand dismissively. "You confuse honor and morality, my dear. A grave error. To be sure, what I have done is not strictly legal, and some men would call it unkind."

"Some women would call it monstrous and cruel," Katie said evenly.

"No matter. I gave my word you would come to no harm, and I then compromised your reputation. There was no other path open to me but marriage."

"I do not care about my reputation, my lord. You are protecting something worthless."

Brynston felt himself become angry, angry enough to lash out, to hit, to destroy. Instead he curled his hand tightly around the back of a Hepplewhite chair, ignoring for the moment the gouges in the legs from where his wife had dashed out the windowpanes. "This has nothing to do with *you*, madame. It is of no importance what you value or do not value. It is my duty to protect the name of my family, and my title. You have attempted to drag me through the muck with you, and you have paid a price for your efforts. If that price is too steep, I pity you."

She shook her head, as if amazed. "No, my lord, I pity you. This code of honor is a pile of fool's gold, and you hold on to it as if it were real."

There was the anger again, hot and strong, and for a moment Brynston saw Jo Cargill in Katie's place. Beautiful Jo, laughing at the value he placed on his name, laughing at his tediously conventional morals. He had been a dashing young rakehell when Jo had been as much a part of him as his own breath. But not such a rakehell as to forget who he was, who he would become. Not enough of a rakehell to throw his name away on a woman who threw dice as if it were food to her, and who paid her debts with whatever she had to hand. Her body, his soul.

"You need not believe in honor, Katie," he finally said, keeping his voice quiet in order to keep the lid clamped firmly down on his anger. "You need not believe in the name of this family, in this marriage, in right and wrong. But you will behave as if you believed in these things, or I swear to you you will live to regret it."

Katie swallowed hard, but she stood her ground. "I thought you gave your word to Graves that I'd come to no harm. Or does that not apply any more, now that I'm your *wife*?" She all but spat the last word.

"On the contrary, it applies so long as you are alive," Brynston said simply. "I do not have to harm a mare to break her to my will. That does not mean she will never feel the touch of my whip."

Katie paled visibly. "If you beat me, I swear I'll kill you. I'd rather hang than live as a whipped dog."

"You take me too literally, wife. Though I appreciate the warning," Brynston said dryly. "There are other methods than beating to bring a shrew to heel. You do not care to discover them."

"Go to the devil!" she said, her voice harsh.

"Impossible, my dear," he said with a bitter smile. He reached out to cup her chin, ignoring her flinch. He brought her face to his, and kissed her lightly on the lips. "I *am* the devil."

Her heart hammered, and she felt the now familiar warm drowsiness settle over her. There was a weakness in her that longed to give in to him, even when she knew that it was impossible.

He pulled away with a reluctant expression. "However, we are expected down to dinner in—" He checked his watch, and Katie wondered when he had found time to replace the one Finch had stolen. "Twenty-eight minutes precisely," he finished. "The family is never late to dinner. Good day, madame."

"I won't be at dinner," Katie announced.

"Yes, you will," Brynston said pleasantly.

"I—I don't have anything suitable to wear," Katie said, faltering for a moment.

"We are terribly informal at Willowby Hall. Surely you can find something of Portia's to your taste." He checked his watch again. "Twenty-seven minutes. Do not be late."

Katie all but had to sit on the maid to keep from being dragged to the dinner table on time. At about a quarter past eight, she came down to the main dining room. She was glad for Portia's loan of a few gowns. Katie's own all smelled of tavern smoke and cheap ale, and she would be glad when she could burn the lot of them and all the wretched memories that went with them.

"Is that her?" an angelic voice piped. Katie was surprised to see a lovely child of about eight, a perfect miniature of Brynston, seated at the table with the rest of the family.

"Hush, brat, or Julius will beat you black and blue," stage-whispered a pixieish girl of about fourteen. She had the reddest hair Katie had ever seen.

They were a good-looking family. Three ladies and three gentlemen—one albeit a quite small gentleman—sat at the long, formal table. Brynston sat at head, naturally, and the seat to his right was Katie's. Lady Milvia, to Katie's relief, was nowhere to be seen.

"Pleasure to see you again, madame," Val said, flashing a grin.

Katie was distressed to see that she would be wedged between the earl and his reckless younger brother. "How . . . nice to see you, Lord Valentine," she said demurely. The second-to-last person on earth she wanted to sit with was Val Willowby, whom she had taken for fifteen thousand pounds.

"My brother is much cleverer than I am," he said, leaning conspiratorially close as she slid into her seat. "All I could think of when you and I, er . . . met, was to run home with my tail between my legs. But Jules had the good sense to up and marry you!"

"Shut up, Val," Brynston said irritably. "The countess does not want to listen to your blather."

Katie thought she heard a twinge in Brynston's voice. Jealousy? "On the contrary, Lord Valentine," she said, gazing deep into his eyes. "I find your conversation to be most fascinating." She did not quite dare to bat her eyelashes, but the night was young.

"Julius, I want to know why Lady Brynston gets to come to dinner late," grumbled the angelic boy. The plate in front of him was a masterwork of architecture—ramparts made of mashed potatoes and palisades of green beans.

"She doesn't," Brynston replied. "The rules at dinner apply to Lady Brynston just as they do to all of us."

"Oh, Julius, no, not her first night here!" Katie recognized the speaker as the middle sister, Portia, the one who had lent Katie all her pretty gowns. "And after that long trip from Scotland."

"Miss Phipps told me that Graves told *her* that the roads were perfectly dreadful," piped the youngest girl.

"You will tell Miss Phipps that I do not approve of gossip among the servants," Brynston said frostily.

"Good heavens, Jules, that's hardly gossip, it's conversation," said a tall, proud-looking beauty with dark auburn hair and her brother's flashing blue eyes. That would be Titania, then, the eldest sister.

Katie sat silently through all this, wondering what the dreadful punishment might be for coming late to dinner. She only hoped whatever it was would not keep her from eating for very much longer, because she was starving. She caught the attention of one of the footmen. "I'm ready for my dinner now, please."

The footman looked panicked, and he shot Lord Brynston a helpless look.

"He can't bring your dinner," Brynston explained.

"Well then, who can?"

"No one. We do not tolerate lateness to the table, it is unfair to the cook and to your fellow dinner guests."

Katie felt anger throb in her throat again, dampened by the fact that she really was ravenous. "Very well. I will retire to my room and have a tray sent up at the cook's convenience."

She started to stand, but Brynston grasped her firmly by the wrist and made her sit again. "You will sit at table and converse politely with my family, and there will be no tray. We eat at regular hours in Willowby Hall, not willy-nilly like a band of gypsies."

"Surely we do not need to struggle over this matter again, my lord," she said. "It seems we are always at odds about my eating habits." How would he explain *that* to his loving family?

"As I recall, the struggle resolved itself without undue . . . incident," he said quietly.

Suddenly the room seemed to darken, as if the only light in it came from his eyes. Her breath caught in her throat, and her head swam alarmingly.

"See, look there, Julius, the girl's ready to faint off her chair," Titania said reproachfully. "Cook won't mind and you know it. Let her have something to eat."

"The *girl*, as you put it, is of an age precisely with yourself, Ti," Brynston said.

"There isn't any chance she might be—how shall I put this, Jules?" Titania asked, her eyes sparkling.

Katie choked on the glass of wine she'd lifted to her lips. Titania thought she might be breeding. Good God, what a wretched farce this was.

"Don't be coarse, Titania, we were only married this morning," Brynston said irritably.

"And naturally ice-cold Jules would never permit himself to take liberties," Titania said, catching Val's eye with a discreet wink.

"Do you feel faint?" Brynston snapped at Katie.

Katie set her wine glass firmly on the table. "Of course not. I feel very well."

"The one thing I dislike more than a liar is a bad liar," Brynston said. "Very well, tonight there shall be an exception. Frederick?" He motioned to the footman. "You may bring madame her dinner."

Frederick positively beamed. "Oh, yes, sir. Thank you, sir."

Katie stared at him. He had given in. The Brimstone Earl *never* gave in. He did not even look particularly put out.

"Forgive me, madame, I have not yet introduced you to my incomparable family," Brynston said. "Somehow, it is wretchedly difficult to observe the niceties at Willowby Hall. Very well, then, this is my sister Titania," he said, gesturing to the sparkling creature. Her thick mane of hair looked as if she had carelessly swept it up with a few pins, and a few dark curls escaped here and there to frame a classically beautiful face. "Then there is

Portia," he said, gesturing to the pretty strawberry blonde, "and Rosalind," the girl with the flaming red hair. All three murmured polite greetings.

"You already know Val," he said, and Val grinned at her.

"And finally there is Tybalt, who was prophetically named because he is the most villainous little terror since Cromwell."

"You do me a grave injustice, sir," little Tybalt said, the words sounding strangely precocious in his small voice.

"I do not, sir," his brother replied easily.

Tybalt turned his small, angelic face to Katie's and said, "Pleased to make your acquaintance, madame," with such perfect manners that Katie wondered if Brynston might not be kidding.

"I disapprove of the practice of serving children their meals in the schoolroom," Brynston said, by way of explanation for Tybalt's and Rosalind's presence at the table. "Governesses are far too likely to be lax in their correction of table manners."

"We think Jules is a changeling," Titania said, spearing a delicious-looking bite of beef on her plate. "There's no one else in the family who's anything like him."

"Father was like him," Val corrected. "The rest of us," he whispered loudly to Katie, "are heathens."

"Portia's not so bad," Rosalind pointed out.

"That's true, she takes after mother," Val said. "Sweet and sensible. But certainly not a cold fish like our beloved brother."

"That's enough, Val," Brynston growled.

"I think madame will fit into this family very well," Rosalind said, trying for an innocent look.

"Rosie, you must mind your tongue," Portia chided. "Do you have any idea how that sounded?"

"She knows very well how it sounded," Titania said. "And what's more, she's right. There's no sense in tiptoeing around it, we all know the countess tossed all her furniture out the window." She leaned over Val and patted Katie's arm. "Don't let us frighten you, Katie. We like you."

The footman discreetly set Katie's plate in front of her.

"That's enough from the lot of you!" Brynston growled, casting a quelling glance around the table. "If I hear another peep, I'll lock the lot of you in the coal cellar."

This was greeted by laughter from everyone but Katie, who was convinced he truly *would* lock them in the coal cellar. Hadn't he abducted her, tied her up, threatened her, and—

And kissed her? That strange warmth began to build again under her breastbone. The more time she spent in Brynston's clutches, the more confused she became.

To her complete astonishment, Brynston joined their laughter after a moment. "They're abominable, aren't they?" he said to Katie.

A green bean sailed across the table, apparently flung by Rosalind at her youngest brother. Tybalt prepared to load a spoon with mashed potatoes in retribution.

"Tibby!" Brynston said, in a voice that could have frozen milk. "You know that I draw the line at hurling food about the dining room."

Tybalt obediently set down his spoon. "I must point out, sir, that it was Rosalind who threw the first bean."

Brynston nodded indulgently. "I know, Tibby, it's unfair. But women—" at that he cast a savage glance at Katie, "—are notoriously unscrupulous."

"I could throw a green bean at you myself for that," Titania grumbled.

"Try it and you'll see you're not too old for a caning," Brynston said with the ghost of an evil smile.

"I can promise you would regret that very deeply," Titania said, and for a moment she looked truly like her brother's sister.

"Gad, we're squaring off for a battle of titans," Val said. "Bound to be a bit rough on us poor mortals, eh, countess?" He gave Katie a conspiratorial wink.

"I suppose the rest of us will simply have to devise our own defenses," Katie said, giving her brother-in-law a dazzling smile. He really was rather sweet, now that she wasn't facing him across the gaming table. He was all lanky, puppyish ease, from his long, lean form to his heavy-lidded, topaz-brown eyes.

"Valentine," Brynston growled in warning.

"Julius?" Val replied with a lazy smile.

"Eat your green beans," Brynston said.

Valentine cast Katie another glance, sparkling with good humor. "With relish, beloved brother. With great relish."

18

Katie was on pins and needles all through dinner, and was grateful when she could get back to her now sparse room. Some time after ten, she heard the rattle of carriage wheels. It was impossible not to—without glass in her windows, the sound of wheels and hooves on paving-stones rose clearly from the entry yard. She could hear the scuttle of servants rushing up and down the stairs, the hushed bark of the butler admonishing a parlor maid. She sat upright on the edge of her bed, shivering from the cold, telling herself she did not care who the guest was.

But her curiosity began to get the better of her. Arranging her hair as best she could in a jagged piece of windowpane still stuck in its frame—for she had jettisoned both mirrors long before—she decided she was presentable enough for Lord Brynston's guests, whoever they might be. Who knows, she might have the opportunity of behaving so truly badly that even pigheaded Brynston would see this marriage was impossible.

The man was addled, clearly. The worse she behaved,

the more self-controlled he became, though the fire banked in his eyes smoldered dangerously.

She touched the heavy silk draperies, tracing the brocade pattern with her fingertip. And what if she stayed? What if she remained his countess, turned her back on everything she had been before? As soon as the thought came to her, she chased it away. There were too many people who knew the truth, too many wealthy, gullible men she'd rooked. Eventually the truth would leak out, dribble by dribble, and as Brynston pieced it together he would come to hate her even more. He tolerated her now because he thought she was, though spoiled and dishonorable, one of his own kind. The titled, the privileged, the rich. It was one thing to be a wealthy young woman paying off a blackmailer. It was another altogether to have been a professional criminal since she'd been old enough to wear long skirts.

She shut her eyes against the wishes she dared not wish, the dreams she didn't quite dare to dream. Lord Brynston had guests, which meant that Lady Brynston had a ruckus to raise.

She caught her husband's eye as she swept into the grand, formal drawing room, and saw that he was scowling. It took her only another blink of an eyelash to see why.

"Alex!" she cried. She hurled herself into the big man's arms, forgetting everything but the overwhelming rush of joy she felt at seeing him there. She would be all right now. She would be safe. Alex Manners had come to rescue her after all.

She disentangled herself and embraced her father, kissing him on the cheek. "Dad, it's so good to see you. I hope your trip was pleasant?" she asked.

"Demmed roads—beg your pardon, Katie—nearly shook me to jelly," Phineas grumbled.

"I apologize for taking your daughter so far away from you," Brynston said smoothly, stepping forward from the fireplace. "But as you can see, Mister Feathering, I found her utterly irresistible."

He stretched and shot Manners and Phineas a pointed look. "I'm sure you have a great deal to talk about. Pray forgive me—I have estate matters to tend to, and I retire early in the country. Katie, come and let me kiss you good night."

Katie's cheeks were hot, but she stood dutifully. She turned her head as he bent to kiss her, but misjudged his intentions, and ended by feeling the warm brush of his mouth against hers, and by smelling the familiar sweetness of his breath.

Her mind reeled, confused, but she composed herself in an instant. "Good night, Lord Brynston. I will see you tomorrow, then." She dared him to suggest otherwise, to suggest that he would see her tonight, that he would try to claim his right by marriage to her body.

But Brynston said only, "Good night, madame," and bowed lightly to her as he left the room.

She sat back on the sofa, still disturbingly aware of the touch of his lips on her own.

"Damn, but this is well done of you, Katie!" Phineas said once Brynston had safely closed the door. His face nearly split in two with pleasure.

"Was it?" Alex asked, his scarred face dark with concern. "What's happened here, Katie? Why did you marry him?"

Katie's shoulders sagged. "Because I had no choice. He's taken it into his head that some blessed rule of honor or other required that he marry me, and once he'd decided, there was no talking him out of it. God knows I tried."

Phineas frowned. "You tried—to talk him *out* of marrying you? Why the devil would you do that?"

"Because she would not sell herself to the highest bidder like some overpriced tart," Alex said, his voice low but angry.

"Alex, please," she warned. She did not want to have her father and her dearest friend coming to blows in Brynston's drawing room. "It's all right." She took a deep breath and turned to face her father. "Dad, Brynston is much too clever to rook. We never should have tangled with him in the first place. He's not like most of these English, he's intelligent and he's dangerous. I need to get out of here."

"Over my dead body," Phineas said flatly.

"You make it sound irresistible," Alex muttered.

Phineas ignored him. "We're still down seventy thousand pounds, Katie love, and the Turks won't be put off forever."

"No," Katie said, swallowing hard. "They won't be. You haven't seen them recently, have you?"

Phineas shook his head. "We left London as soon as we heard the news about your engagement."

"Lord Brynston shot them," Katie said.

Phineas brightened. "Are they dead?"

She shook her head, no. "They held us up on the road. I suppose they must have followed me that morning."

Alex paced in front of the fireplace. "Brynston had the Turks in his sights and he didn't shoot to kill?" He made a sound of disgust. "Amateur."

Katie shrugged. "He thought shooting them would be enough to frighten them off."

"That's like shooting a bear to frighten it off," Phineas said, worried. "They'll be worse than ever now. We need those bloodsuckers off our backs, Katie. You've got to pry that money out of your husband."

Katie felt the blood drain from her face. "That's impossible. You're talking about a good-sized fortune. And I told you, he's not some gullible Lord Mumblethorpe."

"Brimstone has the money, everyone knows it," Phineas argued. "He'll never miss it. Just write a draft or something."

"He'll miss it," Katie said flatly. "Father, you're not listening to me. Lord Brynston is not a gull."

"Did he harm you, Katie?" Alex asked, blurting the words. His face was grave, his eyes dark with concern.

Katie shook her head. "Not really. He's got some

confused idea that he's supposed to do this. And when the Turks showed up, I told him they were blackmailing *me*—it was all I could think of."

Phineas chuckled. "Fast on her feet, that girl. What'd you tell him you did?"

"I told him I was illegitimate, that you were not my father. And that the Turks had threatened to tell you that."

Phineas scowled and turned a little red. "I say, Katie, that was a bit much, wasn't it?"

"I was backed into a corner. It was the only thing I could think of. I shouldn't have said it."

"Damned right you shouldn't have," Phineas said gruffly, his feelings clearly hurt.

Katie shook her head. "No, no, Brynston thinks you're some kind of unbending moral stickler. The kind of man who beats his children for stumbling over their prayers. He was afraid you wouldn't take me back after he had . . . ruined me."

"Katie, he didn't—?" Alex stopped his pacing to search her face.

She shook her head. "Nothing like that Alex, don't worry. He's talking about my name, that's all. My reputation." She smiled weakly. "These English seem obsessed by their reputations."

Alex nodded. "It's all some of them have."

"But not Brynston," Phineas said, obviously uncomfortable with all this talk of morality and good name. They were, after all, subjects he knew nothing about. "Brynston has land, lots of it, and money. You just need to pluck some of it from under his diligent nose."

"I can't," she said.

"You mean you won't." Phineas looked bitterly disappointed in her.

"I mean I can't. He's too shrewd, and I'm in this too deep already. You've got to help me get out of here, and we can start over abroad. Italy, maybe."

"We'll be able to travel to France again soon," Phineas said grudgingly.

"Paris, then. That's a city we know, a city we fit into. I can't stay in England any longer, it—" Katie broke off, thinking of the long stretches of gray and brown from outside her carriage window. "It oppresses me."

Alex bit off a curse. He faced the fire and folded his big hands behind his back. "We can't wait until they open travel to France. You do understand what's at stake here?" he asked Phineas, looking over his shoulder to stare the smaller man coldly in the eye.

Katie suppressed a shudder. What was *at stake* was her maidenhead, as she knew very well. So far as Brynston knew, they were married, and he had every right to take her to his marriage bed.

Phineas huffed and waved his hands, dismissing their concerns. "Katie can take care of any *Englishman*. Let the fellow try to make unwanted advances, she'll have him singing soprano before he can set one English paw on her."

"I appreciate your confidence, father," Katie said, "but what I need is your help. I've told you, Brynston's not like the rest of these English fools. He's not weak, or soft. In fact, he's one of the most bull-headed men I've ever met. I can't handle him alone."

"You're not alone now, Katie," Alex said quietly. "From this point on, wherever you go, I'm standing guard over you. Whether you can see me or not. If Brynston thinks to claim his rights as your husband . . . "

Alex trailed off, and Katie did not press him. Alex would die for her, she knew, and he would also kill. Brynston was a powerful man in any sense of the word, but Alex had learned ruthlessness in schools Brynston could only dream about.

Katie nodded. "I don't think it will get to that point."

Alex shrugged and bowed his head. "Nonetheless. One squeak from you and I'm there, Katie. Always."

She smiled, despite the worries that prickled the back of her neck, despite the damp thrill of fear that went through her every time she thought of Brynston demanding his rights as her husband.

Her *husband*. She swallowed painfully.

"Until the peace is signed, then?" Phineas asked. "Can you play at being countess that long? Boney won't last long, he can't. And we have no contacts in Italy. We can't depend on the Turks' patience any more, now that your hotheaded earl has managed to get them riled."

Katie's mouth felt dry at the idea. "He is not *my* earl. How long do you think the war will go on?"

"Two weeks, three at most," Alex said. "But I don't like the idea of leaving you to the mercy of that English—"

"It will be all right," she said heavily. "I can manage. Two weeks, no longer," she warned.

"We've got two men in Marseilles," Phineas said. "First-rate chaps. For a cut, they'll arrange for our rooms and carriages, smooth out our introduction to the locals."

"And they can keep the Turks at bay for a little while longer, which we can't on our own," Alex said heavily.

"What if they show up here?" Katie asked.

Alex shook his head. "This place is a fortress. No one's getting in . . . or out."

"I do think Brynston would shoot at them again if they approached," Katie said. "Or Graves would. Unexpected depths, that man."

"Puffed-up English windbag if you ask me," Alex muttered. "He tried to get me to come in the servants' entrance."

Katie smiled wryly. "He's a little overzealous about the proprieties," she admitted. "All right, then, it's settled. You two make sure we can leave here no later than two weeks from today. I think I can handle Brynston that long. If the peace isn't signed, we can go to China for all I care, but I'm not spending another instant in this place. Fair enough?"

Both men nodded, Phineas looking pleased and Alex's brow crumpled with concern. But neither of them, Katie thought, really understood what she was up against in the Brimstone Earl.

19

Titania clapped her hands sharply together, bringing the motley gathering to attention. "All right, all right, that's enough. I called you all here for a reason."

"You called us here because it fits your cloak-and-dagger way of doing things, dear sister," Val drawled, perched negligently on a cask of brandy. "You thrive on an air of mystery."

"She called us here to talk about Katie," Rosalind sniffed, not yet past the age of being proud to carry grown-up news.

"Precisely," Portia said. "Now we all know that Julius and Katie are inclined to have their little spats."

Val suppressed a sputter. "Is that what you'd call it? It'll be a miracle if they don't bloody well murder one another."

"And *you* are not helping, brother dear," Portia said pointedly. "What, if I may ask, did you think you were accomplishing by flirting with Katie at dinner?"

"The creature's life is dreary enough, shackled to Julius the Morose," Val said offhandedly. "I thought I'd let the girl have a bit of fun. Anyway, I'm still the slightest bit vexed with her for taking me for all that ready. Julius nearly boxed my ears for it."

"It's what you deserve, you oughtn't be gambling with the family money anyway," Rosalind sniffed.

"A lot you know about it, infant," he said with a scowl. "And I won't be lectured by a spoilt brat."

"Oh, do shut up, Val," Portia said. "We're here to figure out what to do about Katie, remember?"

Tibby sat cross-legged in the corner, looking angelically perfect, as always. His blue eyes wandered to stare at a spider spinning her web in a dark corner.

"Now then," Portia said primly. "The problem, as I see it, is that they have not taken sufficient time to get to know one another."

Val snorted. "He's done nothing *but* spend time with her since she rooked him for all that cash."

Portia was unperturbed. "That can scarcely be called getting to know one another, since Julius was behaving exceedingly badly."

"The poor girl probably thinks he's a lunatic," Titania put in.

"He acts like one, around her," Rosalind said. "I haven't heard him shout so loudly since Tybalt put toads in Milvia's chamber pot." She brought her hand to her mouth to stifle a giggle.

Portia smiled. "People often behave foolishly when they're in love."

"She reminds him of Jo Cargill," Val said.

The cellar went quiet. They all knew it was true, or at least all but Tybalt, who had slipped off and was squatting on his haunches in the corner, getting a better look at his spider.

"It isn't fair," Portia said. "She's nothing like Jo, not really."

"Jo had far more sense," Titania said tartly. "She didn't find herself trussed up like a Christmas goose and hauled in front of a bribable parson to be married."

"But Katie doesn't really *mind*, does she? To be a

countess, after only being an American?" Rosalind shuddered delicately. "I'm glad *I'm* not an American."

"You've been paying too much attention to Julius," Titania said. "I'd rather like to go to America. I should love to see the Red Indians, and ride a horse bareback."

"America's mostly a jolly lot of shopkeepers," Val said. He had been to America once, traveling to Philadelphia and Boston when he was twenty. "Never once saw a Red Indian, I'm afraid, Ti."

"They're in the West," Rosalind said, with all the scorn and confidence born of the schoolroom. "Miss Phipps taught us all about them last week."

"I should ride west, then," Titania said. "On one of those queer spotted ponies. And take a war bonnet for my headdress, and a tomahawk instead of a parasol!"

They could all easily imagine their headstrong sister galloping with the American savages, for all Titania had the manners and demeanor befitting an earl's daughter.

"Now then, this is not getting us anywhere," Portia pointed out gently. "What we need is a plan to bring them together, in some pleasant atmosphere where they could enjoy civil conversation."

"They could go driving," Val suggested.

Portia shook her head. "Katie distinctly told me she would never agree to get into a carriage with Julius again so long as she lived."

"*Quelle surprise*," Titania said dryly. "Why not just a walk in the countryside?"

"They won't stop yelling at each other long enough to get the idea," Rosalind said. "We should *tell* them to take walks together."

Portia raised an eyebrow. "Do you truly think telling Julius to do a thing is the best way to make him do it?"

"And Katie's cut from the same cloth," Titania said, approval ringing in her voice. "She'd rather jump into the fishpond in the dead of winter than do as someone tells her to."

"Unlike, say, yourself," Val drawled.

Titania put out her tongue at him. "You're just jealous because I'm not a lazy sod like you, brother darling."

"Better a lazy sod than a willful wench who'll lead apes before she'll grant so much concession to a man as to allow him a dance." Val grinned at his proud, headstrong younger sister.

Titania tossed her head. "I simply require that my husband not be a spindle-shanked weakling who quakes at the first sign of spirit in a female," she said airily.

"I'd hardly call 'em weaklings, Ti. You caused more bloodshed your first season than Boney's army."

"If men will duel for stupid reasons, that is hardly my concern." Titania arranged the ruffles on her gown fastidiously, bending her head to hide her blush.

Rosalind giggled again, as she always did when the subject of marriage came up, and then clamped her hand over her mouth to suppress it.

"All right then," Portia said, casting a reproachful look around the cellar. "Tybalt, where are you?"

"Here!" came a small voice from a corner.

"What are you doing?" Portia asked.

"Examining the construction of this spider's web."

Portia nodded, satisfied. "We are agreed, a lovely long walk in the country would be just the thing. Perhaps a picnic."

"With lots of asparagus and oysters to act as aphrodisiacs," Val said with wicked relish.

"Oh, you're wretched!" Titania told him, punching him in the arm. "You ought to be displayed in a zoological garden, you great baboon."

"What's an aphr— an aphr— One of those things?" Rosalind asked, suddenly very interested.

"Never you mind, Rosalind," Portia said, flushing deeply as she was not *entirely* sure herself, but knew it had been a most improper comment. "Now then, the question is, how are we to convince them to do it?"

"We don't convince them, we trick them," Val said. "Lure them out somehow."

"We could take Katie riding," Rosalind said wistfully. Rosalind loved to ride and took advantage of any opportunity to do so.

"And I can tell Julius I want to accompany him on his rounds," Val said. "Of course, the shock may kill him."

"Then we've got to ditch them both somewhere they're sure to find one another," Titania said with a gleam in her eye.

Val cleared his throat roughly. "There's, em, an abandoned croft a few miles from the village—quite pleasant, really, and the atmosphere is most . . . romantic."

Titania raised an eyebrow. "Have you been making rendezvous with the village girls, brother dear?"

Val assumed a look of unsullied innocence. "Me? Not at all. I heard some gossips talking about it, that's all."

"You have a care for those girls, Val," Portia said sternly. "Julius won't like your scattering brats around the county, and neither do I."

"Fear not, Portia, I am exceedingly careful about such matters," Val said.

"Careful? How do you mean?" Rosalind asked.

"None of your business," Titania and Val said together.

Portia cleared her throat. "Ahem, I suggest we return to the business at hand." She paused, and sniffed at the air. "Tybalt?"

"Yes?" The voice was very small indeed, and muffled.

"What are you doing?"

"Conducting an experiment," said the small voice.

"What kind of experiment? Don't tell me you've gotten into those—oh Tibby, no!"

The air filled with the unmistakable scent of expensive brandy, and Tybalt emerged from behind a pillar with an enormous cork in his hands. "It seems to have come loose," he said simply, as his brothers and sisters danced around him, Portia snatching the bung out of his hand to find the uncorked cask, the rich scent of brandy already beginning to mix with the earth of the cellar.

Portia winced, feeling the brandy ooze into her slippers as she shoved the bung back into its hole, stopping the river of brandy from flooding the cellar floor. "I suppose," she said, shaking off her wet hands, "it is time to formulate a plan of action."

Katie shivered as she stood at the window of her oddly sparse room. The morning light was winter gray, making the room look even more cold and desolate. She looked out onto the courtyard. Most of the debris had been swept away, but she could still make out a faint glittery dust where the shards of window glass had wedged themselves beneath the paving stones.

She was going to stay here. She was going to pretend to be the countess of Brynston, as she had pretended to be so many other things—a tobacco heiress, a banker's daughter.

Her own things had arrived with Alex and Phineas, and she opened her jewel box, taking out the green glass ear bobs Brynston had won for her those weeks long ago at the Frost Fair. She held them up to her ears, and peered at her reflection in the jagged piece of window glass. They made her look cheap and flashy, a common bit of street trash. Had he known? Had he, of all the men she had fooled, been the only one to see her for what she really was?

A knock came at her door, and she quickly thrust the ear bobs back into the jewelry box. "Come in," she said.

Brynston stood at the door, gleaming from head to boots. "Madame," he said in greeting. "Is this a convenient moment?"

"That depends," she said, her heart pounding.

He lifted one black eyebrow, and fixed her with those burning eyes. "It comes to my attention that you, being American, are doubtless not yet versed in the duties and demeanor befitting a countess. Therefore, I am here to conduct your education."

Katie frowned. "You? Why didn't you send one of your sisters, if you thought I needed educating?"

"Because my sisters are untrustworthy hoydens," Brynston said patiently. "Portia is better than the others, but any of them would fill your head with a pack of rubbish about how to *handle* me."

"And how should I handle you?" she asked, flushing warm at her own boldness.

"Why, you should obey me without hesitation, of course," he said, flashing her a white, dangerous smile.

"If you wanted a milk-and-water miss, my lord, you married the wrong bride."

Brynston let out an impatient snort. "Yes, yes, I know. You really are becoming quite tiresome on the subject, madame. Now then, you can either commence your education as countess or I can lock you in your rooms until you see common sense."

Katie kept firm control of her temper. "I will take your lessons, but not because of your odious threats. I'm bored here, that's all. There's nothing else worth doing in this musty house."

"I keep a veritable army of servants to ensure that the house is not musty, madame, but I take your point. And I should not want you, under any circumstances, to become bored."

"Why not?" Katie asked warily.

"Because, madame, you are already entirely troublesome enough. Now then, I shall pretend to be some visiting lady of good family, and you will receive me for tea."

"You?" Katie asked, incredulous. "As a lady of fashionable society?"

"Forgive me, I suspected you of possessing an imagination," Brynston said, impatient.

Katie suppressed a small smile. "And I had never suspected the same of you. Very well, you may begin."

Brynston put on a ludicrous expression, more suited to a French vaudeville comedian than a lady of fashion.

"My dear," he said in a flutey contralto. "How good of you to receive me."

Katie crossed her arms in front of her chest. "You're dreadful," she said.

Brynston dropped his pose. "I rather doubt that is the best response to make to a lady of fashion. *How do you do* might have been more appropriate."

"You're doing it all wrong," Katie insisted. "Here, it's more like this." She composed her features into a mask of perfect hauteur, modeling herself on that paragon, Lady Holland. "There you are, my child," she said with a regal tilt of her nose. "Come and let me have a look at what you're wearing. Good heavens, organza in March? What can your mother have been thinking?" Katie fanned herself with the fervor of a woman all but ready to faint dead away.

Brynston laughed aloud, and the sound startled Katie out of her pose. He looked different when he laughed, younger and strangely free.

"Where the devil did you learn to do that?" he asked. "Don't tell me you're secretly an actress?"

Katie's good humor dissolved like bitters in water. "No, my lord, not an actress. Just a natural mimic, I suppose."

"You were playing a role the night I met you," he mused. "I suppose I shall have to watch for that."

"I suppose you shall," she said, her mouth suddenly dry.

"Come on, then, Katie," he said good-naturedly. "I didn't mean to devil you. Let's continue, and if you will forgive me my bad acting, I'll forgive you your good." His face assumed the expression of the haughty dowager once again. "My dear, can one abide by this dreadful weather? One feels it sink into one's very bones."

Katie found that she wanted to play the game, that she wanted to convince him she could play the countess as well as she'd once played the goose-headed fool. "Just so," she said, taking him convivially and leading him to the settee, one of the few seats that had been too large to push out the window. "Why, just the other morning I was walking with Lady Perrin, and we agreed that the humors are especially damp and unwholesome at this time of year. One can only look forward to spring, when all shall be gay and bright again."

Katie mimicked the skillful pouring of tea, sitting straight-backed on the settee.

Brynston pretended to sniff at his tea, wrinkle his nose faintly, and sip. "Of course, when one is my age," he said sadly, "the spring brings only memories of youth."

"Surely a lady as lovely as your ladyship must look forward, not back, to such memories," Katie said, taking an invisible cake from an equally invisible footman.

"You are too kind, child," Brynston said with a hideous giggle, as he also took a cake from the ghostly footman.

"That is really too much," Katie protested, dropping her pose. "That giggle! I cannot believe a lady of fashion ever cackled that way."

"In how many drawing rooms have you been received? Of the highest *ton*, I mean?"

"A few," Katie admitted.

"I have been received in rather more than a few," he said dryly. "I can assure you, the giggle is drawn directly from life."

He reassumed his attitude of the haughty dowager. "I hope you will permit me to offer you my good wishes on your marriage, my dear. The *ton* is quite a-twitter over it! The earl must be swooning of love for you." He punctuated this with a sort of genteel leer.

The thought made Katie's cheeks burn, and she switched to a broad gutter accent. "Nah, 'e's put me in the puddin' club, that's all." She laid her hands broadly over her belly. "I've a bloomin' bun in me oven, hain't I?"

"That is not true!" Brynston thundered, becoming all at once his usual black, volcanic self.

"And it's not true that you're swooning with love for me, either," Katie retorted. For some reason, the idea irritated her.

"It's the kind of nonsense these harpies like to spout," he said. "She's fishing, she wants to know why I *did* marry you."

"And she suspects the very reason I gave," Katie said with a grin.

"That is why you will do your utmost to convince her otherwise," he said with a growl.

"Are you high *ton* English really too infirm to count?" Katie teased. "Surely time will tell the old dragon she's guessed wrong."

"That's not the point." Brynston's tone suggested he was losing his patience. "I'm beginning to think you don't take this seriously."

She lifted a hand to her cheek in mock horror. "Heaven forfend. Pray go on, Lady Cowflop."

"Katie!" Brynston said warningly.

"My lady?" she said sweetly, fluttering her eyelashes. "Would you care for more tea?"

Disgruntled, he again arranged his features to resemble the dowager's. "He must be in a perfect swoon of love for you," he trilled.

"Oh, in apoplectic fits of it," she agreed.

"Katie!"

"Sorry." She composed herself, shrinking her grin to a demure smile. "Yes, I suppose it is unfashionable for husband and wife to adore each other so, but we are simple people, after all, my lady."

"Simple people?" Brynston asked, sounding a little huffy but maintaining his persona. "Surely one cannot call the inhabitants of Willowby Hall *simple*, child. You make the earl sound a positive yeoman."

Katie smiled blandly. "Oh, we are perfect rustics, you know. We do not stand on ceremony here at Willowby Hall. May I pour you another cup?"

"Thank you, my dear," Brynston said sweetly. "Was it a very lovely wedding, then?"

"Very," Katie agreed with a sugared smile. "Quite traditional. One might even say . . . medieval."

Brynston lifted one eyebrow in silent warning.

Katie laughed. "Sorry," she said, not feeling at all contrite.

"Such a beautiful girl, I can see how you enchanted the earl so utterly. Pity about these short hairstyles the girls are wearing now. In my day, no *respectable* young lady would ever wear her hair so short."

Katie smiled, thinking that in Lady Cowflop's day, no respectable lady was seen without a powdered wig. "And you have such lovely hair, Lady Cowflop. I vow, it's as full as any village milkmaid's."

"Oh, thank you," Brynston said, patting his hair with a grotesque simper. His eyes sparkled with mischief. "I wash it every morning in rosemary water and bull's urine."

Katie was silent for a stunned moment, then burst into a highly unladylike gale of laughter. Brynston joined her. As soon as he began to get control of himself, she broke into a renewed fit of giggles, starting him off again.

"It's a recipe my grandmother used," he said finally, wiping tears from his eyes. "She used to swear by it."

"I can't believe your grandfather ever got close enough to produce any heirs," Katie said, still laughing.

"The seventh earl of Brynston was renowned for his courage," Brynston said, erupting into laughter again.

After a moment, Katie managed to compose herself. She turned away from him, and sucked in a deep breath. "No, don't look at me. My stomach's sore from laughing."

"Anatomical references are very low *ton*," Brynston said in his Lady Cowflop voice.

"Unlike formulas for shampoo made from bull's urine," Katie said, biting hard on her lower lip to keep from laughing again.

"You must forgive an old lady her reminiscences, child," Brynston said.

"I do forgive you," Katie said, turning back to him. It occurred to her that she was alone with her volcanic husband—had been for some minutes—but she did not feel menaced by him today. He was freer here, easier. Less the chilly gentleman and more a man of—what? Good humor? Warmth? These were words she never would have associated with the Brimstone Earl.

"Do you trust me to play my role yet?" she asked lightly. It was beyond absurd to want to please him, and yet she did.

"If you can keep your impishness under control, you will be entirely convincing," he said.

"Is that what you want me to do?"

"In the company of guests? Most certainly," he said flatly.

"And when we are alone? Should I still control my impishness?"

"I haven't laughed so much in a long time," he admitted. "I don't laugh enough, I know. But there are responsibilities attached to a title. And you will need to learn them as well, and to take them seriously."

"You've thrust a heavy burden on me," she said, meeting his gaze levelly.

"I know. I won't pretend it was right. It was merely the least wrong thing I knew how to do."

Katie shut her eyes, desperately reaching for the old walls she kept around her feelings. They were harder to maintain with a Brimstone Earl who was gentle and funny.

She threw up the only barrier she could think of. "You were wrong. You've done me a terrible harm . . . Julius." She spoke his Christian name for the first time, and it felt curiously intimate on her tongue. *Julius.*

His eyes chilled, and he sat a fraction straighter. "Perhaps. Time will tell. I am inclined to think that we shall both be less miserable, eventually."

Katie took a deep breath to calm her pounding heart. He did not know there would be no *eventually*. Perhaps it would be kinder to be so obnoxious, so temperamental and wretched, that he would be glad to see her go.

But she could not quite manage it today. "Thank you for my lesson, my lord."

Realizing he was being dismissed, he stood abruptly. "If you promise not to chuck it out the window, I'll have some new furniture brought in tomorrow."

"If you like," she said quietly.

He stood a long moment in the door frame, as if there were something he wanted to say. "Katie," he began, then stopped and began again. "Some day, someone might—" He broke off.

"What is it, my lord?" she asked.

"If anyone should ever tell you about a girl—a girl I used to be engaged to, you needn't listen. I used to think you were something like her, but I was wrong. You're nothing like Jo, not in the least."

"I don't think I understand," Katie said.

Julius smiled a strange, melancholy smile. "It doesn't matter. Good day, Katie."

"Good day . . . Julius." And with that, she softly clicked the door behind him.

20

Alex Manners climbed the back stairs two at a time, lost in thought. He was sick with worry, wondering what was to become of Katie Starr in her precarious position at Willowby Hall.

He nearly collided with Brynston's valet, who wore a dove-colored coat and an expression as bland as a dishful of tapioca.

Alex disliked tapioca.

"I beg your pardon," Graves said stiffly.

Alex looked up at the smaller man. "Done polishing your master's boots, are you?"

"His lordship's boots are polished every morning, as has been the case in this house since before you were born, sir," Graves said curtly. He started again down the narrow stairs, but Alex put out a hand and stopped him.

"I guess you know the earl better than most. Just between you and me, why is he doing this? Why won't he let Katie go?"

Graves looked shocked. "The countess is his wife. Where would she want to go?"

"She's miserable here. She's miserable with *him*. Didn't you see all the furniture she tossed out the window? Does that seem like a happy, blushing bride to you?"

"Her ladyship has always displayed an exceptionally lively temperament," Graves said, allowing a trace of rue to creep into his voice.

Alex smiled wryly. "Is that what you'd call it? Katie's a little firecracker when she's crossed, no doubt about it."

"You must call her *the countess* or *her ladyship*," Graves said, frowning. "You set a bad example for the other servants."

"She is my friend, and the closest thing to a daughter I've ever known," Alex said softly. "We are Katie and Alex to one another, and always will be."

Graves shook his head disapprovingly. "Americans."

Alex did not give a damn what this puffed-up little monkey thought of Americans. "You traveled with them, is that right? After he kidnapped her the second time."

Graves looked uncomfortable, as if his cravat were suddenly too tight. "He only wished to speak with Miss Feathering, to assure himself as to her safety and ascertain why she had left so precipitously."

"He was in a rage because she had slipped free of him, and he wanted to know how," Alex corrected.

Graves shrugged faintly. "In any event, he did not believe at that time that he would seek Miss Feathering's company for a prolonged period of time."

"And then he forced her to marry him."

The valet positively squirmed. "I would not like to say *forced*."

"I know you wouldn't like to say it, but it's the truth. I only want to know why he did it."

Graves glanced down at his impeccably shined shoes, as if he were ashamed of something. "I do not hold with gossiping about our betters. It's a filthy habit from which no good can come."

"He despises her, he can't bear the sight of her. I want to know why he forced her to marry him."

Graves's head shot up, startled. "Oh no, that isn't true! I believe he loves her."

Alex's face twisted in disbelief. "Loves her? He's got a funny way of showing it."

Graves waved his concerns aside. "His lordship can be a . . . volatile man, when crossed."

"So the answer is not to cross him?" Alex said sarcastically.

"Yes, of course," Graves said, not understanding the joke. "But he is not so fearsome as he seems. He married her for honor's sake, partly, and because he had given his word she would come to no harm."

"Given his word?" Alex jumped on the phrase. "To whom? Who knew he had her in his clutches?"

Graves swallowed twice, and plucked an invisible speck of lint from his jacket. "To, er, myself."

"You?" Alex could scarcely believe his ears. "Why should you care? You serve that surly devil."

"I am very fond of the countess," Graves protested. "You might say I serve her ladyship now as well. As loyally as I do his lordship."

"But your *first* loyalty is to Brynston," Alex said.

The valet shook his head. "You are seeing only what you want to see, Mr. Manners. His interests and hers are not so far apart as you imagine."

Alex snorted disdainfully. "She can't bear him, Graves. She can hardly endure his presence in the room."

Graves looked at him owlishly for a long moment. "As any good servant could tell you, Mr. Manners, sometimes there is more to be learned through quiet observation than in grilling one like a Bow Street Runner. I must attend to my duties now. Good day to you, sir."

And with that, Graves edged past him, neatened the lapels on his coat, and trotted down the stairwell without a backwards glance.

*　　*　　*

After lunch, Lord Brynston was called away by his agent to inspect some newly built cottages near town. Katie found herself in the library fighting for wakefulness. The novel in her lap seemed to consist mostly of shrill sermons on the appropriate demeanor of young ladies.

Katie yawned and closed the book. Brynston's "lessons" and her own disguises to the contrary, she was not at all interested in becoming a proper young lady.

She looked out the window. The day was gray, but she doubted they would see more snow this year. Winter was melting into spring, and soon the trees would be covered in tight green buds. Where would she be to see them? France? Italy? She pulled her shawl tighter around her shoulders, though the room was not at all cold.

A small knock came at the door, and a blazing red head peered into the library. "Hullo, Katie. Are you bored? I am. I hate being in the house after Christmas."

"Come in, Rosalind," Katie said, smiling as she set the book aside. "I suppose I was a little bored, yes."

"Is Julius off fixing things?" Rosalind asked, plopping herself in a comfortable chair as she yanked at the bell.

"I believe he said something about some cottages."

Rosalind rolled her eyes. "They're looking at the roofs. They spent all last winter talking about the best roofs for the cottages, and Julius *never* wanted to go riding, or have picnics, or do anything interesting. I hate roofs."

"It doesn't sound very lively," Katie conceded. "But I suppose it is very important."

Rosalind sat straight up in her chair, mimicking the ponderous voices of adults. "Do they leak? Are there mice living in them? Do they rot? Are they full of swallows' nests?" She collapsed back in her chair with a huff. "*Dreary.*"

The butler appeared at the door, and Katie asked him to bring tea and cakes, and a pot of coffee for herself.

"So what do you think is interesting?" Katie asked, unsure how to treat her youngest sister-in-law. Rosalind was neither a child nor a woman, but at that difficult place between the two. A place Katie had never really known—she had gone from the heartless, rowdy innocence of childhood to haunted adulthood in the blink of an eye.

She repressed the thought. There was no sense in dwelling on the past, there was nothing she could do to repair it now.

Rosalind thought about this question, then slid Katie a sideways look. She bit her lip shyly for a moment, then blurted, "Is it really true that Mr. Manners is a ruthless killer?"

Katie was taken aback. "I beg your pardon?"

"Miss Phipps said that she talked with Graves, and Graves said that Mr. Manners was a ruthless killer. Is that really true? Aren't you afraid he'll murder you one night while you're sleeping?" Rosalind's eyes were wide as she considered the chilling possibilities.

"It doesn't sound to me like Miss Phipps is very good about minding her own business."

"She's not," Rosalind said. "Just last week, she told me our old parlor maid had to leave because she was expecting. But she wouldn't tell me *what* she was expecting. You don't have any idea, do you?"

Katie relaxed as she realized Rosalind's curiosity had more to do with the unearthing of interesting adult secrets than it did with unmasking Katie and her family.

"I can't imagine," she said with a pleasant smile. "As for Mr. Manners, I don't think you have any reason to be frightened of him. He's awfully partial to little girls. I don't think he's killed one in her sleep for, oh, ages."

"I am not a little girl," Rosalind sniffed. She thought about this a moment. "You're teasing me, about Mr. Manners killing people."

"Yes, I'm teasing you," Katie said, smiling.

"I expect Miss Phipps was just saying it to sound important," Rosalind said, a little haughty. "My brother would dismiss her for gossiping, but it is very difficult to keep governesses here. Tibby keeps frightening them away."

"Little Tibby? But he seems like a perfect gentleman," Katie said.

Rosalind made the face of someone who had swallowed violent poison. "Tibby is *awful*!" she cried. "One day, he locked all of Milvia's hounds in the sewing closet, and they made a terrible noise trying to be let out, and when they *were* let out they nearly knocked me over and they put their muddy paws on my dress. And he set a fire in the drawing room that almost didn't get put out, and there's a great big black mark on the floor under the blue carpet. And last year, he cut off my hair so that he could do one of his horrid experiments."

"I see," Katie said, nodding soberly. "You're right, he does sound awful. But your hair looks very nice now."

Rosalind looked at her wistfully. "I wish I could get it cut like yours. Miss Phipps says it would make me look like a harlot."

Katie colored. Miss Phipps seemed to be a woman of little reticence. "Perhaps she means you're still a bit young to wear this style."

"I hate being young," Rosalind said, kicking her legs against the legs of her chair. "I can't wait until I come out, and have splendid dresses and things. Titania came out last year, and she's had four duels fought over her already."

"Your sister seems like a remarkable person," Katie said, and Rosalind nodded silently, still kicking her chair.

The butler knocked discreetly at the door and then opened it, bearing the tea tray and a heap of pretty almond-shaped cakes. "Lady Milvia Trowsedale is in the front parlor, your ladyship."

Katie frowned. She was having a very nice time with Rosalind, and the last thing she wanted was to do battle with Lady Milvia.

Rosalind sat up straight in her chair and folded her hands in a most ladylike fashion. "Tell her we are not at home, Granby," she said, sounding like a princess.

"Very good, Lady Rosalind," the butler said, bowing faintly.

"Lady Milvia is—" Rosalind began in a stage-whisper.

"Let me guess," Katie whispered back with a conspiratorial wink. "Dreary."

Rosalind grinned. "Very, very dreary."

Lady Milvia pushed her way past Granby, removing her gloves. "Katie, darling, how divine to see you!"

"Lady Milvia," Katie said mildly, standing and presenting her cheek to Milvia's to be kissed.

"Don't tell me you've been sitting all alone in this drafty house!" Milvia cooed. "My dear, you will expire of tedium."

"I'm not alone, Lady Milvia. I have been having a most stimulating conversation with Lady Rosalind," Katie said.

Milvia flicked a glance over the child. "Charming. Granby, bring me a pot of oolong, will you? You know the kind I like best." Milvia settled herself on the sofa as if she intended to take up residence there. "Forgive me, dear, for ordering your servants about. But I come to Willowby Hall so often, I sometimes forget I don't live here."

"It must be a difficult adjustment for you," Katie murmured.

"I was about to say the same of you, my dear," Milvia said. "Word has got round, you know, about that naughty prank you played. All that exquisite furniture, quite ruined!" Her eyes widened as if she were describing the horrors of war. Then they narrowed again. "But perhaps you are unfamiliar with what such trifles cost."

Katie shrugged faintly. "You must not put any stock in lovers' quarrels," she said evenly, though she felt her cheeks warm at the word *lovers*. "I can assure you, Julius does not."

Milvia went rather pale, and snapped her fan open and shut irritably. Before she could think of another barb, Granby returned with a fresh pot.

"I can't bear tea," Katie explained, pouring herself a cup of coffee.

"How patriotic of you," Milvia said, stirring milk into her oolong. "What do your people call it, that little riot they had over the tea?"

"The Boston Tea Party," Katie said. "They dressed as Indians and took tomahawks to the English barrels." She smiled sharply at Milvia.

"Did they truly?" Rosalind asked, plucking three cakes off the tea tray. "It sounds like a perilous adventure. Was anyone horribly maimed?"

"I suppose there is something savage about the American character, isn't there?" Milvia said, shuddering delicately.

"No one maimed, sorry, Rosalind," Katie said. "But they did spoil rather a lot of tea."

"The more I think about it, the more I think the Americans sound perfectly interesting," Rosalind said, before sinking her teeth thoughtfully into a cake.

Milvia looked sour as she drank her oolong in tiny, stabbing sips. "I was wondering if Katie might not be bored here. You know how dreary these winter sojourns can be, especially for someone unfamiliar with the countryside."

Rosalind looked almost startled, and sat up. "Oh yes! She might be bored. I almost forgot—Katie, would you like to go riding with me next week? I think the weather will hold, and you haven't seen the dales. They're just beginning to come awake from the winter, it's like something out of a fairy tale. Oh, please say you'll come!"

"You make it sound so romantic," Katie said with a smile.

Rosalind's cheeks glowed as brightly as a Christmas candle. "Yes, very romantic. Will you? Please?"

"It would be nice to get some fresh air—" Katie mused.

"Wonderful!" Rosalind clapped her hands happily. "You will be glad you did, I can promise you that."

"I think that sounds very agreeable," Milvia said. "If

you'll permit me to tag along, my dear, I believe I can show you the unique features of this landscape as few people could."

"No!" Rosalind blurted, almost choking on a cake. "I mean, I had hoped it would just be Katie and me, Mil. You know, to get to know each other as sisters. You can come next time."

Milvia's wintry blue eyes were as chilly as the March sky outside the window. "Of course. I did not mean to intrude."

"You weren't intruding, Lady Milvia," Katie said, wanting to smooth over the faux pas. She didn't want to go riding with Milvia any more than Rosalind did, but it seemed unkind to be so blunt about it. "Perhaps we can go riding another time. I'm sure you have a most unique perspective."

"Yes, another time!" Rosalind said, brightening. "That would be all right."

"If you like," Milvia said with a dainty lift of her nose. She sipped her tea, visibly offended but unwilling to acknowledge the slight. After a moment she changed the subject. "Your family name is Feathering, isn't that right, my dear?"

Katie nodded. "Yes, that's right."

"Odd that I shouldn't know them," Milvia mused. "I know so many of the best families in America."

"America is a big country," Katie said neutrally.

"And your father has made his fortune in . . . what was it? I'm so terribly muzzy about such matters."

"Textiles," Katie said. "And other imports, but mostly fabrics from Italy and France. Ladies in Philadelphia have as great a desire to be fashionable as you do here in England." Katie was not nervous—she had worked out the details of the Featherings' background long ago—but she did wonder why Lady Milvia was so curious.

"It must be wonderful to feel so useful," Milvia said, the look of distaste on her face apparent. To the English aristocracy, there was little more shameful than the taint of trade.

"I'm very proud of my father. He started out in life with

very little." *And now he has a hundred thousand pound debt and a daughter who tells lies for a living,* Katie thought.

"Fascinating," Milvia purred.

"Does your father import English wool?" Rosalind asked, eager to be part of the conversation. "Miss Phipps says that English wool formed the backbone of our system of government and trade, going back to the time of Chaucer."

Milvia shuddered delicately, brushing an invisible particle from her skirts. "How terribly learned of you, Rosalind dear. You are becoming a perfect blue. I do hope that woman doesn't have you reading Chaucer—I've been told it's most indelicate."

"I'd rather be a bluestocking than one of those boring girls who fly about Almack's like a pack of butterflies," Rosalind said.

"Those butterflies prove very attractive to eligible young men," Milvia said. "Why, Katie here must have fluttered most enticingly to attract the attentions of the earl of Brynston."

"I don't flutter," Katie said, tightening her grip on her cup.

Milvia gave her an appraising look that seemed to say, *Wrong accent, wrong clothes, wrong hair.* "No, I don't suppose you do. But then you are a lady of myriad hidden charms."

Katie was becoming distinctly annoyed. Lady Milvia might be heartbroken over the loss of the Brimstone Earl, but she was taking it out on entirely the wrong person.

"Waaaahl," Katie drawled, leaning back in her chair as if it were a carved rocker, "as my old granny used to say, hide yer light under a bushel and you won't git nothin' but a burnt basket."

Milvia blinked. "I say. Excuse me?"

Katie thrust her feet out in front of her and rested them on the footstool, setting her cup on a side table. "What I mean is, you cain't make cider without a few rotten apples."

Milvia peered at Katie, flipped open her fan, and fluttered it against her cheek. "Yes, I see."

Katie waggled her eyebrows significantly and leaned forward in her chair. "Whar thar's chickens, thar's chicken sh—"

"My goodness!" Milvia said, interrupting. "You are a very . . . colorful people, you Americans."

"I hope I didn't embarrass you none," Katie drawled. "I put my foot in my mouth so often I reckon my tongue's got bunions."

"Not at all, I shall have to remember those quaint expressions for another occasion," Milvia said quickly.

Katie stood. "If you don't mind, ma'am, I reckon I'll mosey on upstairs and check on them chickens."

"Chickens?" Milvia said weakly. "Upstairs?"

"Are there truly?" Rosalind said, her voice hopeful.

"In my room, of course," Katie said. "How else kin I keep an eye on 'em? Thar ain't nothin' like fresh raw eggs first thang in the mornin'. I jest snatch 'em out from under the hen, crack 'em in a cup, and down they go."

Milvia looked a little green. "Good heavens, I've never heard of such a thing."

"No, ma'am, I reckon it ain't the custom over here in England," Katie said. "You wouldn't be hankerin' to come up and pet them chickens, would you, Lady Milvia? Cause you're more'n welcome. I'd be plumb honored."

"I want to, too!" Rosalind said. "I would be plumb honored as well." The words sounded doubly ludicrous in Rosalind's plummy accent.

Milvia shook her head quickly, no. "Thank you, Katie, but I don't think I can stay."

Katie grinned. "Suit yerself. I'll be seein' you, Lady Milvia. Rosie, you kin come up another time."

"Yes," Milvia said, trying to compose herself. "Indeed. Good day, Katie."

"Good day, Lady Milvia," Katie said, and the smile on her face was genuine.

*   *   *

Katie ran into Alex on the landing, and she plucked him into her room, sighing with relief as she shut the door. She watched at the window, careful to keep behind the curtains until Milvia's carriage was gone.

"What's wrong?" Alex asked. "You look jumpy."

"Lady Milvia Trowsedale is what's wrong," she said. "She knows something, Alex, I'm sure of it. Or she suspects, which is just as bad."

"How much, do you think?" Alex frowned, squinting out the window to catch a glimpse of her carriage.

Katie shook her head. "Not enough to hang us just yet. She won't go to Brynston until she has something solid."

Alex nodded. "He won't be pleased."

Katie shivered at the thought. "He won't be pleased?" she said with a little laugh. "He'll explode like a bomb. A very big bomb."

"So what do we do? I could send a few boys over, urge her to keep quiet," Alex said soberly.

Katie walked away from the window, arms crossed in front of her chest. "She's not some guttersnipe we can clout over the head, Alex. She's an earl's daughter, she has connections. We need to get out of here. As quickly as possible."

Alex nodded. "It was stupid to stay. We ought to have gone to Spain, and crossed over the Pyrenees when the time was right, and hidden in some little *taverna*. The Turks can't turn an entire country upside down looking for us."

"Of course they can," Katie moaned, pressing her hands to her temples. "But if Brynston finds out I'm a sharper, he'll make the Turks look like a Sunday School picnic."

The wind blew cold through the broken window, and Katie rummaged through her armoire, finding a fur-lined pelisse. Perhaps breaking all the windows in the middle of winter had not been the smartest thing she'd ever done. Even now, the curtains were roiling as if they wrapped around some small person.

Even as this thought formed in Katie's mind, a lump fell out of the curtains and onto the floor. Katie suppressed a scream as the lump stood, dusted itself off, and adjusted the majestically large chapeau bras on its head.

The small figure bowed and swept the hat off again in a grandiose gesture. "Good afternoon, and at your service, countess."

21

"*Tom? Tom Finch?*" Katie said, not quite daring to believe it.

"At your service, your ladyship," the boy said.

For a moment Katie was too stunned to comprehend. She rushed over and embraced him. "Tom! How did you get here? You're so far from home! How did you know where to find me?"

At the same time, Alex rumbled, "What the blazes are you doing here, you little rogue? Get back to the stables before I give you the leathering you deserve."

Tom extricated himself with all the pained dignity of a ten-year-old boy. "That old zouch Manners ain't told you, then," he said with a baleful look at Alex.

"Told me what?"

Tom sketched a faint bow. "I has the honor of bein' the new stable boy to the Starr family, also known as the Feathering family, also known as the Featherstones, the Stoneshaws, and several other aliases on top of that."

"You're our new stable boy?" Katie blinked. "Alex, why didn't you tell me? Didn't you know Tom and I were friends?"

Alex scowled. "The brat never mentioned it. Not," he added with a glower at the boy, "that it would have been proper for him to come up here even if he had."

"I would never take advantage of the acquaintanceship of a lady," Tom said, dignified despite the broad London accent.

"But why are you working for us? You haven't had an accident, have you? Has something happened to your hands?" Katie took Tom's hands in her own and examined them, worried. The Starrs took in criminals who could not longer practice their illicit trade, not ablebodied young cutpurses like Tom.

"I guess you could say me infirmity was philosophical in nature," he said. "I didn't want to nick purses no more. Lawk, it's cold in here."

Katie took him by the arm and led him over to the settee. "Sorry, it's my fault. I knocked out all the windows."

Tom looked at the curtains billowing about the jagged windowpanes, and then at Katie again. "Pardon my sayin' so, your ladyship, but you're just a scrap of a thing—you could have escaped out that window without knockin' 'em all out."

"I wasn't trying to escape—it would be impossible, anyway. Brynston guards this place like a fortress." Katie rifled through the armoire for something warm for Tom, coming upon a pretty little velvet-lined spencer. "Here, you can wear this. It'll keep the chill off."

"I been cold before, your ladyship," Tom said with great dignity. "But I ain't never put on no gentry-mort's winter frock, and I ain't likely to. Beg your pardon for any offense, your ladyship."

Alex made a sound like a strangled cough, and covered his mouth behind his big hands.

"I'm not offended, though I do think you're being a dolt," Katie said. "I never realized how *cold* these big English houses get."

"An' they do seem so lovely and warm from the outside," Tom said wistfully. "I couldn't hardly believe me eyes when I saw them great front steps, and bugger if there ain't a hundred windows in this place."

"Ninety-nine now," Alex corrected with a glance at the window. He retreated to the far corner and leaned against the wall with his massive arms folded in front of him, looking like some kind of harem guard.

Tom stood abruptly as if he had just remembered something. "I hope you will allow me the honor of congratulatin' you on the occasion of your marriage," he said, enunciating the words with great care.

Katie frowned. "Oh, Tom, not you too. Everyone but me seems to think this wretched marriage is actually a good idea."

"W—well, ain't it?" Tom asked, nonplussed.

"No, it is not," Katie said firmly. "I find Lord Brynston every bit as disagreeable now as I ever did." She felt a pang of guilt, and took Tom by the hand. "Tom—before, in the flash house—I'm sorry I didn't tell you about me. About what I am."

His eyes were steady and trusting. "That you was one of us, you mean? A sharper?"

Katie nodded. "I wasn't trying to put on airs, I just couldn't take the risk of Brynston finding out. I honestly think he would have seen me hang, if he could have managed it."

Tom nodded thoughtfully. "He's a rum'un. But it's all different now." He gestured to her room, then wrinkled his forehead as he really took it in for the first time—the sparse furnishings, the bare walls. He whistled beneath his breath. "Lawk, you did a right job on this place."

"I threw all the furniture out the window," she said, feeling a little sheepish now.

"All of it?" Tom asked, incredulous.

"Everything I could fit through the window frame."

"Mirrors? Vases, pictures?" He looked pained.

"Those, too."

Tom rolled his eyes and sat back in his chair. "And in

a bloody swank house like this one. You could have had a rum cod for that lot."

"She is familiar with how much such things cost," Alex growled. "Mind your manners, brat, especially about what's not your business."

Tom shot Katie a sideways glance. "This is one of them questions of principle, ain't it?"

"As a matter of fact, it is," she said. "I never chose to come here, it's the last thing I wanted."

"But he's an earl," Tom said, clearly not able to grasp the notion of refusing such a plum prize. "And that makes you a countess, right? Everything's different if you're a countess."

"Nothing is different. Brynston would despise me if he knew what I truly am," Katie said.

"An' you must keeps your horrible secret," Tom said, leaning back in his seat as understanding crossed his face. "Or else be forsaken by your true love."

"Tom, pay attention," Katie said irritably. "Brynston is *not* my true love. This marriage is a sham."

Tom's eyes widened. "Then you ain't truly the countess?"

"No. Well, maybe yes, for the time being, but I don't think so really," she said, looking down to find she was wringing her lace handkerchief to bits. "He forced the marriage, which I don't think is legal even in Scotland, and anyway I didn't use my real name."

Tom whistled again, looking totally mystified. "I see, your ladyship."

"Oh, Tom, won't you please call me Katie? *Your ladyship* gives me the collywobbles."

"Oh no, ma'am, I couldn't."

"Please? While we're just having a friendly conversation? You may *your ladyship* to your heart's content when we're playing a game for the rest of the world."

"Don't push the boy, Katie," Alex said, giving Tom a severe look. "It's only right that he speak to you with respect."

"It ain't no game with me, ma'am, I promise you."

Tom's freckled face was earnest. "I'm a bloody good stable boy."

Katie looked at him appraisingly. "Hmmm, I suppose you would be. You're smart and you pay attention, and you aren't easy to push around."

"Thank you, ma'am," he said, tucking his chin and blushing fiercely.

"Katie."

"Katie," Tom said, in a small, awed voice.

Alex grumbled faintly in the corner, but he let it lie.

"So tell me why you gave up picking pockets."

His eyes widened. "Why, it was meetin' you, your ladyship."

"Katie," she corrected.

"Katie," he agreed shyly. "It was seein' how fine you was, with your refined manners an' the way you stood up to old Brimstone. It turned over me new leaf, it did."

"You can't mean that." Katie frowned. "Tom, it was a lie, a jostle. All of it. You know that now."

Tom shook his head. "Don't make no never mind, Katie. You might not be no legal countess, but you're a proper lady, an' I'll fight any bugger what says you ain't."

"He's right, you know, Katie," Alex said, his voice strangely warm.

She took Tom's hands suddenly in her own, wanting him to understand the truth. "Tom, I grew up just as you did. Stealing, cheating, running wild in the streets. It's only luck that kept me out of the bawdy-house."

She felt her hands grow cold, remembering. Remembering the moment when she had ceased to be a snapping little wolf cub, and had been seen as a woman. There had been no pride in it, only danger and the threat of degradation.

Tom's face was serious. "I know that, Katie. It weren't 'til I knew that that I figured I could change."

"What do you mean?"

Tom's eyes were still wide and round with youth, but he spoke with the dignity of a much older man. "If I hadn't

known a thievin' little judy could become a great lady
like yourself, I would never have known what I could
grow up to be better than that bastard Lyme. It was you
what taught me that, Katie, and I owes you everything
for it."

Katie felt the sting of tears come to her eyes, but she
blinked them away. She could not make him see that she
was no great lady, that she was still the same grubby
urchin who stole pennies from fine gentlemen and spent
them on rum, or throwing dice.

Tom had gained something precious from her—from
this cobweb of sticky lies. She would not deny him that,
though her own redemption seemed as far away as heaven.

"I can't stay," he said, smiling as he squeezed her
hand. "Kittredge'll warm me arse if them harnesses ain't
polished."

Katie was outraged. "Kittredge? That ungrateful
wretch! You tell him if he lays one finger on you, he can
very well go back to stealing old boots and shoes."

"He's just doin' his job for you proper, same as what
I is."

"Listen to the boy, Katie," Alex said, stepping forward.
"He's not such a cheeky brat as I suspected, though he
could still use a few lessons in keeping his place." He shot
Tom a savage glower.

Katie frowned. "Well, I still say Kittredge ought to
treat him with respect. Tom, you be sure and tell him I
told you that."

"I will, ma'am," Tom said with a grin. "Anything you
need me to do to old Brimstone? Saw through the axle
on his rumble-tumble? Or maybe you'd like to see his
lordship have a bit of a riding accident . . . "

"She doesn't need your help now, boy," Alex said.
"She's got me for that. You just look after the horses."

"Absolutely not," Katie said firmly. "You're reformed,
remember? Anyway, riding accidents are terribly dangerous.
You'll make me a widow if you go fooling around like that."

"You sure that ain't what you want, Katie?" Tom's

eyes were so sweet, so pure. "Sounds like it would solve all your problems, if his lordship was to pike off."

"You're not in that line of work any more," she said gently.

"Me soul's black with sin as it is, Katie," Tom said. "One more won't damn me, unless what I'm damned already. An' I owe you the world."

She shook her head. "I don't wish the earl any harm. He's a good man." She was surprised to hear the words leave her mouth, but they were true. He *was* a good man, despite his faults. Too good for her.

Tom nodded soberly. "You know I'd do anything for you, Katie."

"Not too grand to give me a hug, I hope?" Katie said, holding out her arms.

The boy felt too thin, his bony shoulders sharp, but she told herself he was safe now. Safe from the depredations of animals like Lyme, and safe from the dank horrors of a prison hulk.

"All right, then," he said gruffly, pulling away and clearing his throat. "I'd best be off, but don't you worry none, Katie. Tom Finch is keepin' watch over you, and Tom Finch is a gentleman what don't forget his obligations."

"Thank you, Tom, I feel better knowing that," she said.

"Right then." He slung one skinny leg over the windowsill, looking out for the broken glass.

"Oh, Tom?" Katie called out to him before he could lower himself to the stone courtyard.

"Yes, Katie?" he said.

"Remember not to let Lord Brynston see you. He's bound to ask all sorts of questions if he recognizes you from London."

Tom looked disgusted. "What kind of goosecap do you take me for? His lordship won't see me. He won't even see me shadow."

Katie let out her breath in relief. "Thanks, Tom."

And in a moment, he had shinnied down the drainpipe, landed lightly in the courtyard, and was gone.

* * *

Julius had taken his tea to his study to review Willowby Hall's accounts in peace, but as he placed the stack of ledgers on his desk, his younger brother appeared in the door frame.

"Toiling in the vineyards, eh brother?" Val asked, strolling to the desk and rifling casually through the big account books.

Julius resisted the temptation to slap Val's hand away, removing it instead with his own, as one would pick up and eject a dead mouse. "I know it must be trying, Val, having nothing to do all day but lie about the house, but do try to keep your paws off the estate papers."

"You don't know, you really don't!" Val protested. "I suppose you think it's nothing but routs and deep play, the life of a younger brother. Well, it ain't, I'm telling you. Damned difficult to keep up any sense of the meaning of one's life. I'm seriously considering taking up a profession."

"Splendid idea, the very thing to turn you from a rowdy pup to something resembling a man," Julius said dryly.

Val made a face. "Of course, I shouldn't care to have people say the Willowby estate couldn't support one paltry younger brother. People might think we were wanting for the ready, that we had to scramble."

"I doubt anyone would think that," Julius said blandly. "Besides, you've forgotten Tibby. That makes two paltry younger brothers."

Val shuddered. "Tibby's not a brother, he's a . . . some kind of family curse."

Julius smiled. "True enough. Rather reminds me of you at that age. Perhaps we should drown him now."

"I wish you would. The runt poured a pint of treacle into my new boots last week. I'd only worn them twice."

"He's teaching you the dangers of vanity," Julius said, amused.

"He's teaching me the temptations of fratricide," Val corrected. "Or he would be, if I could catch him. Quick little chap."

"Did you have something you wanted to discuss with me, Val?" Julius asked. "Because otherwise . . . " He gestured to the tower of ledgers on his desk.

"Just making conversation," Val said, easing into an armchair. "Furthering brotherly harmony and all that." He studied his fingernails, then fiddled with the buttons on his waistcoat.

"I see," said Julius, deciding he would simply have to be patient until Val worked up the courage to spit it out, whatever it was he had come here to say.

"I must say that Katie—" Val began.

Ah, so that was it. "Spare your breath, Valentine. I'm in no humor to hear what an ogre I've been to my wife. She will accustom herself to life here well enough, it's not such a hardship as all that."

Val looked startled, then swallowed twice. "Oh, no! Not at all, brother. I wouldn't dream of interfering between you and your wife."

Julius raised an eyebrow. "Wouldn't you?"

Val sniffed and took out his pocket watch. "Of course not."

"If you're not planning on interfering, then what did you come here to talk about?" Julius asked, becoming a trifle impatient.

Val studied his watch carefully, bringing it to his ear with every twist as he wound it. "She's been giving Milvia a tolerable run for her money lately," he said. "Rosie said she frightened her clear out of the house this afternoon."

"I daresay she did," Julius agreed. "Katie has her strengths, and dealing with difficult people is one of them."

"Bit hard on old Mil, though, ain't it?" Val mused.

"Milvia has been more than a bit hard on Katie. I'd say she got what she deserved."

"Still," Val said, avoiding Julius's eyes, "you can see her point. Mil's, I mean. She's bound to be hipped."

"Milvia has behaved abominably since we arrived," Julius said flatly. "I would have credited her with more sense. And better manners."

Val shrugged. "She's disappointed. What woman wouldn't be? We all thought you were to marry."

Julius felt a tic that betrayed his impatience. "I know what you all thought, and it can't be helped. I hadn't offered for her, as you know very well."

"But she was waiting for you," Val pressed. "You as much as implied that you were *about* to offer for her."

Julius shut his eyes and counted to ten for patience. "Milvia Trowsedale may be an old friend, but she is not a member of this family. My first duty is to the Willowbys, and it was to preserve the honor of that name and the title that I married Katie Feathering. If Milvia can't understand that then it's just as well I didn't marry her, she would never have made a countess."

"And Katie will?"

Julius turned a lethal glare on his brother. "What do you mean by that question?"

Val lost his nerve for a moment, his gaze fluttering down to his feet, but he raised it again to meet his brother's. "She did throw all of her furniture out the window," he said, by way of explanation.

Julius snorted dismissively. "Fit of pique. Perfectly natural in a new bride."

"Is it? I was under the impression that she couldn't bear the sight of you, that she would rather perish than submit to your will."

Julius felt a painful twinge, which he repressed. "Her father has calmed her down nicely, if you will notice. She will learn to do as she is told, and all will go very well."

"Will she? I wonder, Julius. Tell me, is she truly your wife? In every sense? I'd wager a hundred guineas she'd never been touched, by you or anyone else."

Julius slammed the ledger shut and pinned Val with his eyes as he would pin a fencing opponent into a corner. "Damn it, Val, you go too far," he said, his voice lethally quiet. "Do not think that just because you are my brother, I won't call you out. You will refrain from making insulting speculations about my wife, and you will consider yourself as bound to respect her as you would any countess in England. Do I make myself perfectly clear?"

Val blanched. "Of course, naturally, I meant no offense," he stammered. "She's a lovely girl, I think the world of her."

"Very well," Julius said, opening the ledger again. "Now, if you haven't any other offensive insinuations to make, I have a great deal of work to do."

Val stretched and yawned. "Ah, yes, I can see that," he said. He stood and made to go, brushing a speck of lint from his inexpressibles. "Er, Julius?"

Julius raised his gaze with slow deliberation. "Yes, Val?"

"You're making the tour of the estates next week, aren't you? Galloping about finding out who in the village needs blankets, making sure the mill's in order, that sort of thing?"

"Yes," Julius said, nodding. "Katie will tend to the tenants' needs when she has learned her duties, but until then I'll continue as I have always done. Why?"

"D'you think you might take me with you?"

"Take you with me? Whatever for? You'll be a monstrous nuisance."

Val looked put out. "I say, that's putting it a bit strong. I just want to help."

"You've never wanted to help a day in your life, why start now?"

Val shrugged. "You work too hard, everyone here can see that. And it'll be some time before Katie is—" Val cleared his throat, looking at a loss for words. "Before Katie is ready to assume her duties as countess."

Julius scanned his brother's face, looking for the lie. It was there, somewhere. He could sense it, but he couldn't begin to guess at the reason for it. "I start at seven. If you are late, I will leave without you."

"Good God—couldn't you make it eight? Nine would be better."

"Seven," Julius said flatly. "If you'd rather sleep in, go right ahead. I'll manage without you." He tried to speak the words without excessive sarcasm.

"Right," Val said, taking a deep breath as if steeling himself for battle. "Seven o'clock sharp. I'll be there, brother."

"Suit yourself," Julius said, watching with mixed suspicion and amazement as his brother strode confidently out the door.

22

The earl of Brynston was not the sort of man to tolerate flightiness, in himself or in anyone he might rely on. But after Val left he found that the figures in his account books danced and flitted like sparrows. He could not add a column of figures to come out the same way twice, and the more he tried to apply himself, the farther afield his mind skipped.

His mind grew no clearer during dinner, when he was chiefly occupied with keeping Rosalind and Tibby from starting a small-scale war. Titania was almost as bad as the children, and at one point Julius had to threaten her grievously to keep her from jettisoning a spoonful of peas at Val.

He went to bed that night with a peculiar heaviness in his stomach, and when he awoke the next day it was worse. When he should have been reviewing his agent's plans for next year's planting, he found himself thinking of wild green eyes. And when he should have been reading the morning paper to sort out Schwartzenberg's progress against Paris, he found himself musing about whether his wife's hair was more the color of a tawny port or vintage sherry.

He finally gave it up, sighing and setting the newspaper aside on his desk. He stood to look out the window, his hands braced on the sill. Spring was beginning to thaw the winter landscape, the snow drifts melting back to the shadows, and the first shoots of green beginning to warm the dark earth. Another spring at Willowby Hall, a new beginning.

A new beginning as a married man.

Julius shut his eyes against it for a moment. Married. Shackled to a hoyden who seemed to thrive on defying him. What had made him think he could tame the wilderness in her eyes? A fox kit would have made him a better countess than this untamed little American.

He sighed and stood straight. It had been his own hammer-headed stubbornness that had got him into this mess, and he would use the same to repair the damage. The countess Katie *would* learn her duties, and she would carry them out with all the grace and delicacy the title demanded.

He took himself quickly to her rooms, not wanting to give himself time to make excuses. He rapped sharply at the door.

"Come in," she said.

When he saw her he nearly forgot why he had come. She was curled in a settee near the window, all but buried in an enormous green wool shawl. She had chosen it for warmth, not style, and indeed it was far sturdier than the filmy, fashionable draperies à la mode in London. But it suited her, making her look like some timid elf-child, and the color sweetly echoed the woodland green of her eyes.

The brute Manners was with her, standing against the wall like a guard. The forked white scar on his cheek stood out clearly in the morning light.

"Yes, my lord?" she said, standing and pulling the shawl around her as if it were an amulet against him.

Julius cleared his throat. "If it is not inconvenient, I believe it is time for another lesson."

"Lesson?" she asked. "Ah yes, the transformation of an American sow's ear into a good English silk purse."

"I have no hopes of making you English," he pointed out.

"But you do cherish some faint hope of making me civilized," she said.

Brynston found himself smiling. "A glimmer of hope, yes."

She returned his smile shyly. "Only a glimmer? Surely you have more confidence in your skills than that, my lord."

"Should I stay, Katie?" Manners said, his voice a menacing rumble.

Katie smiled at the man and gave his hand a squeeze. It was uncanny—the brute Manners would have given any halfway impressionable child nightmares, but Katie seemed to think of him as more indulgent uncle than hired assassin. "No, Alex, you can go. Why don't you see if Hannah would like some company? She's making some alterations to the gowns Portia lent me, it can't be very interesting for her."

"I'll be in the sewing closet," he said, casting a meaningful look at Brynston. "It's within easy earshot, if you should need me." He bowed stiffly in Brynston's direction and was gone.

"Imposing brute, isn't he?" Julius asked, when he was gone.

"Alex? He's a silly old mother bear, and I wish he wouldn't hover so. He never does anything to amuse himself unless I strictly order him to. Now then, my lord, what shall our lesson be today?"

"I do wish you would call me Julius," he said, wanting suddenly to touch her. Wanting to brush aside the expanse of green shawl, the modest wool dress, the flannel underthings he knew she would wear beneath. Wanting to see just what this wild fairy child was hiding, after all.

She must have read the hunger in his eyes, for she brought her arms to her chest like a shield. "Julius, then."

He reined his reaction to her. It was stupid to frighten her, it would do nothing to further his own ends. "May I come in?"

She nodded.

"I see the servants have made your accommodations more, ah, comfortable," he said. The room now had two chairs, a small table, and a writing desk, and thick blankets hung behind the curtains over the window, billowing faintly in the wind.

She nodded. "The only thing they haven't managed is the windows—the glazier's ill with fever. They've sent to York for another."

"Don't you get cold?"

She shook her head no, and pulled her shawl up around her shoulders. "I'm very comfortable."

He looked down at her feet, which were bare. Tiny and sweetly formed, like the rest of her. He thought of what it would feel like to rest his hand on her cool ankle, to slide it up her bare leg.

He frowned, flustered. "My sister must have a pair of slippers she could lend you, Katie. You'll catch your death. I won't have you making a widower of me before I'm truly a husband."

Her breath caught in her throat at that, and he looked up into her eyes. She looked lost, but not exactly frightened. He was caught by ancient instinct, the instinct a hound feels when he catches the scent of a rabbit. *Chase her.*

"I tell you, I am not cold, my lord. I can feel the spring in the air already. And the fire takes the edge off the chill."

He leashed his control, fighting the blood that pounded in him, that impelled him to forget reason, to forget civilization and society and foolish promises. He knew just where the ravening scent of blood would lead him, what would happen if he gave in to the instinct that screamed in him now. *Take her.* He would lose all reason, this hunger would devour him whole. *Take her, damn you. Take her.* It had happened before.

It would not happen again. He stepped abruptly away from her, turning to face the blankets over the windows. "Yes, I can see now, they look quite—substantial. Very warm indeed, I must commend whoever thought of it."

"Lizzie Hamp," Katie said, sounding puzzled.

"I beg your pardon?" Julius counted silently to ten, over and over, as he crushed every trace of feeling with the practice of long years. Repress desire, repress tenderness. Repress . . . love?

"Lizzie Hamp, she's one of the cottagers. Or she used to be, she's a house parlor maid now. Surely you know her—the one with the gap between her front teeth."

Julius could feel the mask of self-control settle over his features once again, and he turned back to his wife. "Ah yes, Lizzie. Clever girl. I'll see that she gets a little something extra this quarter."

Katie nodded, seeming puzzled. "You're generous with your servants."

He blinked. "But not with my wife?"

"I didn't mean that."

He shrugged. "Perhaps I am disturbing you. I will come again another day."

"No—don't," Katie said, then bit her lower lip.

Julius raised one eyebrow.

"I was . . . lonely." The words seemed to escape her mouth without her wanting them to, and she looked down at her bare feet.

"I thought your Mr. Manners was keeping you company."

Katie smiled weakly. "He does, but he drives me to distraction if we spend too much time together. He's always nagging me about being sure I get enough to eat, and am I keeping warm enough." She broke off with a blush, perhaps remembering Julius's own concern for her bare feet.

"And my sisters? Do not tell me they have been less than friendly company to you—"

Katie shook her head. "They have been nothing but kind and welcoming. Your family is wonderful, my lord—Julius."

He felt suddenly warm, hearing his name come from her lips. He coughed in his hand to cover any color that came to his face. "They ought to be locked up," he said gruffly. "I asked Prinny to have the lot of them beheaded, but he seems to find them amusing."

Katie grinned. "I'm glad to hear there are a few limits to what a rich English earl may and may not do."

Julius found himself returning her smile. "A few."

Katie smoothed her shawl and squared her shoulders. "I'm ready for my lesson, my lord."

"I really must insist you put on at least a pair of slippers," he said, not wanting to look at the tiny bare feet again, not wanting to think about the delicacy of her bones, the curve of her instep.

"Yes, my lord." She scurried to her dressing room to find a pair of slippers.

"How do you feel about a royal visit?" Julius called to her, picking up the novel on her table. Some ghastly tale of fashionable society one of his sisters had brought into the house, no doubt.

"You mean, today?" Katie's head popped out of her dressing room, covered in a huge muslin mob cap. "That sounds like the very thing."

"Why, if I may ask, are you wearing that hideous object?"

"In my day," Katie intoned, dropping into a priggish mezzo-soprano, "No respectable young lady would have appeared before a *gentleman*—" At that she gave Julius a long, quizzing stare, "—without her head *decently* covered."

"In your day," Julius repeated, smiling. "And when, if I might ask, would that have been?"

Katie stepped out of her dressing room, bright silk fan in one hand, and she rapped him hard across the shoulder with it. "Impertinent fellow!" she said. "It is beyond disagreeable to demand hints about a lady's age."

"Forgive me madame—I was bedazzled by the delicate flush of youth that creeps across your cheek. And yet, if I am not mistaken, your wisdom is far too great for some schoolroom chit."

Katie dropped her eyelashes and raised her chin. She gave Julius another powerful bat with the fan. "Trifler!" she cried with a horrid giggle. "You flirt with all the ladies so, do not attempt to deny it for I have seen it with my own eyes."

"I have tried in vain to distract myself with other, lesser beauties, my lady, but I find that I cannot."

Katie snorted at that, and broke her pose. "Oh, you really are too much. *Tried in vain* my eye. Who would believe that?"

"You'd be surprised," Julius said with a grin. "Anyway, I can't believe you of all people accuse me of being *de trop*."

"You are, though," she said, looking up at him thoughtfully. "Entirely *de trop*, my lord."

"Julius."

"Julius," she agreed, her voice soft.

Kiss her, his blood urged, but he fought it. Her eyes were sparkling and warm with laughter, and he would not chase that from her now.

"Are you ready?"

"I am," Katie said, adjusting the ridiculous cap.

Julius shut his eyes and mentally transformed himself into a swaggering, pompous, spoiled child in a man's over-stuffed body. "I say, Lady Brynston," he said, when he was ready. "Marvelous what you've done with Willowby Hall, what? That painting's new, ain't it?" Julius mimed a peer through a quizzing glass. "Looks like a Titian."

Katie laid her hand prettily on Julius's elbow, guiding him to the sofa. "I'm afraid I couldn't tell a Titian from a Turner, your royal highness, but I *do* think it's awfully pretty. Is it an *important* painting?" She settled herself in the chair opposite him, hanging on his every word.

Julius felt a bit taken aback to be staring into those

huge green eyes. They were like a thicket, ready to swallow him up in brambles and the perfume of spice and wild roses. He coughed to cover his discomfort, and peered again through the imaginary quizzing glass. "Ehhh—" he said, with the air of a man accustomed to speaking without interruption, "I daresay the subject is not altogether an unusual one." He squinted at the painting with a discerning eye. "But the—ehhh—brush strokes, you see, and the composition—there, you see the chiaroscuro, in the corner? Prettily done, stap me if it ain't. And a Titian, you know," he said, turning his quizzing eye on Katie, "is always—ehhh—a Titian."

"You are so very wise on so many subjects, your royal highness," Katie said, sounding perfectly serious. "I do not see how you can find the time, with all the demands the monarchy must press upon you."

Julius eased back in his chair with the air of a very lazy, very fat cat. "Bless you, child, you cannot imagine the—ehhh—pressures placed upon me. Now that we have that upstart little French mongrel on the run—" he paused to allow himself a dyspeptic-sounding chuckle, "—we may begin the process of rebuilding this great nation so that it may become—ehhh . . . " He looked at a loss for a moment. "Ever greater!" he said, brightening.

"And yet, with all that rests on your shoulders, you find time for art and refinement."

Julius gave her a positively greasy smile. "Life should be unbearably tedious, my dear, if one did not partake in the occasional—ehhh—pleasure."

Katie laughed and fanned herself. "Oh, your royal highness, such a wit!"

Julius broke his pose. "He didn't say anything witty."

Katie blinked. "He hasn't said anything remotely interesting since he's been here," she said pointedly.

"Well, of course he hasn't, he's the Prince Regent."

"He's a crashing bore," Katie said.

"Well, you'd never know it to watch you," Julius said, disgruntled.

Katie leaned back in her chair, visibly amused. "What do you mean?"

"Just because he's a prince doesn't mean you have to throw yourself at the man."

Katie laughed. "I wasn't throwing myself at him, I was flattering him with my attention. There's a difference."

"Not the way you do it, there isn't," Julius said. "That thing you do—with your eyes—it's indecent. Don't do it any more."

Katie smiled, then bit her lower lip to hide it. "Don't tell me you're jealous of the Prince, my lord."

"Of course not, don't be ridiculous. Anyway everyone knows he prefers mutton over lamb."

Katie raised an eyebrow. "So I'd heard."

"Anyway, the Prince isn't here. It's only me, it was just a game," Julius said, feeling like a prize-winning ass.

"That's right," Katie nodded.

"We can have that lesson later," Julius decided. "The Prince has only come to Willowby Hall twice since he became Regent. We will have opportunity to practice this later should the need arise."

Katie looked into her lap, and spread her fan to conceal what Julius thought might very well be a giggle.

"Are you laughing at him, or me?" he growled.

She peeped out at him from over the fan. "Neither, my lord."

"Julius."

"Julius," she agreed, straightening and fanning herself. "Very well then, if you don't care to play-act the Prince, what will you do?"

"We shall review the correct demeanor for dealing with servants," Julius said, glad to get the matter in hand again. "Now then, suppose you have a parlor maid who has allowed her appearance to become slatternly."

"You mean like this?" Katie thrust one shoulder forward, lowered her eyelids, and jutted her lower lip in a pout.

"Don't do that, Katie, it makes you look like a half-witted harlot."

Katie broke the pose, indignant. "Half-witted? She was supposed to be drunk."

"I suppose most of us are half-witted when we're drunk. Are you ready to be serious now?"

Katie sat up straight and fixed her cap. "I am, my lord. Julius. Sorry."

"Very good." He stood, and motioned for her to do the same. "I will be the slatternly maidservant, and you shall chastise me."

Katie bit her lip, but she said nothing, only nodding.

Julius assumed a pose something like Katie's own, but with, he hoped, a bit more dignity.

Katie took a deep breath. "Now then, Brunhilde, it has come to my attention—"

Julius interrupted her. "Brunhilde? That's ludicrous, we would never hire a maidservant named Brunhilde."

"You'd never hire a maidservant over six foot tall who thumped around the house in Hessians, either," Katie said, her eyes alight with mischief.

Julius frowned. "Very well then. But I will thank you to take this seriously, wife."

"I do, husband, I do," she said soberly.

He reassumed his pose. "I don't know what you mean, mum, I'm sure. At my last position my demeanor was spoke of in the 'ighest regard."

"Yes, Brunhilde, but your last position was with Lady Cowflop, and we both know very well what kind of a household *she* runs."

Julius gave her a warning look. "I ain't done owt wrong, mum, an' you can't say as I 'ave."

"You have done nothing wrong, Brunhilde, but your skirts are torn, your bodice is much too low, and you are severely in want of a shave."

Julius turned his warning look to a full icy scowl.

"And furthermore, your expression would make the fattest pig in Yorkshire go off his feed," Katie said, her tone silvery and composed. "Now then, if you wish to remain in my employ, you will clean your fingernails, wipe your muddy boots before you come in the house, and desist from wearing my husband's cravats. Do I make myself clear, Brunhilde?"

Julius felt the corner of his mouth twitch into a smile, but he repressed it. "Oh my lady, my lady, you maun nay turn me out! I've got me old crippled mother to feed, and seventeen little brothers and sisters, and if you turn me out we'll 'ave nothin' to eat but the grass in the fields."

"Understand me, girl," Katie said, her light eyes fierce as her voice deepened to the darkest baritone she could manage. "If I catch you or your family grazing in my fields without permission, I will have you clapped in irons and the lot of you hanged, and then fed to the hogs without benefit of Christian burial. Do I make my meaning perfectly clear?"

"You're awfully 'ard, me lady," Julius squeaked.

"If I am hard, it is because honor requires it of me, child. Do not question your betters, and do not speak any word of reproach, and while you are about it, do not look at me with those pitiful cow's eyes or I'll have you thrashed."

Julius stiffened in protest. "That is entirely unfair. I am not like that."

Katie grinned. "I see you recognize the portrait. It wasn't mockery, it was homage."

"You make me sound like an unbending arrogant brute."

"Perhaps." Katie shrugged.

"Damn it, woman, there are days when I could throttle you. You don't know the first thing about me, and yet—"

He broke off, because Katie looked as if she were ready to burst into a gale of giggles.

He smiled sheepishly. "I suppose I can be a bit of a brute, sometimes."

"Once in a very great while," Katie said, repressing a grin.

"It's not as if you don't give me cause, wife," he said, but his tone was gentle.

"No, my lord—Julius. It's not."

"I suppose you think you are very clever," he said, moving toward her, wanting suddenly touch her cheek, to feel if the roses there were warm or cool.

She scooted nervously past him toward the window. "I think nothing of the kind, my lord."

He turned and trapped her there, between his body and the faint chill of the blanket-covered windows. "If you were in my shoes, what do you think you would do, Katie?" He gave in to his impulse, and stroked her cheek with the back of his hand, lightly, very lightly. She was warm, and her cheek flushed bright.

"I think I should probably trip and fall, husband. Your shoes are a good measure too big for me."

"You are trying to distract me," he said, refusing to be distracted. He brushed a strand of hair from her forehead. She had silky hair, soft as a child's, and as unruly. At the moment, he was finding the little curly wisps that stroked her face as seductive as the most elegant coiffure at Almack's. More seductive. She was fresh, alluring.

"In your place," she said, her voice very small, "I would turn me away. I have no place here, Julius."

"I disagree." He brought his thumb gently down to trace the outline of her ear. His breathing was beginning to quicken, and so, he noted with satisfaction, was hers.

"I am—" She took a deep, shuddering breath. "I am not good enough for you, Julius. That is the truth."

"You are an idiot," he said softly, cupping the sweet curve of her jaw in his hand, tipping her mouth up to meet his own. "But an exceptionally sweet one."

The touch of their lips was like a spark flying into kindling. His desire burst forth with a heat and a fury that surprised him. He banked it, pulled back from her an instant to quell his own hunger, then brought his mouth down on hers again. She was his wife, and the knowledge burned him like a brand. She was his wife, and to give way to him was only her proper place.

Take her. Take her! His blood screamed in his ears,

but he fought it, forcing himself to make love only to her mouth, her sweet rosebud of a mouth, to stroke and coax her to willingness with the touch of his lips. Her perfume, the faint scent of spice and roses, drove him half out of his mind. With his tongue he parted her, and with his tongue he teased hers, probing, demanding.

His blood quickened as he passed his hand possessively over her, over the ripe tautness of her flesh and the tender dip of her lower back. His hands explored her as if the kerseymere gown did not exist. She was new territory to be marked out and explored, and she was *his*.

Her tongue darted away from him, then came round again, with all the questioning sweetness of innocence.

He broke roughly away from her, murmuring into her mouth, "I want to devour you, Katie. Every inch of you."

"You do devour me. There will be nothing left, when you are done."

He pulled away from her, checking his hunger. It would not do to plunder his new bride. Instead he would coax her, tempt her, seduce her with all the slow sweetness befitting a countess. "Do I still frighten you? And you the bravest American hellion these English shores have ever seen."

The green eyes shone moss-wet with tears. "My lord, you terrify me."

The words were like a pail of icy water, and he took her by the shoulders, pressing her to arm's length.

"Why, Katie? Why should you be so frightened? I know I have treated you ill, but I promise you, I swear it on my honor, you will not regret your life here as my countess. You can be happy here, Katie, if you will only let yourself be."

"I am—I am not ready for . . . this." The answering sparks in her own eyes told him what she meant.

"You are unhappy, madame?" he asked, his voice colder than he had intended.

Her eyes, those eyes the precise color of a meadow on midsummer's day, registered the pain she felt at his words. "You frighten me," she said again.

"I am sorry, I did not realize," he said stiffly, clamping down on the last vestiges of his desire. "You did not behave like a frightened woman."

She paled visibly, and he was sorry he had said it. He'd made her sound like a wanton, when he'd meant only that she'd kissed him as . . . as a bride kisses her husband.

"This is all too soon, too sudden," she stammered. "Please . . . " She left the last word there to float on the air.

"You think I am some drunken sailor tipping an alehouse wench?" he asked, suddenly angry. "Should I force you, would that make me live up to your expectations?"

She shook her head. Her face was smooth, almost impassive, but the green eyes were wild with fear. "I trust you will not behave so dishonorably, my lord."

An ugly oath formed in his throat, but he swallowed it. "A husband does not dishonor his wife by taking his pleasure of her."

"I am not your wife," Katie said. "I have never consented to this marriage."

"But you will," he said, regaining control of his temper. "Your demeanor in these past days proves that."

"Do not let yourself be hurt by false expectations," she said, and for a moment her eyes gentled.

He found himself smiling down at her. "I appreciate your concern, countess, but it is ill-placed. You will consent to this marriage, you will be a proper wife to me and a proper countess for Willowby Hall."

"I can't," she said simply.

"Do not be contrary, it ill becomes you," he said. He took her chin in his hand. "Katie, listen to me."

Her gaze tried to slide away from his, but drifted up again, as if caught by some inexorable tide. "I always listen to you, my lord."

"Julius," he corrected.

"Julius," she said, and her eyes darkened softly at the word, as if brushed by twilight.

"You are my wife now, a Willowby. Do you know what that means?"

Her gaze slid away from his. "What?"

"It means," he said gently, "that you are one of my family. I do not allow my family to come to harm, at anyone's hands. I will protect you as long as you draw breath, or die in the effort."

She looked at him again, and pulled lightly free of his grasp. "I never asked for your protection."

"I never asked to be the earl of Brynston," he replied. "We do not live in a world in which we choose our fates. I'm sorry yours has caused you distress, but I swear to you I will not add to it."

"It's your blasted stubbornness that condemns me to this fate, nothing more."

There it was, a hint of the old snap. He was glad to see it in her.

He shook his head. "I've told you, I protect my family. You cheated Val, and you cheated me. I could not permit that. You've made your bed, pretty Katie, and now you must learn to lie in it."

The terror in her eyes flared. "No—I can't—"

He shut his eyes, cursing himself for a fool. "I'm sorry, a poor choice of words. Katie, I will not force you to my bed."

She took a wary step away from him. "You won't?"

"Of course not."

"Will you give me your word?"

He made a disgusted sound. "I do not lie, wife. Anything I tell you you may consider as my bond. But if it will make you feel better, yes, I give you my word. We will not consummate this marriage without your consent."

Her eyes warmed as she relaxed, but her voice was still cool as she said, "Thank you, Julius. I am glad to see you agree to be a gentleman about this."

"You have a high opinion of gentlemen, sweeting. Most would have left you deflowered and weeping back in the flash house."

She looked as shattered as if he had struck her to the ground.

"I'm sorry," he said quickly. "That was coarse and unkind. Forgive me."

"Of course," she murmured. "But I am very tired. I should like to rest until dinner, if I may."

"Of course," he said. "Forgive me for overtaxing you." He moved quickly to her and kissed her lightly on the cheek, before she could have time to be frightened, and then he walked briskly to the door. "Good day, Katie. I will see you at dinner."

"Good day, Julius," she said with a distracted, distant smile, closing the door behind him.

23

It took every scrap of Katie's will not to sink to the floor and give in to sobs. She was trapped here, with no place to hide, no place to run. She had finagled, tricked, or lied her way out of dozens of tight spots, but she could not see an escape route out of her marriage to the Brimstone Earl. He was too stubborn to let her go, and he saw through every lie she'd told him. Every one except the cursed one that had led him to think he had to marry her.

She went to the dressing room to wash her face, washing away his light touch on her jaw, the heat of his kiss. He was entangling her, drawing her into a web she could not fight her way free of.

As she dried her face, she thought of his words. *You are one of my family. I will protect you as long as you draw breath.* She had never heard anyone say such things. To Katie, family was an accident of birth, a loose collection of co-conspirators who helped each other when they could, but didn't worry overmuch when they couldn't. Her childhood had taught her how to take care of herself, and she was grateful for that. It was stupidity to expect anyone to shield one from harm—that was for pigeons, people whose soft lives allowed them to be weak.

Setting the linen towel aside, Katie trailed a finger along the pale painted dado of the pretty dressing room, tracing a line from the lacy peignoir hanging from a hook by the tub to the translucent porcelain ewer. This was what Brynston was trying to do to her—make her delicate and fragile, as a proper lady was supposed to be. But Katie was a tougher bird than that, and the silks and laces of this place would not be enough to make her soft. All she had to do was to survive a little longer in this place, and then Willowby Hall and all temptation to softness and luxury would be behind her.

She thought of summoning Alex, of confiding her fears to him. For all her determination, she was afraid of what Brynston might do with his kisses and his caresses and the warm possessive thrill of his voice. She was afraid of what she wanted him to do.

She absolutely could not talk to Alex about this, she realized. The very idea left her strangely mortified. Somehow she would pull her feelings together. Alex had sent word on ahead to the men in Marseilles. They would give the letter a week's head start, then somehow follow it. They would find a way. They had to.

And when they left, Katie would put Brynston behind her forever. She was who she was—Katie Starr, street rat and sharper extraordinaire. No one in the world could change that, not even the Brimstone Earl.

A few minutes before midnight that night, Phineas Starr felt the unmistakable rumble in his belly that told him he needed to be fed. Dinner had been a pleasantly extravagant affair—the chocolate *pots de creme* had been especially tasty—but that had been hours ago, and Phineas was not a man to go for hours at a time without replenishment.

It was too late to ring, there would be no one left in the servants' hall. Phineas slipped on a violet silk dressing

gown, cadged from Brynston and therefore a trifle small
in the waist and long around the calves, and crept out of
his comfortable room and down the hallway.

The candles were still lit, expensive beeswax burned as
carelessly as if it were the cheapest tallow. Phineas nodded approvingly, padding down the hallway and noting
the heavy gilt frames on the pictures that crammed the
walls. Katie had a nose for wealth, like a bloodhound, and
she had turned up a proper gold mine this time. She was
shying a bit at the notion of really slipping the noose
around that blasted earl, but she'd come around. She
always had before.

The house, which had been bustling all day with the
murmur of servants and the laughter of Brynston's hell-
born family, was silent now. Phineas could hear the faint
ticking of a clock, and that was all.

The sixth door from Phineas's room had been left an
inch or two ajar. This was Brynston's private study,
Phineas knew, for he had heard the earl and his brother
arguing there the other day. The door was thick and
solid, so that he had been obliged to press his ear firmly
against it to hear what was being said.

Phineas would have to watch that Val, he was cleverer
than he seemed. He'd played the devil's advocate and
tricked Brynston into defending Katie as vehemently as
he had once cursed her. The Willowbys showed a touching desire to make Katie part of their family. They would
be disappointed, of course, but it was a sweet sentiment.

Phineas cleared his throat now to warn anyone who
might hear him that he was wandering about. For some
reason people often suspected Phineas of sneaking up on
them. He thought Brynston might be apt to be especially
touchy on the subject.

There was no stir from the room, not the faint dry rus-
tle of paper or the soft creak of an old chair. Nothing.
Phineas cleared his throat again, in a soft but distinctly
audible *ahem*. Still nothing.

He stretched up on his toes to wrest a candle from a

sconce, cursing softly as the hot wax spilled over his fingers. Holding it out in front of him like a torch, he rapped gently on the door, thinking perhaps that Brynston had fallen asleep over his desk. The man was not sharing a bed with Katie, though surely he meant to eventually. The thought made Phineas squirm inwardly a little, and so he squelched it.

The study was empty, left open, perhaps, by a careless servant. Phineas shut the door quietly behind him, lit the lamp on the desk, and blew out the candle. This was a rare opportunity. He had tried the door several times, when no one was looking, and it had always been locked.

That was the advantage, Phineas mused as he picked the desk lock, of taking one's servants from the criminal classes. Being waited on by thieves and card sharps was not always comfortable, but it kept one's wits honed. While another household worried about the cook stealing a few capons, Phineas knew for a fact that his servants would pick him clean as an old skeleton if he relaxed his guard for an instant. He found an odd comfort in the knowledge.

Brynston's papers seemed at first glance as dull and deadly serious as the earl himself. No packets of pornographic etchings, no letters hinting at dark scandals. Phineas had hoped to find some record of debts owed, given the prodigious sum the earl had dropped in Katie's lap, but the thirty thousand Brynston had lost to her seemed his only foray into deep play.

Phineas rifled through ribbon-tied stacks of letters with practiced hands. There were some promising-looking old ones, still carrying a faint whiff of scent, but they'd turned out to be from Brynston's mother, and were full of dreary platitudes about the duties of the title and other similar balderdash.

Finally, tucked into the very back of the drawer, he found a packet tied with a dark red ribbon. These, too, were scented, their perfume both lighter and more seductive than the previous. Smeared across the top letter of the stack was an ugly inkblot, marring the creamy paper like a bruise.

Phineas made note of the elegant handwriting, the charming slight quirk to the ps and qs. "Julius, my own darling love," he read silently at the top of the first letter.

Now that was more like it. Phineas read through the letter quickly. There seemed no hint of scandal anywhere to be found in it. The writer, an apparently vapid, wildly smitten young lady named Josephine Cargill, went on at length about Willowby's myriad perfections, settling mostly on the span of his manly shoulders and the gentlemanly way he controlled his baser passions.

"Even then you were a bore, Brynston," Phineas muttered, thinking that Willowby would have done much better to sample the wares before agreeing to buy. Because this Jo had clearly been panting for him.

Phineas scowled at the stupidity of a world that placed such high value on trifles such as height and broad shoulders. These were simple tricks of fate—any dolt could tower above a girl like some kind of elm tree. But cleverness, wisdom, subtlety—these were things honed over time, becoming sharper and sweeter with every year. Phineas prided himself that he had developed these qualities in spades. And the young Julius Willowby had not seemed to possess them in any great degree.

A thought crossed Phineas's mind—why should Brynston still have the letters in his possession? He had not married the girl, Katie had been Brynston's first bride. The right thing to do would have been to return the letters when they had parted, and Brynston seemed addicted to doing the right thing.

Except that business about abducting Katie, of course. Phineas wrinkled his forehead, puzzled, and read on. Perhaps something in one of these letters would make sense of things.

It was hard to say when Phineas began to suspect that Jo was a member of his own criminal tribe, but by the tenth letter he was sure of it. She was not vapid, as he had earlier assumed, but calculating, stroking Brynston's vanity with practiced ease. She had begun to pry presents out of him—expensive presents, and twice she made mention of borrowing against her own dowry, and would Brynston please be so kind as to guarantee her debtors would get the money back again when they married. It was just as well Brynston had never married the baggage, or she would surely have cleaned him out of every penny. And then where would Phineas and Katie be?

Phineas felt a paternal swell of pride, that his little champion had been able to take Brynston while this Jo creature, clever and tricky though she might be, had not.

But it was clear from Jo's letters that she had led young Willowby a fair way down the road to ruin. He had taken up gambling in earnest, winning more often than not, but staking sums high enough to cause his thrill-seeking fiancée to clap with glee.

"Here we go," Phineas murmured, reading the final letter in the stack. It was in a different hand than the others, and bore no sign of feminine elegance.

Dear John—

It pains me to have to break such distasteful news to you, and to do so at a distance, in the impersonality of a note. There are no words I can use to soften the blow, so I will come out and tell you that Miss Josephine Cargill has been apprehended selling information to an agent of the French government. This information can only have come from your household. I know your son, Julius, considers himself affianced to this creature. He must be warned at the earliest opportunity that Miss Cargill is nothing better than a French spy, and that he must consider himself in no wise bound to her. She is, in fact, married to a French citoyen, and has three children by the man. May God have mercy on them, as they will not know their mother's love for some years, if ever again. At this moment we have the woman in our custody; we have not yet determined what is to be done with her. Fippingsworth is all for having her hanged, but the king finds the idea distasteful.

It will be to our advantage if you should come down to London with your son, and reconstruct any vital information this creature may have apprehended while taking advantage of your hospitality. Bear in mind that she is well versed in the picking of locks and other secretive measures, and may therefore have laid her unworthy and treasonous hands on such items you would not have shared even with trusted family members.

I hope that Julius will not be overset by this wretched business, and pray that he may find another more wholesome Englishwoman with whom to share his life and his title.

> *Your old friend,*
> *Ld. William Castlingdon*

Phineas whistled softly as he rocked back in his seat. Well, well. So pretty gifts weren't all little Jo had been after. Somehow, she'd pried state secrets out of Brynston's father, then eighth earl of Brynston and Member of Parliament. Clearly Julius had been the weak link. It was easy enough to imagine—soft words, tender glances, and it was all a young man could do to keep from puffing up and crowing like a bantam rooster.

Phineas folded the letter carefully and tucked it into his dressing-gown pocket, tying the rest with their red silk ribbon and placing them back in the drawer where he had found them. His fingertips brushed against the smooth coldness of metal, and he fished out a small round silver frame, a miniature, perhaps, of the duplicitous Jo.

He held it to the lamp. She had been a lovely girl, flirtatious and feminine, with a saucy sparkle in her eye. And, more interestingly, she bore a glancing resemblance to Katie. The hair was not the same—Jo had a profusion of strawberry ringlets—but the chin and the shape of the brow were similar. The girls could have been cousins.

Phineas replaced Jo's miniature in its hiding place and slid the drawer noiselessly shut. Hard to know what to make of these new discoveries. The information was a trifle stale for blackmail, but if the family had taken pains to suppress news of the matter, the profits could still be considerable. And Katie would want to know about the girl. Brynston would be on the watch for similar games. Phineas realized with a start that the earl was probably already on his guard—he had been burned once before by a spirited, pretty girl, and would be wary of one now. Katie had been right to be cautious.

"Try and ransom my little champion, will you Brynston?" Phineas said softly to himself, chuckling as he shut the study door behind him and padded down to the kitchens. "We'll just see who ransoms whom, Lord High and Mighty." And quietly, happily, he laughed and laughed.

24

It took the combined efforts of two footmen, three scolding sisters, and Val's long-suffering valet to manage it, but Val Willowby was out of bed, dressed, and breakfasted by seven the next morning.

Julius, who had, according to his custom, eaten a light breakfast in his dressing room at six o'clock precisely, cast an appraising look over his younger brother.

"Give it up, Val, you'll never last the morning," Julius said, thinking to be kind. "You needn't follow me around, you won't be any help. Go back to bed."

Indeed, Val's eyelids looked like wet laundry drooping over his eyes, and his face was cut in three places where he had tried to shave himself to save time. "Fustian!" he muttered, indignant. "You act as if I'd never been up at this hour before. Gad it's bright out here."

"That's called the sun, Val. It's always bright." Julius quieted his mount, a powerful coal-black brute called Tempest, who was pawing the earth, anxious to begin.

"It's all this snow," Val sniffed, mounting his own favorite, a flashy, high-strung bay called Firefly. "It throws off a wretched glare."

"Hmm," Julius said, trying to be amiable. "Think that fluttering creature can keep up with Tempest?"

Val patted his horse's neck. "He steps a damn sight higher than that wretched Bucephalus you insist on riding. I can't see why you don't put him to pasture, Julius. He's really a perfect disgrace."

"He's ugly, but I'd set him against a thousand of your Butterflies." He nudged Tempest into a canter.

"Firefly!" Val corrected, shouting after him.

Julius rode hard and fast, as he always did mornings. It helped him sharpen his wits, clearing away the fuzz of house party chit chat, and the poring over of account books late into the night.

And, lately, it cleared his mind of the potent distraction of an intractable American countess whose reluctance to the marriage bed was proving more piquant than the most seductive courtesans in Christendom.

The snow was mostly melted, Val's indignant huffings about the glare to the contrary, and the earth was scattered with the yellow and violet of crocuses. The winter had been a long, hard one, and the villagers had needed his help to a far greater extent than they usually did. But it looked as if spring had truly come at last.

Julius looked appraisingly out over the fields, wondering if he should try a new crop of red wheat. Off in the distance, Val was jumping hedgerows with Firefly.

It took the better part of the morning to make their rounds in the village. Every house they entered was full of questions about the new countess. Was she as lovely as everyone said? Was it true she came from America? Was it true they didn't have any earls, or even a king, in America? Julius answered the questions with good humor, and asked a few of his own. Old Zachary Monk's leg was healing nicely, and Mrs. Monk was making pies from the bushel of apples Julius had delivered from Willowby Hall's stores. She tried to press one on him, but he had no place to carry it. Mrs. Toby, the blacksmith's wife, had wrestled with an ugly cough all winter, and they had feared consumption, but this morning she looked as bright and fresh as a spring pansy, and said she had never felt better. Julius left her a bottle of the new medicament his doctor in London had recommended.

After the village came the cottagers, and it was these Val seemed especially interested in. He asked innumerable questions of the folk who lived in the rough cottages—how far they stood from the village proper, how did they keep warm on cold nights such as these, and whether there were any mules to be had in these environs, or did everyone get about by walking. Julius had to admit, he was impressed by his brother's interest in these simplest of Willowby Hall's tenants, although the effect was somewhat marred by Val's checking his watch every ten minutes.

"By Jove," Val called, when they were a few miles past the last cottage. "Beg your pardon, brother, but if I don't piss soon, I'll burst."

Julius smiled and reined Tempest in near a thick copse of birch trees, sliding down to join his brother. "Sorry, I forgot you weren't used to riding on a full belly."

"It's not my belly that troubles me," Val said with a grin.

After they'd relieved themselves, Val's head shot round with an anxious look. "I say! What's that over there? Good Gad, I think it's a fire!"

Julius's senses were suddenly as keen as a hound's, as he moved to where his brother was standing. "Fire? Are you sure, man? Where, show me."

"Off there ahead, there's a great plume of smoke. You'll see better from that hill." He pointed to a low rise on the other side of the copse.

Julius took the hill in long, quick strides. The ground was damp with snow-melt, and he doubted a fire would spread far, but the best assurance of that would be to mount a fire brigade at the earliest opportunity.

"Where do you mean? You're daft, there's no plume of smoke. I don't see a thing!" he called, squinting through the bare trees to where the horses were standing.

Val said nothing, but Julius could hear the thunder of hoofbeats.

"What the hell—?" Julius asked, coming down off the hill and around the copse. He was just in time to see the billowing whisk of Firefly's dark red tail, with Tempest's black flank beside it. They galloped off as fast as two fast horses could gallop, Val holding Tempest's rein in his left hand.

"Get your wretched skinny arse back here, Val Willowby!" Julius bellowed. "I'm not in the mood for nursery games!" But there was no reply, and within minutes, his brother and the two horses had rounded the bend in the road and were out of sight.

Rosalind and Katie had spent the morning exploring the Willowby holdings, Rosalind pointing out the most picturesque ruined cottages on the north side of the estate, replaced now by warmer, more modern models to the east. Everywhere the land showed tender signs of approaching spring—the drifts of crocus, the beginnings of tight buds appearing on branches. Hard green spears sprung everywhere out of the earth, and Katie could imagine the scene in a few month's time, the abandoned cottages overgrown with daffodils and roses.

The morning air was still crisp on Katie's cheeks as she rode, but there was a sweetness afield that held the promise of the spring to come. She had not planned to be in England for the spring, but in this moment, riding Willowby Hall's excellent mare while Rosalind rode happily beside her, she was glad to be in this place, with its tender colors and soft gray light.

Rosalind pulled to a stop in front of a particularly lovely ruined fence, overgrown now with a thicket of wild roses and blackberry. The canes were still bare, but Katie only had to shut her eyes to imagine a riot of cream and red roses against the glossy dark berries, and the mingling of their sweet, fierce perfumes.

"You don't really think Willowby's so dreadful, do you Katie?" Rosalind asked.

Katie smiled. "Don't you think it's a bit unfair, to ask me that here?" She gestured to the landscape, with its breathtaking combination of wild and tame, harsh and sweet.

Rosalind glanced at Katie from the corner of her eye. "I don't think it's unfair at all. I want you to stay and live with us forever. So I'll only show you the lovely things."

"It is lovely," Katie said, more serious now. "But Rosalind—you mustn't let yourself be disappointed. If things don't work out between the earl and I."

"You think he's a very hard man, don't you?" Rosalind asked, eyes narrowed as if she were summing Katie up.

"Isn't he?"

"Sometimes. When he's angry. He can be absolutely rotten when he's angry," Rosalind conceded.

"I make him angry."

"You wake him up," Rosalind corrected. "He used to spend all his days looking after this place, and then going to the city so he could sit in Parliament. He's never cared about anything but his duty, since he was smaller than Tibby."

"I don't think that's changed much," Katie said, trying to smile.

"It's still important to him. It has to be. He takes care of everything, you see."

Katie raised her eyebrows, but said nothing.

At the look on Katie's face, Rosalind said, "Oh, no, you don't understand! I don't suppose you have people like him in America. It's not me I mean, or even the family. He looks after us, but we'd rub along well enough without him, I suppose. One can always be a governess or something, if things get really awful. I mean *Willowby*. He keeps track of all the corn and the pheasants and the rabbits. He goes to every wedding in the village and sends a silver cup to every christening. He even goes to all the funerals, or if he's in Parliament he sends Val and

Titania. He's part of this place, and it's part of him. They'd die without each other."

Katie looked out over the fence covered with brambles, out past the rolling fields and the still-snowy valleys dotted with crocus. She did not want to think about this verdant, rambling landscape being part of her husband, being the huge outward manifestation of a generosity and spirit kept firmly in check. It was easier to think of him as the Brimstone Earl, bitter and hard.

"I can't imagine Lord Brynston caring much about daffodils," Katie said, trying to laugh away her unease.

"They belong to him, and he loves them. He loves everything that belongs to him," Rosalind said simply.

Katie's heart felt pierced with sweet, singing pain. She was a well-trained sharper who had gotten herself in over her head. That was all. She did not belong here, she was not a countess, and she definitely was not in love with the Brimstone Earl.

That would be impossible. Unbearable.

"I am not something to be possessed, like a candlestick or a music box," Katie said. "I'm sorry, Rosalind. I don't mean to speak ill of your brother, but you must know I never agreed to this marriage. I will stay for a little while longer. But I cannot make my life here, no matter how beautiful a cage your brother has devised for me."

Rosalind ducked her head, conceding the point. "I hope you don't think I've been a scold."

"You?" Katie smiled, swallowing down the lump at her throat. "Rosalind, you're not a scold. I'm flattered that you would want me to stay, that you all would accept . . . someone like me as your brother's wife."

Rosalind cocked her head to one side. "Grown people can be awfully thick, sometimes, Katie. You're exactly the sort of wife my brother needs." And with that she urged her mare forward, and they rode on.

*   *   *

They found a beautiful wooded spot for an early lunch, and Rosalind hobbled the horses while Katie unpacked the picnic basket. She had to laugh at Rosalind's idea of a rustic meal. "What were you thinking? You've got enough here to feed a small army."

Rosalind cocked an appraising eye at the massive willow basket, her brown kerseymere gown and blaze-red hair making her look like a spring robin. "You never can tell, Katie. There might be perils out here in the wilderness."

Katie laughed. "I don't think you know what wilderness is."

Rosalind shrugged. "Maybe not. But unexpected things can happen out on these dales."

"Well, I suppose we might get chased by a cow," Katie said dubiously.

"They can be quite dangerous," Rosalind said serenely, buttering a slice of bread.

Lunch came and went, and the early hours of the afternoon passed companionably. Katie almost managed to forget the shadows teasing at the back of her mind as Rosalind chatted about Willowby, about the house and the local folklore and the meddlesome fairies who were supposed to live beneath the toadstools at the base of the old oak trees.

"It doesn't seem real," Katie murmured as she rested her head against the soft roll of quilted blankets. It was peaceful out here, with no sound but the peeping of birds. She watched the clouds roll lazily across the pale blue spring sky until her eyelids grew too heavy to keep open, and she drifted to sleep.

It was much cooler when she woke up, and the breeze chilled Katie so that the fine hairs on her arms and the back of her neck stood up. She looked around for Rosalind as she rubbed the sleep from her eyes—they should be getting back. The day's deceptive mildness was beginning to fade into a cold, damp night.

"Rosalind?" she called, smoothing her hair and

wondering if she had deep red blanket-creases in her cheeks. Her mind was still pleasantly sleep-fogged. She looked around for her friend, and wondered offhandedly where the horses could be. "Rosalind? Where are you hiding?" Perhaps her sister-in-law was off picking flowers. She could have gathered a wheelbarrow full of crocuses by now.

Katie stood and stretched her arms, shaking the pins and needles from her left hand. She tried to smooth the wrinkles from her gown, but it was hopelessly rumpled where she had been lying on it.

She walked over to a low stone fence and tested its stability with her hand. It seemed sturdy enough. She hoisted her skirts and climbed to stand on it, squinting out over the rolling landscape to see if she could catch a glimpse of Rosalind.

Nothing. And no trace of either Rosalind or the horses.

Puzzled, she hopped down and returned to the basket and the picnic blankets, and knelt to rummage through the basket for a bit of cheese. Pinned to the basket's lid she found a note in large, looped handwriting:

Katie—
  I'm awfully sorry, but perhaps one day you'll for-give me. Head west down the narrow road a quarter mile, and you will find something to your advantage. Do not dawdle too long, as the nights here are quite cold and I should feel dreadful if you were to catch a chill.
  Yr. very affectionate sister,
  Lady Rosalind Willowby

Katie scowled fiercely. The girl probably thought this was a clever joke, to abandon the new member of the household in the middle of the dales and let her find her way home again.

But that did not ring quite true. Rosalind was impish, but this prank verged on cruel. Stung by the seeming nas-tiness of the joke, Katie gathered up her bonnet, which the breeze had taken off some fair distance into a meadow. The quilted blankets and the wicker picnic basket, still three-quarters full, made an unwieldy armful, and Katie was glad as she stumbled toward the road that she did not have to walk far. With a glance at the setting sun to decide which direction was west, Katie set off with grim determination to find whatever destiny her mischievous sister-in-law had planned for her.

Julius was in a blind, crockery-smashing rage. Unfortunately, the abandoned cottage he now found himself in had no crockery. Nor did it have a working pump, food in the cupboards, or anything resembling a conveyance back to Willowby Hall. It did have clean sheets and warm blankets on the bed, two good beeswax candles in the cupboard, and a neat stack of dry wood in the fireplace.

Julius was unimpressed by Val's idea of a joke. Perhaps this was a message that Julius should take life lackadaisically, as Val did. Perhaps it was just a bit of Val's usual useless tomfoolery. In any event, Julius would be stuck here unless he decided soon whether to spend the night or to return home on foot.

He would walk, he knew instantly. He would not postpone for even a few hours the pleasure of kicking Val's arse from the drawing room to the courtyard and back again.

As he strode out of the cottage, slamming the door behind him, his jaw dropped to see a swinging vandyked wool skirt walking down the road, the rest of the body hidden by a stack of blankets and an enormous wicker basket. The effect was something like a very fashionable, charming peddler.

And from the cut and color of the skirts, the feminine peddler's diminutive height, and that light, dancelike gait he had come to know very well, Julius knew that the figure struggling down the lane was none other than his own fascinating, maddening wife.

25

"What the hell are *you* doing here?" Julius blurted before he could stop himself.

Katie gave a little shriek, and the blankets and the wicker basket came tumbling down to the ground, silver forks scattering in all directions and two china cups smashing to bits.

She glowered at him, looking ready to do him serious physical harm. "What the blazes do you think you're doing, scaring me that way? Are you out of your mind?" Grumbling, she knelt to the ground and began to pick bundles from the shards of broken china.

Chastened, Julius knelt with her, plucking forks from the tufts of grass at the side of the road. "Forgive me. I was startled. But I'd still like to know what you're doing here."

She shot him a venomous glance. "As if you didn't know. Very amusing, my lord."

"I do not advise that you test my patience, *wife*. I'm in no humor for it," he said angrily.

"And what kind of humor do you think I'm in, *husband*?"

Katie's eyes were spitting fire now. "Carted out here like some gullible infant and then left to conveniently stumble across you? Don't think I don't see through your scheme. It's pathetically transparent."

"And why," Julius asked coldly, "should I bother myself to trick you into coming out to the middle of nowhere?"

"Because you want—" Katie's voice faltered, but it was with anger, not uncertainty. "Because you wanted to seduce me, and it was easier to get me out of the way of the rest of the family," she spat.

"Confound you," Julius said softly. "When will I make you realize that when I have made a promise, I keep it? This is not my doing, Katie. Use that feverish little brain of yours for five seconds."

She was silent a moment, continuing to glare at him like a fox caught in a trap. Julius almost expected her to bare her teeth. "I've thought about it," she said, "and I still don't trust you."

"Fine," he snapped. "That makes two of us, I don't trust you either. But if you think I like being stuck out here with no food or drink just for the chance at a tumble with my own wife, you're out of your bloody mind."

She bit her lip and frowned, and looked down at the picnic basket. "Well, they worked out that much, at least." She looked up at him again. "There's enough food in here to feed Napoleon's army. I wondered why Rosalind asked the cook to pack so much."

Julius nodded grimly. "Rosalind. I see. And Val contrived to get me out here, with no way home but my own legs. I'm beginning to smell a rat—five rats, to be precise, in the form of my hell-born family."

Katie sat back on her heels as she thought. She gave him an appraising look. "This really isn't your doing, is it?"

"If I wanted to take you, Katie, I would take you," he said softly. "I am not a man to resort to tricks and games to get what he wants."

She shivered faintly. "It's getting cold."

"The wind off the dales has a nasty bite, and it's damp as well. We'd best get inside."

The sky was lead gray above them, and the wind seemed to pierce through Julius's coat to his very bones.

Katie hoisted the wicker basket and moved to carry it into the cottage.

"Here, let me take that," he said, setting his hand on the handle.

She jerked it away from him again. "I'm not an invalid," she snapped, walking down the garden path with a very straight back indeed.

"Yes, little wife, I can see that," he muttered, picking up the sturdy blankets and following her through the front door.

Katie began to build a fire with surprisingly practiced movements.

"I didn't know heiresses lit their own fires in America," he said, watching her for her reaction.

He was disappointed.

"There's a great deal you don't know," she said tartly. "And you are such a stubborn block of wood I doubt very much you'll ever learn."

He began to unpack the wicker basket. Katie was right; there was an astonishing quantity of food. "You're not much of a flatterer, are you?"

She gave him a cold look. "I should think a pampered English earl gets more than enough flattery."

A splinter of china gouged his thumb, and he yanked it back and sucked it. "As it happens, you are entirely wrong about that. Growing up to be earl consists mostly of clouts to the head, interspersed with endless rounds of duties that are tedious in the extreme."

"And so you wished me to be countess? To share your clouts and your tedium?"

He allowed himself a small smile. "Most women would have thanked me. But you see very clearly, wife. Yes, I want you to share my clouts and my tedium. And you are right, I have done you no great kindness."

She seemed disarmed at this, and busied herself with the fire, keeping her face turned away from his.

He looked at the array of food he'd set on the table—sandwiches, custard tarts, a bottle of claret, a bottle of port, two kinds of jam, a marvelous-smelling paté, a few apples. "Good God, how did you manage to haul this thing down the road?"

She looked at him evenly. "I'm stronger than I look."

"Apparently so." He returned her gaze. He could see she was angry, and humiliated. She was prickly, and did not like being tricked.

Neither did he, if he thought about it.

"How did Rosie manage to ditch you?"

"It wasn't hard. I was so full from lunch that I fell asleep." She blushed dark pink, like the underside of a rose petal. "I suppose they thought it was a very funny joke."

"What they thought was that they could encourage us to . . . become better acquainted," Julius said dryly. "It's hard to believe, I know, but they probably imagined they were doing us a favor."

"Funny kind of favor," she said, turning away from him as if she wanted to escape. She found an apron, white and spotless, hanging near the hearth. "They've thought of everything, haven't they?"

"Almost everything. It's only about eight miles back to the house. I'm walking."

She turned to face him, startled. "Oh! I suppose—I hadn't thought of that."

"Neither had Val. Mostly, I suppose, because the boy would rather be horsewhipped in the village square than let someone see him using his legs to get around. But I have a different sort of pride than my brother's."

"I'll go with you. It won't take us more than a few hours."

Julius shook his head. "No, stay here. It's nearly dark, and it's going to get quite cold. You'll be safe and warm here, and I'll send someone for you in the morning."

The flash of lightning could almost have been a trick of his eyes, but a few seconds later, as if to mock them and this whole ludicrous predicament, a crack of thunder came from outside the door. Immediately rain began to spill down in soft pats.

"Your family is devious, Lord Brynston, but I think this was beyond even their powers," Katie said.

Julius sighed. "Perhaps they've been making offerings to some fiendish pagan rain god."

She looked dubiously up at the ceiling. "I suppose the roof leaks."

Julius pulled his collar higher around his neck. "Almost certainly."

She gave a small, defeated-sounding sigh. "You can't walk home in a thunderstorm. You'll freeze solid."

"I don't mind." He did mind. Since Katie had come, the need to thrash his brother had receded in Julius's mind, replaced by tenderer notions. But he would not let her think he was pleased by this trick, would not let her count him among her deceivers.

The rain was building quickly to a resounding drench, slopping down the thatch to form small waterfalls in front of the windows.

She shook her head. "For once in your life, don't be a hammer-head. I know how cold it gets here at night. We'll both stay here."

He tried to repress his smile, but he could feel it slipping out around the edges. "You do have a way with words, wife."

"And you, husband, have a damned fool expression on your face, which I advise you to wipe off before I take a skillet to it," Katie said, but her face held the ghost of a smile as well.

Brynston had promised to take himself off as soon as the storm subsided, but as if the sky itself was conspiring against them, the rain continued to pour down in a heavy, cold sheet. Katie built up the fire to a fearsome blaze, sitting on the settle and letting the hearth's heat scald her face and toes, while behind her the cottage grew steadily colder and danker by the hour.

She could not very well refuse to let him sit at her side, nor did she truly want to. But the presence of him so near, the powerful muscles of his legs in their snug deerskin breeches, the sensual and compelling scent of a man who had been riding hard all day, made her feel faintly dizzy. She stared into the fire, feeling her cheeks warm until she knew they must be red as cherries, trying not to think about the intoxicating physical proximity of her unlawfully wedded husband.

They ate dinner together there, in front of the fire, not speaking. They shared claret from the last unbroken china cup, and the sandwiches tasted doubly good with the wind and rain howling outside and the fire roaring like a beast within. The tarts were devoured and pronounced marvelous by both parties, and, to Katie's surprise, they were. She should have had no appetite. Her nervousness, the dangerous intimate spark that threatened to blaze between her and this man, should have made the food taste like pasteboard in her mouth. But she was hungry, and she ate with gusto.

Finally, the cottage grew black, and it seemed they had no choice. They must go to bed. Katie dared a peek at Brynston, who looked remarkably mild and contented, the darkness in him warmed by the glow of the fire.

Feeling as fragile as the china cups they had shattered earlier, she asked, "Do you think you will feel sleepy soon?"

He looked at her and smiled, and she felt ridiculously warm and happy. "I think I will. Shall I move the bed near the fire?"

She swallowed, her throat dry. "I . . . you take the bed, if you like. I can sleep on the settle, you're far too tall for it."

"You may be tough as an old boot, Katie Willowby, but you're not sleeping on that thing. Don't worry, I'll stack a pile of blankets between us four feet high. Nothing will happen that you don't want to happen."

That was exactly what she was afraid of, but she bit her lip and nodded. The words were still echoing a little crazily in her mind: *Katie Willowby*. She was intoxicated, confused by his proximity and the claret and the hot blaze of the fire.

She intended to say, No, absolutely not, I will sleep here and you will sleep there. Instead she found herself nodding and saying, "All right."

Brynston took off his coat and pushed the heavy bed nearer the fire. He rolled the picnic blankets into a fat bolster, setting it dead down the middle of the bed. "There you are, the marital equivalent of Hadrian's Wall. You won't even know I'm on the other side of this."

You're crazy if you believe that, she thought, slipping between the cool sheets, thinking only briefly of how uncomfortable she would be sleeping all night in her gown and stays. She would not be able to forget, even for a moment, that the beautiful, hard-eyed, intoxicatingly dangerous Brimstone Earl was only two blankets away.

Katie did not think she would be able to sleep at all, but she slipped quickly into a fitful doze, chased through her nightmares by skinny snapping dogs, by menacing Turks, by an ugly, thick-lipped face belonging to her childhood. She struggled against them all, tangling herself in the sheets, thrashing against the rolled blankets between her and her husband. When her eyes fluttered open from her restless sleep, the roll looked more like a heap of mashed potatoes than Hadrian's Wall.

She rearranged it as best she could, and lay there on her back. The fire still burned low in the grate, and she could just see the rough timbers of the cottage ceiling. The roof had not leaked after all, at least not much, though the rain still fell outside. The air smelled of the freshness of the rain and of the dark, thick smoke of the fire. The mixture soothed her back into a dreamy state that was not quite sleep, but a kind of aimless mental meandering.

Later, when she tried to remember just how it had started, she never could. She had been asleep, and so, she supposed, had he. Her demons still chased her, the thick-lipped face laughed its ugly sniggering laugh, she ran and ran, as she did every night. But this time, as she reached out to strike away the evil things that chased her, there was warmth there, flesh and blood and bone. Another hand met hers in the darkness, and the sensation was so delicious that even in sleep, she curled toward it, as a cat curls cozily by the fire.

The hand stroked hers gently, so gently, and she edged closer to it, bumping up against the firm roll of blankets as if they were another body. She was not awake; she was not asleep. She was in the tentative, magical place between those two worlds, and she knew only that to feel another hand touching hers in the darkness was a thing she had yearned for her entire life.

The hand stroked hers softly, gently. It was so pleasur-able that she wanted to reach out and see if it was as lovely to touch as to be touched. She splayed her fingers the tini-est bit, and there the hand was, the play of skin over bone. She ran her fingertips over it, over the lean hard shape, and up the forearm that was corded with muscle, covered lightly with hair.

There was a small sound, an exhalation of pleasure, and a shifting. The hand became an arm, the arm wrapped itself around her, reaching past the roll of blan-kets to caress her shoulder and the tender flesh beneath her ear.

She gave herself over to this, tucking her head like a cat asking to be petted, and perhaps she made her own small sound of pleasure. She reached past the roll of blankets and found the angular line of a hip and the hardness of a lean torso. The hip was still covered by deerskin, but the torso was gloriously bare skin.

She explored him as a blind girl might, delighting in the softness and the smoothness of his skin, the hard sculpted planes of muscle. His scent filled her, metallic and masculine. He was nothing like her, this other, this beautiful nameless creature of the darkness.

There came another shifting, a small groan. The roll of blankets shifted, and suddenly a warm surrounding mass of muscle and sinew settled next to her. His movements were so slow, so gentle, that she could not be afraid. Part of her knew that she could wake up from the sweetness of this dream at any instant. She could sit bolt upright and send it scattering to the skies like a flock of blackbirds. And so she lay there, still stroking him languidly, discovering him, discovering the answering warmth building low in her body that she did not want to dispel.

His hands were slow and easy, so that the shock she felt when they moved to her breasts was not sharp, but a sweet lazy trickle like summer honey. He cupped her breast, brushed his hand across the nipple that was stiffening beneath the fabric of her gown. His touch was like the taste of melted chocolate, and she was sorry when he stopped.

He rolled her over, as deftly as another man might have straightened his cravat, and the hands were on the back of her neck, kneading, caressing the wings of her shoulders. She made no protest when he unbuttoned the tiny buttons of her gown, no protest as he brushed her gown away and resumed his stroking. She felt cherished, protected. Loved. She was like a potted flower desperate for water. She drank his touch greedily, happily, and it nourished her and made roses bloom deep in the soft darkness of her belly. She could feel their petals unfurl as he stripped the dress away, smell the intoxicating summer's heat of their fragrance as he rolled her onto her back again, working deftly at her stays.

Her first free breath there beneath him, freed of the light pressure of her stays, freeing now of the thin fabric of her chemisette as he slipped it over her head, was like the blossoming of a million flowers out past her fingertips, her toes, out through the top of her scalp through her hair, until she was lying in a bed of petal-soft, fragrant pleasure, all the while giving herself up to his stroking, to the delicious nourishment of touch, to the intimate language of hands that said, *I want. I need.*

I love.

He left her there alone for a moment, cool and bereft, and she felt an instant's piercing loneliness. But then he was with her again, and he lowered himself gently over her, the touch of his bare skin against hers almost more pleasure than she could bear.

It was now that he kissed her, now that she was already melted to a soft summery sweetness. The taste of his lips carried her further into the madness. The rain whispered outside as he curled his fingers in her hair, stroked her scalp and her neck and her shoulders, came around to cup her breasts again, bare this time, and all the while he kissed her.

He curled his hand behind her head and unfastened the catch on her locket, sliding it free of her. For a moment she felt frightened without it, as if it were the only way she could find her way back to daylight. But when his hands returned again to her throat and her breasts, she sighed and gave way to him.

She allowed her eyes to flutter open and she could see him there, darkly golden in the dying light, lying over her like the last rays of the sun. She arched her back lightly to tilt her breasts up to him, to offer herself, and he bent down and took one nipple into his mouth.

The blooming grew stronger, almost violent, a twisting of dark green vines at the base of her belly. The throb that went through her left her damp and limp, but he showed no mercy. Gold as a gleaming, sinful idol, he bent over her, suckling her, nipping gently, so gently, and his teeth shone white in the dark firelight. She heard an animal sound, a soft growl of need, and realized it was her, not him, who had made it.

The hands moved lower now, to span her hips and then to slide down to her thighs. They parted her only a fraction, testing her slickness, and then he answered with his own growl. Slowly his touch grew bolder, fiercer, and the need echoed in her like a wild animal calling out to its mate. A finger slid into her slowly, so slowly.

She cried out, and moved beneath him. She had never been caught in a current so deep or so strong. The hand began to move rhythmically against her, thrusting with slow, devastating precision, and the blooming became a fierce tangle of clawing and fighting and desperate need. She moved hard against his hand, she was hungry, she fought for something she did not understand.

And he gave it to her. The hands that had whispered of love and cherishing now fed her want nakedly, now thrust against her and insinuated into her and brought her to the brink of a wide, deep pool that seemed to have no bottom.

And then she jumped into the pool, and everything was gold and warm and bright all around her, and her hunger was fed with pure gold joy.

His hands slowed their movement, and she lay there dazed for a moment. The enchantment had not broken in the golden frenzy, but had been strengthened by it. She swam in warm sweetness, safe and comfortable, until the insistent small movements of his hands lit another spark of hunger in her.

She arched up and twisted her body slightly to meet his touch, and he made a small sound of approval. There came a shifting, and his body was over hers again, the warm heaviness of him surrounding her. She arched her back up to brush his chest with the bareness of her nipples, and his gasp echoed her own. Only a few moments ago, she had been so dazed and drowsy she thought she must surely sink into sleep, but now she felt alive again. The blooming was beginning anew.

"Stay with me, little fox kit," he murmured, brushing her hair with his lips. "I'm not half done with you yet."

"You'll burn me up, and there'll be nothing left but cinders," she said softly, but she was not afraid of him tonight. Tonight he was golden and tender and he had led her to mysteries she'd never dreamed existed.

"I feel that way too," he said. "You've set a fire in me, little Katie, and I don't know how I'll quench it."

"It's not possible to quench volcanoes," she said, with a small smile on her lips. "Didn't you know that? They just burn hotter and hotter until they explode."

He gave her a lazy, wolfish grin. "What a perfectly splendid idea."

She looked up at him, puzzled, but he bent over her again and kissed the questions from her lips, until she was too dazzled even to remember what she knew and what she did not.

His fingers teased at her, stroked her wetness until she felt her breathing go quick and shallow, and she squirmed beneath him.

"Do you want me, then?" he whispered, his voice husky with need, its roughness washing over her like a length of sheerest silk.

"I want you," she said, her voice breathless from the terrible pleasure of it. There was no sleep left in her now. He had chased it all away, along with all of daylight's reasons they must not do this.

"Yes," she said again, reaching up to press her lips to his, curling her hands around the broad strength of his neck to pull him down to her. "Yes, I want you. I want you."

He came down on her, ravenous, and the warm surrounding weight of his body became not gentle protector but fierce invader. But she was not frightened. The blooming within her chased away the fear. She arched up to him, meeting his crushing kisses with her own ferocity.

He poised himself to enter her, and she felt a moment of shock. She was being prodded by something very rude and very uncomfortable. She frowned and was about to protest when he slid his hands down again to work their unholy magic, and then she felt only melting and the dizzying sweetness of the blooming.

He pushed himself into her a fraction, and she felt a knife cut through the sweetness.

"Ah, no, you can't!" she cried, certain that if he continued, he would split her in half.

"I'm sorry, sweeting," he murmured, as he drove into her without mercy, tearing all her pleasure as if it were the fragile petals of a poppy.

Her eyes welled with tears. She had thought it would be so lovely, had wanted it so much. And it was uncomfortable, and he was too big, and she hurt. She wished suddenly he would leave her alone so she could cry.

"It hurts the first time," he said gravely. "Is it very bad?"

"No," she said forlornly. "I mean, yes. It's wretched."

He bent down to kiss her forehead and temples. "Relax beneath me, sweeting."

She dutifully tried to relax, wondering if now was the time she was supposed to start reciting the Lord's Prayer, or thinking of God and country, or whatever proper ladies were supposed to do. Her throat burned with unshed tears.

He began to move within her, and at first she was more annoyed than before. Then, very quickly, she realized that this was not some distasteful aftermath of the delectable sensations of the blooming. The hunger returned, but deeper, fuller, and as he satisfied it, the hunger built apace, so that desire outran fulfillment. Small, soft sounds began to escape from her lips.

"Christ, sweeting, what the hell have you done to me?" he murmured in her ear. "You've bewitched me, I never had a chance."

She reached up to curl her fingers in his hair, and was struck with a sudden, forceful blow by how *beautiful* he was. His shoulders were wide and well muscled, the dark gold of the firelight painting deep shadows across them. His chest was broad and lightly furred with dark hair, lowering down in a vee to that mysterious part of him buried deep within her, moving softly, teasing her, building her pleasure and satisfying it.

She dared a look down at him, at where they were

joined, at the way her legs wrapped around his hips. A thrill shot through her like molten metal, and she bucked beneath him, not to please him or to tantalize him, but because some darkly primitive corner of her own soul *wanted* her to.

He groaned, and drove deeply into her, and the force made her toss her head back. "Yes," she managed. "More." And then words melted in the volcanic heat building between them, and she could say nothing else.

They threw themselves against one another, fighting as much as loving, and if her virgin's body was still too tender for such fierceness, she did not know it. She knew only that she must lose herself in this, must burn away the excuses and the reasons of daytime.

And as he bore down on her, hard and fast and ruthlessly beautiful, he slid his hand between them and he touched her, and the blooming became an explosion, an annihilation that threatened to shatter everything she was, so that there was neither him nor her, but only an unending explosive melting.

As the last sparks of her pleasure floated out into the night like sparks from a bonfire, he stiffened in her arms. A strangled cry escaped his throat, and then he was heavy and quiet against her, and she was quiet within herself, floating like a dandelion seed on a puff of wind. He stroked her hair and kissed her, gently, lazily. They said nothing, but after a long time lying together that way, they slept.

26

The morning came too soon, and Katie buried her face in the pillows to keep the sun from her eyes. She felt lazy this morning, languid, like some pasha's wife in a harem.

A deep, contented groan came from beside her, and a hard masculine hand settled lightly on her bare hip, stroking her absently.

Katie's eyes shot open, and she clutched the covers to her bare breasts, scooting her hip away from the possessive hand.

The movement was enough to wake Brynston, and his eyes fluttered open. His intensity was softened this morning, gentled by what had happened between them in the night, but his gaze still pierced her. "Good morning," he said.

She felt her cheeks grow hot, and she pulled the sheets tightly around herself. "Good morning," she said stiffly.

He gave her a long, appraising look, taking in the tightly wrapped sheet and the scalding flush on her cheeks. "You're unhappy." It was a statement, not a question, but his eyes seemed to plead with her to tell him it was not so.

"I'm confused," she said, and it was true. Before last night, it would have been easy enough to walk away from this mock marriage, easy enough to turn her back on him and live out her life as a cheat and a thief.

Or perhaps it would not have been so easy. But now, after last night, knowing that if she wanted to, she could curl up in the protective circle of his arms and let him love her body, let him take her to that place of warmth and joy—

She scooted quickly off the bed, not wanting to think about it any more.

"Hey!" he cried in protest, reaching out to grab a fistful of coverlet before she dragged it off the bed with her. "I'm not modest, sweeting, but it's damnably cold this morning."

She dared a glance at him. He leaned back against the headboard, watching her, the covers barely concealing his hips and thighs and the wonderful mystery of his sex. His chest was bare and proud, and every inch as lovely as it had been last night.

"Do you like what you see?" he asked. There was a faintly teasing smile on his lips, but his eyes were still worried.

She could not lie to him, not about this. "Yes," she said quietly.

"It wasn't so terrible," he said, pushing himself forward.

The covers slipped from his hips, and Katie quickly turned her eyes away. "It wasn't terrible. But it wasn't what I wanted."

He stepped out of the bed, gloriously bare, and moved to her. He tapped on the covers with one finger. "It's cold out here."

She shook her head violently and took a step away from him. "You'd better get dressed."

"I'm bloody well freezing my arse off," he said, taking

one corner of the blanket and gently unwrapping her, before wrapping the covers again around them both, pressing her nakedness to his.

"We can't—" she began, her voice faltering. His hands had crept around to caress her buttocks, and he was nuzzling her hair. He smelled magnificently of their love-making.

"We can, little fox kit," he said, smiling as he bent down to kiss her again, a gentle kiss, with more greeting than passion in it. "Many times. You're my wife."

The thought of his moving inside her again, of the magic he had worked with his mouth and his hands and his sex, made her feel a little dizzy, and she leaned against him. "I need to—to think about this," she murmured, her cheek pressed against his chest.

"I know this isn't easy," he said, his voice rumbling in her ear. "But you will see, Katie. We'll be happy together."

The words twisted cruelly in her heart. They would not be happy together. He was an honorable-to-his-toes English earl, and she was a common cutpurse. She could no more be a proper countess to him than she could fly to the moon.

But in that moment, wrapped up in the delicious warmth of him, she wanted to. She wanted to very badly.

His arousal pressed gently against her belly. She felt an answering call of desire, low and warm. "Please—" she said, trying to push him away. "I can't think like this."

"Neither can I, that's why I like it," he said with a grin. His face was transformed when he smiled like that, and all his stony severity seemed a half-forgotten dream.

He let her go. As she grabbed at the sheets to cover herself, he was left bare and unselfconscious. He walked over to the bed to find his clothes, and she could not keep herself from peeking at him.

His sex was proudly aroused, curving thickly upward, and yet he showed no shame as he walked around the bed picking up shirt and breeches. The muscles of his buttocks were as hard and lean as those of any classical statue, but he was lightly covered with dark hair, more satyr than Apollo.

He caught a glimpse of her, and shot her a grin over his shoulder. "Can't help staring, can you, wench?"

She blushed again and stared at the floor.

"I can't keep my eyes off you either," he said. "You snatched up those covers before I could learn what color your nipples are, or whether your breasts are as exquisite as they seemed last night."

The cottage was filled with the scent of their lovemaking, and she stared resolutely at the floor, trying desperately to think of something else. "Please stop talking that way."

"I love the way you're made," he continued, ruthless. He stepped close to her again, wrapping her in his arms. "I love the way my hands span your waist, the feeling of my thumbs on the bones of your hips. You're so tiny, you seem so fragile, and yet you were fiercer than I could have imagined."

"If you don't stop right this minute, I'll walk home just like this," she said, ashamed and flustered and feeling the blooming begin to warm again at the base of her belly.

He looked down at her and frowned. "I'm sorry. You think I'm teasing, don't you?"

But she was afraid he was not teasing, that he meant every word. And that thought pierced her with a sadness she could hardly endure.

They ate breakfast in silence, washing the slightly stale remaining custard tarts down with swallows of claret. Katie wished dearly for a cup of coffee, for something to clear her mind and help her understand what she must do now. Now that everything was dazzlingly, heartbreakingly wrong.

The day had been bright and clear after the night's rain, and when the morning sun grew high, a carriage had appeared on the road, drawn by an exquisite pair of matched isabellas. Val and Rosalind had been nowhere to be seen as the footman stepped down from the carriage and wordlessly escorted Katie and Brynston inside. Katie had held her head as high as if she were the Queen of Sheba, and said little on the ride home.

And now she had been left to her own devices. Brynston had been called away almost as soon as they'd arrived at Willowby Hall, to help deal with a riot of angry farmers some twenty miles away. Left alone, Katie imagined the servants sniggering behind their hands at the lascivious evening 'is lordship and 'er ladyship had spent at the cottage.

A knock came at her door. "Katie?" came Alex's voice, concerned. "Are you all right? I'm here if you want to talk."

Katie felt a scalding flush to the roots of her hair. She could not face Alex Manners, she absolutely couldn't. It was impossible. He would look at her and *know* what had happened, and he would want to know if she was sad, if she was frightened.

In an odd way, she was both of those things. But if she told Alex that, he would get entirely the wrong impression. She didn't want his protection. When had she stopped wanting Alex's protection?

"I'm fine, Alex!" she called out. "But I'm dreadfully tired—can we talk later?"

"Are you all right?" he repeated, and Katie could almost see his big hands wringing.

"I'm fine," she said. "I'm just going to have a nap—we can talk before dinner."

But you're not fine, and you're not going to take a nap, a tiny voice nagged as she tied a wide bonnet onto her head and changed into sturdy walking boots. She hoped a brisk walk would clear her thoughts.

She did not want Julius. Did she? She had been seduced, tricked when she was half asleep into giving her body to a man she hated.

You do not hate him, the voice whispered as she closed the door behind her, keeping a guilty eye out for Alex, and headed downstairs.

He held her prisoner at Willowby, and that was intolerable. Katie was no man's captive, and she never would be.

He holds you prisoner because you love him, the voice dared.

She tried to chase the thought away as she walked out the door and down the lane, but she found that she could not. It clung to her like a burr to her skirts.

She loved him. God help her, she truly loved him.

She broke into a run, wanting only to forget the touch of his lips, the gentle sweetness in his voice as he'd murmured to her in the night. To remember why she must return to the loneliness, the long empty nights in which she had no one to cherish her.

She was so lost in her musings that she scarcely noticed, some time later, the pair of peddlers hobbling down the road, dyed red from head to toe in the characteristic manner of the reddleman. She shivered a little at the dark red faces, out of which eyes blazed like coals. Poor fellows, they must have been very poor, for their cart was meager and ill-stocked.

They wheeled their creaking cart slowly down the narrow path. One was thin and shrunken, an old man, perhaps. The other was fat enough, his arm wrapped in a bulky bandage. Katie felt a chill spring breeze blow on the back of her neck, and she slowed her pace. How would a poor reddleman get so fat?

At that moment, the two men looked up at her, dark eyes flashing. Her blood froze, every instinct telling her to bolt before even she could consciously recognize the pair of dyed red faces.

She broke into a run, and they took off after her. She could not run back to Willowby Hall—it was too far, and there was no shelter if she tired before they did. So she veered off the road, leaped the low stone fence, and escaped into the wood.

It was cold here, far colder than on the bright road, and the bare oaks bent their tangled branches down toward her like grasping fingers. The gray trunks whipped past her as she ran, and once a low branch caught at her cloak, and she shrieked, thinking it was a human hand.

She could hear the two voices, shouting at each other in Turkish. Her lungs burned like fire, but still she ran, bolting in zigzags like a chased rabbit, blind to everything but the need to get away from the voices, away from the dark, cruel eyes in the red faces.

She dared a glance behind her, and the skinny one was coming fast behind, his teeth bared in a feral snarl. She pushed her legs to run faster, her muscles ripped by white-hot pain, her lungs screaming in protest. There was nothing left but instinct in her, and instinct made her run.

The skinny one yelped and snarled behind her like a rabid hound. His longer legs meant he could lope more easily, and he was waiting for her to tire.

If she were a fox, she would have had a burrow to run to ground in, but as it was there was no hiding place for her. She could not climb a tree to escape them, they would only come up after her. Her mind grew wild with panic, as if she were drowning, and still her legs pumped on, propelling her through the forest.

The trees grew more thickly together here, and even in winter's bareness it became dark and gloomy. She was awash in sweat, but she had to slow now to dart between the thick roots, feeling the soft rotted leaves give way beneath her boots.

She dared another glance behind her, and was startled to see that no one followed her. The skinny one had dropped back, less agile than she, perhaps. The fat one she had not seen for some minutes.

The trees gave way to a broad, rain-swollen stream above a waterfall. She stumbled through it, feeling the icy water seep up around her boots. Her feet slid on the slippery rocks, and she shot out her hands to brace herself. She regained her footing and crossed the stream, shaking her wet hands and shivering with the cold. Where were they? Had they followed her this far?

As her panic began to subside, searing pain slicing

through her heart and lungs, a red figure stepped out from a tree in front of her. His eyes shone black and cruel as lit coals, and sweat trickled through the red dye on his face to paint bloodlike stains on his shirt collar. Katie tried to change direction, darting back toward the stream. He was too close. Her ankle twisted and she tripped, thrashing against the rush of cold water, into his arms.

27

Khalil was above her, his plump hands around her throat. He ducked her head into the icy water, and she felt it enter her nose. She held her breath and went still, not fighting him, saving every ounce of breath. It seemed a thousand years before he let her up again, and the cold made her ears sing with pain.

"You have not been attending to your work," he said, puffing slightly from his exertion but keeping his smile horribly bland.

Mehmet came up behind him, looking over his shoulder and speaking rapidly in Turkish.

"It's the earl," she managed, choking and coughing. "He's had me since—since you saw him take me off the docks."

"And does he hold your father and the big man, your Manners, as well?" Khalil asked pleasantly. His grip tightened around her throat, and he moved as if to dunk her in the icy stream again.

"No!" she gasped, clawing at his hands. "We were planning our escape. To Europe. We have men in Marseilles."

Khalil looked appraisingly at her and relaxed his grip on her throat. "You think to escape from us, perhaps, as well as from your earl?"

"Not you, only from Brynston. He is a clever man, too clever for me," she said. "As soon as I am free of him, I will work hard to repay you." *Believe me*, she willed, trying to keep from giving way to desperation. *Believe me, you wretched bully bastard.*

He released his grip suddenly, and she sat upright, shaking the icy water from her ears. Her hands were numb with the cold and she began to shiver, clenching her teeth to keep them from chattering.

Khalil hauled her out of the stream as if she were a sodden doll. She stumbled to keep up with him, her feet tripping beneath her.

"You have been playing a game with us," Khalil said brusquely. "The earl is a formidable opponent, it is true." He winced and touched the unwieldy bandage on his arm. A bright bloom of blood had appeared during the chase, brighter than the reddle dye that stained both men, and he frowned down at it.

"He is a devil," Mehmet said, in a thicker accent than Khalil's.

"I would never trifle with the men who serve Ali," she said bowing her head subserviently. "I honor him too much for that." *Let me get out of this in one piece*, she prayed. Khalil was murderously angry.

"I know this," Khalil said, taking her hand in his. "I know that you honor Ali. I also know that you are a thief. And a thief will steal wherever she can, yes? You must learn, little thief, that you cannot steal from Ali."

"I would never try to steal from Ali," she said earnestly.

"It is unseemly," Khalil mused, "for a woman to be in such a dishonorable profession. Women should be sheltered from such matters."

"I will pay back your money, Khalil," she said, not knowing what else to say.

He closed his hand around hers, gently at first, then he tightened his grip on the bony part of her hand.

His grip was like the pinch of crab-claws, and Katie felt a sharp sting at first. Then his fingers found a nerve she didn't know she had, and suddenly the pain was so intense she dropped to her knees.

"You will pay Ali what you owe him, with interest," Khalil said pleasantly. He released his grip. "That is a taste. There are a thousand such places on the body, where the merest pressure produces great discomfort. And there are other, equally unpleasant things that may happen to an American whore who thinks to do a man's work."

"I understand," she whispered. She looked down at her hand, which was red with smeared paint. "You will get your money. I swear it."

Khalil motioned to Mehmet and they made to leave. "Understand," Khalil said before they went. His voice was soft, but carried in the clearing like a shout. "It is not only you who will taste Ali's anger."

And with that, he and Mehmet melted into the woods like a pair of red specters, leaving Katie on her knees, shaking and alone.

The earl of Brynston stretched out in front of the fire at the Spotted Dog Inn. He was pleasantly aware of every muscle, every sinew of his body. If he closed his eyes he could remember where Katie had touched him, her hands made bold by the half darkness. His wife. His maddening little puzzle-box of a wife.

His work here was finished, the rioting farm workers quieted. The squire who owned these lands was a hard man, inclined to scoff away the harshness of the winter and the needs of his hungry tenants. But through a combination of cajolery and plain intimidation, Julius had convinced the squire to be freer with his hand now, so that the stingy fool might have more from his lands in the long run.

Julius had thought to stay the night at the Spotted Dog, an especially cozy and hospitable lodging house, and ride back in the morning. But he decided against it. It was safe enough to ride at night—this was not country much traveled by footpads. And he wanted very much to be next to his bride again, to taste the intoxicating sweetness of her and feel her body, slim and trembling, beneath his own.

He would ride back tonight. At full gallop.

The door to the parlor opened behind him, and he turned, startled, to see Milvia Trowsedale standing in the door frame.

"Mil!" he called in greeting, not displeased to see her. She had been a close companion to the Willowbys for many years, and he had never wished her any ill. Indeed, he would happily have married her, if Katie had not come along. Odd that, lately, he had come to think of Katie's arrival in his life as more blessing than curse.

"Good evening, Julius," Milvia said primly, stepping forward and slipping off her willow-green pelisse. "I am glad to have found you here."

"You're lucky you did. I'm planning on riding back tonight."

Milvia sat down in the wing chair beside him, her usually tranquil brow wrinkled by concern. "Julius, I have something . . . difficult to tell you, and I'm not sure how you'll take it."

He felt a lump form in his throat the size of a goose egg. "Is it Katie? What's happened to her?"

"I shouldn't say anything has *happened* to her—" Milvia began, clearly uneasy.

"The family, then? Good God, there's nothing happened to Tibby, is there? Or one of the others?"

She shook her head. "No, no, nothing like that, rest easy Julius. My news is not so . . . catastrophic."

He sat back in his chair, his heart slowing back to its usual beat. "I'm sorry to leap at you that way, Mil—it's just that the idea of something happening to them drives me half out of my wits."

She bit her lip nervously. "That's just it, you see, Julius. I've discovered something, well—unsavory. And I'm afraid if I tell you, you'll be angry. But if I don't tell you, well, you shall go on making a terrible mistake."

Julius narrowed his eyes. "Whatever you have to say, spit it out plainly, woman."

Milvia flushed, visibly annoyed. "It's about . . . Katherine. The woman you call your wife."

He felt the sudden urge to bellow at Milvia as another, weaker man might. Instead, he restrained his temper, letting it leak out through the tiniest cracks like molten metal seeping through the seams of a mold. "I have heard enough of your insinuations about my wife, Lady Milvia. I know that I have hurt you by marrying, and I am sorry for that, but you will not speak her name again if you care to remain welcome at Willowby Hall."

But she was not to be put off so easily. She met his gaze steadily, the silver eyes gleaming with something like triumph. "I'm sorry, Julius, but I cannot keep silent. I have made inquiries in London, and you must hear what I have learned. The woman is nothing better than a common sharper."

Even as anger threatened to propel him to his feet, he controlled himself. His hands gripped the arms of his chair until he could no longer feel his fingers. "I know that. It's an unfortunate habit, and one I fully intend to break her of."

"Julius, you of all people must see the need to have a care about such creatures!" Milvia said, shocked.

The rage was nearly blinding now, and Julius honestly thought he might strike her. The impulse passed in an instant, though he had to wait a few more seconds before trusting himself to speak. "Please go, Mil."

"I think you have misunderstood me, Julius," she insisted. "I do not mean that she is a well-bred girl who plays at card sharping. I have had a long conversation with the Bow Street Runners. The girl is a professional blackleg. Her family, her fortune, her name—all lies.

There are no Featherings of Philadelphia, everything she owned in London was had on credit. Credit which has yet to be repaid."

"If a collection of bad debts were proof of ill-doing, half the upper ten thousand would be unmasked as mountebanks and charlatans," Julius said through gritted teeth.

"She is a fraud," Milvia said evenly. "She took Lord Mumblethorpe for ten thousand last summer, and Count Fowler for sixteen thousand the Christmas before. Different names, different identities, but the same woman."

"The Runners cannot know that," Julius said, staring numbly into the fire. "How can they know it's her?"

"Her servant," Milvia answered. "He's distinctive enough. A plain little wren like her might wear a thousand disguises, but the servant would be recognizable to anyone who had seen him. She ought not to keep him, but she must have some affection for the man. Her lover, perhaps."

Julius turned on Milvia, anger burning through him like vitriol. He thought of the way Katie had stiffened in his arms when he had taken her maidenhead, the way her voice had trembled.

"No!" he thundered, his control slipping dangerously.

Milvia jumped back in her seat, frightened. "Very well, then, a servant," she said quickly. "Only a servant. But she is a *criminal*. Nothing better than a common thief. I'd wager she didn't even use her true name on your marriage license. You are married to nothing, Julius. No one. At least, no one real."

The rage tore at him, clawed at his breast until his heart was in bleeding tatters, but it was no longer directed at Milvia. And, surprisingly, it was not directed at Katie. He turned the full force of it on himself, for being the most gullible, simple-minded fool since Adam himself.

*   *   *

With the night had come a drenching blanket of near-freezing spring rain, but Julius did not mind it. It suited his mood. Milvia's word grated on his mind like the rasping squeak of bats. *You are married to nothing. No one real.*

As the rain poured down around the brim of his hat like an icy waterfall, the white heat of his temper began to cool. A fraud, a common sharper. That made a great deal of sense. For the first time since he'd met Katie Feathering, he thought he understood her.

Not Katie Feathering. There was no such person. Katie Willowby, then. Because he was not going to let go of this marriage. She belonged to him, and even this egregious pack of lies was not enough to tear them apart.

She had tried to tell him, he remembered now. Before the wedding, when the fear in her eyes had been like the cries of a trapped animal. And he had mocked her, dismissed it, waved it away as yet another of her excuses.

"Oh, Katie, Katie love. What the bloody hell have you done to me?" Julius cried aloud into the night. His words were swallowed up by the heather, ignored by the cold pale light of the moon. Beneath him Tempest took the road in hard, fast strides, bringing him back to her.

When he saw her, he would know. Know if they could repair the fabric woven of lies and dishonor, or if their marriage was doomed to be a lifeless thing, stillborn and unnatural.

But God help him, he wanted her again. Wanted her laughter, and the wild light shining in her eyes. He wanted his felonious countess, though she was as disreputable as a pack of gypsies. When she had given herself to him last night, there had been no duplicity in the soft curve of her embracing arms, no shame in the way she had unfolded to him like a chaste white flower. There was truth in that, at least. Whatever name she had given him, whatever the illegality of their wedding vows, they were joined by something holy and true.

And Julius would be goddamned if he was going to give that up without a fight.

He arrived late, soaked to the skin. The stable boy started when he saw him, as if Julius were more ghost than man. But ghosts didn't feel the cold threatening to crack their bones. And ghosts weren't susceptible to heartbreak.

"Graves!" he bellowed, taking the front stairs two at a time. He bellowed a great deal more since Katie had come into his life. He still was not sure whether or not he approved of the change.

Graves emerged from his room, cravat tied untidily around his neck. He struggled for his habitual cool expression. "Your lordship?"

"I will speak with the countess at once. I do not care if she is still asleep, and I do not care whether or not she is dressed. She will be in my study in ten minutes precisely, or I will drag her from her room myself."

Graves nodded hastily and swiped a hand over his rumpled hair. "Yes, my lord. I will awaken the maid, my lord."

Julius paused to pull out his watch. "Ten minutes," he said again. "You need not attend to me, I'll see to my own boots."

Graves looked quietly horrified, but, seeing that his master was in no humor to be crossed, he made his way to the servants' bedrooms with great efficiency.

Nine minutes and thirty seconds later, Julius watched his boots steam in front of the fire. The miniature of Jo Cargill lay half-forgotten on his thigh, as he stared into the fire's blaze and wondered how he could have done it again. Entangled himself with a woman who would disgrace him. Put the Willowby name and the Brynston title at risk of dishonor, bring shame on himself and the others in his family. Intolerable. Impossible.

And yet—he was impatient to see those wild green eyes, to hear what explanation she would make. God help her if she lied to him. He would not hear any more lies. But if she told him the truth . . .

He stood up and savagely flung Jo's miniature across the room. It hit a small portrait of his four-times great grandfather, which came crashing to the ground. Damn it all to hell. He took out his watch—it had been eleven minutes. Time to drag the little thief from her lair.

His hand was on the door when Graves opened it, startled to see Julius there so close.

"You have brought my wife?" Julius asked coldly.

"I have not, sir."

"I thought I made myself clear. She will not buy herself time with feminine protests—I will go to her room and bring her back here myself, if I have to drag her naked and screaming."

Graves looked worried, and his normally placid brow furrowed. "I regret that your lordship will find that impossible, sir."

"What do you mean?" Julius asked, suspicious.

"Her ladyship, sir. The maid said the countess came back from her morning constitutional looking very overset and pale, and ordered that she not be disturbed for the remainder of the day. Her father and their servants made themselves similarly scarce."

"Spit it out, damn your eyes. What the hell are you trying to say?"

Graves swallowed, then smoothed the lapels of his waistcoat nervously. "She's gone, sir. The lot of them—Mr. Feathering, the servants, that hulking fellow Manners. All of them have vanished without a trace."

28

The sweet scent of potted jasmine floated on the air above the chateau's gardens. The Comte d'Urbaigne leaned closer to Katie, his thin lips curled in a faint smile, the cloying smell of his scent threatening to drown out the jasmine.

"Are you enjoying yourself, Mademoiselle Wilde? You seem a thousand miles away."

Katie put a sparkling smile on her face, and turned her attention entirely to the comte. "It's just that I'm so bedazzled, Monsieur le Comte," she said. Her French was good, she knew, though strongly accented. But a heavy American accent was all to the good in the game she played with the Frenchman.

D'Urbaigne sniffed deeply and smiled. "Very good, my dear, very good. I pride myself on Montpleur's little amenities."

She gazed out over the marble fountains, the lush beds of massed red and white forced lilies, the hedge of rosemary and lavender clipped to a massive labyrinth. Just on the other side of the tall stone fence were freshly scarred battlefields, as Bonaparte desperately clung to the last shreds of his empire.

"It is all very beautiful," she sighed, while inwardly she thought that she wouldn't have given a rotten egg for the lot. She felt caged here, suffocated.

"The gardener, he shows a small talent, I think," the comte said, giving her a greasy smile.

Katie wondered how such a wealthy man could have such dreadful teeth. The comte's were like a mouthful of rotting seed corn. But he had not been wealthy, Katie knew, before the revolution. He had merely been shrewd, and effective. When Napoleon had granted a generous number of titles to reestablish the aristocracy, humble Jean-Jacques le Gros had become the Comte d'Urbaigne to reign over Montpleur, one of the more sumptuous chateaux in Provence.

"Everything shows the most exquisite taste," Katie said with a smile, leaning on what she knew would be the comte's weakness. He had come to wealth and power late in life, and would be eager for reassurance that he led life *comme il faut*.

"Jou-Jou," Mariane said, pouting down at her glass. "That beastly man has allowed me to run out of claret."

Mariane was the comte's mistress, a plush creature rather like a very fat yellow songbird.

"Poor Minouche," the comte crooned. "Etienne!" he rapped out sharply. "Come attend to your duties, you lazy sod."

Katie did not want to be here, everything in her screamed that it was wrong. But she had no choice, no choice at all.

Perhaps she could somehow have pried the remaining money she needed from Brynston. Could have told some lie that would make everything all right for a little while longer. But the thought of facing those flame-blue eyes with another game, of taking his body into her own and all the while knowing she had cheated him, was unendurable. Better to let the Turks cut out her heart.

And so she played the old game again. This time she

could not afford to make any mistakes. She was a red-head now, Catalina Wilde, tobacco heiress. Her accent was not at all Southern, but no one knew that here. As an American she was intriguing, foreign. And an apparently enraptured witness to all the gaudy splendor the comte could lay at her feet.

"Monsieur le comte?" came a voice from behind Katie's shoulder. Katie turned to see the elegant figure of d'Urbaigne's wife. From the pleasant expression on her face, she must have just come from her lover, a petty nobleman who lived in an *apartement* adjoining the chateau.

"Oui, madame?" the comte said pleasantly, sliding his hand absently to Mariane's plump thigh.

"The dressmakers will be coming in an hour—do you think Catalina would like to have a few gowns made? The French mode is so . . . different from the English," the comtesse said, a thin, superior smile on her lips.

Katie blinked and smiled brightly at the comtesse. "You are so kind, I don't know how I shall ever repay your hospitality. You must come to my home some day to visit. You can't imagine how lovely it is this time of year."

The comtesse shuddered delicately. "We should be devoured by wild Indians, no doubt. It sounds enchanting, but I fear I lack my husband's courage. Will you let us make you a present of a few gowns, then? Those gray things the English made for you will never do for a springtime in France, child. You must have color, and freshness."

Mariane narrowed her eyes appraisingly. "Yellow, perhaps. Like an early jonquil. Very pretty."

"Good heavens, not yellow," the comtesse said disparagingly. "It invariably makes one look jaundiced." She looked pointedly at Mariane's own canary-colored silk dress.

Mariane shrugged. "Green, then, to match her eyes."

"Hmmm," the comtesse said, pressing her fan to her

lips and studying Katie as if she were a painting. "Yes, perhaps green. Something very light and delicate, like a gown of new spring leaves."

"Have a care, or your d'Arcy will snatch her up," Mariane said with a cool smile. D'Arcy was the comtesse's lover.

The comtesse slid ruthlessly prying eyes over Katie's small, thin form in her gray kerseymere gown. "I do not think she is to d'Arcy's taste," she said with a nasty smile.

Katie sat mutely between the two women, trying to keep a vacant smile plastered to her lips. She had to get out of here. A few more nights, a few easy games with d'Urbaigne to loosen his purse strings, and then she would go in for the kill. She needed at least seventy thousand pounds, and she would take it ruthlessly. She was the same tough sharper she had always been.

And then she would be gone. Perhaps she would go to live on some remote, wild island, and to hell with her father's predilection for getting himself in too deep. She could not play the old game any more, it was destroying her soul.

Her father stepped through the glass double doors to meet them, a disagreeable expression on his face. He greeted the comte with a half smile, then plopped down in a chair, looking morosely out over the gardens.

The comte stayed to chat a few minutes, then took himself off to attend to some duty, Mariane in tow.

Katie could hardly wait until he was gone. "Father, you must pay attention to the game at hand," she hissed once d'Urbaigne was safely out of earshot.

Phineas looked up. "Eh? Oh yes, game at hand. Quite right. Only I can't help thinking about that Brynston fellow. He was a lovely catch, Katie, first rate. We could have taken him for a hundred thousand if we'd played our cards right. Maybe more."

"I'm not discussing this again," Katie said coldly.

"I saw the letters, Katie!" Phineas said plaintively. "They let military secrets leak to the French, for the sake of a woman. A pretty little jostler, as it turned out. But not of your caliber, Katie. Couldn't hold a match to you."

"Keep your voice down," she said with a frown.

"They can't understand our English," Phineas said blithely. "It's the accent. Throws 'em off something terrible."

"That's no excuse for carelessness."

"You could have made him do it, Katie," Phineas went on, lowering his voice but otherwise ignoring her protests. "He'd grown to like you, to trust. You were his wife, he'd have listened to you."

"I was never his wife." She snapped her fan irritably. "Anyway, Brynston was no pigeon. He was too smart and too suspicious. We'd all have ended up at the end of a rope."

And she loved him. That was the real thorn that pierced her heart. There were things even a street rat wouldn't do.

"You could have convinced him," Phineas insisted, sliding down in his chair like a spoiled little boy who's been told he can't have a second dessert.

Katie shook her head. "He saw right through me. It's a miracle he never figured out who we are, or what we do for a living. Anyway, it's too late now. He's in England and we're here." She lowered her voice still further, though there was no one to hear them. "I want to get in, lose a few games tonight, and get out by the end of the week. My nerves are strained and I don't want to strain them any further. It could affect my game."

Phineas sat up straighter, looking concerned. "You didn't tell me you weren't feeling well. What's the matter? Not too tired from the trip, are you? I thought you'd like a change of pace."

He was concerned about her, in his childish, self-centered way, and Katie had to smile. It was true that the trip had not been an easy one, but no trip away from Yorkshire would have been easy. It had torn her heart in half to leave Brynston, to take the fragile thing that had built between them and fling it away.

But the alternative was to dishonor him, to let the

Turks drag his name through the muck until it was as filthy as she was. She wouldn't let that happen. Her own name meant nothing, it was just another costume, another masquerade. But Brynston's name was his sustenance.

And if anything should happen to his family—

She could not bear to think of it. "Anyway, father," she said, placating him in the end, as she always did. "Aren't you happier here than you were in England? The life here is more conducive to your temperament."

"Food's better," Phineas said, smiling a little as he thought of it. "Though Brynston's cook had a way with a custard tart—"

"Never mind that now," she said cutting him off. "The soirée tonight will give me a perfect chance to show my recklessness at cards, and you concentrate on whatever gossip you can pick up. D'Urbaigne's weaknesses seem clear enough, but it always helps to have a little extra information to hand."

"Yes, yes, quite right," Phineas puffed, staring out at the gardens.

"I'll be in my room. I'm woefully out of practice, and I don't think I could palm an ace to save my life."

Phineas looked at her indulgently. "Course you could, Katie love. You're my little champion."

She smiled weakly, but her father's old endearment caused more pain than pleasure. "I'll see you this evening. Wear the new waistcoat you bought in London, and remember—no gaming. We're here to get you out of a hole, not to dig another one."

His face creased with a smile as he waved her away. "I know my business, girl, don't you worry. Your old dad hasn't lost his touch."

She looked at him skeptically, but finally decided he would probably be all right. He usually waited until the future shone bright and rosy before sinking them all into the mire again. And today, despite the bright spring day and the fragrance of jasmine on the air, Katie thought the future looked anything but rosy.

*   *   *

The party was small but elegant, and every silk-stockinged aristocrat in the room vied to monopolize Katie—or rather, Catalina Wilde. Mariane was there, looking decidedly plump and toothsome in buttercup-colored silk, the comtesses's warnings about yellow notwithstanding. The comtesse herself was regal in classic ivory. And Katie wore a gown of shimmering silver, visibly expensive and fashionably cut. Her red hair was an artful pile of curls, and she looked as she wanted to look: rich and carefree.

She did not permit herself to think about the fact that she was neither. Instead, she glanced around the room with a seemingly desultory look. There, the marquis de Bistour, a man who seemed to view all games as purely chance. He spat bile when he lost and crowed when he won. He would do very well when she had finished her game here.

She turned her attention back to her gaming partner, the scandalous duchesse d'Ena, who attracted all eyes. Everyone had gathered around to watch Katie throw her money away at piquet with the duchesse, and to hear Katie's careless, amused laugh as she did it. The old game.

Katie could feel the small weight of her locket between her breasts. She had wanted the comfort it had always brought her. But tonight it brought no comfort, only shabby memories of the years of grasping, lying, cheating. She had thought of the locket as her transport back to her childhood, but now Katie realized she had never been a child. She had been born a tough, cynical old woman.

She tilted her head up and faced the duchesse with all the fierce will and self-control her training had taught her. For tonight, she was Catalina Wilde, rich and careless, and there was no one in this room to challenge her.

"Reeshar Weellowbee, Comte de Breenstun," the footman intoned, his accent sliding painfully over the unfamiliar English syllables.

Katie froze, fixed to the spot with terror. The footman had bungled the name. It was another man. It had to be.

She turned slowly around in her chair to see her husband, darkly resplendent as the devil himself, towering in the high, wide doors leading onto the ballroom.

29

Julius knew just where to seek his countess out, and he was not mistaken. She was in the card room off the main ballroom, her head tilted back as she laughed, showing her cards carelessly to the table as she did so. The flickering gleam of a thousand candles danced off her silver gown, sparkling in the wooded glade of her eyes. She was a redhead this time, the color of a vixen. Apt. Very apt.

She paled when she saw him, and for a moment he thought she might faint. Good. Let her faint. Perhaps she would knock her head against the marble floor and save him the trouble of throttling the life out of her. His Katie. His little fox kit. His wife, God damn her.

She did not faint, but tilted her chin up and focused her eyes behind him, as if she had never seen him in her life. She was frightened, he knew. He had run her to ground, and now she was entirely at his mercy. She would not escape him again. He would not permit it.

It had taken no great trick to finagle an invitation from d'Urbaigne, once Julius had found out where Katie had gone. And that in turn had been surprisingly easy—

American heiresses were not so common as all that, and his errant wife tended to make an impression. She still traveled with the scarred brute, Manners.

Her lover, perhaps, Lady Milvia had said. The very thought made him blindly, irrationally angry. Katie had known only one lover, himself. Her husband. The man who was aching to thrash her to within an inch of her miserable life.

He crossed the room to her, shaking off the attentions of the glittering crowd. In an instant he was upon her, towering over the table, a wolf devouring a lamb before the creature had time to bleat.

She stood and he took her hand in his—so tiny, so delicate. He brought it to his lips. "Madame," he said, meeting her eyes with his own, branding her, telling the room in no uncertain terms that she was his. *His.*

What he intended to do with her was another question.

"Mademoiselle," she corrected, pulling her hand away from him. She was afraid, he knew it from her eyes, but another man would never have seen it. Her eyes were the only thing about her that did not lie. That, perhaps, was why he loved them.

"You have the acquaintance of the mademoiselle?" the Comte d'Urbaigne squeaked, blinking his black little eyes and wringing his hands. He had been happy enough to invite Julius, once word had come that a genuine English earl of old title, not some Empire *arriviste*, had inexplicably come to this provincial countryside. But now he looked put out that Julius had attached himself to the pretty American heiress.

Too bloody bad, Julius thought, smiling coldly at the ugly little comte. His blood sang with the desire for conquest, every instinct cried that he haul his larcenous countess over his shoulder and cart her away to punish her in private.

But he had a bit more finesse than that, after all. And his wife's punishment, at least in part, was going to be excruciatingly, exquisitely public.

"We knew each other in England," Julius explained, daring Katie to deny him. "Frightfully small circle, you know, the best set. Everyone knows simply *everyone*."

She caught his gaze, startled. "The earl is . . . indeed well known in England. His family is a very old one."

"I think madame—pardon me, *mademoiselle*—is better known than she realizes," he said, enunciating the words with severe clarity.

"You flatter me, my lord," she said, tucking her chin to hide her face from him. She knew he could read her eyes, and thought she could hide.

"Not at all, mademoiselle," he said. This was unbearable, he had to touch her. To shake her, to curse her, to kiss her until she lost all reason. To know why she had left him. To kill her for leaving him. To look into her heart and see if she had ever had a true feeling for him.

"If your lordship will permit," she said quietly, we were in the middle of a game."

"Perhaps his lordship would care to join us?" A formidable-looking dragon of a woman in red silk glanced up at him with a nod that said that he was not her social equal, but that he was welcome.

"Oh, I never play cards with mademoiselle," he said, looking Katie in the eye.

"And why not, monsieur?" asked a foppish fellow in a bottle-green jacket.

Julius smiled a predator's smile, pleased to see that Katie had gone white as a bleached sheet. "Mademoiselle is too daring by half, and I hate to win large sums of money from beautiful young women. It makes a man feel ungallant."

The table smiled approvingly at this, except for Katie, who had taken to fanning herself and gulping at her champagne.

He watched her lose a few trifles—though the sums would have seemed significant enough, to a man who didn't know how much she would play for later. Julius scanned the room surreptitiously for Manners, but could make out no sign of the brute. He set himself a chair behind the players, looking on, making vocal comment at the duchesse d'Ena's play.

Finally Katie could stand it no longer, and she excused herself from the table, looking more than a little worse for wear. He followed her out onto the terrace, though she ignored his conversational efforts as though he were a ghost.

"Nowhere left to hide, Katie," he said, when they were outside.

The veranda looked out over the gardens, and Katie stared at the clipped labyrinth as if it were the eighth wonder of the world. "I don't know what you're talking about, and I do not appreciate being approached in this fashion," she said in loud French.

"Don't you?" Julius replied in English. He could feel the muscles in his shoulders tighten like knots of wet rope. "What I'm talking about is that you are my wife, and I will take you back to England with me if I have to kill you first."

Katie shivered in her thin silver gown. "Keep your voice down," she said softly. "What is it you want?"

"Everything," he said simply. "By English law, you belong to me. You are mine to do with as I please." He stroked a strand of red hair—more treachery, more lies— from her cheek.

She swallowed. "I am not your wife. I have never been your wife. I did not consent to that marriage, and I—"

"You what? You lied? You cheated? Like some common doxy rolling dice in a wharfside inn? I know what you are, Katie. And, more to the point, I know what you are not. What's your real name, by the way? I've been dying of curiosity."

Her chin was tilted toward the ground. "How did you find out?"

"Milvia set the Runners on you. She told me a long and sordid story, and I found it quite convincing."

She turned on him, the green eyes chilled with anger.

"Then you will understand why I have no intention of staying shackled to some country earl. You can take your damned house and lands and the blasted title and go to blazes with the lot. I don't want it and I won't take it."

He moved closer to her, close enough to crush her. Again he brushed a bright red curl from her cheek. He wanted to tear it away, to tear down all the falseness. "Was it worth it, Katie? You sold your maidenhead so cheap, my dear. A clever whore would have gotten a far better price for such a valuable commodity."

The pain on her face told him he had hit home. "I'm no whore!" she whispered fiercely.

"If you are not my wife, then you are my whore," he whispered back, the words roaring in his own ears like a furnace blast. "Either way, I came here to get what's mine."

"Get out of here," she said, stepping away from him with a sudden, angry movement. "If you don't leave this house at once I'll scream the place down."

"Go ahead and scream, Katie. Won't they all be interested when they hear what I have to say?"

He had literally backed her into a corner, and she was all but ready to fall over one of the massive granite urns filled with flowers.

"I know people," she said, eyes narrowed. "I can arrange for you to disappear, Lord Brynston. Stay away from me."

Julius snorted. "Not bloody likely." He positioned himself between her and the door. "Why did you run away from me?"

"I left because I cannot bear the sight of you," she said, bravely enough, but with the faintest shiver in her voice.

"You might almost have convinced me of that before the cottage," he said.

"What do you want from me?" The shiver in her voice began to bleed into full-blown panic.

"I want to see you suffer. Why did you run away?"

"None of your damned business. Now let me pass."

She tried to push her way past him, and it should have been like a mouse pushing past an elephant.

Except that at the merest touch of her, Julius found all the dark cold in his heart melted away. The memory of that golden night in the cottage was acting on him like potent brandy, pouring through him with burning sweetness. "Katie," he murmured into her hair.

"Julius, I can't . . . " she pleaded, looking up at him with something like tenderness. "I . . . I just can't."

"Why did you leave?" His words were tender enough, but as she hardened herself visibly to him, he grew angry again and the black coldness returned. "Tell me why, or I'll go into that room and tell every last one of them that you're no better than a common thief. I believe the guillotine is still in use in France."

Her brittle mask was back in place, all trace of feeling vanished. She pushed past him, successfully this time, as he had no will left to stop her.

"Go back to England, Lord Brynston."

"Tell me why you left," he repeated.

"Go to hell," she said, quiet and fierce, and then she was gone.

For three days Katie jumped every time a breeze blew a window shut. Claiming a head cold, she saw no visitors, went nowhere except for long, rambling walks through the labyrinth, and most especially, avoided every opportunity for social interaction with the Brimstone Earl.

She broke off a sprig of rosemary from the labyrinth, and let its perfume fill the air. The Brimstone Earl had found her, and now he would destroy her. Not that she didn't deserve it. The remark about the guillotine had been a nasty joke, something to taunt her with. But Katie did not find the joke at all funny. Fleecing rich, powerful men was always risky. And Napoleon's code of law held that a man—or woman—was guilty until proven innocent, not the other way around as in England or America.

She could rot for a good long while in a French prison before getting the chance to play the role of the tearful, repentant young miss for a magistrate.

And yet she had to act. Soon. They must have that money, and she was the only one with the real wherewithal to get it.

She rounded the corner in the labyrinth, as she had done dozens of times since she coming to Montpleur, when a rustling from within the hedge made her start. She put her hand to her chest, feeling her heart thump wildly. A robin, no doubt, scratching for worms. She had to do something about her nerves.

"You're very jumpy this morning, wife," said an achingly familiar voice behind her.

It took every ounce of will she had, but she schooled her features to a mask of cold indifference before turning around. "Brynston. I thought you would have left by now."

He stepped closer to her, too close. It was like being next to a forest fire. She stepped back away from him.

"Leave my beautiful new countess to this pack of immoral Frenchmen?" he said with an ugly smile. "Don't be ridiculous, *wife*."

Katie resisted the urge to wipe her damp palms on her skirt. "Don't call me that."

"But it's true, little fox kit," he said softly. "You are my countess. You *belong* to me. And I take great care of my belongings."

She backed up again, so that she could feel the harsh prickle of the rosemary hedge against her back. "I don't belong to you or anyone. If you thought I did, that's your mistake."

He stepped closer to her again, and she fought the panic stabbing her stomach. There was nowhere else to go, no place to hide from him.

He took a lock of her red hair and rolled it between his fingers. "I don't like the ginger, Katie."

"You're not meant to," she said quickly. What the hell was wrong with her? She should have been fighting him, fast and ruthless. She wore a tiny sheathed knife sewn into her pockets—not much more than an overgrown stickpin, really, but enough to make him let go of her. Enough to escape him.

"It's false," he said, his mouth close to hers. "I hate falsehood, Katie."

The warm sweetness of his breath brought her back to that night in the cottage, to the dark gold of the fire that had lit them both with beauty, to the blooming that was beginning even now, deep at the base of her belly, though she fought it with all the strength she could muster.

"Go back to England," she said, thrusting out a palm to push his chest away. She could keep the walls up when he was at a distance, could tell herself that she would find a way to live without him. But when he was so close, she wanted him enough to make her head swim. Not only wanted the promise of his body, but wanted *him*—his heart, his soul, the rare, warm sound of his laughter.

"Not until I take back what's mine," he said softly. He cupped her jaw, planting kisses on the pad of her cheek, trailing down to her throat. He was furious with her, and she was terrified of the darkness he opened in her soul.

But fear and fury were no match for the blooming that unfurled in her belly.

"Mine, little fox kit," he murmured, his hands sliding down from her jaw to caress her neck. His thumbs rested menacingly at her throat, as if he would crush life and breath from her, before he slid his hands down to cup her breasts. "And I don't care if I have to lock you in a cage, I do not intend to let you go."

She wanted to fly out at him, to punch him. She was shocked to find that anger did not diminish the blooming, but strengthened it. She hated him in that instant, hated his stubbornness and his high-handed arrogance, and she wanted him with a desire that burned so hot it hurt.

"I don't belong to you or anyone," she said, trying hard to catch her breath.

"If I have to hunt you 'til my dying day, I will possess you," he said, the soft menace in his voice striking her as thundering shouts never would. "I will take you, Katie, body and soul. Wherever you run, I will find you and I will take you and I will mark you as my own."

As if to illustrate, he bent down to kiss her neck in long, gentle bites. She heard herself whimper, felt her knees grow watery, and the desire in her belly blazed.

"Tell me you don't want me," he said, his lips close to her ear as he slowly moved his thumbs to caress her nipples through her gown. "Tell me you don't want this."

"I don't want this," she said, turning her face away from his.

"You lie, wife," he said, before taking her chin in his hands and bringing his mouth down on hers.

She met his tongue with her own, the fierceness of her desire burning away all thought of escape. She met his kiss without restraint, giving in to the tide of fire that swept over her, not caring about the consequences.

Her passion surprised him, and a deep, animal growl of pleasure came from his throat. It shredded the last vestiges of Katie's self-control, and she ground up against him, wanting to be as ruthless as he could ever hope to be. She slid her hand between them and brushed her palm roughly down the front of his inexpressibles, finding his hardness straining there, taunting him.

"Christ," he muttered, breaking away from her. Something akin to pain lit his blue eyes.

She all but snarled as she leaned up to kiss him again, tugging at the buttons on his waistcoat, tearing at his shirt buttons.

He slid her dress down from her shoulders, freeing her breasts and teasing them with his mouth. Burning, she was burning up, and she turned her face up to the weak spring sun to cool herself.

His hands left her to fumble with the fastening on his trousers. Then his hands slid her dress up onto her thighs and he grasped her buttocks, lifting her as if she weighed no more than a kitten. Her arms wrapped around his neck to draw him closer. She wore no unfashionable drawers to impede him as he lifted her up and she wrapped her legs around his hips.

She hesitated only an instant before allowing herself to sink onto his hardness, wincing as the still-unfamiliar heaviness of his sex split her body, before she gave way to the molten river flowing through her.

Their mouths met like warriors as they drove their bodies together. She reached her crisis immediately, then another, and another. She cried out into his mouth, and still he drove into her, as blind with the madness as she was, shuddering even as she exploded around him in mindless fury.

She tossed her head back and he stiffened in her arms, letting out a strangled cry. "Katie . . . love," he said, his voice choked, and then he pressed her close to him, shudders wracking him like sobs.

As his body quieted she curled into the hollow of his neck, not thinking, just wanting to melt there softly against him. For a long moment all was stillness, except for the faint distant sound of larks singing and the shared heaviness of their breath.

After a long moment, Julius lifted her up and gently set her down on the ground, her dress falling to cover her in soft folds. He had come here to break his larcenous wife, to intimidate her into bending to his will. And her passion had left him vulnerable as a new-hatched bird. He shivered as a morning breeze blew over him.

When he looked into the green tangle of her eyes, his heart broke all over again. She was as shattered as he was by what had just happened between them. This had been more than simple lust—it was some kind of possession.

"Get what you wanted, then?" she whispered, her voice bitter as absinthe.

"What?" he asked, trying desperately to regain his defenses.

"You were right, Lord Brynston. A smarter whore would have held out for a better price. I took you for thirty thousand before you had any idea that you would have my body. I wonder what I could have gotten for my maidenhead?"

The words were like sand ground into a fresh wound. "You cold-hearted little monster," he whispered. "How can you . . . how can you speak that filth, after what just happened here?"

"You were the one who said it first, my lord," she said, her eyes shining with unshed tears. "And you were right. You came here to make me play the whore, and you succeeded. You ought to be proud of yourself."

"I ought to kill you for saying that," he whispered. Where the hell were his old defenses? Why couldn't he just erect the usual black, dead wall around his heart? But his heart was a pulsing, living thing now, and it hurt like hell. Damn her. Damn her to bloody hell for doing this to him.

"Is that your *wife* you're talking to?" she snarled, her face half covered by her hands. "Or your whore? Which am I, my lord?"

"For Christ's sake call me Julius!" he said. "What the hell kind of woman are you, to *my lord* me after . . . after this?" What words did he have? He could not call it love-making—it had more to do with fury than with love—and yet it had melted him. Forced him to emerge, wet and raw, from the long chrysalis of his own making, whether he wanted to or not. And she mocked that emergence, tried to make it something tawdry.

"I told you a long time ago what kind of a woman I am," she said, regaining control of her voice. "I told you I wasn't good enough for you, and you refused to believe me. Get it through your skull, Julius. I am not a countess and I never will be."

He looked up to meet her eyes, hardly seeing the echoing pain that shimmered there. "You want your blasted annulment so badly? Fine. I'll make you a bargain, Lady

Brynston. Repay the money you took from me the night we met, and you can have your precious annulment. I walk away without a backwards glance."

She shut her eyes, then, and turned her face away. "That's all I ever wanted from you, Julius. For you to leave me alone."

His heart rebelled, rearing in panic like a frightened horse. She couldn't go, she couldn't let him walk away. Not now that she had awakened his blackened heart.

"Fine," he heard his pride say, throwing the word in her face. "It shouldn't take long to find another flash piece to rid myself of the memory of you."

"I'm sure it won't take you long at all," she said, her voice a murderous whisper. "Now get the hell away from me."

And walk away he did, though the rawness in his heart screamed that he was being a bloody fool.

30

"I can't do it any more, Alex. I just can't."
Katie looked into the full-length silver-framed mirror.
Hannah had just finished her hair, and the effect was
perfect. A sleek, sophisticated cap of curls framed her
face, making her look vivacious and *au courant*. Her
gown was a smooth fall of celadon green silk, the cool,
creamy color playing against the warm forest color of
her eyes.

And her eyes were the problem, because anyone who
looked into them would see that Katie Starr was half out
of her mind with panic.

"You look lovely, miss!" Hannah protested. "The very
picture of fashion. There ain't a toff in France, or
England neither, wouldn't think you was the cream of
society."

Katie closed her eyes for a moment. They felt tired
and scratchy, as if protesting the tears she would not
allow to come.

She could hardly afford to be red-eyed and weepy.
D'Urbaigne was holding a ball tonight, a far larger and

more lavish one than his earlier soirées. Paris had fallen, Napoleon was finished, and tonight, the Provençal aristocracy would drown their terror in decadent frivolity.

When she opened them again, Alex was behind her, looking soberly at her reflection in the mirror. "I know you think it's obvious, Katie, but it's only me who can see it. The rest of them will be dazzled by the gown, the hair, the pose. You're as good as you've ever been."

"He'll see," she said simply, meeting Alex's gaze in the mirror.

Alex flinched almost imperceptibly, then nodded. "He'll see. Let me take care of him, Katie."

She whirled around to face him directly. "No! I don't want anything to happen to him."

Alex stood and walked over to her, taking her in his massive arms as if she were still a very tiny girl. "Hush, hush, I won't harm the man, Katie, I promise. But he won't be standing over your shoulder to ruin your game. Let me do that much for you."

Katie felt her throat burn in what threatened to turn into a snuffle, and she swallowed it ruthlessly back again. She would not cry. She would not. "Swear to me you won't hurt him, Alex."

Alex gave her a gentle squeeze. "Not much, anyway."

She looked up at him in alarm.

He laughed softly. "Give the man some credit, little one. He can take care of himself. If it's a choice between giving him a bump on the head and ending up at the bottom of a ditch, I'm not going to stand back and ponder the matter."

"Only if you really have to?" she said, blinking to force the prickle of tears back. "And only a little."

"Only if it is absolutely unavoidable," he promised.

"Mind you watch yourself, Alex Manners," Hannah said, her round face suddenly creased with worry. "That Brimstone's a bad 'un. Sometimes I vow he's as sinful as the rest of this heathenish family."

Alex looked thoughtful. "Do you know, Hannah, I

think you're right. Abduction, forced marriage, scandalous letters hidden in his desk—the man could be a Starr."

Katie shook her head and extricated herself from Alex's comforting arms. "He's nothing like us. Even when Brynston does the dishonorable, it's for an honorable reason."

"And how about yourself, miss?" Hannah pointed out, her hand on her hip. "I never seen you fleece no mark for yourself. You don't even like them fancy clothes and fine rooms. If you're playin' this game for any reason but to fish your good-for-nothing father out of the muck, I'll eat my hat."

Katie was nonplussed. "Hannah, that's really not your place to say."

Hannah shot a quick glance at Alex. "No, miss, it ain't. But there's times a girl's got to speak her mind, even if it sounds like disrespect."

Katie looked at Alex, expecting him to correct the girl with thunderous disapproval. "Well?"

Alex shrugged. "What do you want me to tell her? She's right. You know it and I know it. If you don't want to play the game any more, Katie, all you need to do is stop. I doubt Phineas will ever mend his ways, but he certainly won't as long as you keep coming to the rescue."

"Perhaps you've forgotten about the Turks," Katie said, annoyed. "If they don't get their hundred thousand pounds, they'll kill me *and* my father."

"Lord Brynston could buy your freedom," Alex pointed out. "He has the money, and it would be worth it to him to get his wife back."

Katie steeled herself against the throb of pain that swept her. "He has no wife."

"So far as he's concerned, you're the countess of Brynston."

"Katherine Feathering was his countess," Katie corrected. "And Brynston knows now that Katherine Feathering was nothing but a pack of lies. She's dead, and nothing he can do is going to bring her back to life again."

She squared her shoulders and looked in the mirror once again. Alex was right. She looked the part, she acted the part, and no one downstairs cared enough to search her eyes for the true feelings there. She could hide her heart long enough to squeeze a tidy sum out of d'Urbaigne, and then it would be on to Paris, if it was safe to travel. The Turks demanded their money, and she had the skills to earn it. That was all that mattered now. "Come on, Alex. We have a job to do."

The party was a glittering success, surprisingly sophisticated for an *événement provençal*. The Duchesse d'Ena was forbiddingly elegant in Chinese brocade, and the Marquis de Bistour strutted about the ballroom in a beautifully cut coat of peacock blue. Katie danced with any number of elegant young fops, some of whom whispered highly improper suggestions in her ear, others of whom were too busy posturing to bother themselves with an exotic American redhead. She paid scant attention to either type—she was too busy watching the door to see if her sham husband would cross the threshold.

But Manners was as good as his word, and in due time Katie found herself in her old, comfortable milieu. She waited for the bloods to drift to the tables first, the worst-addicted who threw their dice in a wild, unseeing fever. Katie had played for high stakes in half the major cities in Europe, and that fever always looked the same. It made men reckless and stupid, and allowed Katie to pick them clean. This was a game like any other, the weak against the strong, and the weak always lost. Katie had learned that before she'd learned to walk, and she would never forget it.

She was pleased that d'Urbaigne was one of the earliest to the tables after the first wave of rash young beaux, and she contrived to drift into a game with him. He was doing well tonight; there was a pile of gold around him like Midas's horde, and it was clear he was intoxicated by the presence of so much cash.

Very good. Katie did much better against opponents who were a little intoxicated.

She lost a fair bit to him, moving rather faster than she usually did. Recklessness was in the air tonight, and she had to match the pace or be left behind. She put stacks of gold coins down against numbers that could scarcely win, and within an hour she was down two thousand *louis*.

Tonight she was no foolish fribble, but a brash American seductress, wild enough to risk a fortune and too rich to care. "Do you know, my lord," she said, casting a seductive glance through her eyelashes at d'Urbaigne. "I believe I have realized my problem. I have been playing too cautiously."

D'Urbaigne roared at that, flashing his dreadful teeth as he threw his head back, the tradesman's son peeking through the aristocratic gilt. "They play for great stakes in America, eh? You think we are too timid, here in Provence?"

"I think you are anything but timid, my lord," she said, giving him a bold look. "Fate favors the courageous, does it not? Half measures are for . . . " She finished the phrase with a silent gesture that suggested, . . . *the little people.*

"You are a most intriguing young woman," d'Urbaigne said, with a glitter in his eye that suggested an interest in a very different sort of game.

"And you," she said, "are a fascinating man. What do you say, my lord? Shall we raise the stakes a little? I feel a craving for a little excitement tonight."

D'Urbaigne did not quite lick his lips, but it was clear he wanted to. He pushed a stack of chits into the circle on the center of the table. "Five thousand *louis d'or*," he said breathlessly.

"Make it ten," Katie said, sliding her own stack to join his. She gave him the look, the look that would make him think it was his own idea to risk such ludicrous sums on the roll of a pair of ivory dice. *Do it*, the look said. *It's what you want. Give in to it.*

He flashed a smile, revealing the mouthful of rotted teeth. "Absolutely. Ten thousand. It is your turn to cast, mademoiselle."

Katie palmed the dice, pressing a tiny lever on the bottom of her cup. She shook the cup with a flourish and threw the dice. "Main point is eight," she said coolly.

D'Urbaigne leaned forward avidly, gripping the sides of the table with his thick fingers.

She threw again. Once again, a five and a three. "A nick, Monsieur le Comte."

The comte stared down at the dice as if they'd struck him.

Katie kept her expression neutral as she blandly scooped up the false dice. She slid her winnings to her side of the table. "Perhaps you wish to quit, now that your luck has turned," she said, willing him to stay.

"Not at all," he said, still staring down at the traitorous dice. "When one plays deeply, one must be willing to lose a few pennies here and there."

Katie gave him a slow smile. "I am glad to see I was not mistaken in you, my lord. Shall we raise the stakes again? Perhaps that will turn your luck. Fifteen thousand?"

D'Urbaigne looked up at her, the fever burning in his dark, snapping eyes. "As you say, mademoiselle, fortune favors the bold." He motioned to a footman for a scrap of paper, and scribbled something on it, pushing it to the center of the table. "Fifty."

A shocked murmur went around the room. Fifty thousand *louis* on a few rolls of the dice? Was d'Urbaigne out of his mind?

Katie's eyes locked on the comte's. "Monsieur le Comte has the heart of a lion."

D'Urbaigne looked at her greedily. "And what kind of heart does mademoiselle possess? A lion, or a sweet little lamb?"

Mademoiselle is a tough little street rat who'll gnaw your bones clean, Katie thought. She nodded, allowing a smile to curve her lips. "I am inspired by Monsieur le Comte's courage. Fifty thousand it is, then. And may fortune reward the greater gamester."

"So be it," d'Urbaigne said, his entire body quivering with the fever. It was something of a miracle, Katie thought, that no one had fleeced him of his house and estates before this. The man was possessed.

She handed him a third pair of dice, seemingly identical to the first. "Your roll, Monsieur."

He threw his dice. "Main point of five," he said, licking his lips. "An auspicious number."

"For one of us," Katie said, smiling and nodding faintly.

He rolled again. Katie held her breath. This was the risky part, as it was not impossible that he would roll his main point again for a win. Unlikely, but not impossible. However, if he should win this round, she would guarantee that she won the next.

The weighted dice fell in her favor, as they did eight times out of ten. Two ones lay on the table. A crab.

There was not a sound in the crowded card room as Katie scooped up her dice and dropped them into her cup. She pressed the tiny lever that would seal the false dice in the bottom. "You are out. I win again, monsieur," she said, her voice quiet.

"I was so sure," he said, staring down at the table. "I felt it in my bones."

"And I, too, felt sure of my own success," she said, wanting suddenly to say something to convince this man never to do something so foolish again. "But only one can win, my lord."

"I had been winning all night!" he cried plaintively, shifting his gaze up to hers.

"Ah, but fortune is a fickle bitch, the most treacherous of treacherous women," came a familiar rumbling voice from behind Katie's left shoulder.

Katie could have leapt out of her skin. Brynston. He had crept up behind her, and had just seen her pluck, skin, and broil the hapless pigeon across the table from her.

"Another game!" d'Urbaigne cried, shaking his dice cup greedily. "Double or nothing, a hundred thousand."

Katie shook her head sadly no. She had taken too much from him as it was. "That game is too rich for me, my lord. I feel suddenly very tired."

"I will play," Brynston announced.

D'Urbaigne looked up expectantly at him. "Yes? A high-stakes roll? You have never felt such excitement, monsieur, I can assure you. The sensation is like no other."

"Not against you," he said. "Against her."

"I am tired," she repeated, pushing herself away from the table. "My concentration is broken."

"You will stay," Brynston said in English.

She could not move beneath the blue fire of his gaze. She could hardly even breathe. His cheek was grazed with a scrape and there was the faint suggestion of a fresh bruise under his left eye, but otherwise he looked imperturbable. "It's impossible—" she began in French.

"It is not impossible," he said in English. "You will stay."

She should have tossed off an impertinent remark and walked away. She should have risked it. She'd truly believed what she'd told d'Urbaigne—fortune did favor the bold. To let Brynston bully her into staying was a bit of weakness she could ill afford.

But even worse than weakness was to underestimate one's opponent. After what had happened between them this morning, he would not hesitate to destroy her. The evidence of her duplicity was in her hand—the false-bottomed dice cup—and he would not hesitate to demonstrate it for the crowd.

"Very well," she said finally. "But I must warn you, my lord. I seem to be in the midst of a powerful winning streak."

"So was d'Urbaigne," Brynston said with an evil smile. "I'll take my chances."

D'Urbaigne made a few feeble attempts to remain in the game, but in the middle of his plea he was hustled off by the comtesse, who dragged him to a side parlor with admirable vigor.

"Hazard, then, my lord?" Katie asked, pulling together every ounce of cool self-control she could muster.

"I don't think so," he said, holding her gaze steadily with his own. He flicked a glance at the dice cup in her hand. "Something tells me dice are unlucky for me tonight. Piquet, I think."

Katie's cheeks burned. "That is a game requiring great skill, my lord."

He smiled at her, but the smile was all cold revenge. "Pray do not underestimate your abilities, my dear. False modesty does not become you."

"Very well, then," she said, sitting very straight in her chair as if preparing to do battle. "Piquet it is."

A liveried footman scurried up with a deck of cards, and Katie cut, keeping her eyes on his.

Katie had been a fool to ever try to gull this man. He was too ruthless—with the world around him, and with himself. Now he dealt the cards with the skill of the cleverest sharper in London, and it was Katie who felt like a prize gudgeon.

"Let's start small, shall we?" he said, almost pleasantly. "A thousand *louis*."

"Your lordship plays very deep indeed if he considers a thousand *louis* small stakes," she murmured.

"I am certain that *mademoiselle* is well accustomed to such play," he said.

She wanted desperately to look anywhere but into his eyes, but the torch blue of his gaze seemed to put her in a kind of trance. There was no light, no beauty, anywhere but in those eyes. She struggled to control her breath, taking slow, deep lungfuls of air.

Brynston set the stock in the center of the table, dividing out the upper five from the bottom three.

Katie stared dully at her cards, unable to concentrate on anything but what had happened between them that morning. The grubby urchin had finally weakened and become a whore, after all. She had joined with him not out of love, but out of some fierce passion born of equal parts lust and fury. There had been nothing romantic or respectable about it.

The memory made the blood sing in her ears as she declared her combinations. She had hardly the will to make out her own cards, much less keep track of who had played what.

"I seem to have won that round," he said pleasantly. "I insist that you have an opportunity to recoup your losses."

"Really, I must go, I am very tired," she murmured.

"Nonsense," he said, sweeping up the cards and shuffling them. "I feel certain a little deep play will revive you."

They played that way for something close to an hour, though to Katie it felt like a lifetime. Unwanted images kept forcing their way into her mind—the ferocity of their joining in the labyrinth, his tenderness the morning after he had taken her maidenhead, the good-natured patience on his face when he dealt with his troublemaking younger siblings. She knew what was behind the mask of Lucifer he wore for society's sake, and that knowledge acted on her with all the bitter sweetness of a draught of laudanum.

And he coolly took advantage of her distraction, taking hand after hand as he moved her pile of winnings slowly to his side of the table.

"Miss Feath—I beg your pardon, Miss Wilde—are you listening?"

She blinked and looked up at him. He was furious with her, he hated her, as she knew would happen when he knew the truth. But, God help her, she wanted it to be different. She wanted things to go back as they had been when he'd thought she was an heiress, when he had taken her to wife and tried to teach her to be a countess.

"I beg your pardon, my lord?" she asked.

His eyes seemed to soften for a moment, so that she could see into the melted, tender place in his soul. Then the mask was back in place, and he shut her out again. "I suggested one last match, to cap the evening. A grand gesture. Ten thousand *louis*, Miss Wilde. Are you agreeable?"

His words came back to her like a slap. He had taken nearly twenty from her already. *Repay the money you took from me the night we met, and I walk away without a backwards glance.* Thirty thousand *louis*, thirty thousand pounds—it was close enough. He was playing for their marriage, and if she lost the hand, she lost him as well.

She looked into his eyes, and she was certain of it. "I agree," she said softly.

It was her turn to deal, and she did so swiftly, not bothering to conceal her skill. She slid the cards off the table and glanced at them, careful to keep her expression neutral. It was a solid hand, a hand she could play to win, if she kept her wits about her.

She discarded a pair of eights, and drew a ten and a king. Excellent.

"Point of five," Brynston said with relish.

She looked down at the cards in her hand. "Good," she said neutrally.

Brynston allowed himself a smile. "A point of five. I score five. A sextet."

Katie looked at her hand. "How high?"

"Queen," Brynston said.

Katie smiled at him dazzlingly. "Not good."

Brynston looked at his hand. "A quatorze of queens."

Katie swallowed hard. "Good."

Brynston led the first trick, a ten of spades. "I start with twenty."

Katie followed suit with the eight of spades. "A sextet, I start with sixteen."

He took the first trick, but she took the next four, knocking out his tens and knaves with a solid run of queens and kings. He took four more, then she took two.

What was she doing? She had fought to be free of him since the first time he'd laid hands on her, and now she was throwing away her opportunity to be rid of him once and for all. To be sure, it was a great sum of money, but money was the last thing on her mind tonight. She had a sudden, ludicrous image of him play-acting the dowager duchess, remembering the way they had laughed together.

They each held a card. Katie led with the king of hearts. He didn't have an ace, she was nearly certain of it. He'd given two hearts to her already.

He shot her a piercing look. "Mademoiselle seems to have regained some of her luck."

"Perhaps," she said, trying for a careless tone.

"But it is not enough." He laid down the ace of hearts. "I take the last trick, and the game."

She stared down at the handful of cards, the lurid red heart hiding her king. She had lost, and he had won. The Brimstone Earl would, by his own agreement, walk away from her forever.

Katie stood and smiled blandly, trying to shut out the room's murmured buzz. She watched Brynston arrange to have his winnings safely transported back to his lodgings and congratulated him with a gamester's sangfroid before walking away from the table.

And all the while, a crazed howling rose up in her soul, screaming into the blackness there.

31

Julius had stayed up until well past four, drinking brandy after brandy in a desperate attempt to escape his own thoughts. He'd intended to sleep the day away, but he was awake again in the early morning, his body poisoned by hangover but his mind too troubled to seek refuge in sleep.

It was over. The complicated mess that Katie had made of his life was finally over. Now he could get back to a world where the demands of honor were clear. She would never lie to him again, never again make him lose himself in the wild, fierce tangle of those green eyes. Never strip away his defenses as she opened her body to him, then throw his feelings in the dirt like so much slop. Perhaps he would patch things up with Milvia and marry her, after all. She would make an excellent countess—had been training for it, in fact, all her life.

So why did the thought of this idyllic existence without his hell-born wife make him want to put a bullet in his head?

Katie had been nervous and distracted most of the evening—astonished, no doubt, to see him there. The brute Manners had accosted Julius on the road before the ball, and it had been the very devil to overcome him. Julius thought he might have cracked a few ribs in the process, and he prodded them now, wincing. Graves could tape his ribs later this morning. For now, Julius wanted to be alone.

That last hand had woken her up, and she had played it to win. She'd known as well as he had that they were playing for their marriage. He'd read it in her eyes, as he had read so many of her secrets before. Though she'd lied to him about every conceivable subject under the sun, her eyes always told him the truth.

And the truth he had read last night was that she did not want him to leave.

Julius head throbbed vilely. The thought that she wanted to stay married to him made his heart race like a frightened rabbit's, and Julius was not at all accustomed to being frightened.

He could not back down from this. He'd told her before that he didn't lie—he'd as much as promised that he would leave her in peace if he got his money back. He could not possibly go back on his word now.

But she wanted him to.

He stood and raked his hands through his hair, fighting the lurching in his stomach, fighting a rising swell of panic. He didn't even know her true last name. But he did know that his fierce little bride had fought him like a cornered animal at every turn. She did not want to be married to him. She could hardly stand him.

But her eyes said something different.

He shut his eyes, hoping to blot it all out. He was pathetic. His strength and honor had been peeled away like the layers of an onion, and there was nothing at all underneath.

A knock came at the door, and even that soft sound was enough to send Julius's head pounding. "Leave me be," he muttered.

The knock came again, a little louder.

"Leave me be!" Julius cried, hardly caring who heard him. He wanted to get drunk, to become an opium eater—anything to shut out these feelings. But even as he thought it, he knew it was futile. When he sobered again, in six weeks or six years, the truth would remain the same. His heart belonged to a disreputable little criminal who didn't want it. Nothing was going to change that.

The door opened, and Graves thrust his serious face into the room. "I have some important news for your lordship," he said, his voice soothingly quiet.

"I'm bloody well tired of important news," Julius said. "Whatever it is, I don't care."

"It's the countess, your lordship."

"There is no—" Julius broke off, giving Graves a searching look. "What's wrong? Has something happened to her?"

"She's gone, your lordship."

Julius felt the blood pound in his head like the surging of ocean waves. His throat was tight, and he could hardly see through the red haze of his rage. He picked up the silver tray and hurled it across the room. It hit the wall in an explosion of glass and brandy. "God *damn* her! God bloody well *damn* her!"

Before he could take the room apart stick by stick, there was the sound of a throat clearing heavily. Julius reined in his fury long enough to see Manners standing behind Graves in the doorway. Julius noted with satisfaction that the man's lip was split with an ugly gash, and that a yellow and purple bruise bloomed across his jaw.

"What the hell do you want? Come to hit me over the head and steal last night's winnings before joining your mistress?" Julius said with a sneer. "You'll have to go thump d'Urbaigne for it instead. I took pity on the idiot and gave the whole thirty thousand to him."

Manners shook his head no. "I don't care what you did with the money. Neither did Katie. She cried herself to sleep last night, but it had nothing to do with the cash."

"Didn't it?" Julius wished for something else to hurl. The writing desk looked promising. "Now why do I find that hard to believe?"

"That doesn't matter now. What does is that Katie did not leave here of her own free will."

That broke through the red fog of Julius's anger, and he fixed the man with a stare. "What the devil are you talking about?"

"If she had, she would have taken her father and me with her," Manners said, clearly working hard to keep his own self-control. "And she had no reason to leave."

"Didn't she?" Julius said. He thought of the way their bodies had clashed together, and of how she had thrown his words in his face.

"I have a good idea where she's been taken, and who's taken her," Manners said.

Julius felt shards of panic begin to prick at him. Had someone really abducted her? Was she in danger? "You overestimate her loyalty, Manners. She didn't want to face me, so she left town. If you're lucky, she'll send you a note and you can catch up with her later."

Manners shook his head. For the first time, he looked sincere, even honorable, in Julius's eyes. Every time he'd seen Manners before, the brute was acting in his capacity as Katie's hired thug. But this morning he seemed more a worried parent than a henchman. "There's a lot you don't know," he said.

Julius felt his lip curl. "You're right about that much at least, my friend."

Manners closed the door behind him and looked Julius squarely in the eye. He spoke with a quiet dignity Julius never would have suspected he possessed. "It's time we changed that. We'll need to move quickly to find her, but first there are some things you should know."

*   *   *

Katie felt as if the rumble of the bath chair beneath her would break every bone in her body. She was hidden by a thick black veil of widow's weeds, her hands bound together in front of her as Mehmet pushed her wheeled chair. They had forced some vile concoction down her throat, so that she could hardly keep her chin off her chest, much less struggle or fight them. She was sure she looked the very picture of a dried husk of an old woman, wheeled about by two careful attendants.

They would kill her, she knew. They had heard about her losses at the table, and Khalil was half out of his mind with rage. Grasping at straws, she had made up some lie about a cache of money she'd hidden in London—a lie they had only half believed. And yet, the lure of gold was great enough that they would risk trusting her once more, would keep her alive long enough to get to London. Once there, she would have no cache of treasure, would have nothing at all to offer them, and they would cut her throat if she was lucky. If she was unlucky, they might take a good deal longer to dispatch her.

They wheeled her to the docks, and Khalil left to arrange their passage. Mehmet remained to guard her, and he amused himself with whispering threats for a few minutes, but quickly tired of that game.

A trio of French doxies drifted by to call out endearments, teasing him and laughing. He laughed with them, matching their banter with his own. Katie tried to lift her head to see them more clearly, but managed only a pathetic wobble. Through her veil she could just see the contemptuous look on his face as he left her there, shooting a worried glance over his shoulder for Khalil before he left with the whores.

All was silent, even peaceful, for what felt like a long time. Katie listened to the sound of the waves lapping the docks, and felt the morning's foggy chill creep past the black drapery of her disguise. The drug they had given her sheltered her from fear or unhappiness. She was in love with a man who could never love her in return. She was bound hand and foot. She would die soon, possibly quite painfully. These realities seemed no more disturbing than the prospect of a pleasant Sunday drive in the country.

A shadow appeared at her left side, and Katie wondered if it was Mehmet, back from tumbling his whores. Perhaps he would resume his threats. It didn't matter. She would simply fold her soul into itself like a sleeping bird, and ignore the relish he took in causing her pain.

"Mother?" came a concerned male voice, in French. "Are you all right? Who has left you here like this? Your old bones will take a chill."

Katie managed to tilt her head enough to see a beefy sailor, his red face touched with concern.

She wanted to beg him to help her escape, to explain to him that she must hide from the evil men who held her. But it was too much, the words would not form themselves in her mouth. "*Le médaillon,*" she managed to croak. *The locket.*

"I don't know what you mean, mother," the sailor said, bending down so that he could see her face. Or would have, if it had not been covered by a thick gauze veil.

"My locket," she said, grasping for the French words, forcing them from her mouth. She used her old gift on him. *Do not question. Believe what I tell you. Take the locket without delay.* "You must take . . . locket . . . earl of Brynston. Will pay you money. Tell him . . . London."

The drug's thickness settled around her again, and she slumped in the wheeled chair. "*Je vous . . . en prie,*" she gasped. *I beg you.*

"You want me to take your locket to this earl, then? Breen Stone?" the sailor asked. "And something about London?"

Somehow Katie managed to lift her chin a fraction of an inch, then let it fall again in approximation of a nod. *Do it,* her gift willed. *Do it quickly, before they return!*

"Where will I find him, mother?" the man asked urgently.

It was impossible. Katie could not find the strength to make her lips move. She tried to lift her bound hands, to take the locket from her neck, but it was impossible. Mehmet and Khalil would come back soon, and probably kill this young man, who only wanted to help an old woman.

Strong hands reached for her throat, and even through the haze of the drug, Katie felt a stab of panic.

But the hands merely lifted the locket from her neck, and the sailor's beefy face said, "I don't know what this is about, mother, but I will do what I can." He stood, and Katie could hear Mehmet's shouts coming from down the dock.

"Hey there, you! What are you doing to my mother? Trying to rob an old lady, were you?" Mehmet shrieked in heavily accented French. "I'll have you thrown in prison, see if I don't."

"You left your mother here all alone on these docks?" the sailor said accusingly. "Don't you know what kind of scum hangs around here? You're the one who ought to be arrested, for putting an old lady in danger."

"Surely you can see that she is too old to get into any trouble. Who would harm such a helpless old thing? She can scarcely move."

"You are a fool if you believe the assassins around here would not harm her," the sailor said, his voice stalwart. "Do not leave her alone again. There are pigs on these docks who would push her into the water as a joke, just for the fun of seeing her drown."

Mehmet's voice took on a kind of oily charm. "A thousand thanks for looking after my blessed mother, sir. I had not realized the dangers. She will be well attended to now. I promise you."

"She'd better be," the sailor said fiercely. "Her locket—"

Mehmet's voice rose to a note of pure panic. "What about it? Did she give it to you? She is like a child, you know, she does not know what she is doing. You must return it to me immediately."

The sailor hesitated a long moment, and Katie mustered every ounce of her strength to shake her head infinitesimally, no.

"I don't have it," the sailor said at last. "Some little pocket-picking bastard snatched it from around her neck before I could stop him. Your carelessness has lost your mother her treasure, friend."

"A pickpocket? A stranger, or did he seem to know her?" Mehmet demanded.

"Just one of the little bastards who cuts purses around here," the sailor said carefully. "Nobody special."

Mehmet relaxed a fraction, though his voice was still tight. "Ah well, it was only a trinket. It had no value at all. Do not trouble yourself about it. Good day, my friend."

"You will not leave her alone again?" the sailor insisted.

"My friend, I would not dream of it," Mehmet answered, and his voice sent a shiver down Katie's limp and crooked spine.

Julius rested his head in his hands as the carriage thundered down the rutted road. Alex had come with him to search for Katie on the docks, while Phineas remained behind to question the servants.

Julius was entirely sober now, but last night's brandy and the thick poison of guilt felt like they would split his skull in half.

Alex Manners clutched Katie's locket in his big hands. A sailor had appeared at d'Urbaigne's chateau gibbering something about having to find an earl called Breen Stone, on behalf of an old, palsied woman bound for London. He'd been led to Brynston's rooms, where he had waved the locket as evidence, saying he had a bad feeling about the woman's son.

"All right," Julius said. "Everything she's done has been for her father. I can understand that, I suppose, though the man is hardly one to inspire such loyalty. But why should she have lashed out at me? I came to France with a good idea of the truth. To remain the countess of Brynston would solve all her problems, and yet—" Julius broke off for a moment, hardly trusting himself to continue. "She threw it all in my face, Alex. The lands, the title—"

"You care for her," Alex Manners said, nodding. "This is more than just stubbornness, isn't it?"

"His lordship is devoted to the countess," Graves put in. "As I told you before."

Julius gave his valet a wan smile. "Surely you haven't been gossiping below stairs, Graves."

Graves assumed an indignant expression. "Certainly not. I merely wanted to let this fellow know that your lordship's feelings were sincere."

"I don't know how you knew that, since it took me a devil of a long time to discover it myself," Julius said.

Alex swallowed thickly, as if steeling himself to say something difficult. "You have to understand, certain matters are . . . difficult for Katie."

"What do you mean, *certain matters*?" Julius asked sharply.

Alex's broad face flushed deeply, his scars white against his dark red cheeks. "The, er, intimacies of marriage."

Julius, who was embarrassed by precious little, found himself at a loss. "I see. Well, yes, such matters are usually . . . awkward for a young bride."

Alex looked grimly determined, as if preparing to hew his way through a mountain. "It's different for Katie. Her background—that is to say, her upbringing—"

Graves put his hand on Alex's forearm, and said, "It's all right. We love the countess, too. We would never think less of her because of something that happened in her past."

Julius stared at his valet as if the man had turned bright green.

But Alex nodded, and swallowed again. "Katie's mother—"

Julius nodded impatiently. "She told me once, that her mother had taken a lover. That her father was not her father."

Alex flinched as if he had been struck hard across the face. "That was not quite the truth," he said, so softly Julius could hardly make out the words. "Katie's mother was a whore."

32

The carriage was quiet for a long moment, as Alex worked to compose himself.

"There's actually not much doubt that Phineas is her father, if you look at the two of them," Alex continued, his voice strangely flat. "He was very young then, cocky as a bantam rooster, and he'd won a lot of money. He took Molly out of the brothel to set himself up as her protector. For awhile they seemed very happy together."

"For awhile?" Julius asked.

"Phineas had lost most of the money within a year, but he seemed to . . . to still care for Molly. They moved into smaller and cheaper rooms every year, and after awhile he began to call her his wife, though to the best of my knowledge they never did get married. Katie came along pretty quickly, and Phineas was fond enough of the child."

"But not as fond as you were," Julius said quietly.

A strangled sob escaped Alex's mouth, and he swallowed it back, clearly mortified. He stared out the window at the rolling landscape while he composed himself. When he could finally speak, he said, "I loved that little girl. She was everything to me. I used to take her for walks around the park, and everyone thought she was my child. I wasn't ugly then, you know, just big. And I used to whisper to her in her pram that I would look after her always, that she would never come to harm so long as her Uncle Alex was close by."

Graves patted the big man again. "You've always done your best for Katie, that's clear."

Alex shook his head. "My best wasn't good enough. When she was eleven—" He broke off, burying his big shaggy head in his hands for a moment.

When he looked up again, his face was hard, almost blank. "We were all living in a place something like the flash houses you have here—whores, thieves, swindlers, all gathered under one roof. Katie was eleven, and the prettiest child you ever could imagine. And her mother . . . " Alex trailed off for a moment, lost in thought. "Molly was still a great beauty. Skin like a dish of sweet cream, and green eyes like lanterns. Phineas was an utter incompetent as a sharper, so there was never any money, but Molly . . . " Alex swallowed. "Molly began to entertain clients again."

Julius felt a cold sickness deep in his stomach. "And you hated her for it."

Alex shook his head violently. "Not hated, no. I never hated her. But I begged her not to do it, tried to get her to see that sort of life was no good for Katie. I would have . . . Well, it didn't matter, she wouldn't leave Phineas, and she couldn't see that he would never make anything of himself. It was bad enough that we were all living in the middle of that cesspit, but for Molly to sink back into—" Alex stopped, and took a deep breath. "Anyway, one night, the bully pimp who ran the place tried to get Katie to follow in her mother's footsteps."

Julius wanted to run, to jump out of the moving carriage and hear nothing more. He could not endure this. He could not sit here and listen to how Katie had been hurt.

But that was cowardice, and nothing more. He willed

himself to sit back and listen, despite the cold sweat that was trickling down his back. "Go on."

"Katie was a wild thing even then," Alex said, the ghost of an ironic smile on his lips. "She'd been raised with the pickpockets, and was no tamer than a little wolf cub. But she was innocent of . . . of what happens between men and women. She was alone with the john before she understood what was expected of her."

Julius found himself forward on his seat, ready to go find the bastards who had hurt Katie, ready to kill to avenge her. "He didn't—?"

Alex shook his head, no. "They seriously underestimated her. The john tried to get rough, and he was dead before he knew what hit him."

"The countess?" Graves said, looking as if he might faint. "She killed him?"

Alex smiled bitterly. "It is the great misfortune of my life that I didn't do it for her, but yes. She used to carry a wicked little dagger, and she took him by surprise."

"And I brought her to the flash house." Julius's mouth filled with the sick, metallic taste of guilt. "I didn't understand why she was so frightened. I thought it was the response any properly bred young lady would have to being amid a pack of criminals."

"It's not just the flash house," Alex said. "All we want is to forget those days. But we can't. Everywhere we go, there are reminders. Katie still has nightmares most nights."

"And what happened to Molly?" Graves asked gently.

Alex's face went starkly neutral again. "After Katie . . . after the john was killed, Katie ran to find me. She was covered in blood and she couldn't stop crying. I wrapped her up in my coat and we ran. I took her to my aunt's house, where I knew she would be safe, and then I went back for Molly."

For a long moment, there was no sound but the rumble of wheels and the creak of carriage springs.

"The pimp killed her," Alex said finally. "As revenge

for what Katie had done, I suppose. He cut her to pieces."

"Your scars," Julius said, suddenly understanding.

"I strangled the bastard, slowly, but he managed to get a few cuts in first," Alex said.

"Oh my," Graves said in a small voice.

Alex smiled wanly. "It wasn't the first time I'd killed a man, my friend, and it wasn't the last. But it was the only time I was glad to do it."

"Katie thinks she killed her mother," Julius said, understanding suddenly flooding him like a wash of light. "She blames herself."

"Katie would take on the sins of the devil himself if she could think of a reason to," Alex said. "She thinks if she'd only begun helping her father to cheat at cards sooner, her mother would never have gone back to whoring. And if she'd let that bastard touch her—" Alex paled, his fists clenching.

Julius gripped the edge of his seat. He needed to be where Katie was, to destroy anything that ever threatened her again. He sent up a silent prayer. *Watch over her. I'll give anything, make any sacrifice, so long as she's safe.*

"You were in love with her," Graves said mildly.

Julius's eyes flew open.

Alex nodded. "I loved Molly from the minute I set eyes on her, and I never stopped. I would have married her and given her anything, but she said she owed Phineas too much. She was a hard-hearted little thing, but I think she did care for him, in her way."

"So you watch over her daughter," Julius said.

Alex gave him a wolf's smile. "There was a time when I gave serious thought to killing you, for Katie's sake. She was so frightened, and you wouldn't leave her alone."

Julius shrugged. "I still don't know why. It would have been easier for everyone if I had."

"I know why," Alex said. "It doesn't matter now. When that sailor showed up looking for you, instead of for me, I realized everything was different."

Graves looked concerned. "I'm sure you are still very important to her," he said placatingly.

Alex nodded. "I am. I know that. But it's not right that a girl cling to someone like me all her life. I'm more a father than a friend to her, and she needs to make a life of her own. A proper husband and family, not this endless wandering. It makes her sick, to run the game, but she doesn't want to think about what will happen if she leaves her father to fend for himself."

"The very first thing I'm doing, once I get her back," Julius growled, "is to give that man the thrashing of his life."

Alex settled back in his seat, his broad face settling into a gargoyle's stony stare. "Sorry, Julius. You're going to have to wait in line."

Katie slipped in and out of consciousness during the long, stormy trip back to England, almost grateful for the drug that dulled her mind so deeply she could not quite manage to be afraid. In the moments when her mind cleared somewhat, she sent a silent wish out to the swirling world around her, that her locket would make its way to Julius, that he would understand what little she had been able to tell the sailor.

The Turks soon appeared in her cabin to pour more of the bitter drink down her throat. Though she commanded her limbs to strike out at them, she could do little more than stir feebly as they forced her head back and tipped the vile stuff into her mouth. She tried to claw her way through the veil of fog that surrounded her, but the drug was too powerful, and she sank again into blackness.

When she awoke, she felt as if every pore of her body oozed poison. Daggers of pain split her skull from back to front, and her body shook with chills and nausea. She was lying on a hard, narrow bed, and she pushed herself slowly up onto her elbows and opened her eyes.

They were not at sea any longer; the ground was still.

The walls in front of her had once been a color, perhaps green. Now they had peeled and faded to a sickly dun. A small table and chair, and the narrow bed she lay on, were the room's only furnishings. She was covered by a blanket that reeked of unwashed bodies and slopped ale, but she was cold, and she did not thrust it aside.

The door knocked, a tiny ineffectual sound, and then opened. A small, reverent person stood there holding a very large tray. "Good afternoon, mum," piped a high voice.

"Where . . . where am I?" Katie managed, her tongue feeling like a wad of thick cotton batting in her mouth.

"Bullsblood House, mum," the child said. "In Spital-fields."

Katie sank back onto the hard bed. "If you tell me you're a pickpocket, I'll kill myself."

The little figure approached her, setting the tray onto the small table. "I hope you won't, mum. It ain't nothin' I chose for meself, but I'd rather pick pockets than get the sooty warts climbin' chimneys."

"Just once," Katie muttered, "why couldn't I get abducted and taken somewhere pleasant? Shopping in Mayfair—now that would be more like it. Child, tell whoever it is who's holding me that I want to be knocked over the head and brought to the dressmaker's."

The child's eyes were wide with worry. "You ain't off your chump, is you, mum? The other blokes'll be that disappointed, they will."

"What other blokes?" Katie asked, trying not to think of her splitting head and rebellious stomach.

"You . . . you is the countess, ain't you?" the child ventured, looking worried.

Katie wanted to laugh, but she was afraid it would hurt too much. "That's me. The countess of criminality. The duchess of deception. The . . . the marchioness of the macers. Hmm, that last one wasn't much good, was it?"

The child shook his head nervously. "No, mum. Countess Katie. You're a legend 'round these parts, even if you does look like you've seen better days."

Katie pushed herself up again, to face the boy. "How do you know my name? Did the Turks tell you to call me that?"

"No, mum. I heard it from Sharper John White, who heard it from Alfie the Pincher over by Newgate, who swears he got it from Tom Finch hisself."

"Tom? You know Tom?"

"No, mum. I knows blokes what knows blokes what knows Tom. An' every rum-kiddy in London knows about Countess Katie. I told you, mum, you're a legend."

Katie sank back on the bed. The pain in her head was beginning to radiate throughout her body, stabbing her like a million bits of glass. "A legend in my own time. Who'd have thought it?"

"Is there anything what I can do for you, mum?" the boy asked earnestly.

"What I would like above all things would be to get out of here," Katie said.

"Ah," the boy said, sounding ashamed. "The blokes what sent you here—they told us you'd say that. The thing of it is, mum, if you escape, they'll stick our spoon in the wall but good. Them as they can catch, anyway."

"Now why doesn't that surprise me?" Katie said. "Not to worry—what was your name?"

"Adam, mum. It's a name from the Bible."

"Ah yes, the Bible," Katie said, smiling despite herself. "I believe I remember that story. Adam, then. I'm very grateful for your offer, but you mustn't do anything that will actually make the Turks angry with you. They're not fellows who take kindly to being made fools of."

"No, mum, don't suppose they would be," Adam said ruefully. "But I brought you some right rum peck."

"Remind me again what that means," Katie said.

"Grub, mum. Victuals."

Katie's stomach lurched dangerously. "I think I'd like to wait a bit before my luncheon, thank you, Adam," she said, taking deep breaths through her nose.

"Feelin' poorly, then, is you?" Adam asked, concerned.

"It's that stuff they used to knock you out. Right nasty, some of it."

"Right nasty," Katie agreed. "But thank you for bringing me the tray. I'll take a few bites in a little while, I promise."

"Me and the other blokes, we'd stand a queer bloody lay for ye, mum," Adam said soberly. "I don't want you to worry yourself none. If anythin' bad was to happen to Countess Katie while I was lookin' after her, I couldn't live with meself after."

"Thank you, Adam. I feel better knowing you're looking after me," Katie said, making an effort to smile at him. "I think I need to sleep now. Will you come and keep me company later?"

Adam's skinny chest puffed out like a tom turkey's. "Oh, aye, mum. I'll be 'round in the darkmans. Sleep well, mum."

"Thank you, Adam," Katie mumbled before her eyes closed and she sank again into the merciful blackness of sleep.

It was nearly dark before she woke again, and the dying light only made the bare, cold little room seem more depressing. Katie sat upright and discovered she felt significantly less terrible than she had earlier. She lifted the cover off the tray by her table. Adam had brought her some sliced bread, now slightly hard, a few chunks of cheese, and a bowl of soup. The soup, stone cold, looked revolting, but Katie devoured the bread and cheese gratefully.

She sat up and winced, prodded herself gingerly, and decided she had not been seriously hurt. Khalil had wanted to cause her pain, not damage. The damage would come after she had delivered her treasure up to them.

A treasure that did not exist. Now that she was more or less conscious, Mehmet and Khalil would come soon to grill her. Where was this trunk of gold coins? How would she get it? How much was inside? She had to think of answers.

A fast knock came at the door, and Katie's blood froze. She lay quickly back down on the bed, covering herself with the filthy blanket, trying to look like someone drugged to unconsciousness.

The door opened, and a familiar young voice said, "Not to worry, Countess Katie. It's only me."

Katie's eyes flew open. "Tom?"

She sat up and swung herself around to face the door, arms wide as Tom flung himself into her arms. Behind him stood a pack of thin children so grimy Katie could hardly make out the boys from the girls.

"Tom, how did you get here?"

"I didn't know where you went, when the lot of you piked it," he said, reproachful. "I was in town playin' High and Low with the Yorkshire lads, and when I got back, the lot of you had bung a whist."

"Oh, Tom, they left you behind? I specifically asked Kittredge if you were aboard the ship, and he said he was sure he'd seen you."

"I'd see blokes what wasn't there too, if I guzzled the lapper what he did," Tom grumbled.

"Sobriety was never Kittredge's strong suit," Katie agreed.

"Anyway, I made me way back to London to ask around and see if anyone could find you. And here you is."

"It's wonderful to see you," Katie said with a smile. "But I'm afraid the Turks are considerably more . . . ill-tempered than Lord Brynston."

"Worse than the Brimstone Earl?" Tom grinned and gave a long, appreciative whistle. "Yer bammin' me."

One grimy little boy behind Tom giggled, and Katie gave him a suspicious look. "Come over here, boy, where I can see you clearly."

The boy shot Tom a look, and Katie noticed that the wretched creature had the bluest eyes she had ever seen.

Save for one other pair.

"Tibby, tell me that isn't you!" she cried, shocked.

"Yes, mum," Tibby said, trying hard to approximate Tom's accent. "I came down from Yorkshire yesterday, to assist Tom an' find you."

"He's a right little needle-point, he is," Tom said admiringly. "Talks funny, but he's sharp as a blade, and quick. Don't know where he could have learned it, living the soft life with old Brimstone."

Tibby giggled again. "Tireless experimentation," he said, by way of explanation.

"Tibby, you've got to go home right away," Katie said severely. "Tom, what could you have been thinking, to let him stay here? Do you have any idea how frantic the earl's going to be?"

Tom cocked her a glance. "I figured it would light a fire under Brimstone's arse, if you'll pardon me language. Bring him down here that much quicker, like."

Katie shook her head. "Tibby, you are to return home immediately. You're the spitting image of your brother, and if the Turks recognize you, they'll feed you nothing but rats and cockroaches until your brother pays your ransom. Does that sound like something you want to happen?"

"I do not believe the gentlemen capable of holding me against my will," Tibby said with an air of greatly injured dignity.

Katie raised one eyebrow. "Rats and cockroaches, Tibby? Even for a day?" She knew it was useless to argue that the Turks might harm or even kill him. For all his naughtiness, Tibby was a sheltered child, and death to him was some useless abstraction for grown-ups to worry over.

Tibby shuddered delicately. "I confess that I would find such a circumstance disagreeable."

Tom gave him a sharp shove in the ribs, and Tibby corrected, "Er, that is, sounds a bloody rum pinch to me, mum."

"Tom, please, for my sake, take him over to Lord

Brynston's house in St. James's Square. The servants will look after him and send word to his family. I'm asking you this as a special favor to me."

Tom looked down at the floor. "If your heart's set on it, mum."

Katie smiled. "Thank you, Tom. I knew I could count on you."

Another small voice piped up from the tribe of small admirers, this one, perhaps, a girl, though it was difficult to tell. "We wants to know what we can do for *you*, mum. Tibby'll be all right, he knows what's what, but you're the one in a pickle."

"You're quite right," Katie said, feeling better than she had in days. "We've got to think of a plan to get me out of here safely—and all of you have got to come with me. If you remain behind, the Turks will be in a horrible temper, and they—" Katie touched her cheek gingerly, where a bruise faintly throbbed. "They can be very nasty when they get angry. I won't have that on my conscience, do you understand?"

The children nodded soberly.

Katie eyed them with satisfaction. Lord knew what she'd do with the lot of them once they'd escaped, but there had to be somewhere they could go. "Very well, then. All of you, come around here and sit by me on the bed. I've got the beginning of an idea. Has any of you ever heard of the Boston Tea Party?"

33

The earl of Brynston and Alex Manners exchanged a look as the maidservant escorted a manfully stoic Tibby from the room. Julius had spent the better part of an hour blistering the boy's ears, and a few moments in a solemn spanking. Now his little brother was to be fed a silent dinner and sent to bed to ponder his sins.

"It will be a miracle if I don't have a complete breakdown," Julius said. "That sounds very pleasant, in fact. I'll just lie in bed all day, and the servants can come feed me nourishing broths. Val can be earl, I don't mind. It would do him good."

"Do you mind waiting until we've rescued Katie?" Alex growled.

"Good point," Julius conceded. "Now then, I have a pair of excellent pistols in my study. Graves, I assume you prefer to carry your own?"

"Thank you, yes, sir, if I may," Graves agreed.

"Very good. Alex, come upstairs to my study and then we'll be off."

Alex stood there, arms crossed, looking for all the

world like an oak tree in the middle of the parlor. "What the hell are you talking about?"

Julius looked up at him, surprised. "We're going to go rescue Katie, of course. Come on, I don't want to leave her in the clutches of those animals for too long."

"And do you have any idea how you're going to do that? Were you just thinking of charging up to the front door and asking them to let her go?"

"Not *asking*, precisely, no," Julius said dryly. "I thought I would be a bit more forceful than that."

"And when they see you there, huffing and puffing like the big bad wolf, they'll either duck out a back entrance or cut Katie's throat." Alex's face had begun to redden with anger.

"Oh, Mr. Manners, surely they wouldn't!" the maid, Hannah, cried. Graves had insisted Hannah join them, saying that a female would help them to understand Katie's "feminine mentality."

Julius was unconvinced that anyone could understand the feminine mentality, especially Katie's, but the round-faced maid was prone to neither giggling nor hysterics, so Julius let her stay.

"I fear they might, Hannah," Graves said, worry creasing his usually impassive face.

"So what did you propose to do?" Julius asked. "Issue an engraved invitation, perhaps? Or maybe we could just leave her there to die, if it's too much trouble to go and fetch her."

"Heaven preserve us," Hannah said quietly. "We must pray for guidance, and that Our Lord may keep her safe."

"That's not a bad idea at that, Hannah," Alex said heavily.

"Fine. The lot of you can stay here worrying and wishing, and I'll go fetch Katie," Julius said. "I'll have her safe and sound by the time you've mustered your courage."

"Are you calling me a coward?" Alex growled, unfolding his massive arms menacingly.

"What would you call it?" Julius answered, shifting his weight, more than ready to fight the big man.

"I thought we wanted to rescue Miss Katie, not brawl in the drawing room like a lot of heathens," Hannah said tartly.

Julius reined his temper, and gave Hannah a scowl. "Saucy thing for a lady's maid, isn't she? If I were you, Alex, I'd remind the girl of her place."

"It doesn't work any more," Alex said ruefully. "Anyway, she's right. Look here, Julius, if you go down there with pistols blazing, you'll either get yourself or Katie killed, or you'll kill the Turks and wind up fighting a murder charge. Now you may not care if you go to prison, but the last thing Katie needs is to see her husband hang."

"There's not a court in England would hang me," Julius said gruffly. "More likely give me a medal. We have to eliminate the Turks permanently."

"That's true enough," Manners agreed. "Katie will only kill herself trying to pay them back if we don't."

"Render unto Caesar what is Caesar's," Hannah said. "This is a matter for Bow Street, not for a bunch of rowdy ruffians."

"But Bow Street has to catch them at something," Julius said. "Katie and Phineas are the only ones who can give first-hand evidence, and they aren't exactly the most credible witnesses one could hope for."

"She's told them she has a cache hidden in London," Manners said. "If the Runners were to intercept them as they were stealing it . . ."

Julius nodded. "Yes, I like that. Very good. Graves, see if you can get a trunk together—a convincing pirate's horde. Hannah, go and find the boy, Finch. I believe he's being fed below stairs. Manners, you accompany the boy back to Spitalfields and be sure he gets there safely. I don't want anything going wrong."

"And what will you do?" Manners asked.

"I'll explain the matter to Bow Street," Julius said. He nodded to the lot of them, sending them on their way.

"We'll get her back, won't we, my lord?" Hannah asked, her round face creased with concern.

"We'll get her back," Julius said. "You don't know me very well yet, Hannah, but I look after my own."

And Katie, he thought with a pang, was utterly and irrevocably his.

Khalil's fat, smooth face was marred by an angry scowl. "Now, then, Miss Starr. You are ready, yes?"

"I need a dark gown, and a cloak," Katie said, checking her lock picks. "I told Mehmet that this morning. It's a full moon tonight, I'll shine like a lantern in what I'm wearing."

"Mehmet did not have occasion to procure you such a garment," Khalil said carelessly.

"If I get caught, you won't see a penny," she reminded him.

Khalil shrugged. "To kill a watchman, it is not so much work. Besides, we have obtained an additional assurance."

"What do you mean?" Katie asked warily.

"Mehmet is watching over the boy you are so fond of. It is Tom, yes? The child with the large hat and the speckles on his face. When we get our hands on this treasure you have promised, the boy will go free. If we do not, he dies. It is a very simple equation."

Katie felt her gorge rise in protest. "This doesn't concern him! Your debt is with me, Khalil, not the boy."

Khalil's mouth settled into a grim line. "We are not fools, Miss Starr. Your own safety is of but trifling concern to you. But the safety of others . . . that is your weakness."

Katie said nothing, only stared blankly ahead. She would have to signal to the children tonight, somehow, that they were to secure Tom's safety. She didn't like it. There were too many things that could go wrong.

But it seemed she had little choice. Khalil pressed a

pistol rudely into her side and walked her briskly downstairs and to the waiting carriage. Like it or not, she was
off to break into her old rooms. And given a little luck,
she would manage to pull this off without anyone getting
killed.

They arrived at well past midnight, and the house was completely dark. It did not take Katie long to pick the lock—she
had done it several times before, coming home late from a
night's gaming and not wanting to wake the servants.

Katie stood just inside the door frame, holding the
lamp as far in front of her as she could manage. The light
threw ghostly shadows over the walls and the covered
furniture.

"All right, Khalil," she said, working to keep her voice
steady. "Now that we're in, I don't make another move
until I see that Tom is safe."

Khalil thrust his pistol rudely into her ribs. "You will
see the boy soon enough. Take me to this treasure of
yours before I lose my patience."

"You want to kill me now?" Katie snapped. "Fine. I
don't care if you ever see that pile of coin, Khalil. I'm
only doing this for the boy's sake. If you can't prove his
safety to me, you might as well shoot me now."

Khalil made a sound of disgust. "Very well." He made
a clucking sound with his teeth and called out something
in Turkish, and Mehmet materialized from the shrubbery,
holding a wicked-looking knife to Tom Finch's throat.

Tom was pale, and his hands trembled slightly, but
he managed to give Katie a wan smile. "Good evenin',
Countess Katie."

Katie started toward him. "Tom! They haven't hurt you,
have they?"

"No mum," he said in a peculiar tone of voice. "I'm
safe, perfectly safe. No need to worry about me none. You
just set your mind to that treasure. If you study the problem, I'm sure you'll be safe." He waggled his eyebrows

significantly, sliding a glance into the house and back at Katie.

"Tom, they haven't hit you in the head, have they?" Katie asked, concerned. "You're babbling."

Tom frowned at her. "I'm tryin' to tell you, mum, I'm *safe*. If you'll *study* my meanin', you'll find that everything will work out."

"Oh!" Katie said abruptly. "Yes, I see now. I shall study it directly, then."

"Enough of this," Khalil said irritably. "Mehmet will wait in the hall with the boy. You will lead me to this treasure of yours."

"Keep your voice down," she said. "You'll have the watchmen on us, and I don't want you killing any more people than you have to. Come on, it's this way."

They walked up the stairs and turned right. Katie hoped this was what Tom had been trying to tell her—she couldn't think of another reason to insist on the words *study* and *safe*.

The door to the study was locked, but Katie picked it easily. The room was much as Phineas had left it. Most of the books had come with the house—obscure treatises and third-rate novels, the sort of shabby miscellany people left in rented houses.

Now the only problem was to find a safe. Phineas had never kept one; he lived with too many criminals to trust his valuables to so obvious a hiding place. Katie began a search of the rooms, beginning with such shop-worn hiding places as behind the pictures on the wall.

"I thought you yourself hid this great treasure?" Khalil said irritably. "How can it be that you must search for it? You are stalling for time, Miss Starr."

"We had our servants . . . relocate the strongbox since we were here. For security reasons," she said quickly. "I'm sure I'll find it any moment."

As she said the words she spied a large metal box wedged under the writing desk, as if hastily crammed there. "There, I'm sure that's it!"

Khalil looked dubious. "Your servants hid this box by leaving it under a writing desk?"

Katie shrugged and set the lamp on the desk. "I never said they were very bright. Come on, help me get it out of there."

Khalil looked at her suspiciously, but finally decided a female one-third his size could do little to physically overpower him. He bent down, huffing a little, and helped her slide the heavy box free of the desk.

The box was locked with a massive iron padlock that looked like it belonged to a cell at Newgate. Katie raised one eyebrow. "That's quite a lock."

Khalil pressed the cold mouth of his pistol to her temple. "You can unlock it, yes?"

Katie waved his gun irritably away. "My concentration is not improved by people holding firearms to my head. Keep your distance, Khalil. I'll get in there soon enough."

She knelt, took out her picks, and tried the first one on the lock. Khalil paced behind her, his weight making the floor boards creak beneath him. The mechanism was more complicated than she was used to, but finally the tumblers fell into place and she clicked the lock open.

She opened the box, wincing at the grating creak of the metal hinges. Then she gave a long, low whistle.

Inside the box was a shabby length of worn red velvet, and wrapped in the velvet were at least a quarter million pounds' worth of diamonds, rubies, and heavy, old gold coin. Khalil thrust his arm into the box over her shoulder, and came away with a fistful of pearls. "Splendid," he said. "And now, Miss Starr, I think you have outlived your usefulness."

Katie had been waiting for this, and she tucked her body tight and rolled to the left, springing to her feet in a snarling crouch. Khalil cocked his pistol and pointed it at her, and she darted from side to side, making herself a more difficult target.

"You will not play these games with me," Khalil said, cutting off her access to the door as he moved toward her. "Stop jumping about so I can kill you quickly. You have earned that much, at least. I will not force you to suffer when you die."

An unmistakable click came from behind Khalil's back. "Kindly step away from the young lady, sir," came a pleasant, working-class voice. "I shall have to ask you to release the pistol in your hand as well."

Khalil shot a wild look over his shoulder to see a neatly dressed young man with two ferocious-looking pistols in his hands, both cocked and trained on Khalil's back.

"Damn it, man, you were supposed to make sure the girl was safe *before* you confronted the bloody Turk!" came a familiar, thundering voice.

Katie blinked to see Lord Brynston step out from behind the curtain, holding his own matched pair of pistols.

Khalil looked at Katie with murder in his eyes. "You treacherous bitch! You have betrayed me! Mehmet!" Khalil shouted something menacing-sounding in Turkish.

"No!" Katie cried. She fumbled in her pocket for the penny-whistle Adam had lent her, and blew it with everything she had.

Suddenly the house boiled over with furious little fiends dressed in loincloths over their long underwear. Their faces were darkened with clay and decorated imaginatively with warpaint, and pigeon feathers were glued or tied haphazardly about their persons.

The Runner could only stand, nonplussed, staring at the explosion of little savages. "I shall have to insist that everyone remain calm and quiet!" he shouted authoritatively.

As if in reply, an arrow whizzed in through the study's open door, missing Brynston's right ear by inches. Someone in the hallway let out a bloodcurdling war whoop, and was answered by a dozen more throughout the house.

"Good God, Katie, what have you done this time?" Brynston asked.

She shot a nervous look at him. He looked as handsome as the night she'd fleeced him for thirty thousand pounds, and her heart gave a wicked jump. "It's the Boston Tea Party," she explained.

Khalil was turning purple with rage. His pistol was pointed directly at the center of Katie's chest. "You have underestimated the strength of my resolve. I have no interest in rotting in one of your English prisons. You will not shoot me, because you are afraid I will kill the girl. You will therefore release me."

"I'm afraid I cannot permit a suspect to leave the scene of a crime without questioning him thoroughly," the Runner said blandly.

"Don't be a bloody ass, Gardner," Brynston said irritably. "He's got us to rights. Let him go."

"Your lordship may be an earl," Gardner said patiently, "but that does not mean I will permit him to subvert English law, which has clearly invested me with the right and responsibility to—"

"Stash it, Gardner," Katie said. "Let him walk, you can catch up with him later. I promise."

Another war whoop came from the hallway, and Katie could just see a slim form sail past as if swinging from a vine. Good God, the street children had outdone themselves. It was absolute bedlam out there.

Gardner frowned, but motioned with his pistol toward the door. "All right, then. You're free to go for now, sir. However, I must ask that you refrain from leaving the city for the next forty-eight hours, as an investigator will be contacting you to—"

"Do shut up, Gardner," Brynston said irritably.

Khalil stepped toward Katie and grabbed her arm, pressing the pistol to her head with his free hand. "The gentlemen will forgive me if I do not trust them to be as generous when the girl is not with me."

"Let her go, Khalil," Brynston commanded, his voice raising the hairs on the back of Katie's neck.

"I will release her when I am gone from this house of madmen," Khalil said, backing toward the door and dragging Katie with him.

"Your life's worth nothing if she comes to any harm," Brynston said, his voice thick with menace. "If I see a scratch on her, I will hunt you down and make you regret the day you were born."

Khalil said nothing, only backed out of the room with Katie in tow. He pushed her roughly toward the stairs. "Move! Quickly! You will not entrap me in this place any longer!"

A wiry figure screeched and swooped down from overhead like an ungainly eagle. The eagle thrust out a pair of skinny legs as it flew past and kicked the pistol from Khalil's grasp before the fat man could register what was happening.

The pistol clattered down the stairs, falling through the railing. When it hit the floor below, it fired, sending a cloud of plaster dust flying.

"Quick, Countess Katie, duck!" chirped a voice from overhead.

Katie looked up to see two thin faces at the balcony, both painted in fierce-looking approximations of the Union Jack. Katie leapt free of Khalil just in time to miss the stream of treacle from overhead. A shower of white pillow feathers followed in the next instant. Before Khalil could so much as sputter and rub the treacle from his eyes, he resembled a half-plucked Christmas goose.

Khalil's eyes glowed with murderous fury as he moved up the stairs toward Katie. Without thinking, she grasped the banister tightly in her hands and kicked him square in the chest with both feet. He went over like a skittle pin, tumbling down the stairs with a ferocious noise. When he reached the bottom, four little Indians threw a damp fishnet over him and began to tie him with soggy ropes. Katie could smell the unmistakable odor of the Thames all the way from upstairs.

"Have you rescued Tom?" she called.

One of the little Indians looked up at her with a bright smile and suspiciously blue eyes. "Oh, yes, madame. The smaller Turkish gentleman is incapacitated in the front parlor."

The Indian next to him frowned and gave him a sharp pinch.

The blue-eyed Indian scowled at his companion, then looked innocently up at her. "That is, I fink 'is ankle's bloody broke, mum."

"What do you mean, rescued Tom?" Brynston said, from very near her left shoulder.

Katie turned. It seemed a hundred years since she'd seen him, and now he was close enough to touch. "From Mehmet," she murmured, trying to remember where she was.

"You hadn't seen Tom since he came back from the house?" Brynston asked, incredulous. "You didn't know we were coming?"

"I . . . I wondered if you might," Katie admitted. "When I sent Tom back with Tibby, I didn't know if you would be there or not."

"Now then, miss, I just need to ask you a few questions," Gardner said, emerging from the study and flipping open a notebook as he licked his pencil lead.

Brynston's head shot up, and he cast the man a look that could have frozen salt water. "Later, Gardner."

"With all due respect, my lord," Gardner said earnestly, "I do find it best to conduct my interrogation when the incident is still fresh in the— Ow!" Gardner rubbed his neck where a red-headed Indian had shot a marble at him.

A bloodcurdling collection of shrieks came from downstairs, as the Indians dragged a thoroughly immobilized Khalil across the floor.

"Good heavens, I wonder what they'll do with him," Katie mused.

"Come on, we're taking cover," Brynston said, plucking her by the sleeve and escorting her to a front bedroom. He closed the door firmly behind them and slid the lock.

"M-my lord," Katie stammered.

"Do you have any idea what you've put me through, Katie Willowby?" Brynston said, his flame-blue eyes unreadable.

She looked up at him. He radiated heat like a stove. "No, my lord," she said in a small voice.

A war whoop came from the hallway, and something hit the door with a sodden thump. "Ow!" came Gardner's voice, muffled by the door. "Now just you wait one moment, you little hooligan—"

"Since I've met you," Brynston continued, the ghost of a smile on his lips, "I've spent more time in a flash house than I had in all my years as a rakehell."

"That is hardly my fault, my lord," Katie said.

"Hush. My family has become even more unmanageable than usual, Lady Milvia's never going to speak to me again, and somehow I managed to get stuck with a stubborn little sharper for a countess."

"That's not my fault either," Katie said.

"I thought I told you to hush."

Katie felt her heart crack. "We're not married, my lord. Julius. You know that as well as I do. You aren't bound to me any longer."

"Not legally, maybe. Not yet."

Katie tried to swallow the lump building in her throat, but it was lodged there and wouldn't budge. "The Brimstone Earl can't take an American street rat as his countess, Julius. It isn't done."

"I don't know if we'll be able to get you into Almack's," he conceded with a grin. "Will that break your heart very much?"

She wanted to melt into him, to shut her eyes to everything she had ever been and simply trust him. "You don't know me, Julius. You might think you do, but—"

His face was grave, but kind. "But I don't know about your mother? I don't know about the man you were forced to kill?"

Katie ducked her head, unable to look at him. "Someone

told you. It must have been Alex." She felt suddenly cold, so cold her teeth were threatening to chatter right out of her head.

Julius folded her in his arms and stroked the wings of her shoulderblades. "He's desperately fond of you. He trusts me, Katie. Why can't you?"

"It's not you I don't trust. Julius, we can't be together."

"Why not, you silly goose?"

"Your name means everything to you," she pointed out, trying to ignore the soft touch of his hands on her back, and the clean, comforting masculine smell of his shirt.

"My *family* means everything to me," he corrected. "Just as yours does to you. You make a perfect Willowby, Katie. Trust me."

She looked up at him then, her heart breaking all over again at the expression in his eyes. "Just what are you trying to say?"

"What I'm trying to say, you daft creature, is that I want you to marry me again. Properly, this time."

She allowed a smile to twitch at her cheek. "I won't have to wear the gag, will I? That was really very disagreeable of you, Julius."

"No, but you must promise to watch your language. The poor parson nearly fainted last time."

"Served him right," she said. "I wish I'd been able to kick him harder."

"You're very brave, aren't you?" Julius said, suddenly serious.

She shook her head, no. "I do what I have to do, that's all. Most of the time I'm scared out of my wits."

"What you have to do now," he said, his voice soft as he bent down to her, "is to be brave enough to be a countess. It's not an easy life, but whenever it feels too hard, I'll be there to help you."

He kissed her softly, very softly on the lips.

"Julius," she said, feeling the cracks in her heart turn to fissures and give way to let all the painful sweet brightness out. "Are you sure?"

"I've never been surer of anything in my life."

"I love you, you horrid English beast," she said, murmuring against his lips as she deepened the kiss.

"I love you too, my disagreeable American savage," he said, when he had kissed her half senseless. "But you know, I am going to be absolutely rotten about one thing."

She looked up at him. "Only one, Julius? However will you choose?"

"Impertinent brat," he frowned. "I am speaking of your darling papa, my dear."

Katie's heart sank at the mention of him. "He still owes seventy thousand pounds to Ali."

"The money is the last thing I'm worried about. I'm going to do something your father will probably find untenable, and I don't want to hear any discussion about it."

Katie bit her lip. "What's that, my lord?"

"I'm putting him on an allowance. He'll get enough to keep his own rooms in London, if he likes, and his tailor will be happy. But that's all he's getting."

"He'll lose five year's worth within the week, I promise you," Katie said.

"Fine. He can come stay with us, if he's got nowhere else to go. But he gets no more money, and you don't rescue him from any more scrapes."

"Julius, you don't know him like I do!" Katie protested. "There's no use being firm with him. I've tried a thousand times."

"No, you haven't," Julius said gently. "I'm sure you've told him you would be firm, I'm sure you've even meant it. And I'm just as sure you bailed him out time and time again."

Katie sank her cheek against Julius's shirt. "But what if he goes to prison?"

"A few days in the Fleet will do him a world of good. It's not Newgate, you know. He won't be locked in with thieves and murderers. And they won't keep him for long, just long enough to sell off his furniture and arrange to pay his debts."

"I don't know," she said doubtfully.

"I know you don't," he said, taking her by the shoulders. "You love your father, though God knows why, and you would like to take care of him. And I'm telling you that he's going to have to grow up. He'll be better off in the end."

Katie nodded. "I'm tired of cheating people, Julius. I'm tired of the look in people's eyes when they've lost a sizable fortune to me."

"You didn't seem overbothered by it the night you took thirty thousand from me," he said crossly.

"You could afford it," she said, smiling. "And you deserved it."

"I probably did, at that," he mused. He bent, and kissed her. And then he kissed her again.

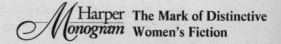

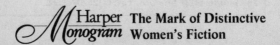